W9-BVD-614

image comics presents

™

LIBRARY
NASH COMMUNITY COLLEGE
P. O. BOX 7488
ROCKY MOUNT, N. C. 27804

ROBERT KIRKMAN
CREATOR, WRITER

CHARLIE ADLARD
PENCILER

STEFANO GAUDIANO
INKER

CLIFF RATHBURN
GRAY TONES

RUS WOOTON
LETTERER

CHARLIE ADLARD
& DAVE STEWART
COVER

SEAN MACKIEWICZ
EDITOR

For SKYBOUND ENTERTAINMENT
Robert Kirkman - Chairman
David Alpert - CEO
Sean Mackiewicz - Editorial Director
Shawn Kirkham - Director of Business Development
Brian Huntington - Online Editorial Director
June Alian - Publicity Director
Jon Moisan - Editor
Arielle Basich - Assistant Editor
Andres Juarez - Graphic Designer
Stephan Murillo - Business Development Assistant
Johnny O'Dell - Online Editorial Assistant
Dan Petersen - Operations Manager
Nick Palmer - Operations Coordinator

International inquiries: ag@sequentialrights.com
Licensing inquiries: contact@skybound.com
WWW.SKYBOUND.COM

IMAGE COMICS, INC.
Robert Kirkman – Chief Operating Officer
Erik Larsen – Chief Financial Officer
Todd McFarlane – President
Marc Silvestri – Chief Executive Officer
Jim Valentino – Vice-President

Eric Stephenson – Publisher
Corey Murphy – Director of Sales
Jeff Boison – Director of Publishing Planning & Book Trade Sales
Jeremy Sullivan – Director of Digital Sales
Kat Salazar – Director of PR & Marketing
Branwyn Bigglestone – Senior Accounts Manager
Sarah Mello – Accounts Manager
Drew Gill – Art Director
Jonathan Chan – Production Manager
Meredith Wallace – Print Manager
Brian Skelly – Publicist
Sasha Head – Sales & Marketing Production Designer
Randy Okamura – Digital Production Designer
David Brothers – Branding Manager
Olivia Ngai – Content Manager
Addison Duke – Production Artist
Vincent Kukua – Production Artist
Tricia Ramos – Production Artist
Jeff Stang – Direct Market Sales Representative
Emilio Bautista – Digital Sales Associate
Leanna Caunter – Accounting Assistant
Chloe Ramos-Peterson – Library Market Sales Representative
IMAGECOMICS.COM

THE WALKING DEAD, VOL. 26: CALL TO ARMS. First Printing. ISBN: 978-1-63215-917-5. Published by Image Comics, Inc. Office of publication: 2001 Center Street, 6th Floor, Berkeley, California 94704. Copyright © 2016 Robert Kirkman, LLC. All rights reserved. Originally published in single magazine format as THE WALKING DEAD #151-156. THE WALKING DEAD™ (including all prominent characters featured in this issue), its logo and all character likenesses are trademarks of Robert Kirkman, LLC, unless otherwise noted. Image Comics® and its logos are registered trademarks and copyrights of Image Comics, Inc. All rights reserved. No part of this publication may be reproduced or transmitted, in any form or by any means (except for short excerpts for review purposes) without the express written permission of Image Comics, Inc. All names, characters, events and locales in this publication are entirely fictional. Any resemblance to actual persons (living and/or dead), events or places, without satiric intent, is coincidental. For information regarding the CPSIA on this printed material call: 203-595-3636 and provide reference # RICH – 688147. PRINTED IN THE USA

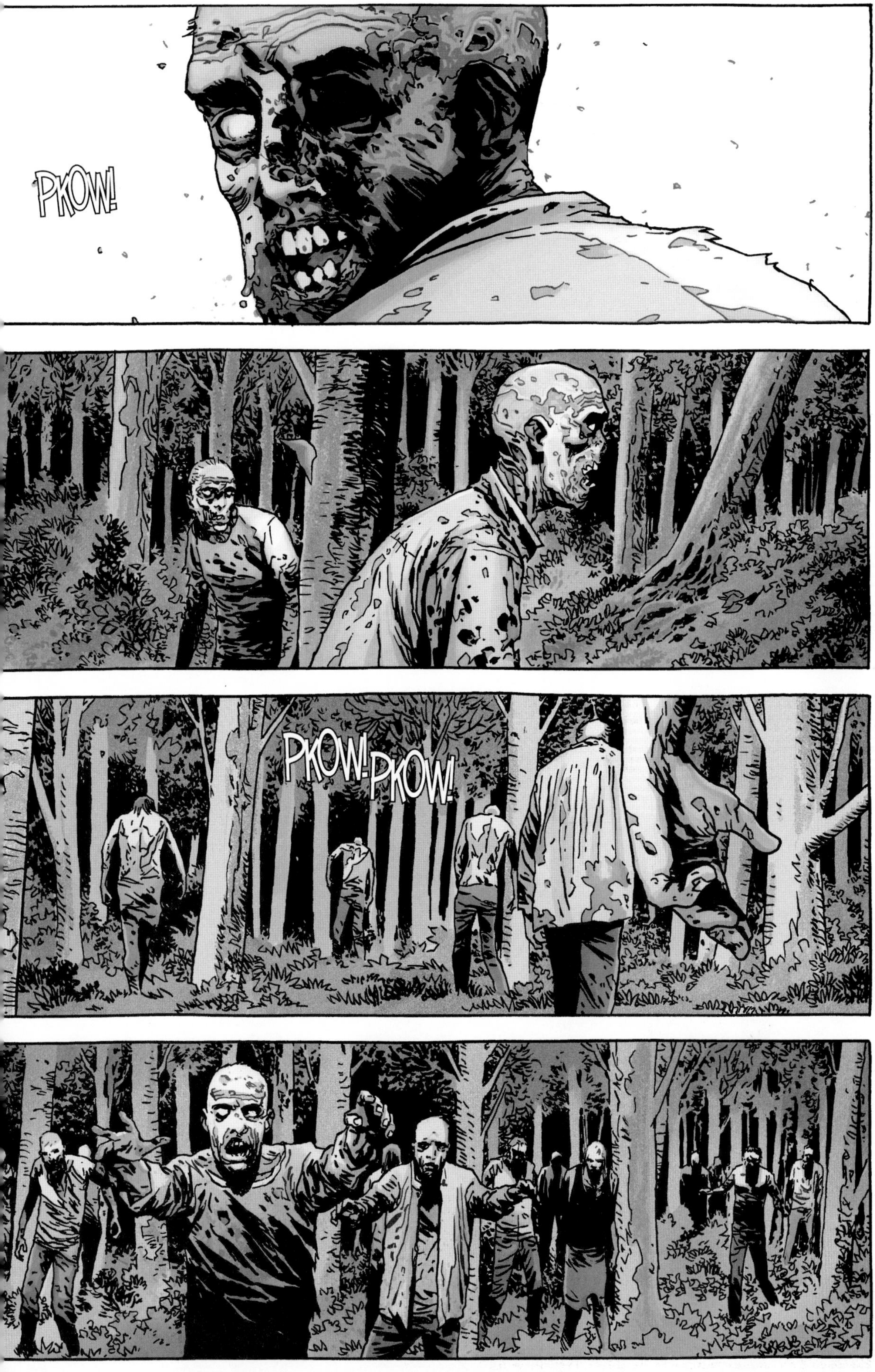
PKOW!
PKOW! PKOW!

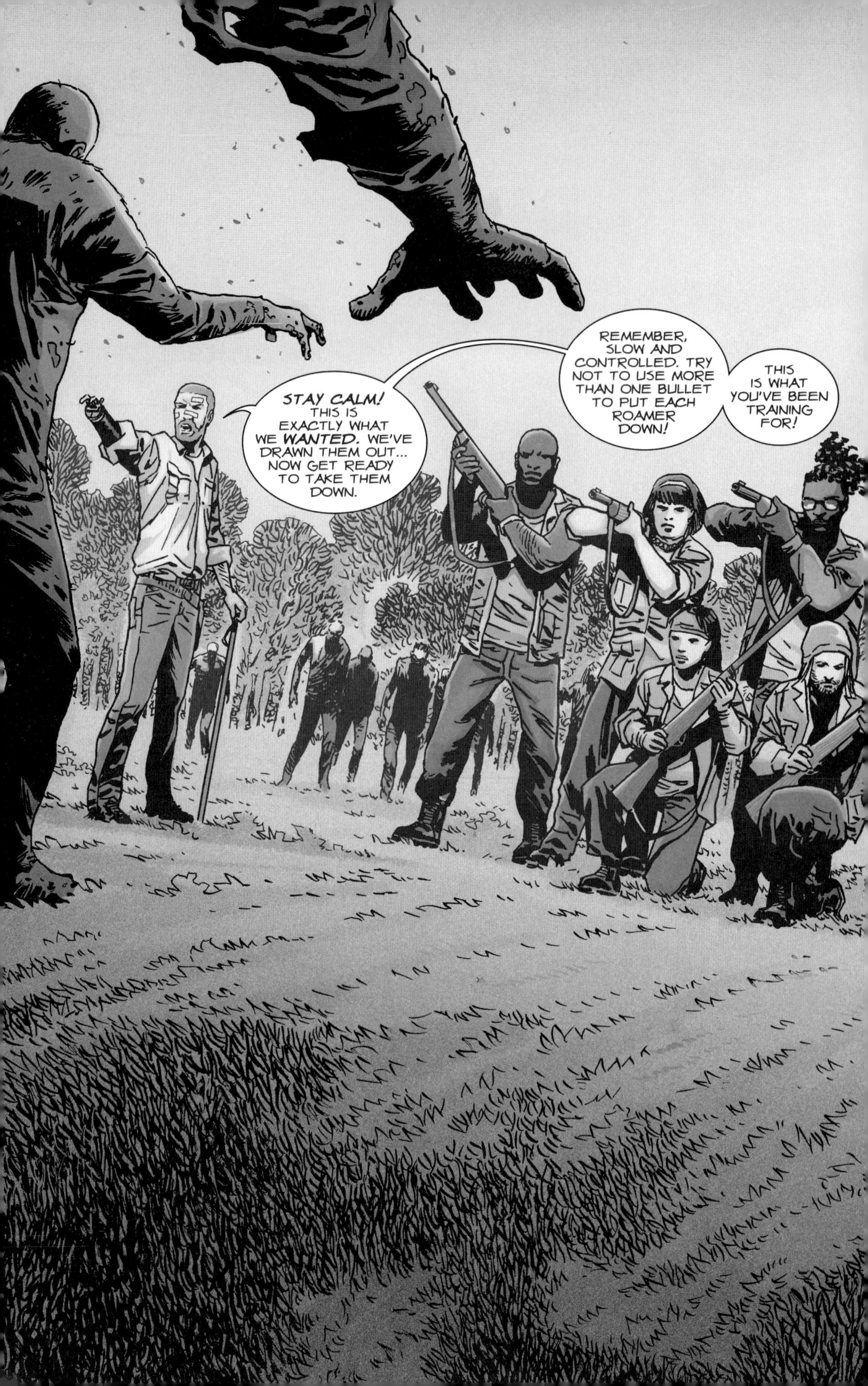
STAY CALM! THIS IS EXACTLY WHAT WE WANTED. WE'VE DRAWN THEM OUT... NOW GET READY TO TAKE THEM DOWN.
REMEMBER, SLOW AND CONTROLLED. TRY NOT TO USE MORE THAN ONE BULLET TO PUT EACH ROAMER DOWN!
THIS IS WHAT YOU'VE BEEN TRAINING FOR!

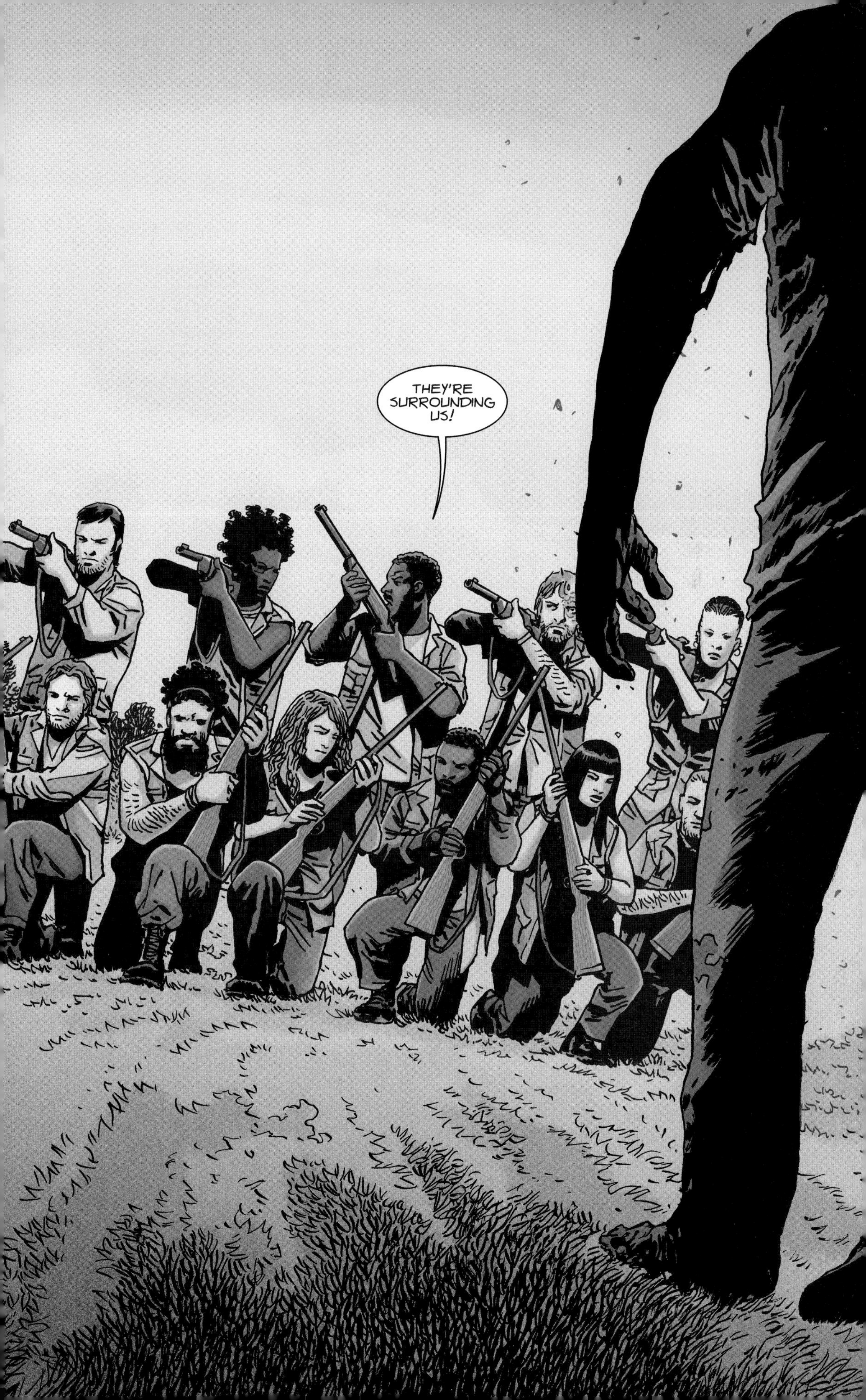
THEY'RE SURROUNDING US!

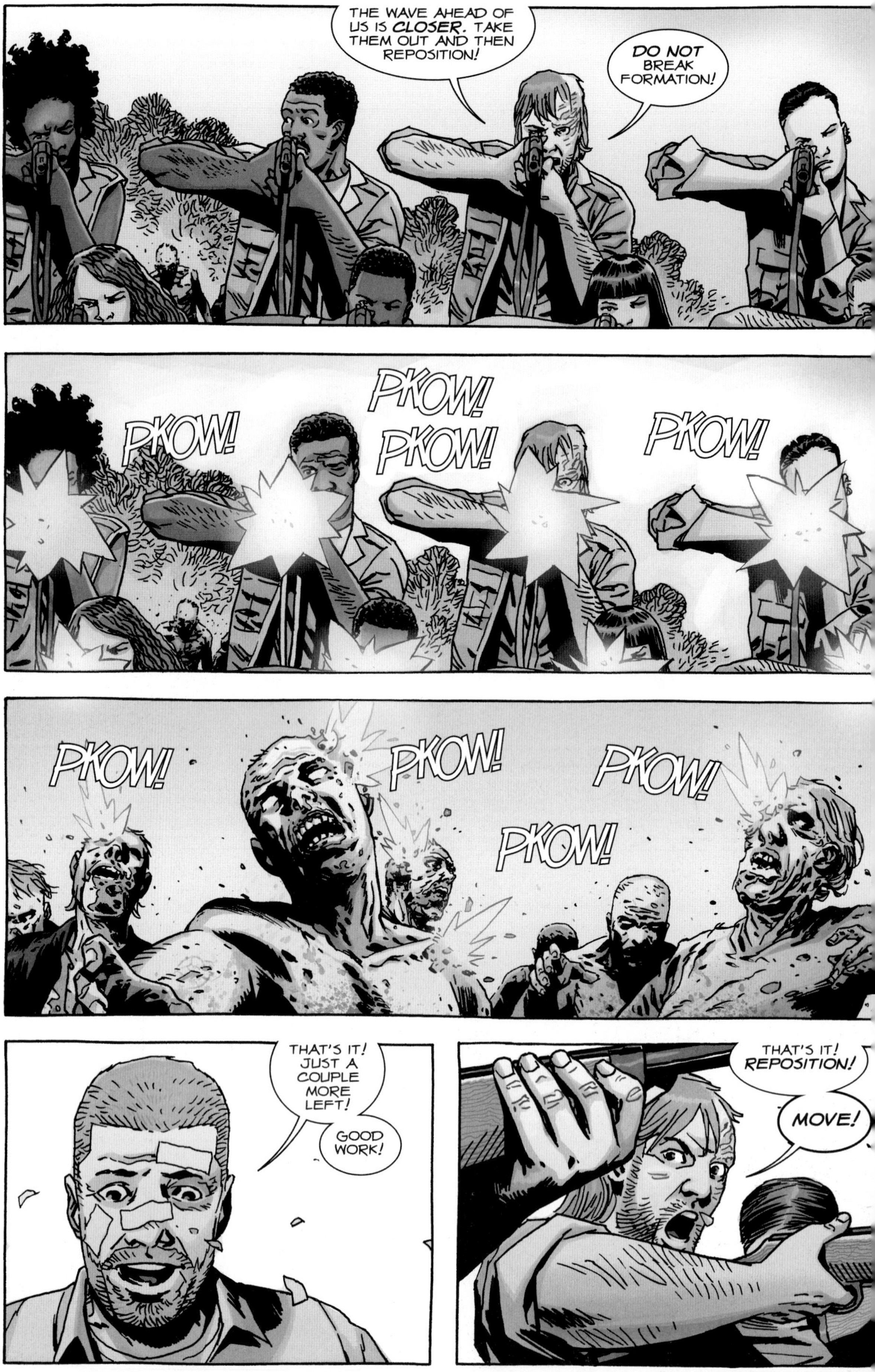
THE WAVE AHEAD OF US IS CLOSER. TAKE THEM OUT AND THEN REPOSITION!
DO NOT BREAK FORMATION!
PKOW!
PKOW!
PKOW!
PKOW!
PKOW!
PKOW!
PKOW!
PKOW!
THAT'S IT! JUST A COUPLE MORE LEFT!
GOOD WORK!
THAT'S IT! REPOSITION!
MOVE!

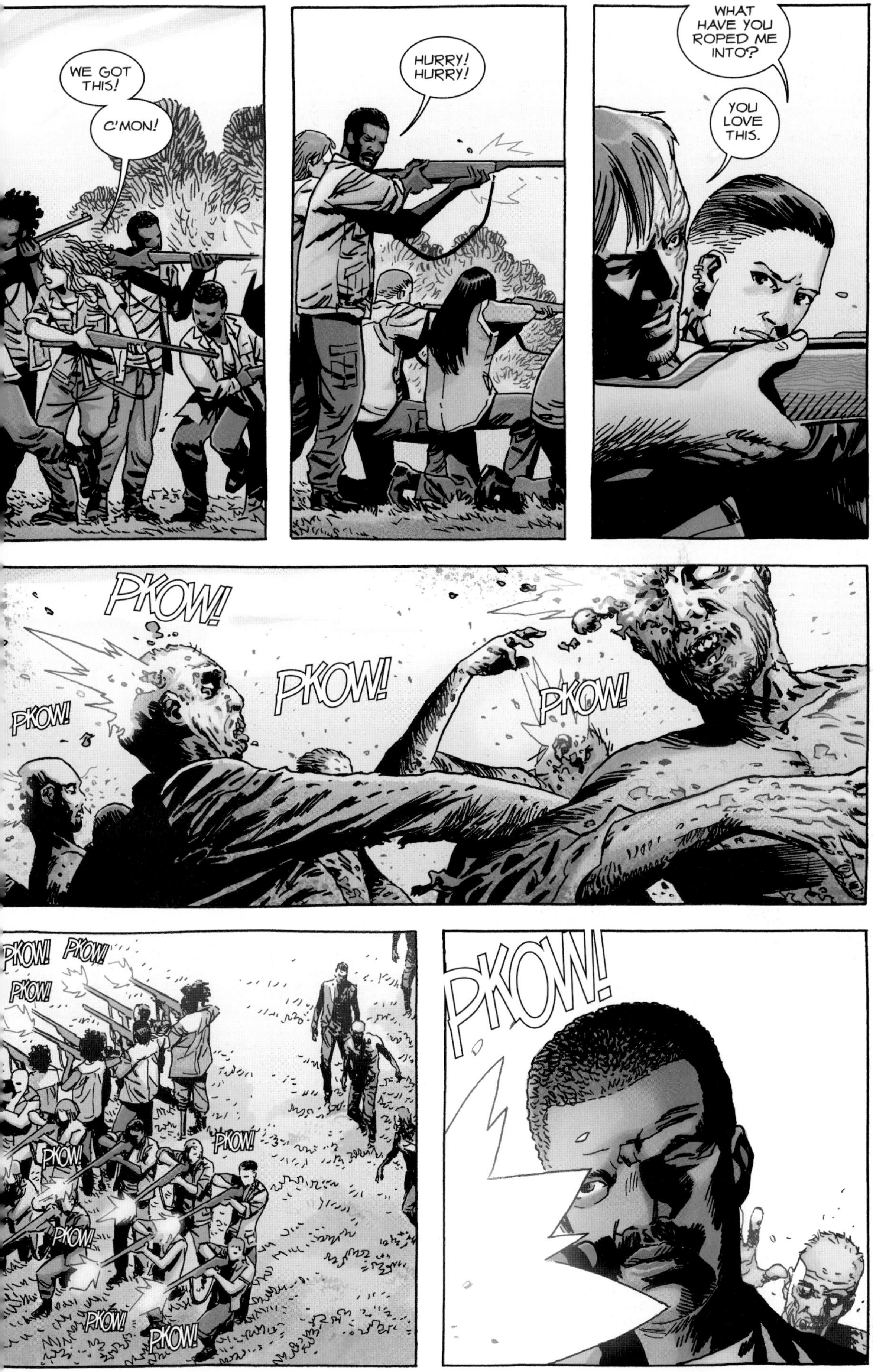
WE GOT THIS!
C'MON!
HURRY! HURRY!
WHAT HAVE YOU ROPED ME INTO?
YOU LOVE THIS.
PKOW!
PKOW!
PKOW!
PKOW!
PKOW!
PKOW!
PKOW!
PKOW!
PKOW!
PKOW!
PKOW!
PKOW!
PKOW!
PKOW!

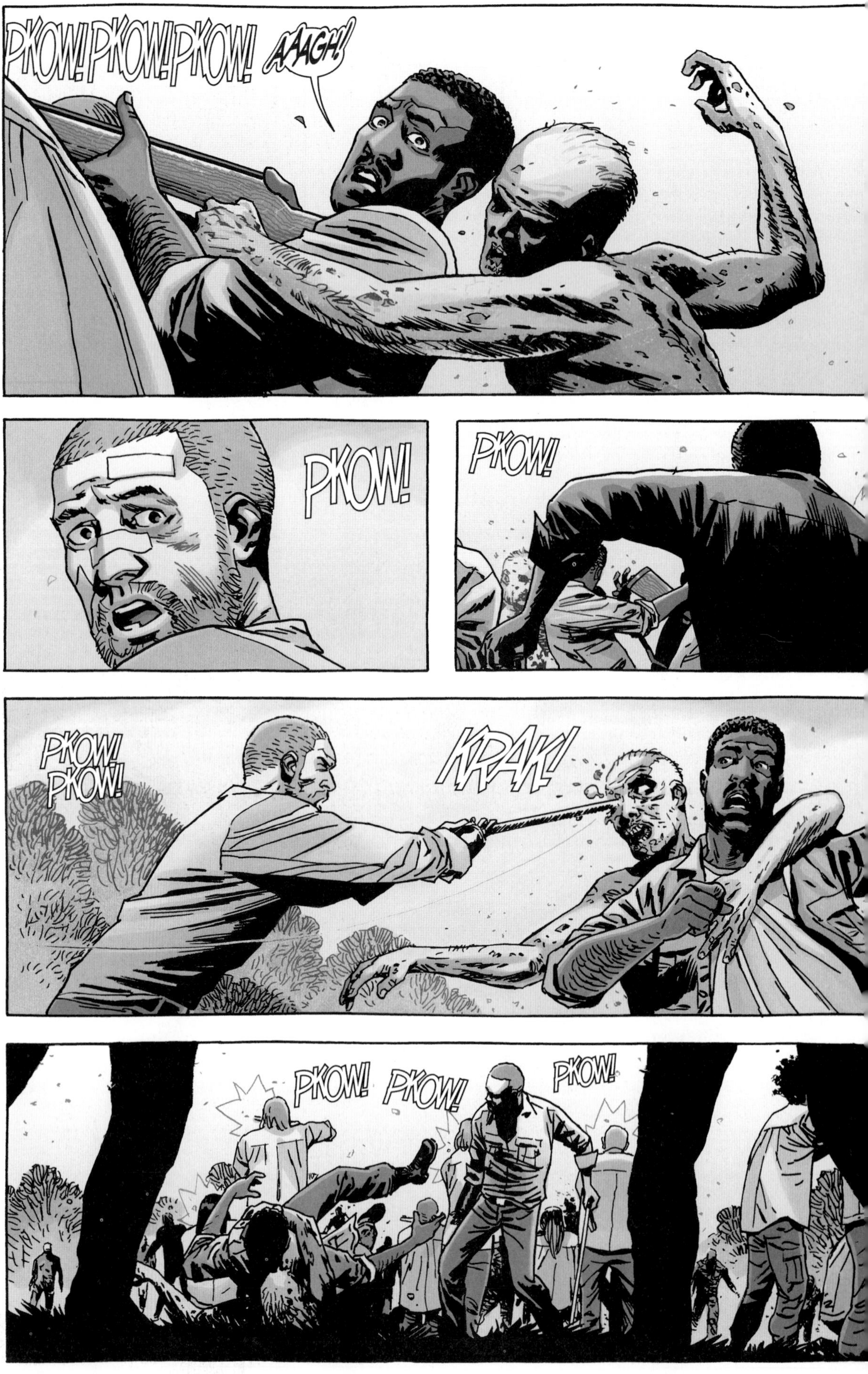
PKOW! PKOW! PKOW!
AAAGH!
PKOW!
PKOW!
PKOW! PKOW!
KRAK!
PKOW! PKOW!
PKOW!

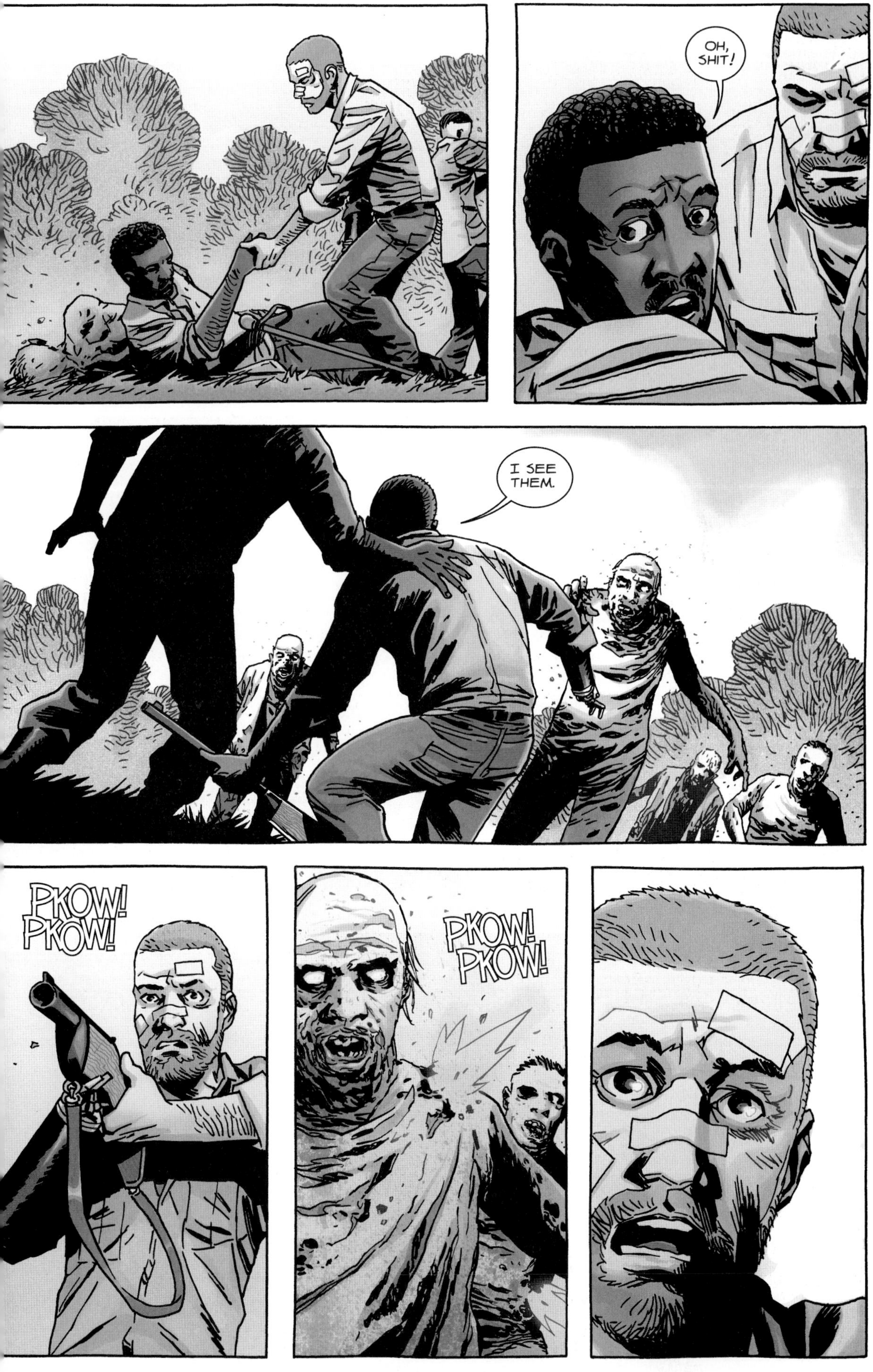
OH, SHIT!
I SEE THEM.
PKOW! PKOW!
PKOW! PKOW!

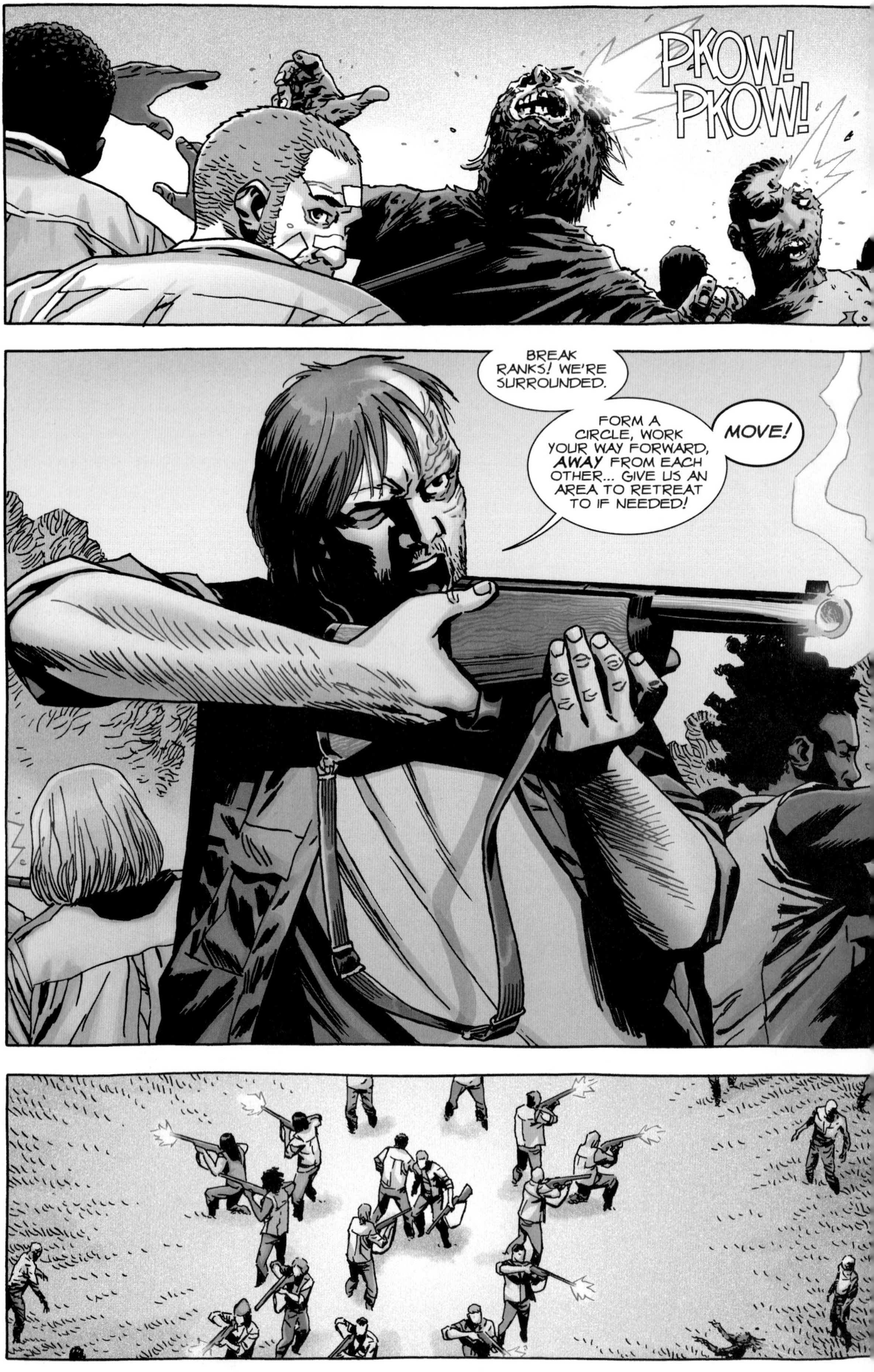
PKOW! PKOW!
BREAK RANKS! WE'RE SURROUNDED.
FORM A CIRCLE, WORK YOUR WAY FORWARD, AWAY FROM EACH OTHER... GIVE US AN AREA TO RETREAT TO IF NEEDED!
MOVE!

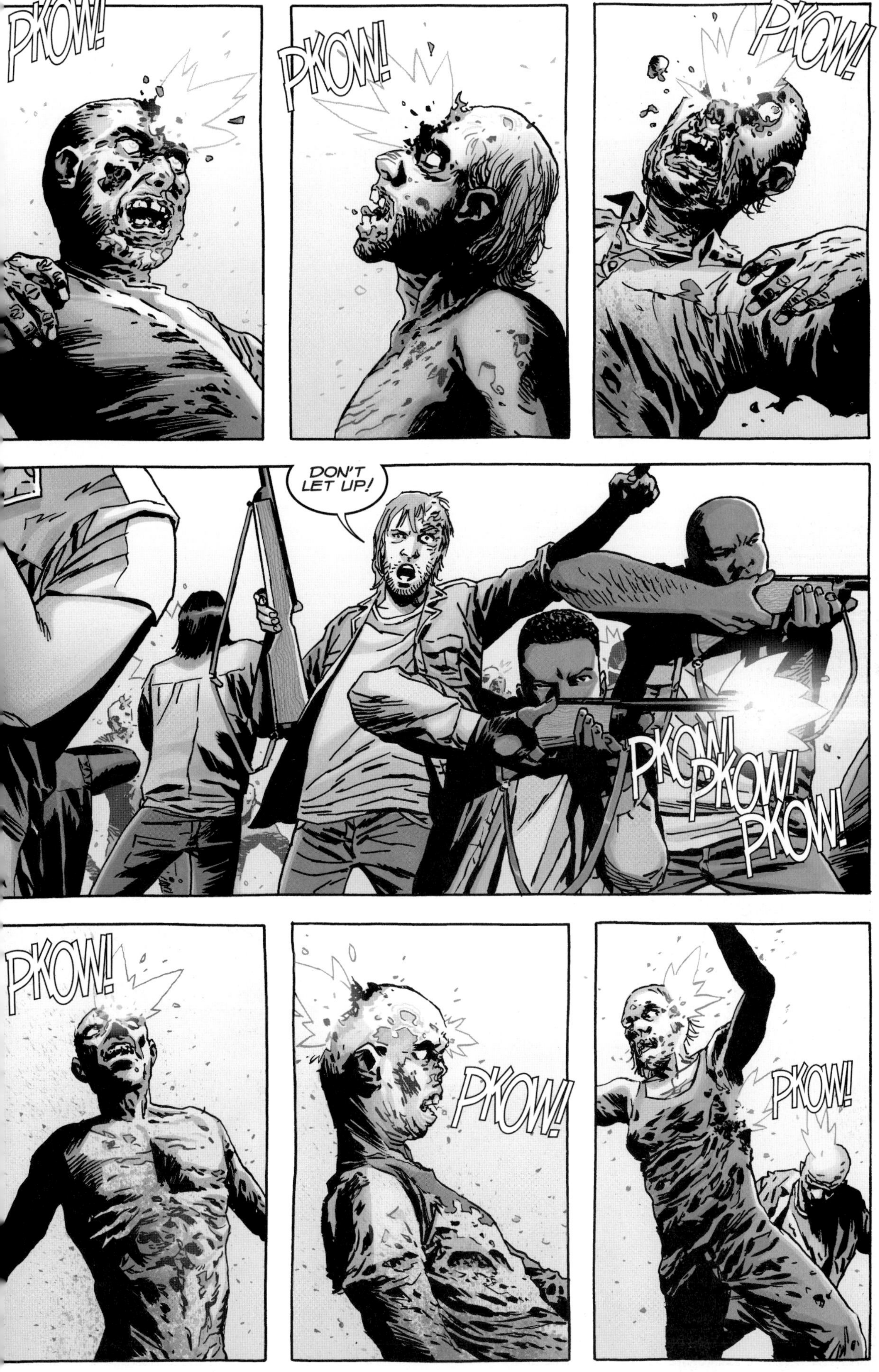
PKOW!
PKOW!
PKOW!
DON'T LET UP!
PKOW!
PKOW!
PKOW!
PKOW!
PKOW!
PKOW!

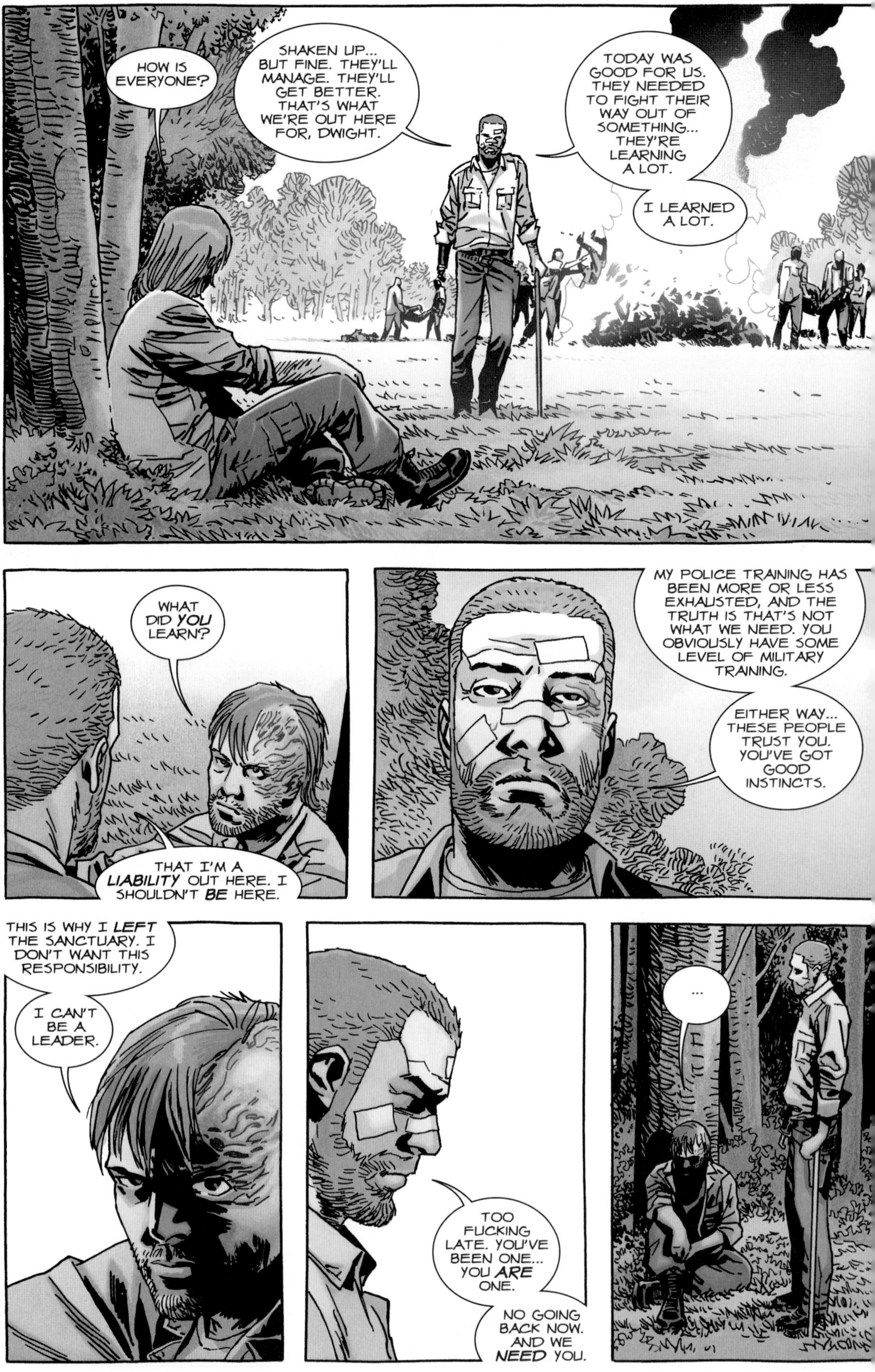
HOW IS EVERYONE?
SHAKEN UP... BUT FINE. THEY'LL MANAGE. THEY'LL GET BETTER. THAT'S WHAT WE'RE OUT HERE FOR, DWIGHT.
TODAY WAS GOOD FOR US. THEY NEEDED TO FIGHT THEIR WAY OUT OF SOMETHING... THEY'RE LEARNING A LOT.
I LEARNED A LOT.
WHAT DID YOU LEARN?
THAT I'M A LIABILITY OUT HERE. I SHOULDN'T BE HERE.
MY POLICE TRAINING HAS BEEN MORE OR LESS EXHAUSTED, AND THE TRUTH IS THAT'S NOT WHAT WE NEED. YOU OBVIOUSLY HAVE SOME LEVEL OF MILITARY TRAINING.
EITHER WAY... THESE PEOPLE TRUST YOU. YOU'VE GOT GOOD INSTINCTS.
THIS IS WHY I LEFT THE SANCTUARY. I DON'T WANT THIS RESPONSIBILITY.
I CAN'T BE A LEADER.
TOO FUCKING LATE. YOU'VE BEEN ONE... YOU ARE ONE.
NO GOING BACK NOW. AND WE NEED YOU.
...

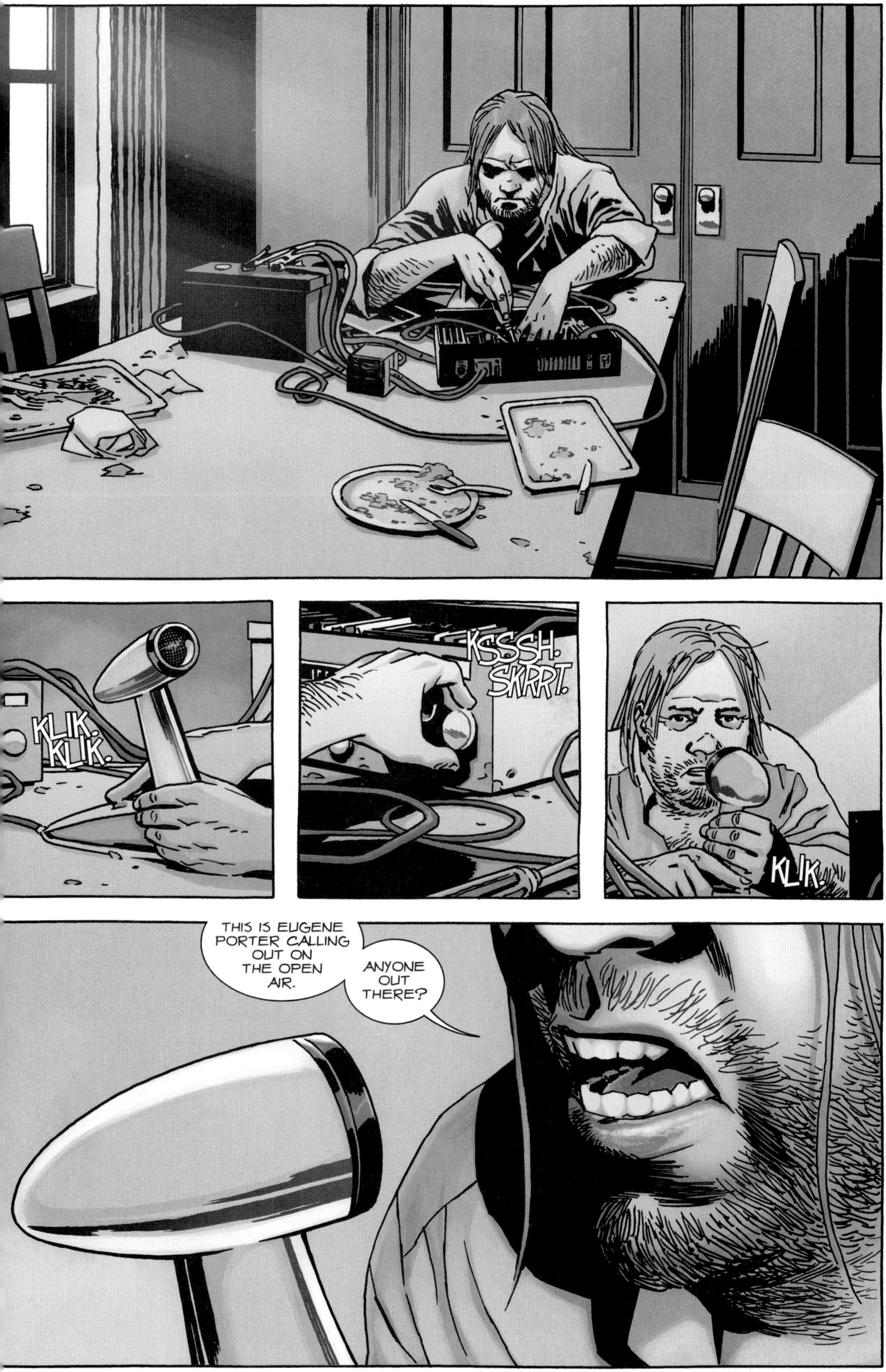
KLIK. KLIK.
KSSSH. SKRRT.
KLIK.
THIS IS EUGENE PORTER CALLING OUT ON THE OPEN AIR.
ANYONE OUT THERE?

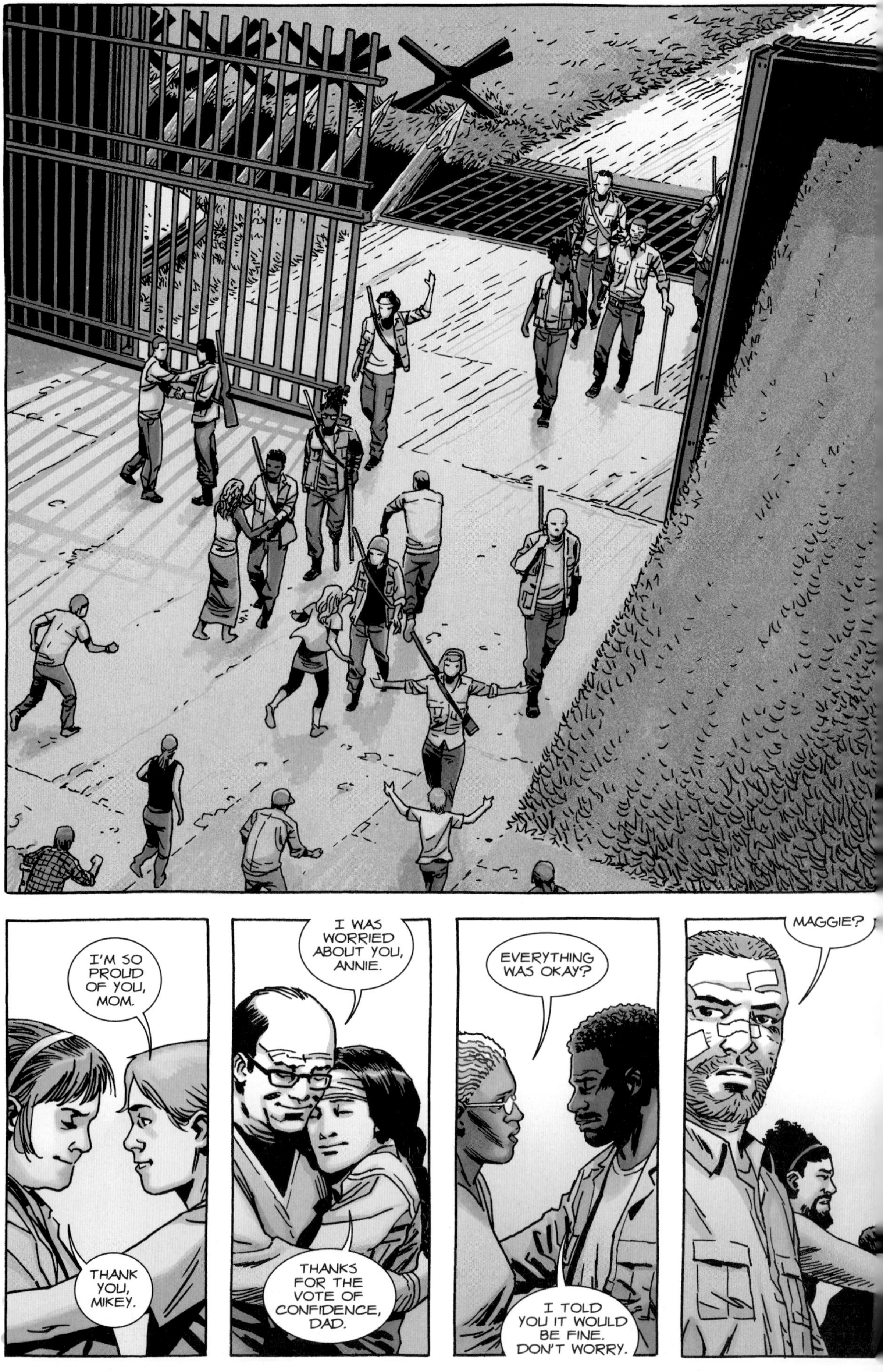
I'M SO PROUD OF YOU, MOM.
THANK YOU, MIKEY.
I WAS WORRIED ABOUT YOU, ANNIE.
THANKS FOR THE VOTE OF CONFIDENCE, DAD.
EVERYTHING WAS OKAY?
I TOLD YOU IT WOULD BE FINE. DON'T WORRY.
MAGGIE?

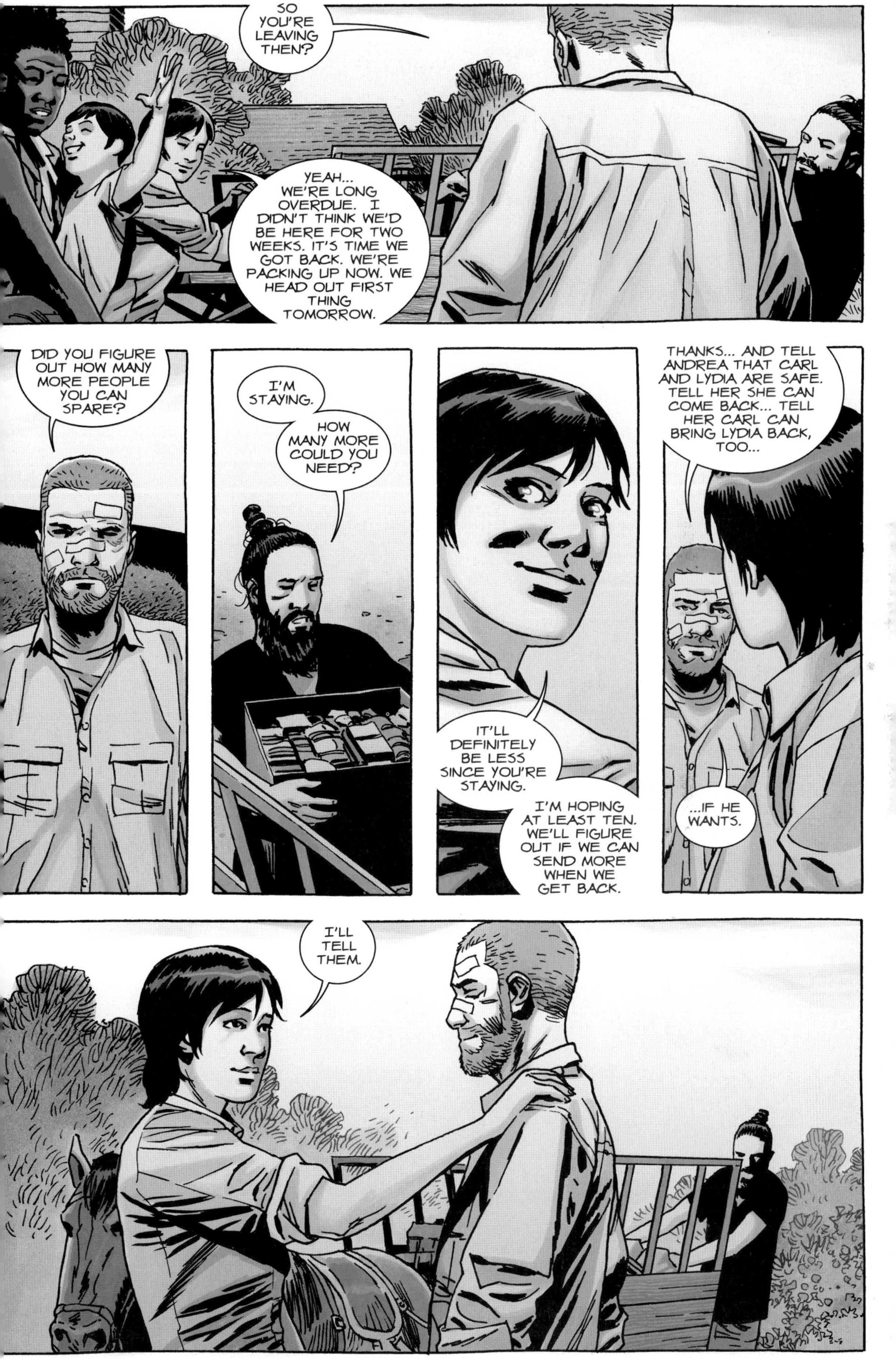
SO YOU'RE LEAVING THEN?
YEAH... WE'RE LONG OVERDUE. I DIDN'T THINK WE'D BE HERE FOR TWO WEEKS. IT'S TIME WE GOT BACK. WE'RE PACKING UP NOW. WE HEAD OUT FIRST THING TOMORROW.
DID YOU FIGURE OUT HOW MANY MORE PEOPLE YOU CAN SPARE?
I'M STAYING.
HOW MANY MORE COULD YOU NEED?
IT'LL DEFINITELY BE LESS SINCE YOU'RE STAYING.
I'M HOPING AT LEAST TEN. WE'LL FIGURE OUT IF WE CAN SEND MORE WHEN WE GET BACK.
THANKS... AND TELL ANDREA THAT CARL AND LYDIA ARE SAFE. TELL HER SHE CAN COME BACK... TELL HER CARL CAN BRING LYDIA BACK, TOO...
...IF HE WANTS.
I'LL TELL THEM.

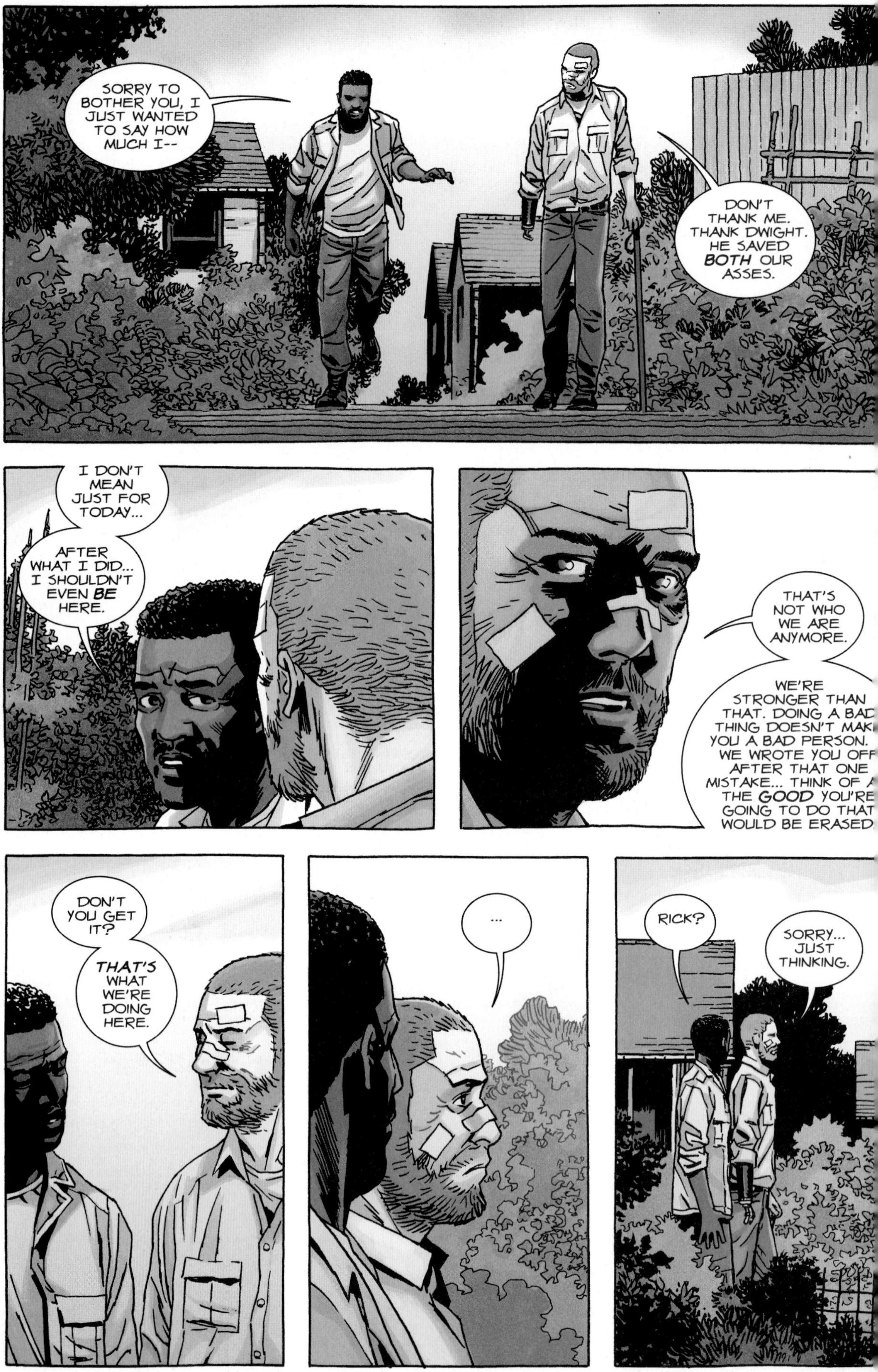
SORRY TO BOTHER YOU, I JUST WANTED TO SAY HOW MUCH I--
DON'T THANK ME. THANK DWIGHT. HE SAVED BOTH OUR ASSES.
I DON'T MEAN JUST FOR TODAY...
AFTER WHAT I DID... I SHOULDN'T EVEN BE HERE.
THAT'S NOT WHO WE ARE ANYMORE.
WE'RE STRONGER THAN THAT. DOING A BAD THING DOESN'T MAK YOU A BAD PERSON. WE WROTE YOU OFF AFTER THAT ONE MISTAKE... THINK OF THE GOOD YOU'RE GOING TO DO THAT WOULD BE ERASED
DON'T YOU GET IT?
THAT'S WHAT WE'RE DOING HERE.
...
RICK?
SORRY... JUST THINKING.

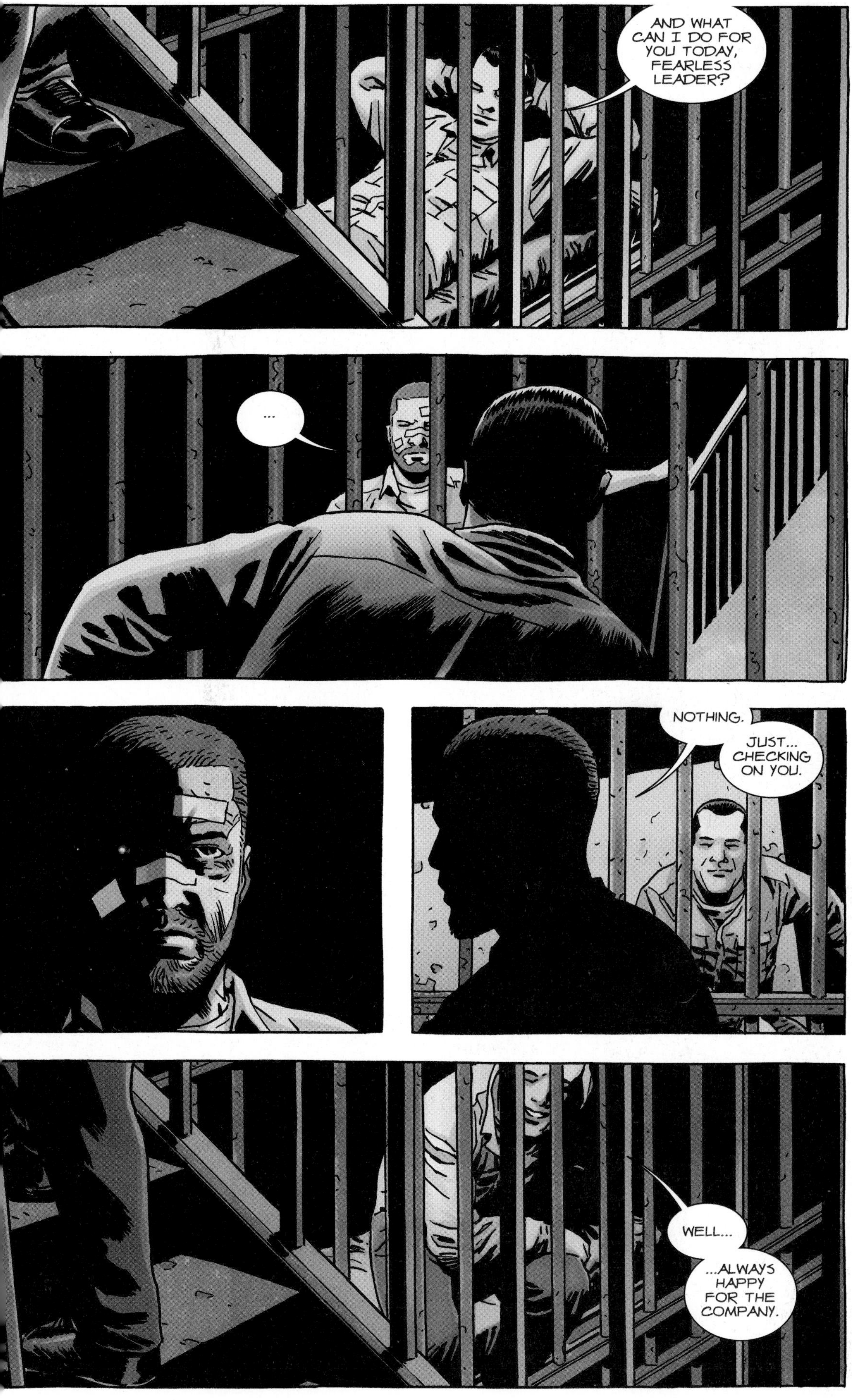
AND WHAT CAN I DO FOR YOU TODAY, FEARLESS LEADER?
...
NOTHING.
JUST... CHECKING ON YOU.
WELL...
...ALWAYS HAPPY FOR THE COMPANY.

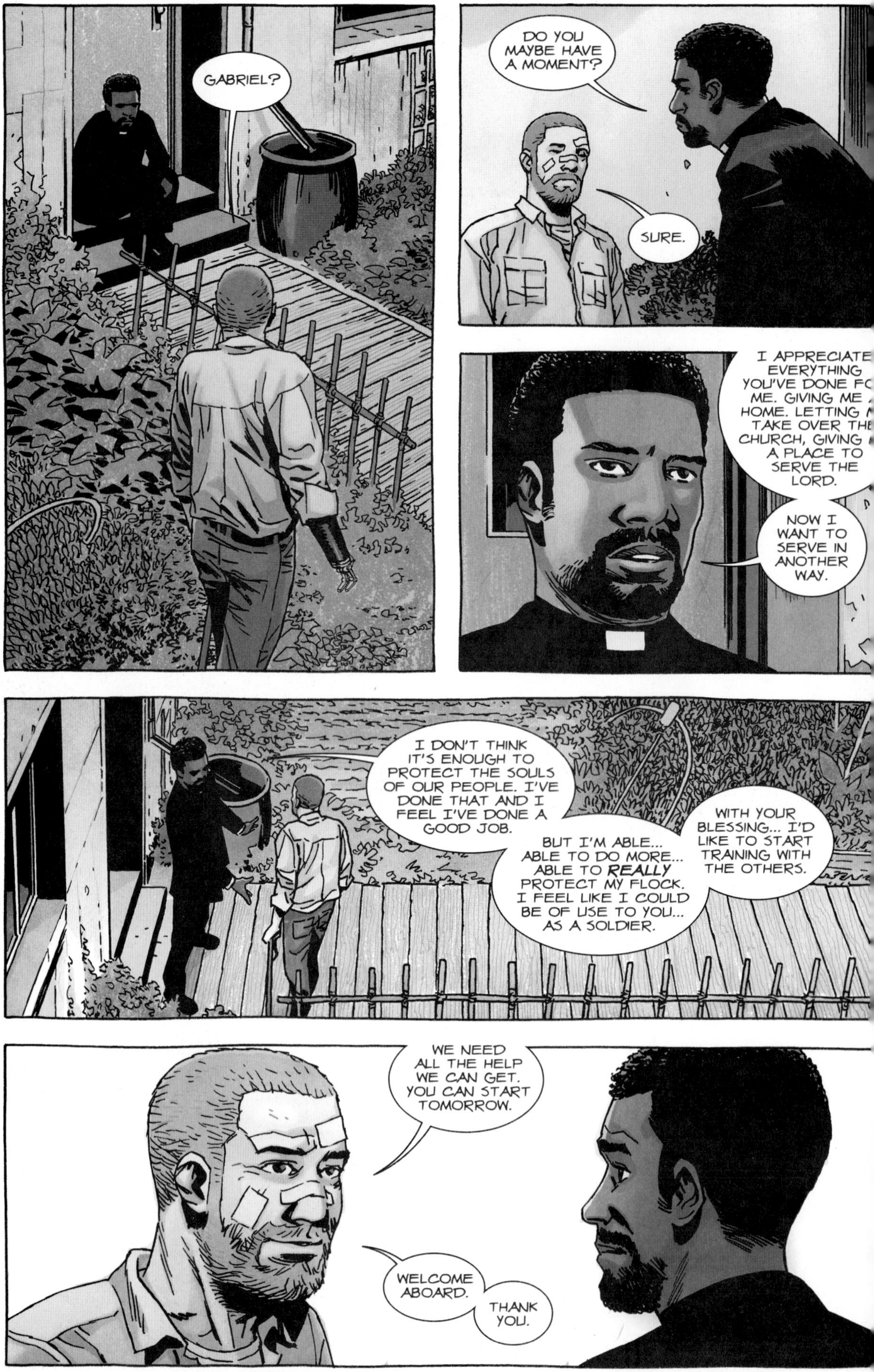
GABRIEL?
DO YOU MAYBE HAVE A MOMENT?
SURE.
I APPRECIATE EVERYTHING YOU'VE DONE FO ME. GIVING ME A HOME. LETTING M TAKE OVER THE CHURCH, GIVING A PLACE TO SERVE THE LORD.
NOW I WANT TO SERVE IN ANOTHER WAY.
I DON'T THINK IT'S ENOUGH TO PROTECT THE SOULS OF OUR PEOPLE. I'VE DONE THAT AND I FEEL I'VE DONE A GOOD JOB.
BUT I'M ABLE... ABLE TO DO MORE... ABLE TO *REALLY* PROTECT MY FLOCK. I FEEL LIKE I COULD BE OF USE TO YOU... AS A SOLDIER.
WITH YOUR BLESSING... I'D LIKE TO START TRAINING WITH THE OTHERS.
WE NEED ALL THE HELP WE CAN GET. YOU CAN START TOMORROW.
WELCOME ABOARD.
THANK YOU.

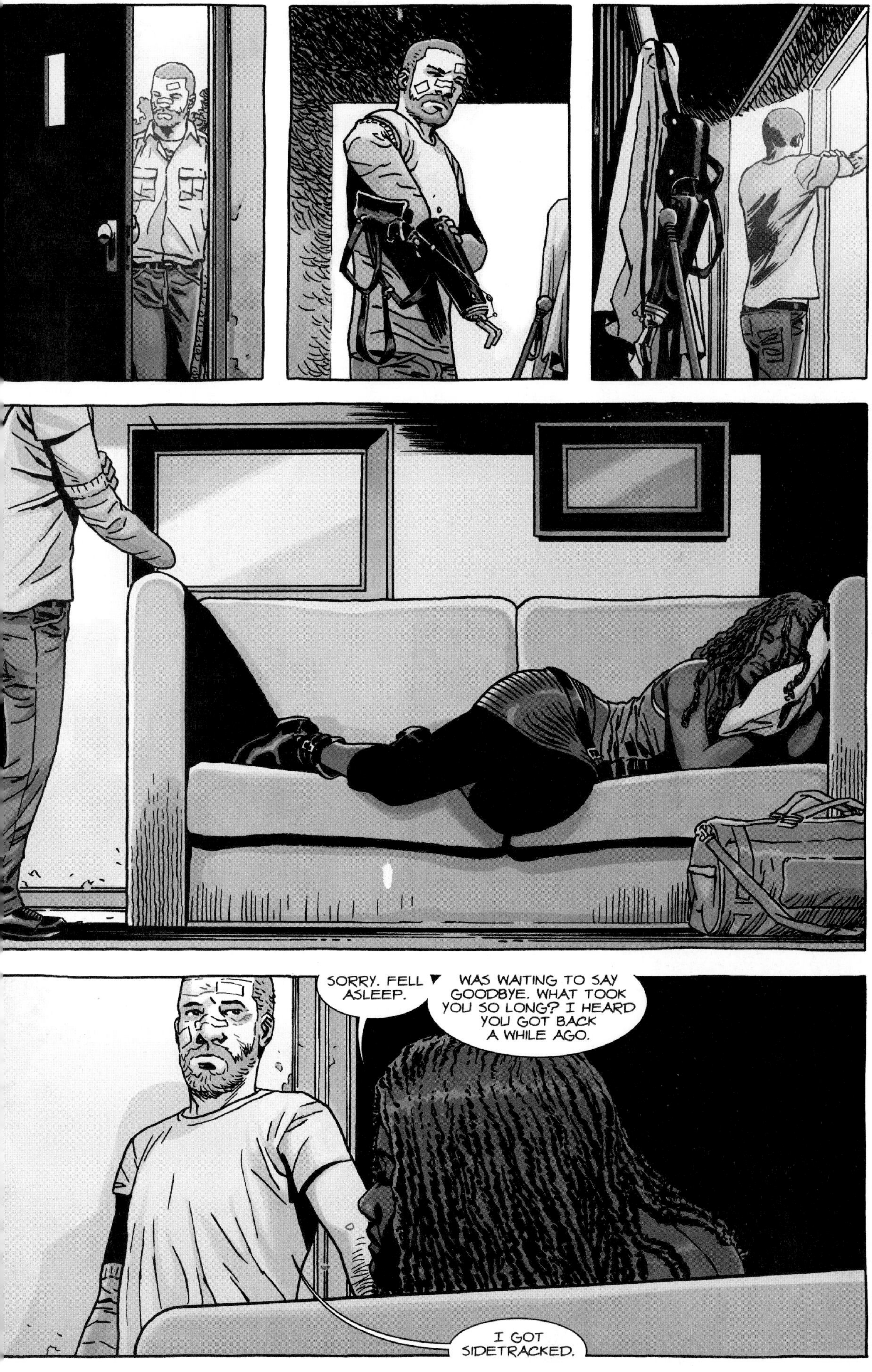
SORRY. FELL ASLEEP.
WAS WAITING TO SAY GOODBYE. WHAT TOOK YOU SO LONG? I HEARD YOU GOT BACK A WHILE AGO.
I GOT SIDETRACKED.

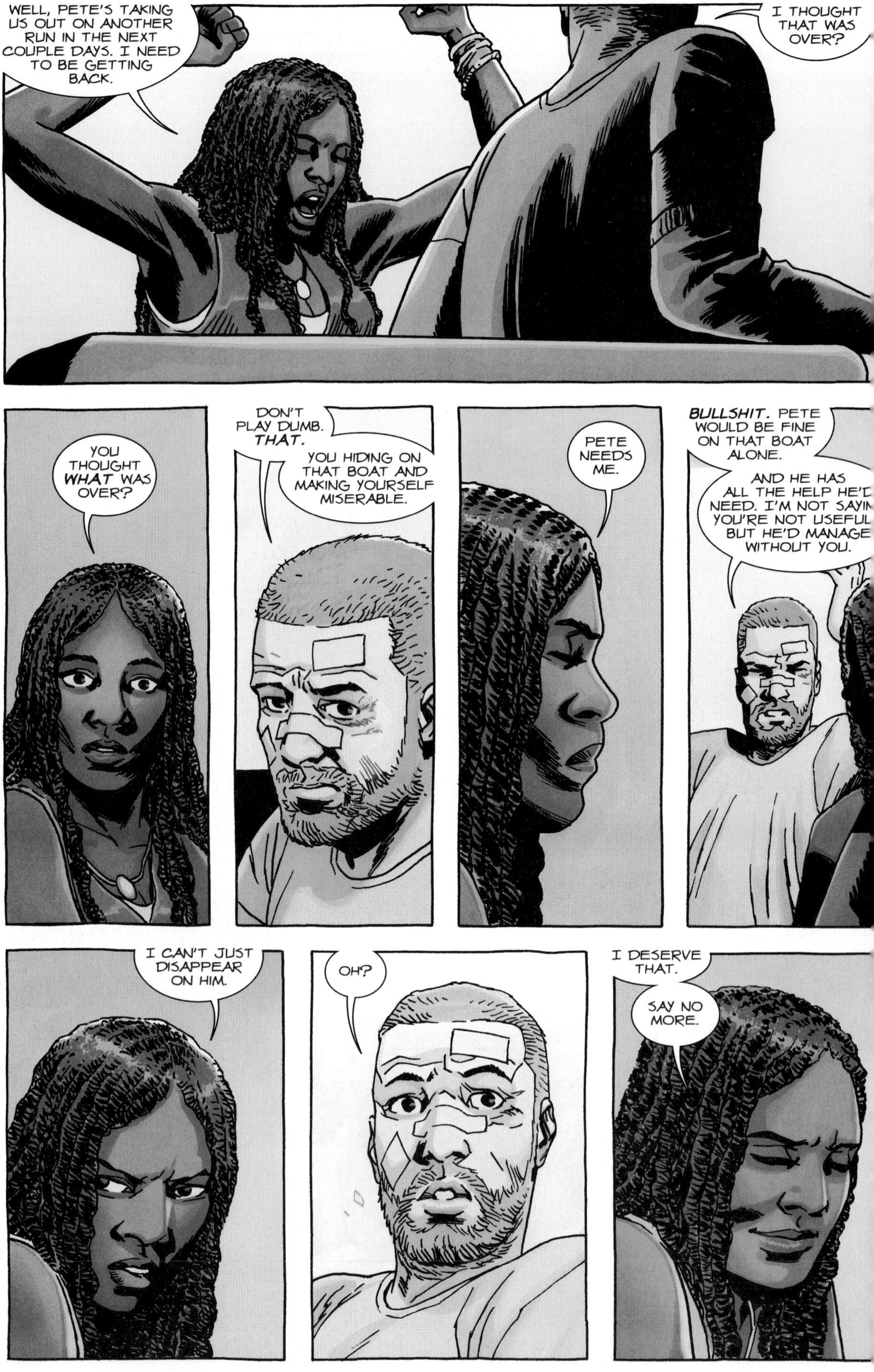
WELL, PETE'S TAKING US OUT ON ANOTHER RUN IN THE NEXT COUPLE DAYS. I NEED TO BE GETTING BACK.
I THOUGHT THAT WAS OVER?
YOU THOUGHT WHAT WAS OVER?
DON'T PLAY DUMB. THAT.
YOU HIDING ON THAT BOAT AND MAKING YOURSELF MISERABLE.
PETE NEEDS ME.
BULLSHIT. PETE WOULD BE FINE ON THAT BOAT ALONE.
I CAN'T JUST DISAPPEAR ON HIM.
OH?
I DESERVE THAT.
SAY NO MORE.

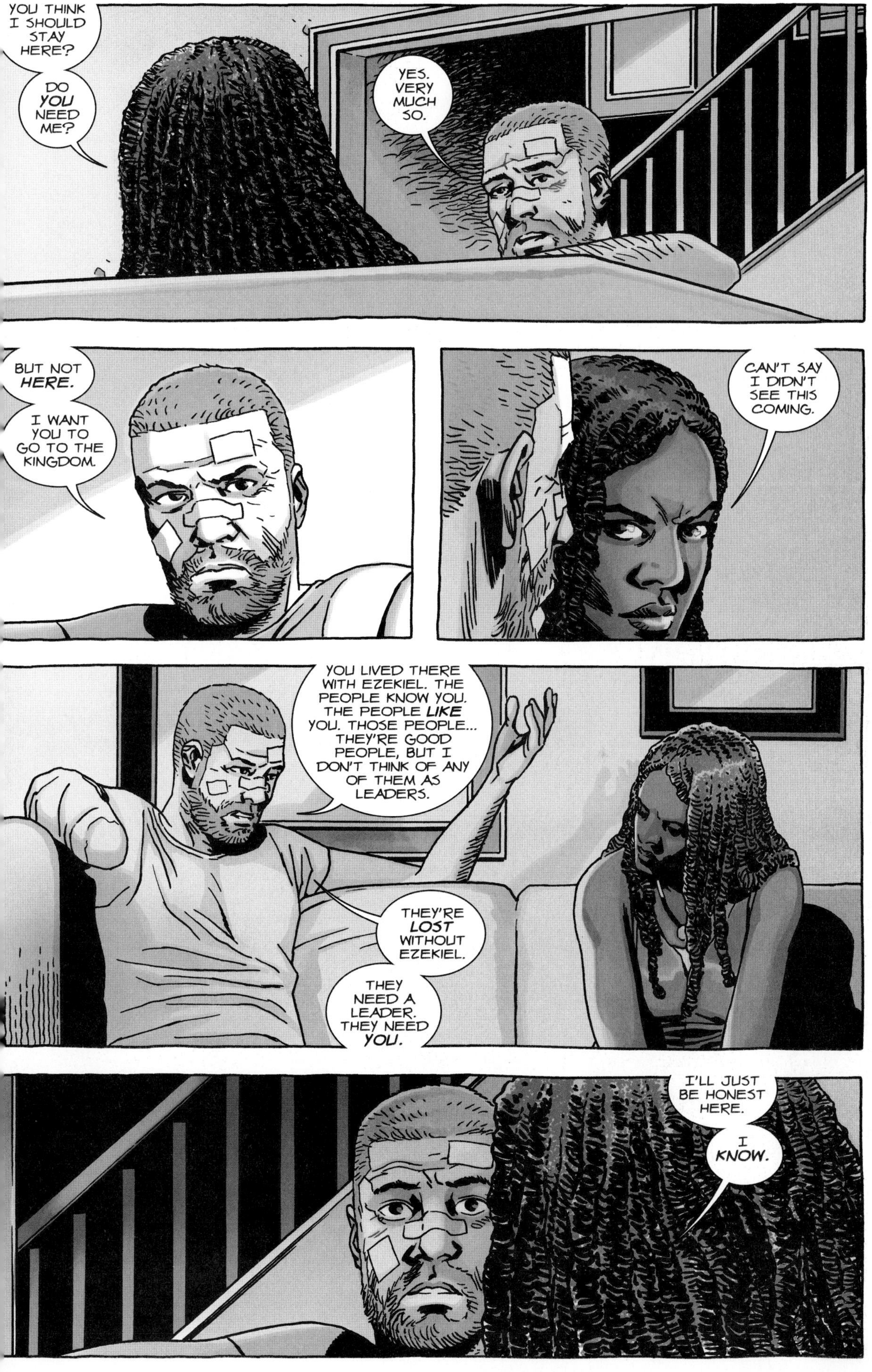
YOU THINK I SHOULD STAY HERE?
DO *YOU* NEED ME?
YES. VERY MUCH SO.
BUT NOT *HERE.*
I WANT YOU TO GO TO THE KINGDOM.
CAN'T SAY I DIDN'T SEE THIS COMING.
YOU LIVED THERE WITH EZEKIEL. THE PEOPLE KNOW YOU. THE PEOPLE *LIKE* YOU. THOSE PEOPLE... THEY'RE GOOD PEOPLE, BUT I DON'T THINK OF ANY OF THEM AS LEADERS.
THEY'RE *LOST* WITHOUT EZEKIEL.
THEY NEED A LEADER. THEY NEED *YOU.*
I'LL JUST BE HONEST HERE.
I *KNOW.*

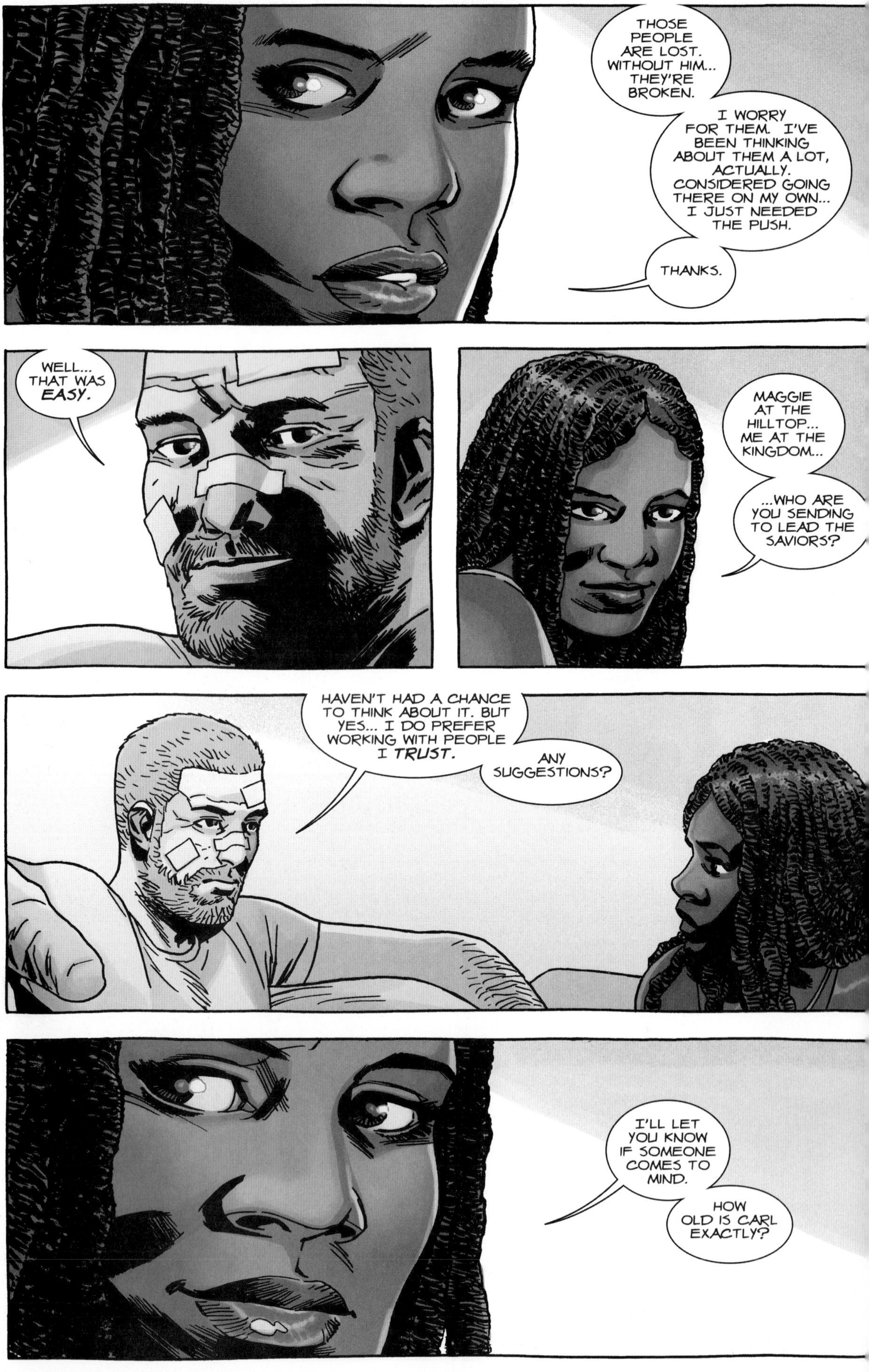
THOSE PEOPLE ARE LOST. WITHOUT HIM... THEY'RE BROKEN.
I WORRY FOR THEM. I'VE BEEN THINKING ABOUT THEM A LOT, ACTUALLY. CONSIDERED GOING THERE ON MY OWN... I JUST NEEDED THE PUSH.
THANKS.
WELL... THAT WAS *EASY.*
MAGGIE AT THE HILLTOP... ME AT THE KINGDOM...
...WHO ARE YOU SENDING TO LEAD THE SAVIORS?
HAVEN'T HAD A CHANCE TO THINK ABOUT IT. BUT YES... I DO PREFER WORKING WITH PEOPLE I *TRUST.*
ANY SUGGESTIONS?
I'LL LET YOU KNOW IF SOMEONE COMES TO MIND.
HOW OLD IS CARL EXACTLY?

THIS IS EUGENE PORTER CALLING OUT LIVE ON THE OPEN AIR.

IS ANYONE OUT THERE?

KLIK.

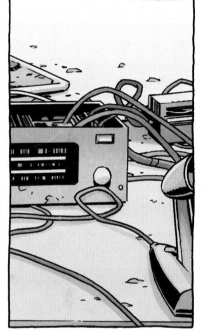

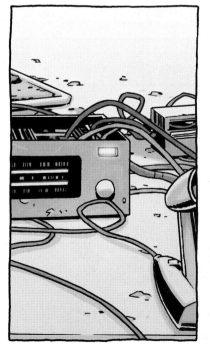

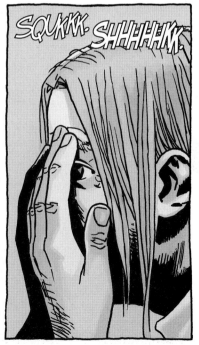

SQUKKK. SHHHHHKK.

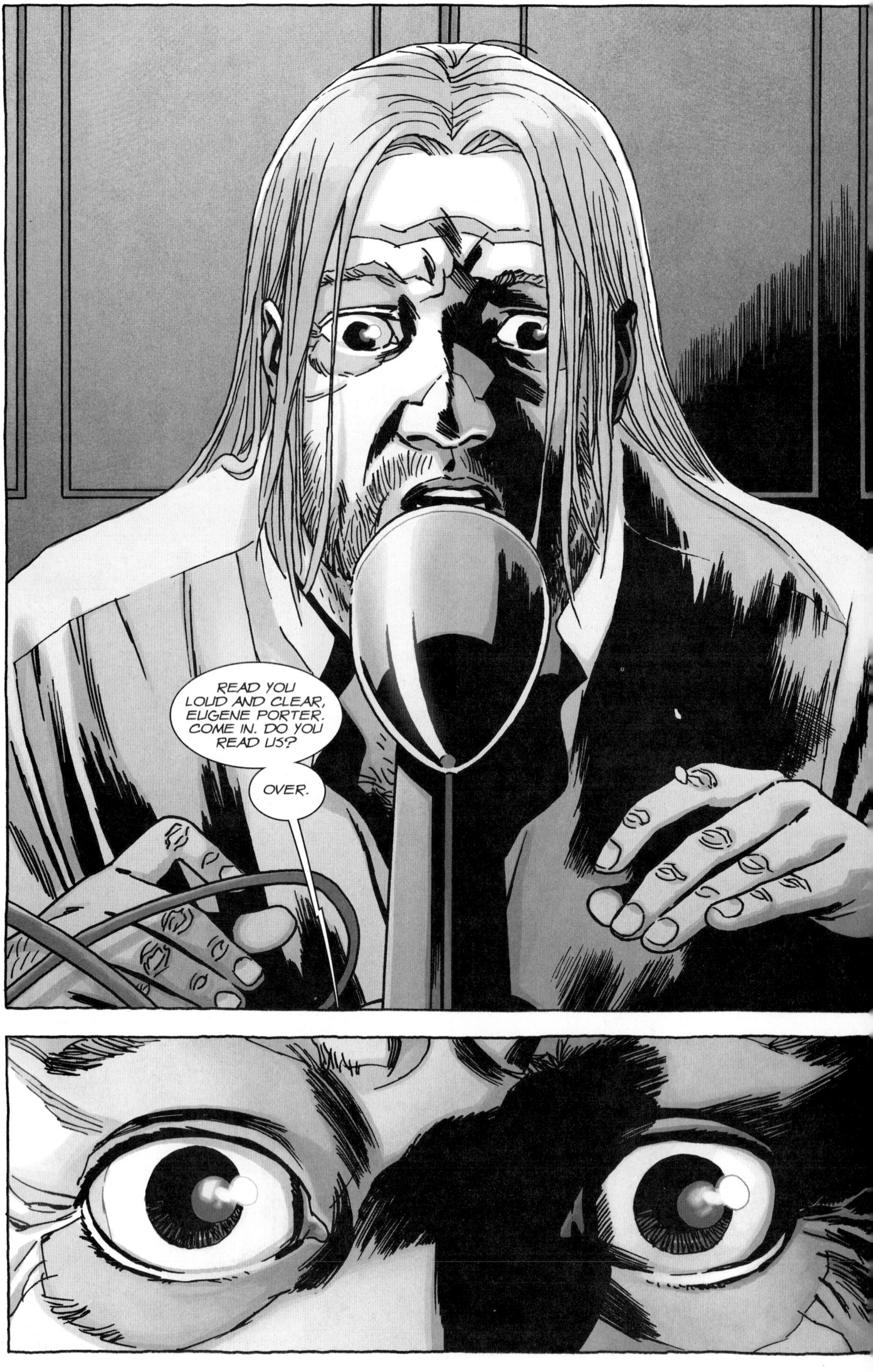
READ YOU LOUD AND CLEAR, EUGENE PORTER. COME IN. DO YOU READ US?
OVER.

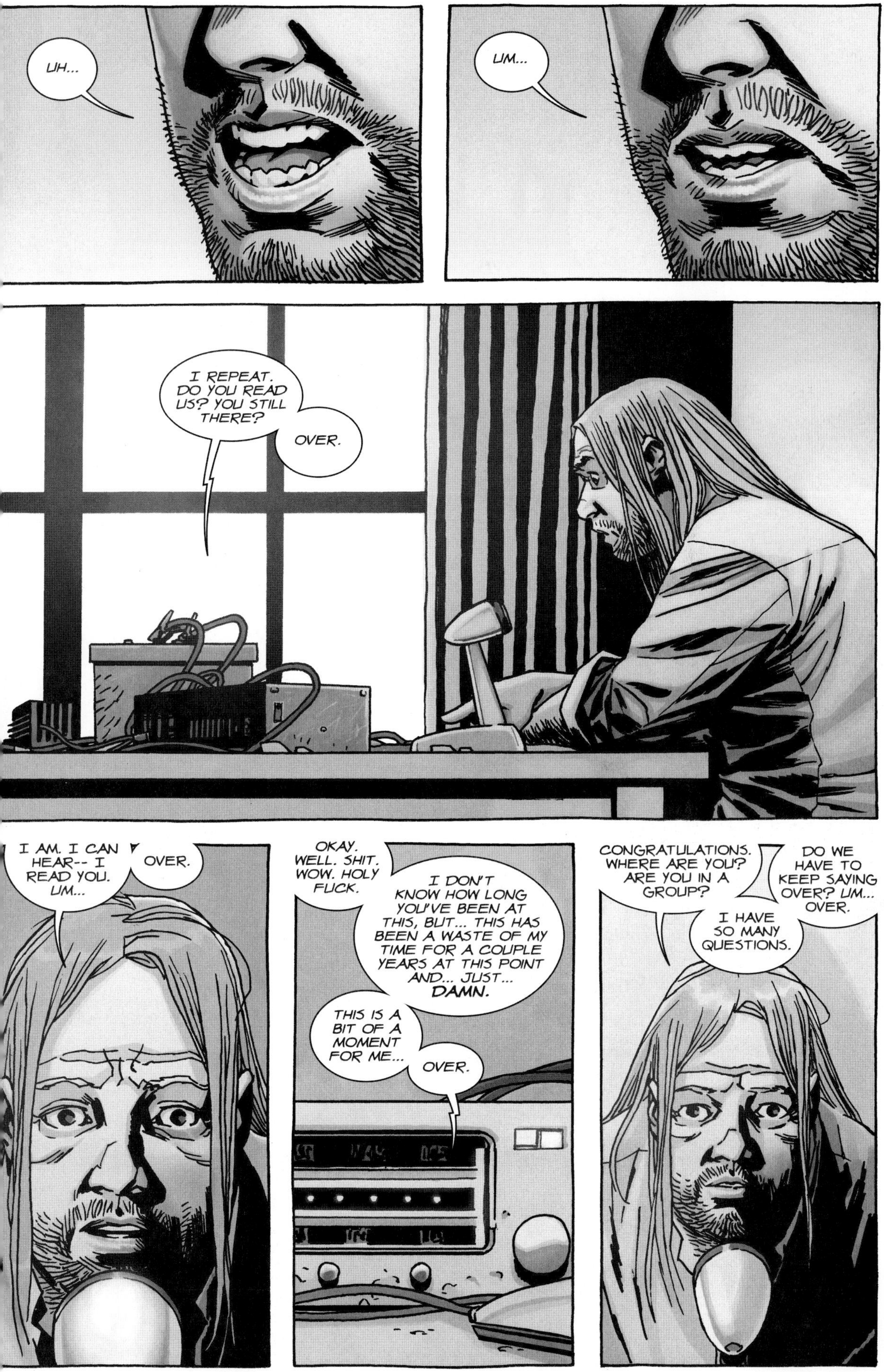
UH...
UM...
I REPEAT. DO YOU READ US? YOU STILL THERE?
OVER.
I AM. I CAN HEAR-- I READ YOU. UM...
OVER.
OKAY. WELL. SHIT. WOW. HOLY FUCK.
I DON'T KNOW HOW LONG YOU'VE BEEN AT THIS, BUT... THIS HAS BEEN A WASTE OF MY TIME FOR A COUPLE YEARS AT THIS POINT AND... JUST... DAMN.
THIS IS A BIT OF A MOMENT FOR ME...
OVER.
CONGRATULATIONS. WHERE ARE YOU? ARE YOU IN A GROUP?
I HAVE SO MANY QUESTIONS.
DO WE HAVE TO KEEP SAYING OVER? UM... OVER.

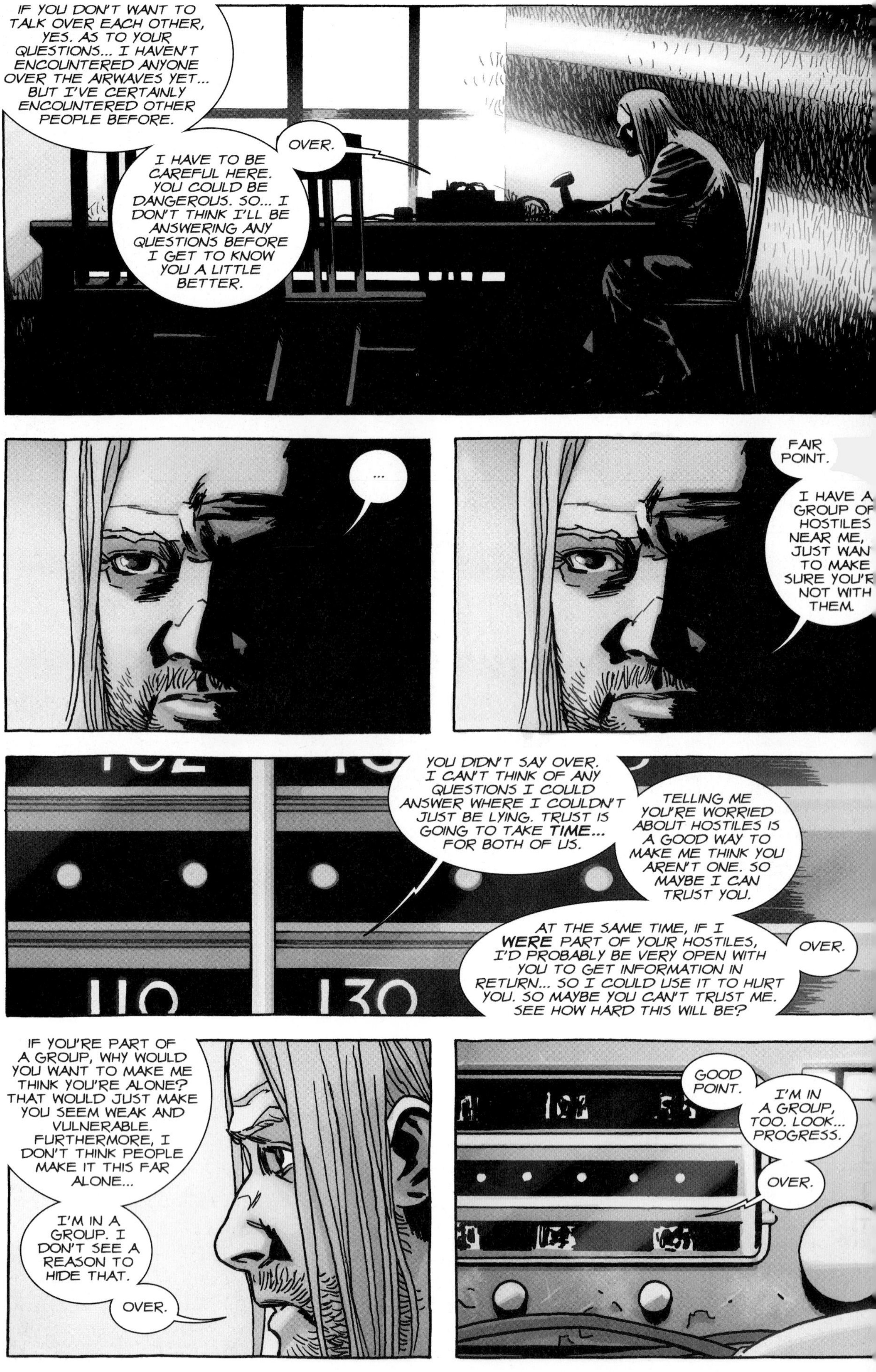
IF YOU DON'T WANT TO TALK OVER EACH OTHER, YES. AS TO YOUR QUESTIONS... I HAVEN'T ENCOUNTERED ANYONE OVER THE AIRWAVES YET... BUT I'VE CERTAINLY ENCOUNTERED OTHER PEOPLE BEFORE.
I HAVE TO BE CAREFUL HERE. YOU COULD BE DANGEROUS. SO... I DON'T THINK I'LL BE ANSWERING ANY QUESTIONS BEFORE I GET TO KNOW YOU A LITTLE BETTER.
OVER.
...
FAIR POINT.
I HAVE A GROUP OF HOSTILES NEAR ME, JUST WAN TO MAKE SURE YOU'R NOT WITH THEM.
YOU DIDN'T SAY OVER. I CAN'T THINK OF ANY QUESTIONS I COULD ANSWER WHERE I COULDN'T JUST BE LYING. TRUST IS GOING TO TAKE TIME... FOR BOTH OF US.
TELLING ME YOU'RE WORRIED ABOUT HOSTILES IS A GOOD WAY TO MAKE ME THINK YOU AREN'T ONE. SO MAYBE I CAN TRUST YOU.
AT THE SAME TIME, IF I WERE PART OF YOUR HOSTILES, I'D PROBABLY BE VERY OPEN WITH YOU TO GET INFORMATION IN RETURN... SO I COULD USE IT TO HURT YOU. SO MAYBE YOU CAN'T TRUST ME. SEE HOW HARD THIS WILL BE?
OVER.
IF YOU'RE PART OF A GROUP, WHY WOULD YOU WANT TO MAKE ME THINK YOU'RE ALONE? THAT WOULD JUST MAKE YOU SEEM WEAK AND VULNERABLE. FURTHERMORE, I DON'T THINK PEOPLE MAKE IT THIS FAR ALONE...
I'M IN A GROUP. I DON'T SEE A REASON TO HIDE THAT.
OVER.
GOOD POINT.
I'M IN A GROUP, TOO. LOOK... PROGRESS.
OVER.

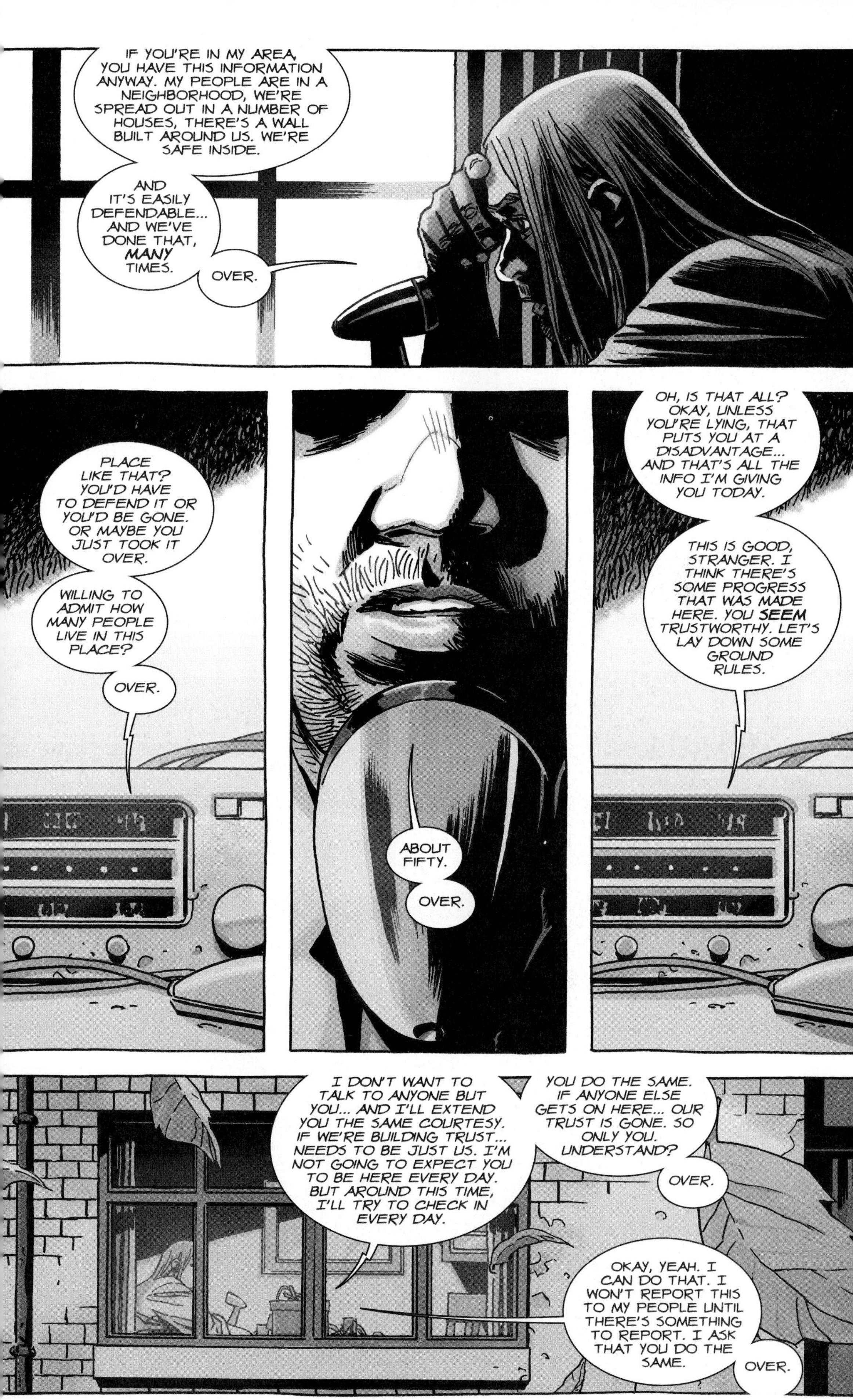
IF YOU'RE IN MY AREA, YOU HAVE THIS INFORMATION ANYWAY. MY PEOPLE ARE IN A NEIGHBORHOOD, WE'RE SPREAD OUT IN A NUMBER OF HOUSES, THERE'S A WALL BUILT AROUND US. WE'RE SAFE INSIDE.
AND IT'S EASILY DEFENDABLE... AND WE'VE DONE THAT, MANY TIMES.
OVER.
PLACE LIKE THAT? YOU'D HAVE TO DEFEND IT OR YOU'D BE GONE. OR MAYBE YOU JUST TOOK IT OVER.
WILLING TO ADMIT HOW MANY PEOPLE LIVE IN THIS PLACE?
OVER.
ABOUT FIFTY.
OVER.
OH, IS THAT ALL? OKAY, UNLESS YOU'RE LYING, THAT PUTS YOU AT A DISADVANTAGE... AND THAT'S ALL THE INFO I'M GIVING YOU TODAY.
THIS IS GOOD, STRANGER. I THINK THERE'S SOME PROGRESS THAT WAS MADE HERE. YOU SEEM TRUSTWORTHY. LET'S LAY DOWN SOME GROUND RULES.
I DON'T WANT TO TALK TO ANYONE BUT YOU... AND I'LL EXTEND YOU THE SAME COURTESY. IF WE'RE BUILDING TRUST... NEEDS TO BE JUST US. I'M NOT GOING TO EXPECT YOU TO BE HERE EVERY DAY. BUT AROUND THIS TIME, I'LL TRY TO CHECK IN EVERY DAY.
YOU DO THE SAME. IF ANYONE ELSE GETS ON HERE... OUR TRUST IS GONE. SO ONLY YOU. UNDERSTAND?
OVER.
OKAY, YEAH. I CAN DO THAT. I WON'T REPORT THIS TO MY PEOPLE UNTIL THERE'S SOMETHING TO REPORT. I ASK THAT YOU DO THE SAME.
OVER.

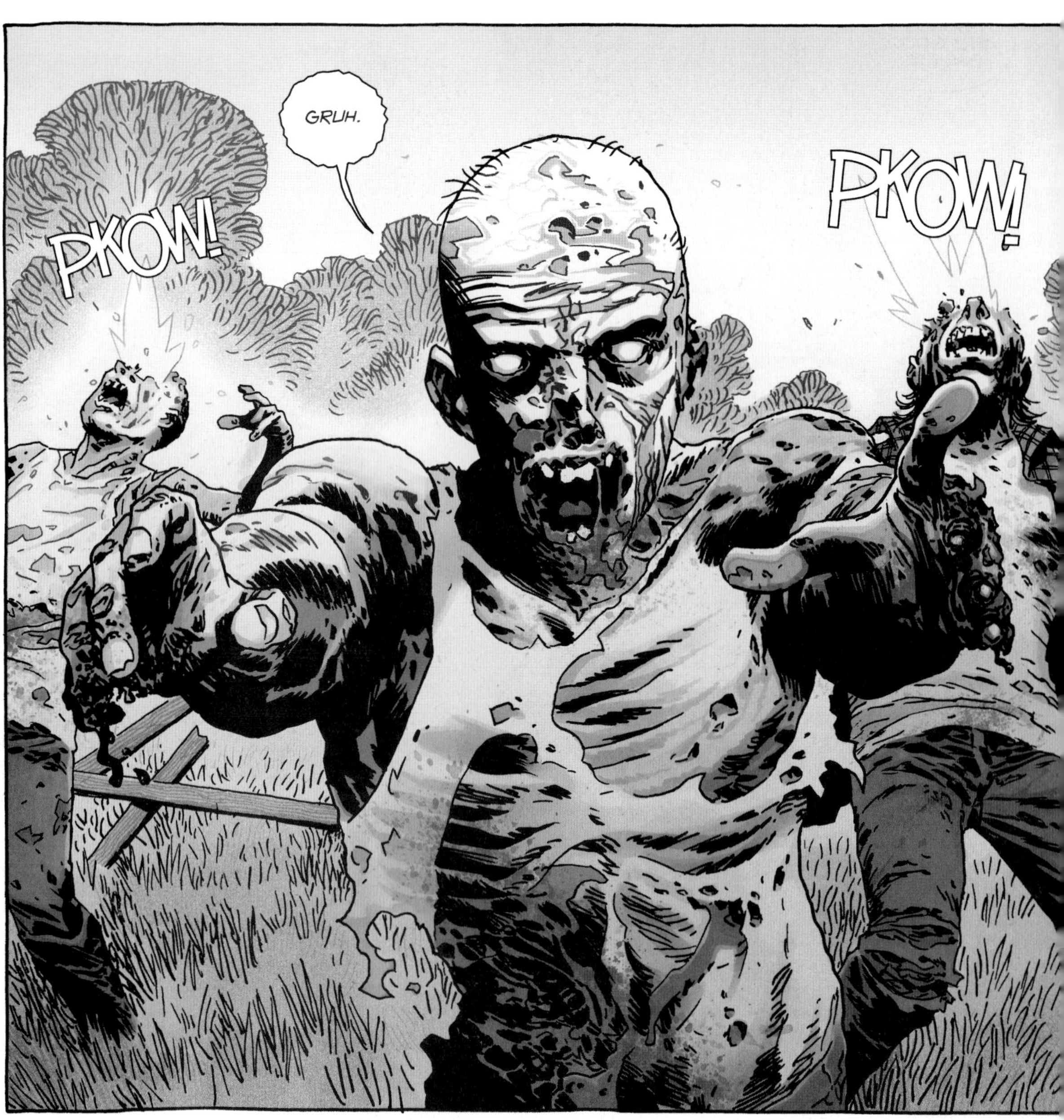
PKOW!
GRUH.
PKOW!

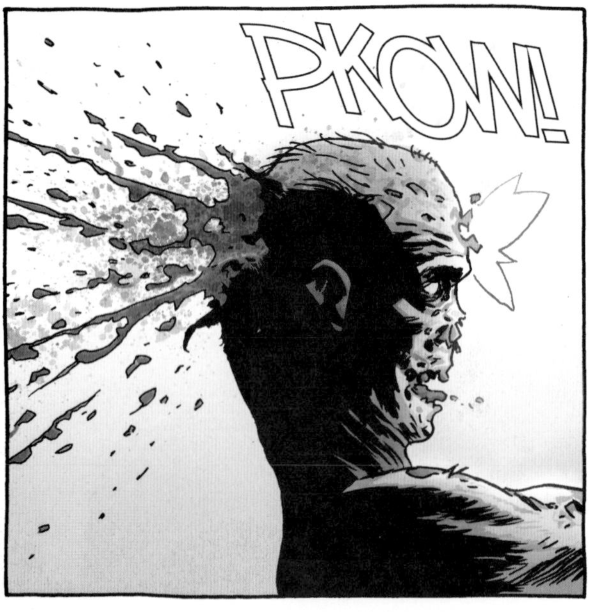
PKOW!

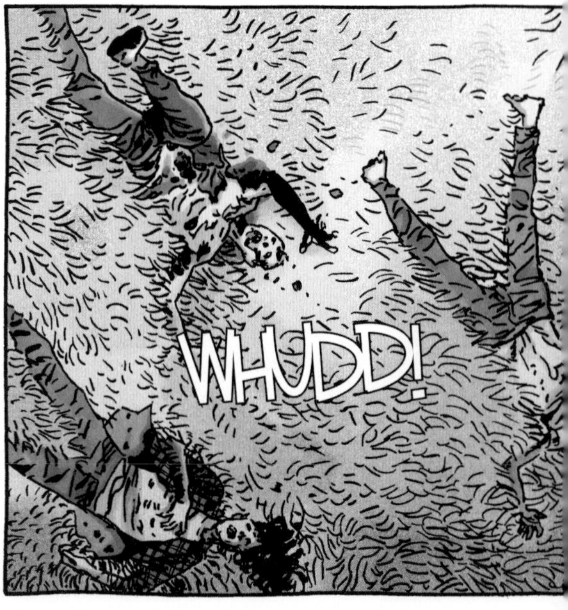
WHUDD!

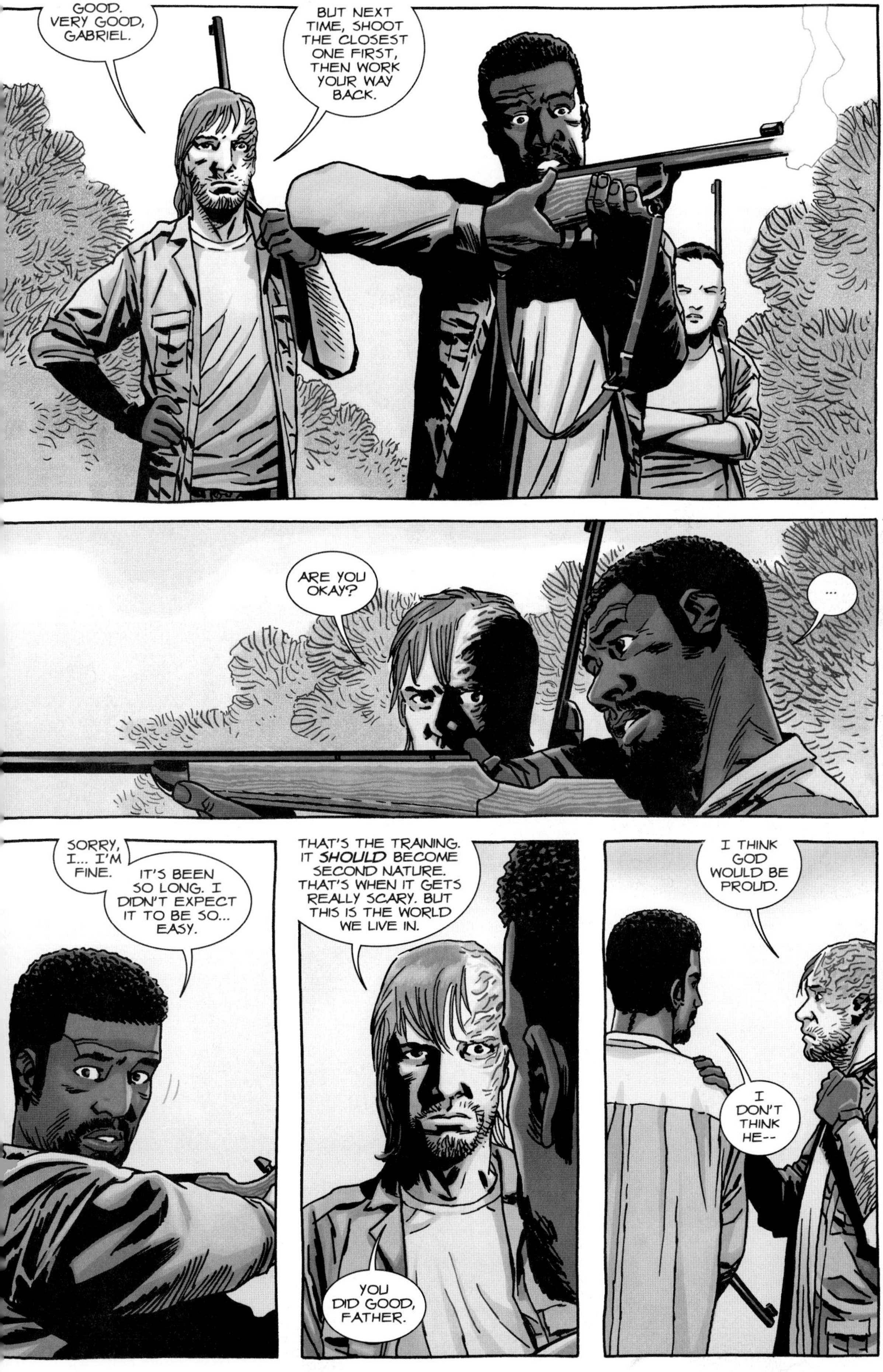
GOOD. VERY GOOD, GABRIEL.
BUT NEXT TIME, SHOOT THE CLOSEST ONE FIRST, THEN WORK YOUR WAY BACK.
ARE YOU OKAY?
...
SORRY, I... I'M FINE.
IT'S BEEN SO LONG. I DIDN'T EXPECT IT TO BE SO... EASY.
THAT'S THE TRAINING. IT SHOULD BECOME SECOND NATURE. THAT'S WHEN IT GETS REALLY SCARY. BUT THIS IS THE WORLD WE LIVE IN.
YOU DID GOOD, FATHER.
I THINK GOD WOULD BE PROUD.
I DON'T THINK HE--

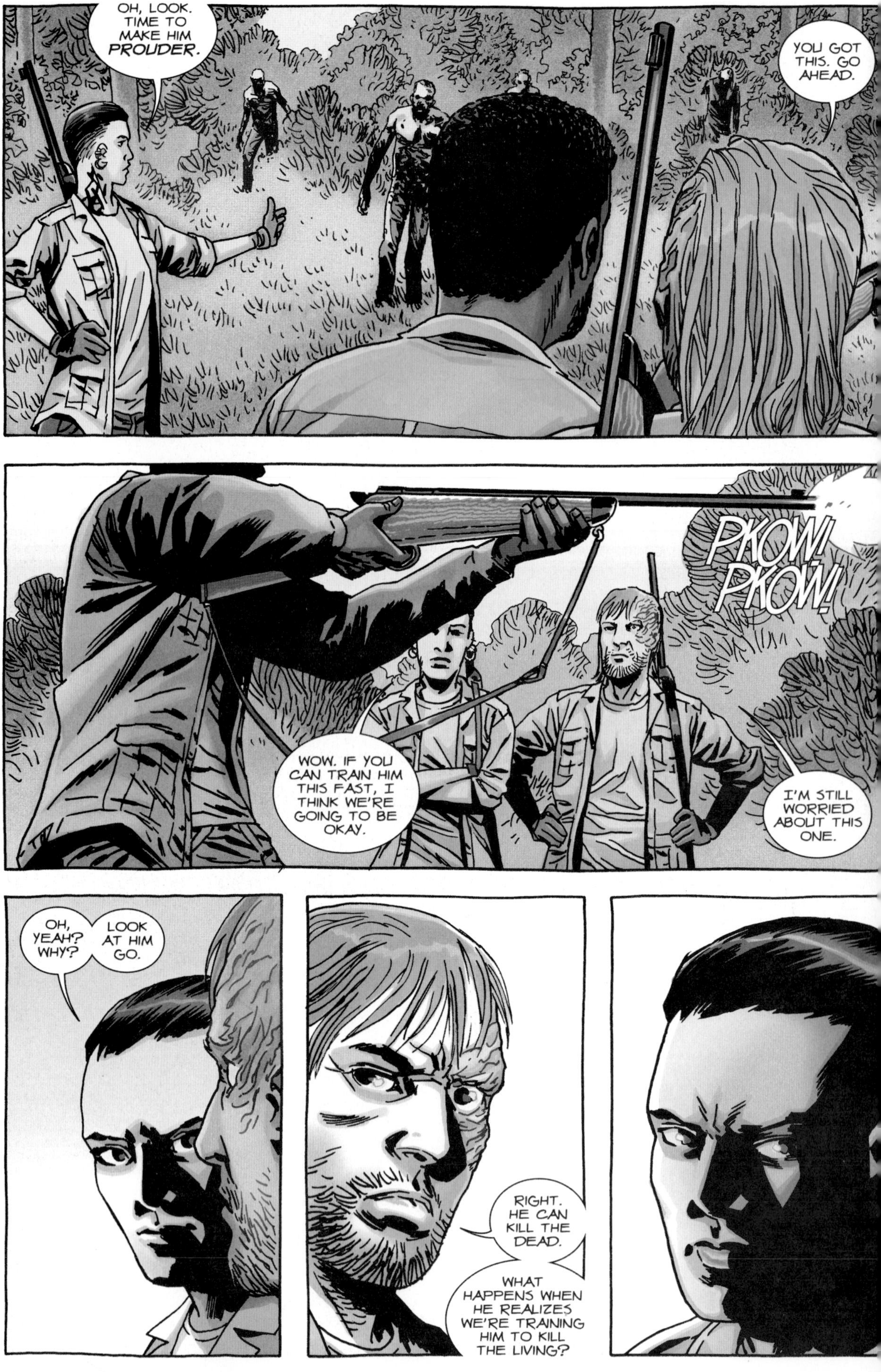
OH, LOOK. TIME TO MAKE HIM PROUDER.
YOU GOT THIS. GO AHEAD.
PKOW! PKOW!
WOW. IF YOU CAN TRAIN HIM THIS FAST, I THINK WE'RE GOING TO BE OKAY.
I'M STILL WORRIED ABOUT THIS ONE.
OH, YEAH? WHY?
LOOK AT HIM GO.
RIGHT. HE CAN KILL THE DEAD.
WHAT HAPPENS WHEN HE REALIZES WE'RE TRAINING HIM TO KILL THE LIVING?

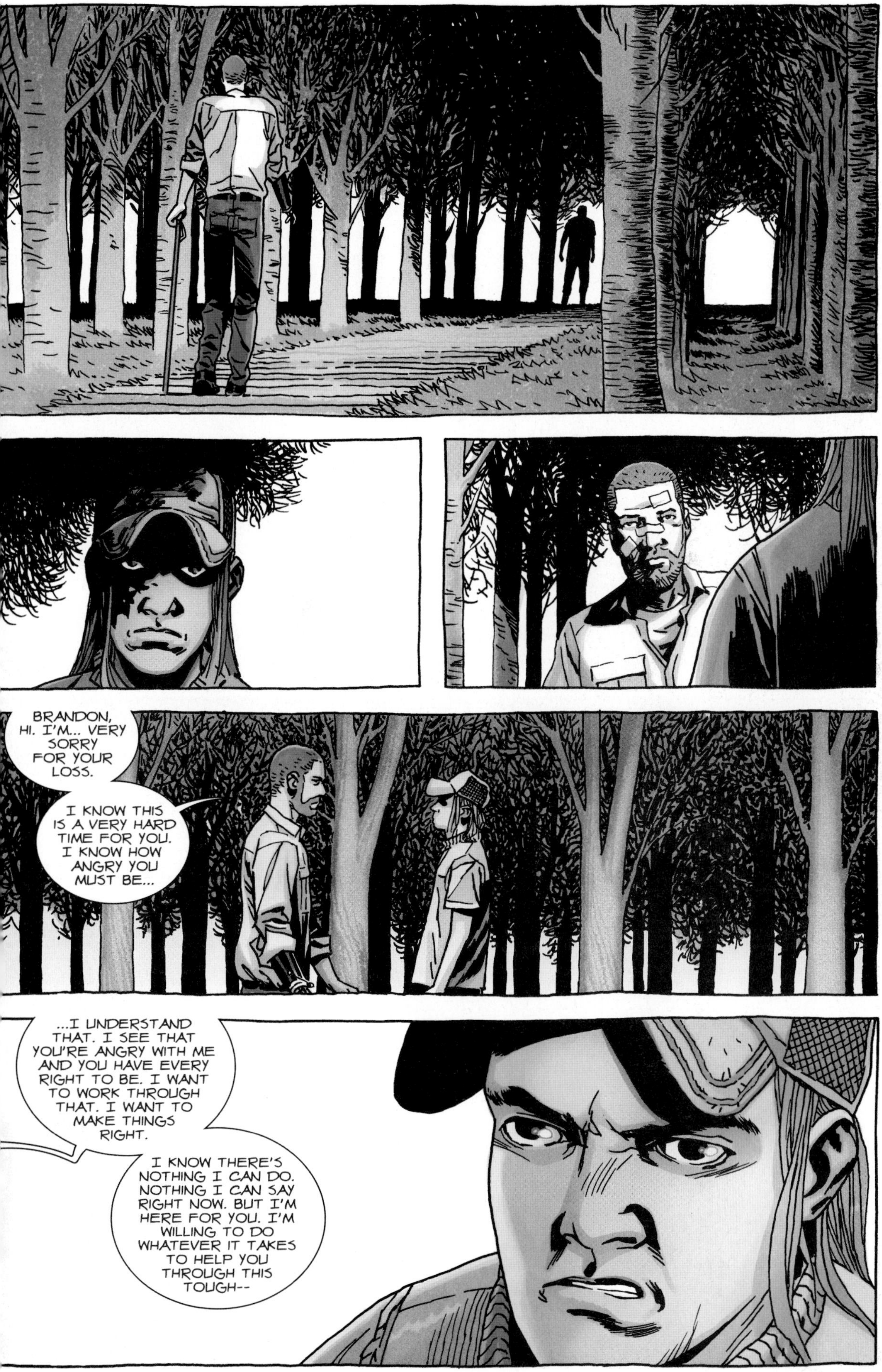
BRANDON, HI. I'M... VERY SORRY FOR YOUR LOSS.
I KNOW THIS IS A VERY HARD TIME FOR YOU. I KNOW HOW ANGRY YOU MUST BE...
...I UNDERSTAND THAT. I SEE THAT YOU'RE ANGRY WITH ME AND YOU HAVE EVERY RIGHT TO BE. I WANT TO WORK THROUGH THAT. I WANT TO MAKE THINGS RIGHT.
I KNOW THERE'S NOTHING I CAN DO. NOTHING I CAN SAY RIGHT NOW. BUT I'M HERE FOR YOU. I'M WILLING TO DO WHATEVER IT TAKES TO HELP YOU THROUGH THIS TOUGH--

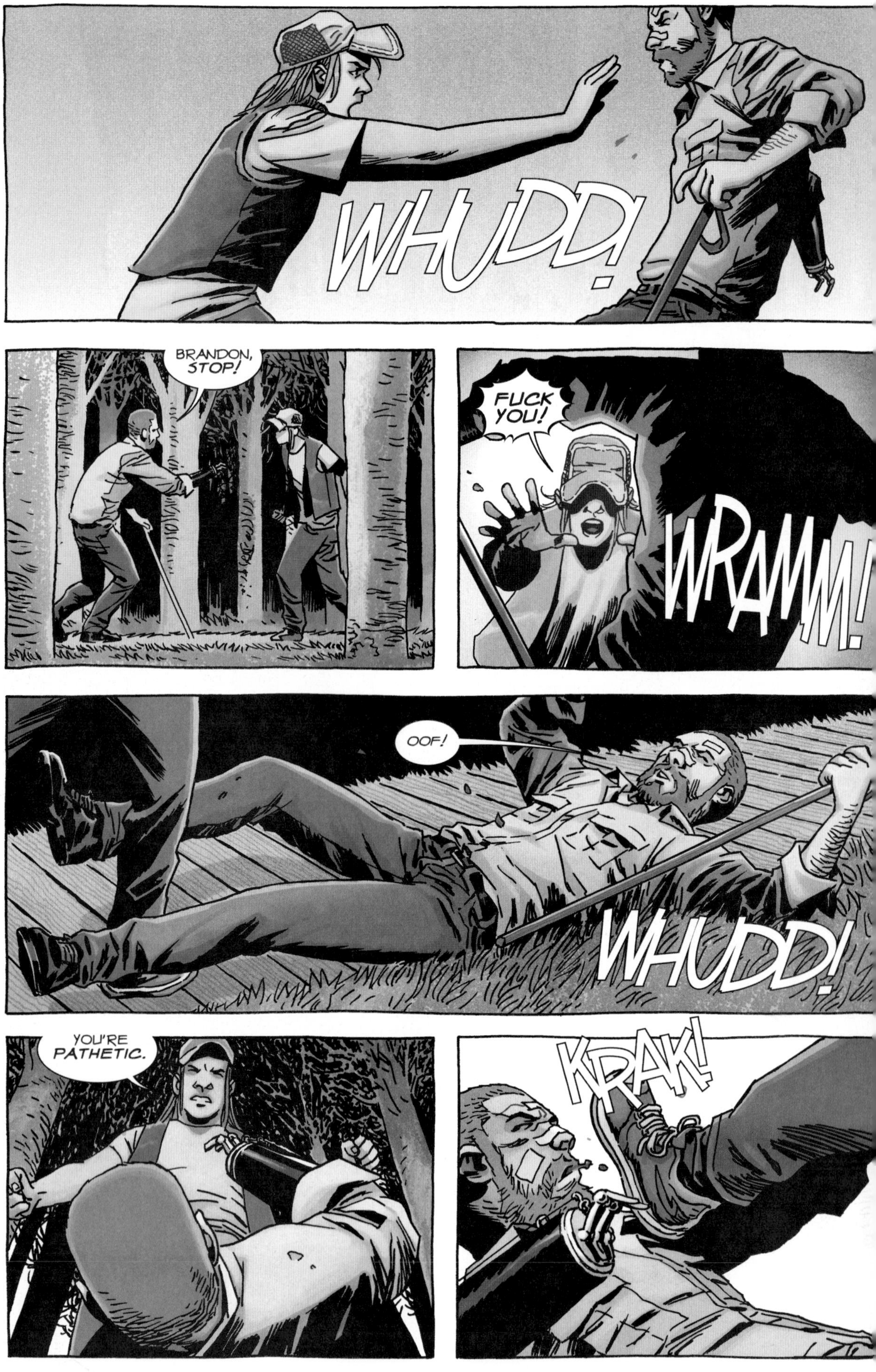
WHUDD!
BRANDON, STOP!
FUCK YOU!
WRAMM!
OOF!
WHUDD!
YOU'RE PATHETIC.
KRAK!

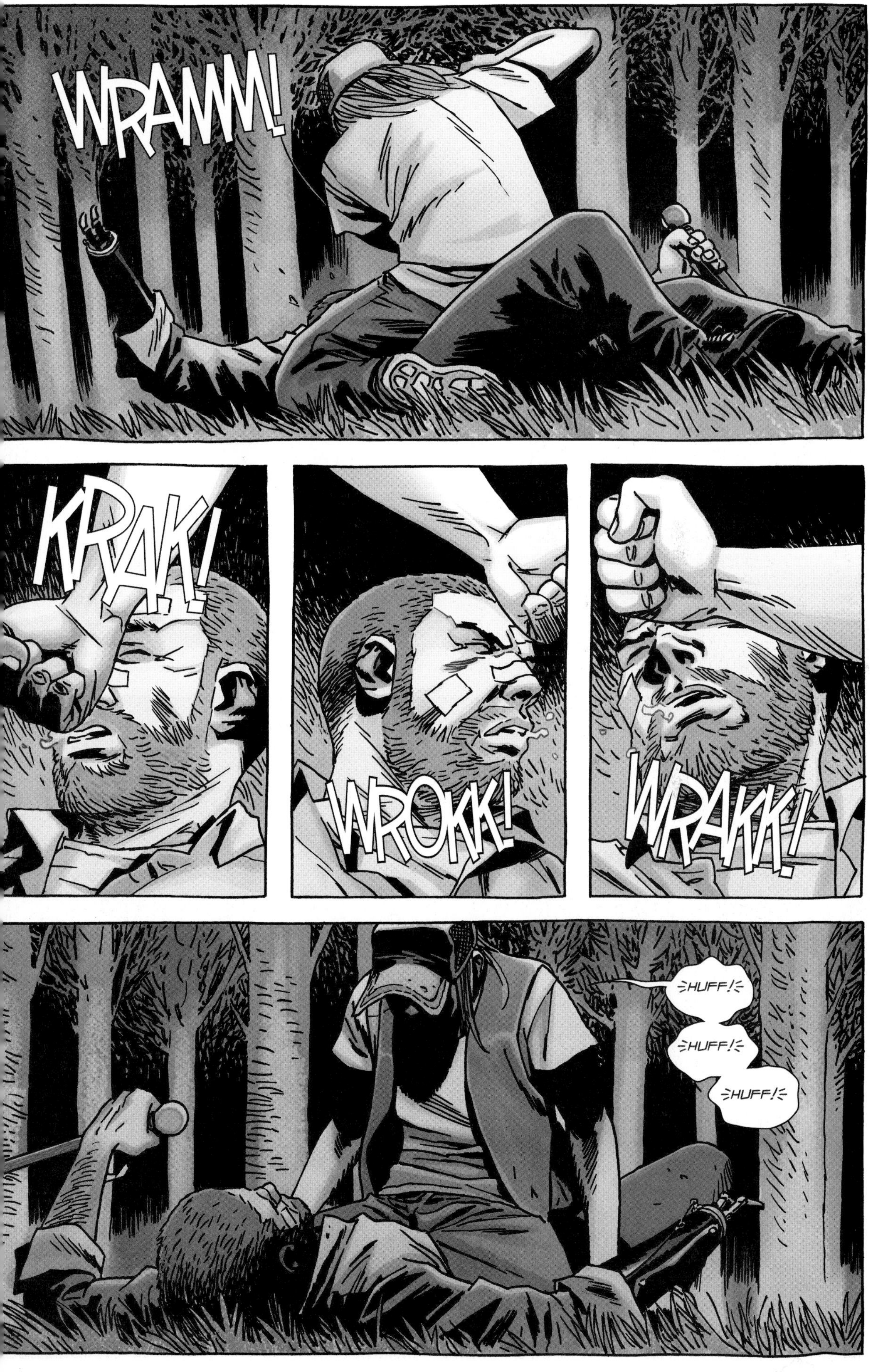
WRAMM!
KRAK!
WROKK!
WRAKK!
HUFF!
HUFF!
HUFF!

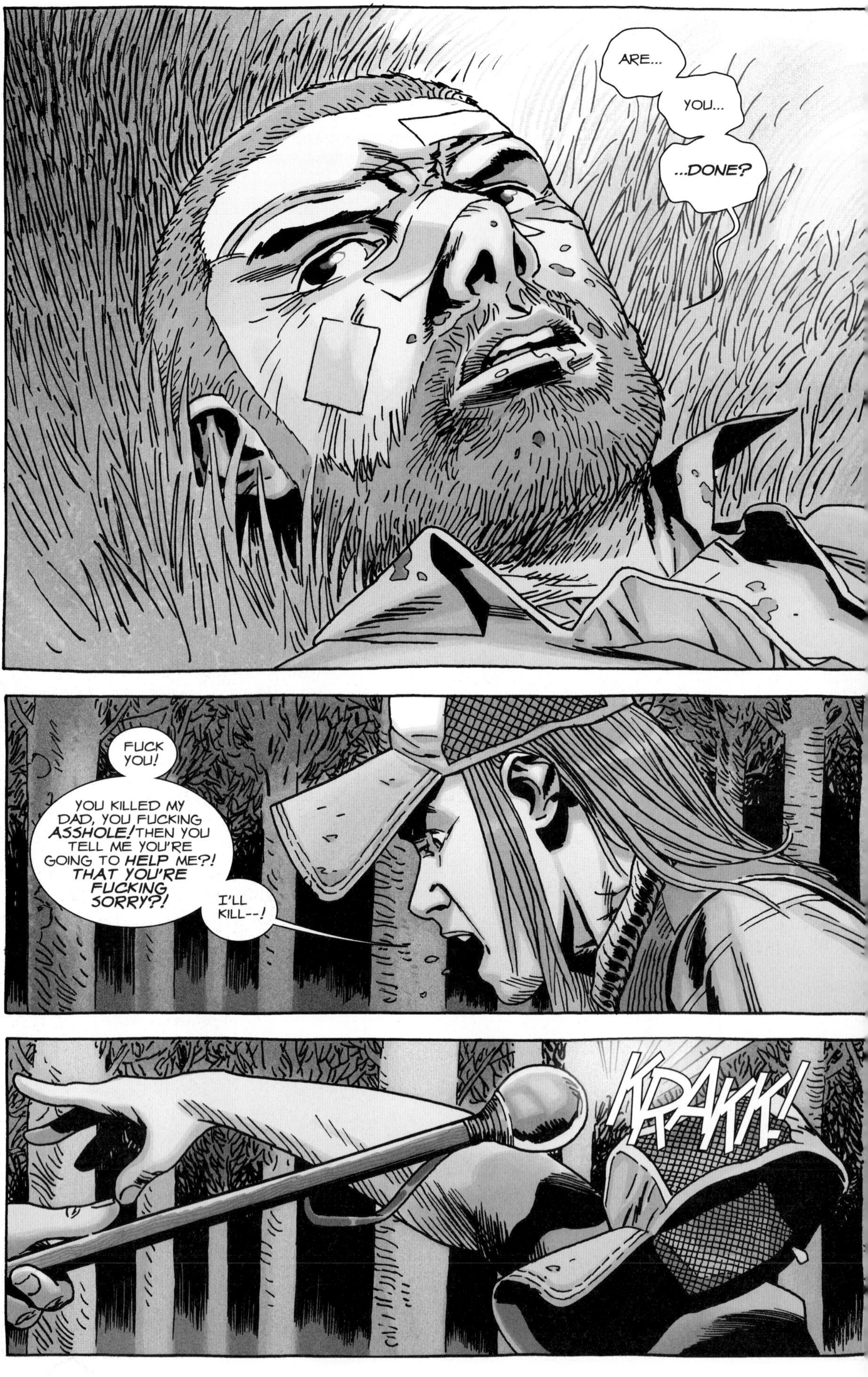
ARE...
YOU...
...DONE?
FUCK YOU!
YOU KILLED MY DAD, YOU FUCKING ASSHOLE! THEN YOU TELL ME YOU'RE GOING TO HELP ME?! THAT YOU'RE FUCKING SORRY?!
I'LL KILL--!
KRAKK!

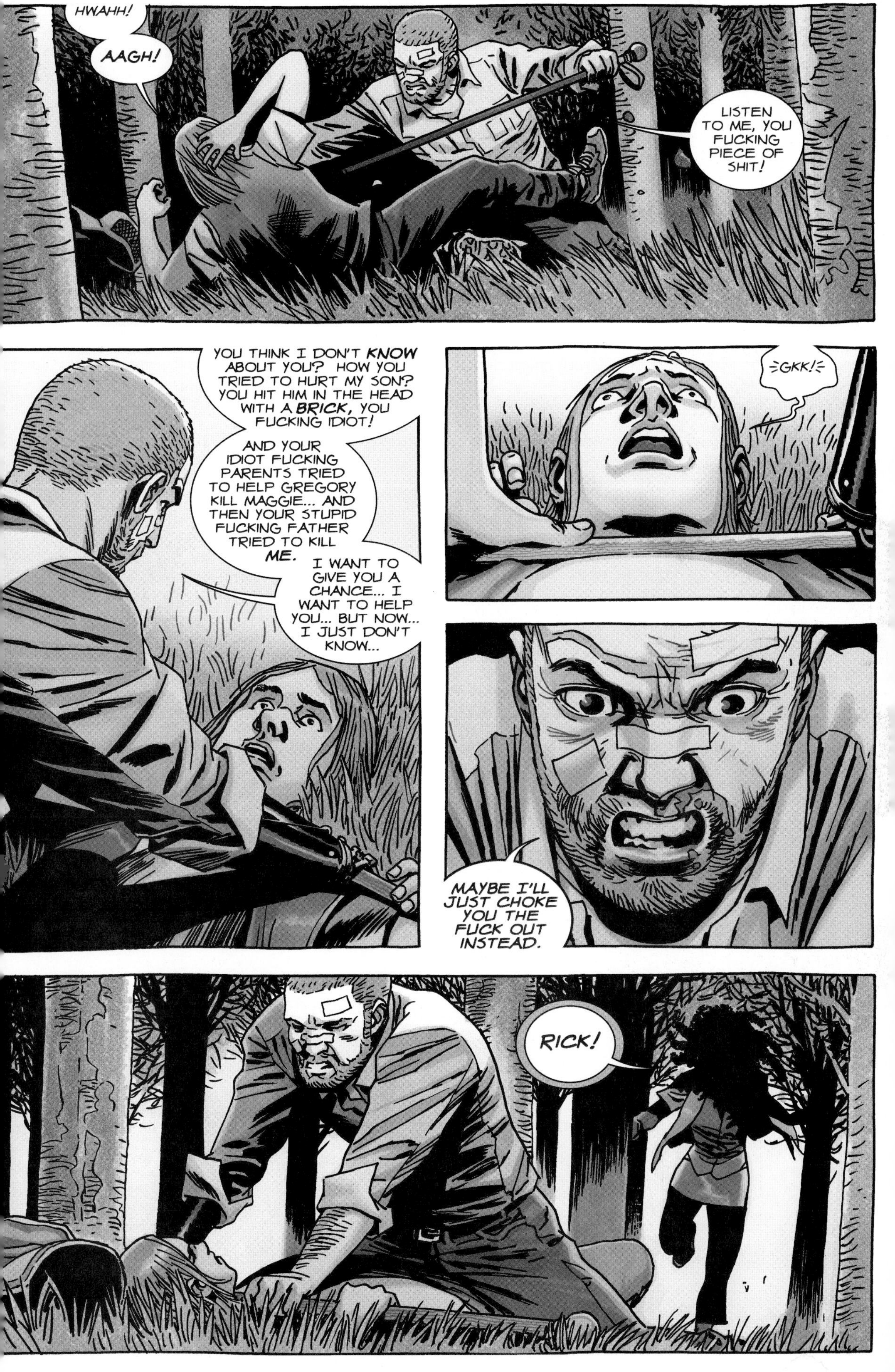

HWAHH!
AAGH!
LISTEN TO ME, YOU FUCKING PIECE OF SHIT!
YOU THINK I DON'T KNOW ABOUT YOU? HOW YOU TRIED TO HURT MY SON? YOU HIT HIM IN THE HEAD WITH A BRICK, YOU FUCKING IDIOT!
AND YOUR IDIOT FUCKING PARENTS TRIED TO HELP GREGORY KILL MAGGIE... AND THEN YOUR STUPID FUCKING FATHER TRIED TO KILL ME.
I WANT TO GIVE YOU A CHANCE... I WANT TO HELP YOU... BUT NOW... I JUST DON'T KNOW...
GKK!
MAYBE I'LL JUST CHOKE YOU THE FUCK OUT INSTEAD.
RICK!

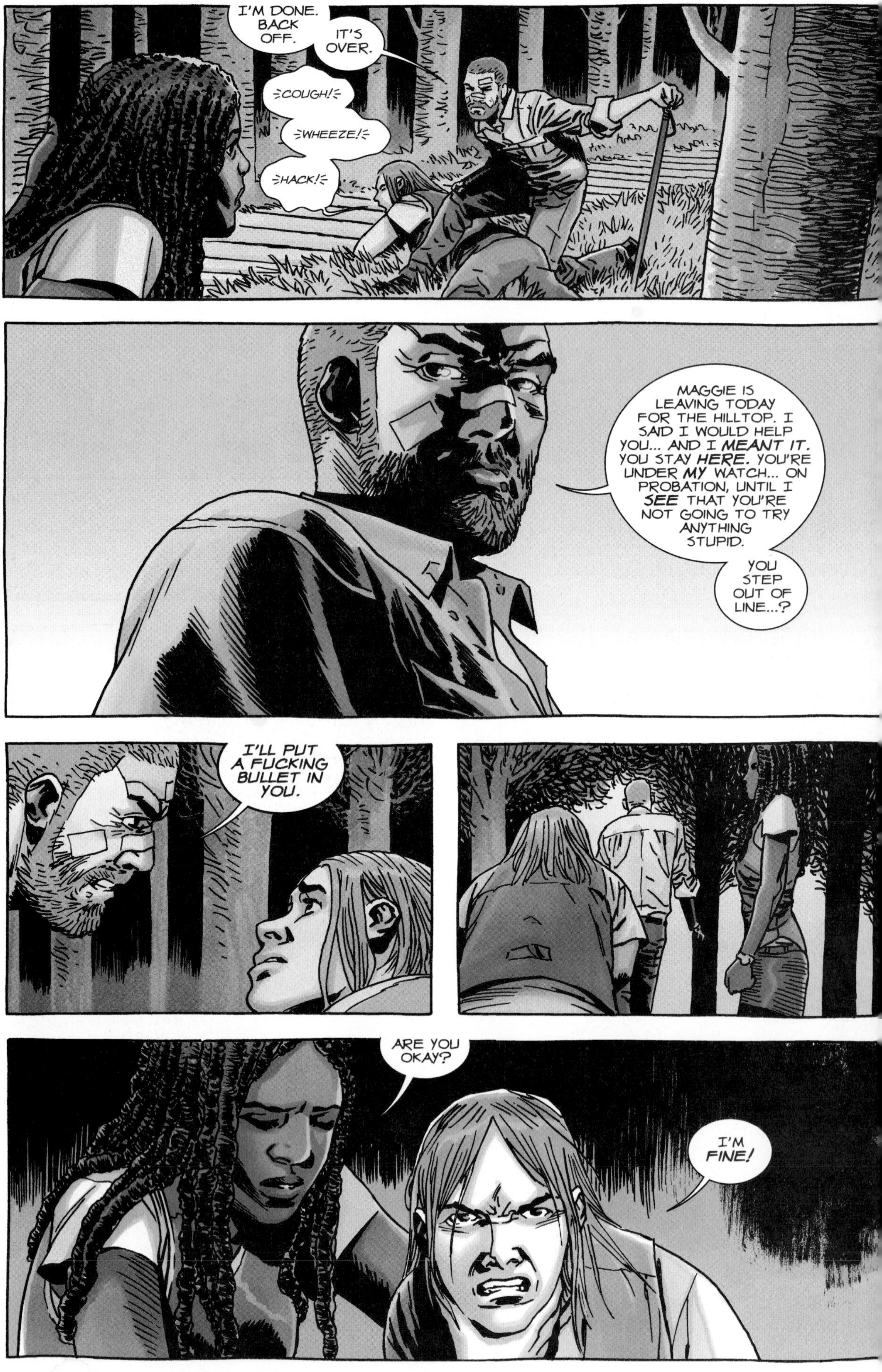

I'M DONE. BACK OFF.
IT'S OVER.
COUGH!
WHEEZE!
HACK!
MAGGIE IS LEAVING TODAY FOR THE HILLTOP. I SAID I WOULD HELP YOU... AND I MEANT IT. YOU STAY HERE. YOU'RE UNDER MY WATCH... ON PROBATION, UNTIL I SEE THAT YOU'RE NOT GOING TO TRY ANYTHING STUPID.
YOU STEP OUT OF LINE...?
I'LL PUT A FUCKING BULLET IN YOU.
ARE YOU OKAY?
I'M FINE!

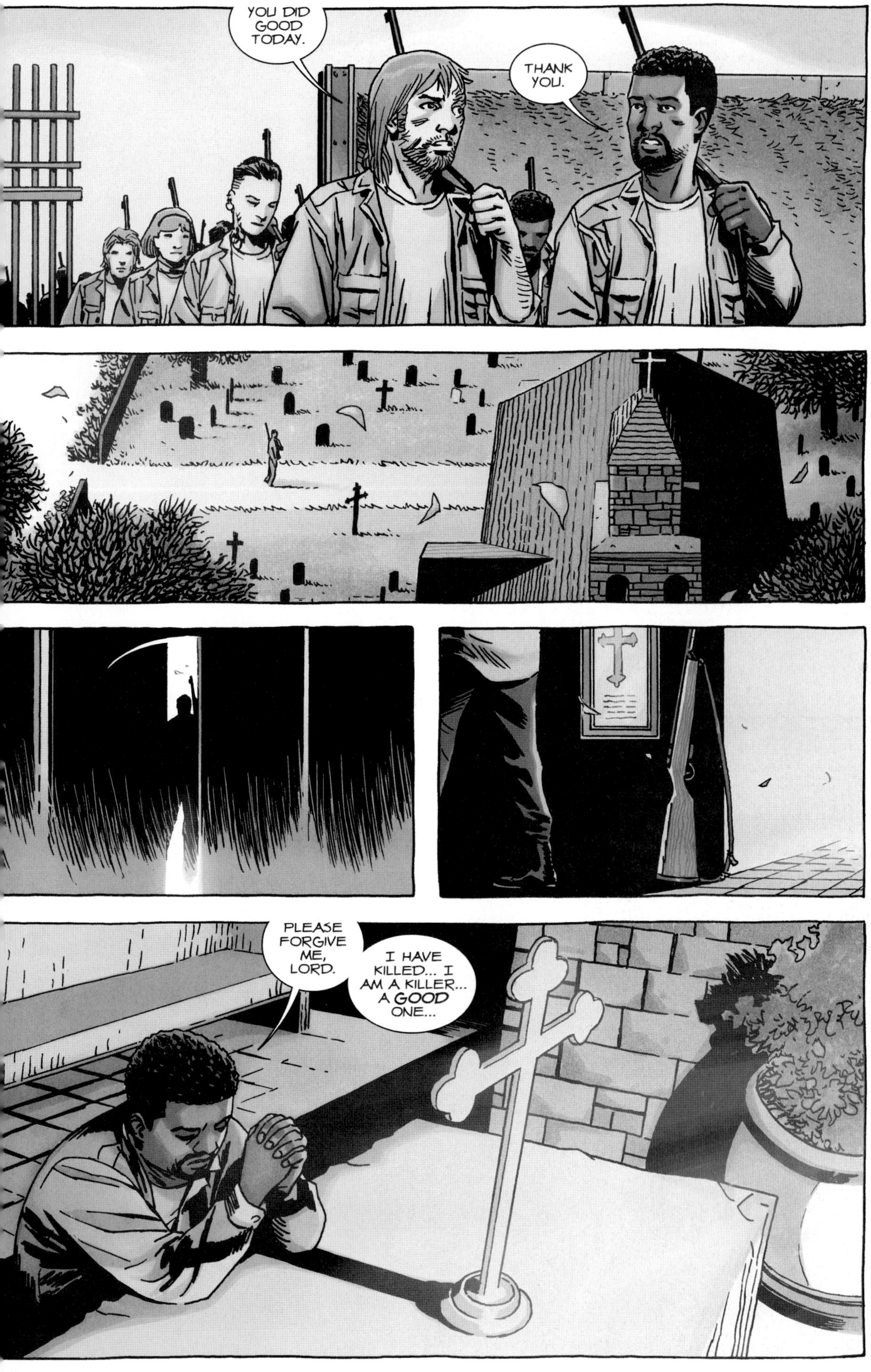

YOU DID GOOD TODAY.
THANK YOU.
PLEASE FORGIVE ME, LORD.
I HAVE KILLED... I AM A KILLER... A GOOD ONE...

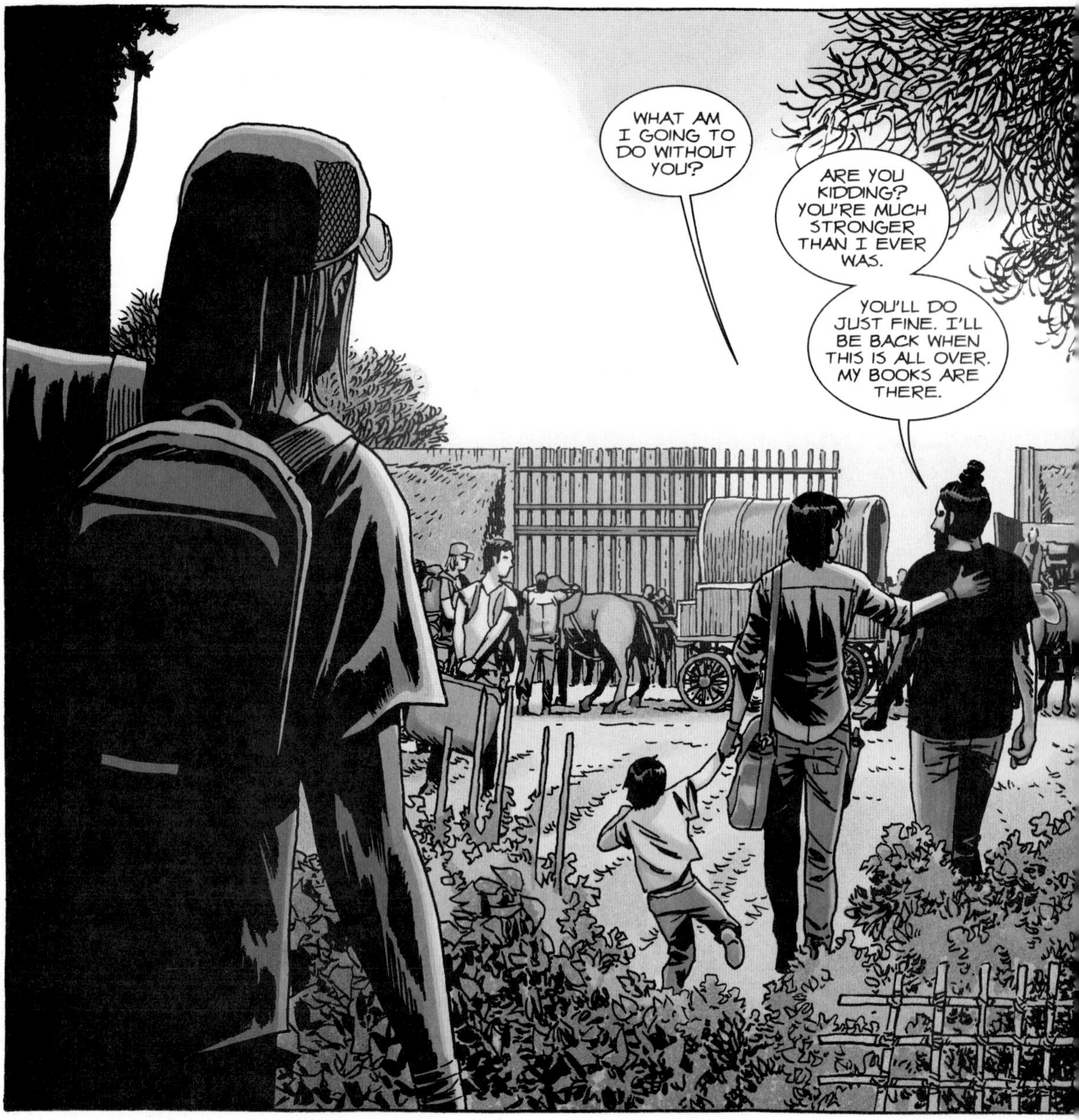
WHAT AM I GOING TO DO WITHOUT YOU?
ARE YOU KIDDING? YOU'RE MUCH STRONGER THAN I EVER WAS.
YOU'LL DO JUST FINE. I'LL BE BACK WHEN THIS IS ALL OVER. MY BOOKS ARE THERE.

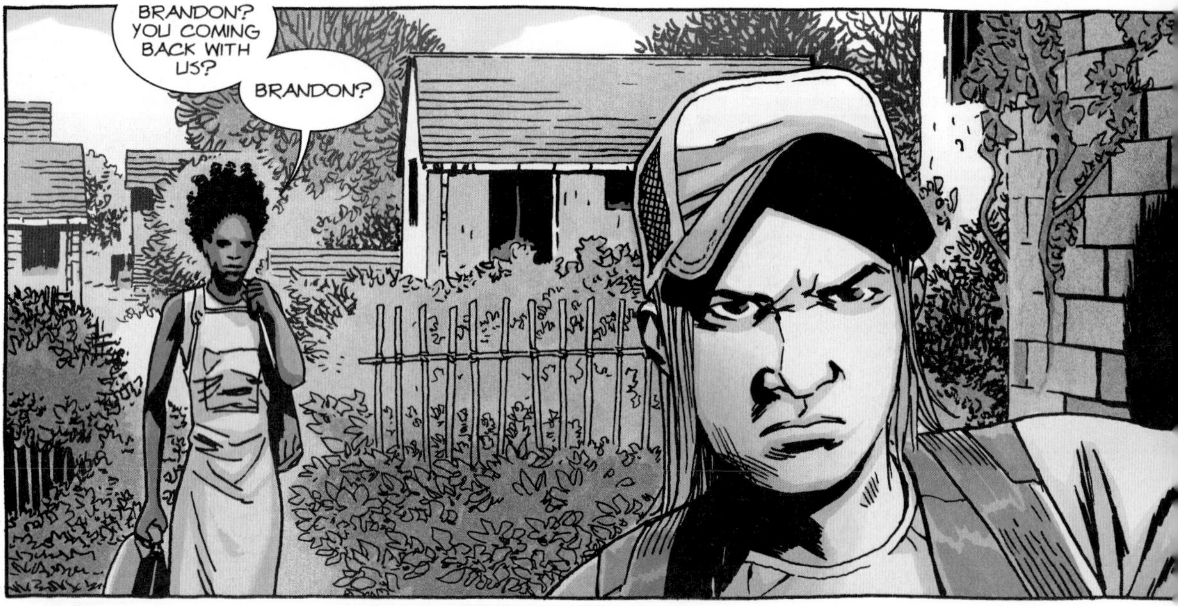
BRANDON? YOU COMING BACK WITH US?
BRANDON?

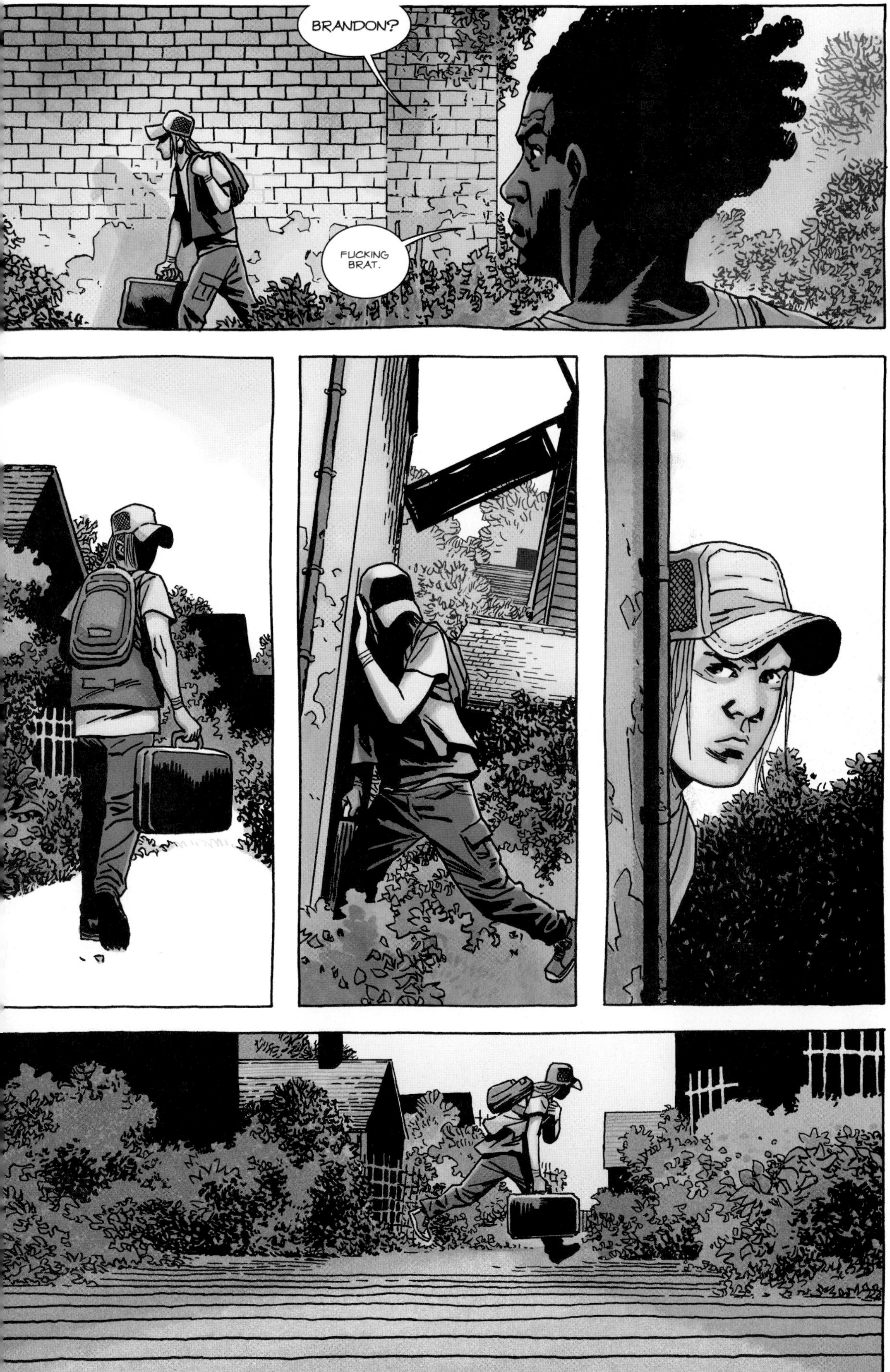
BRANDON?
FUCKING BRAT.

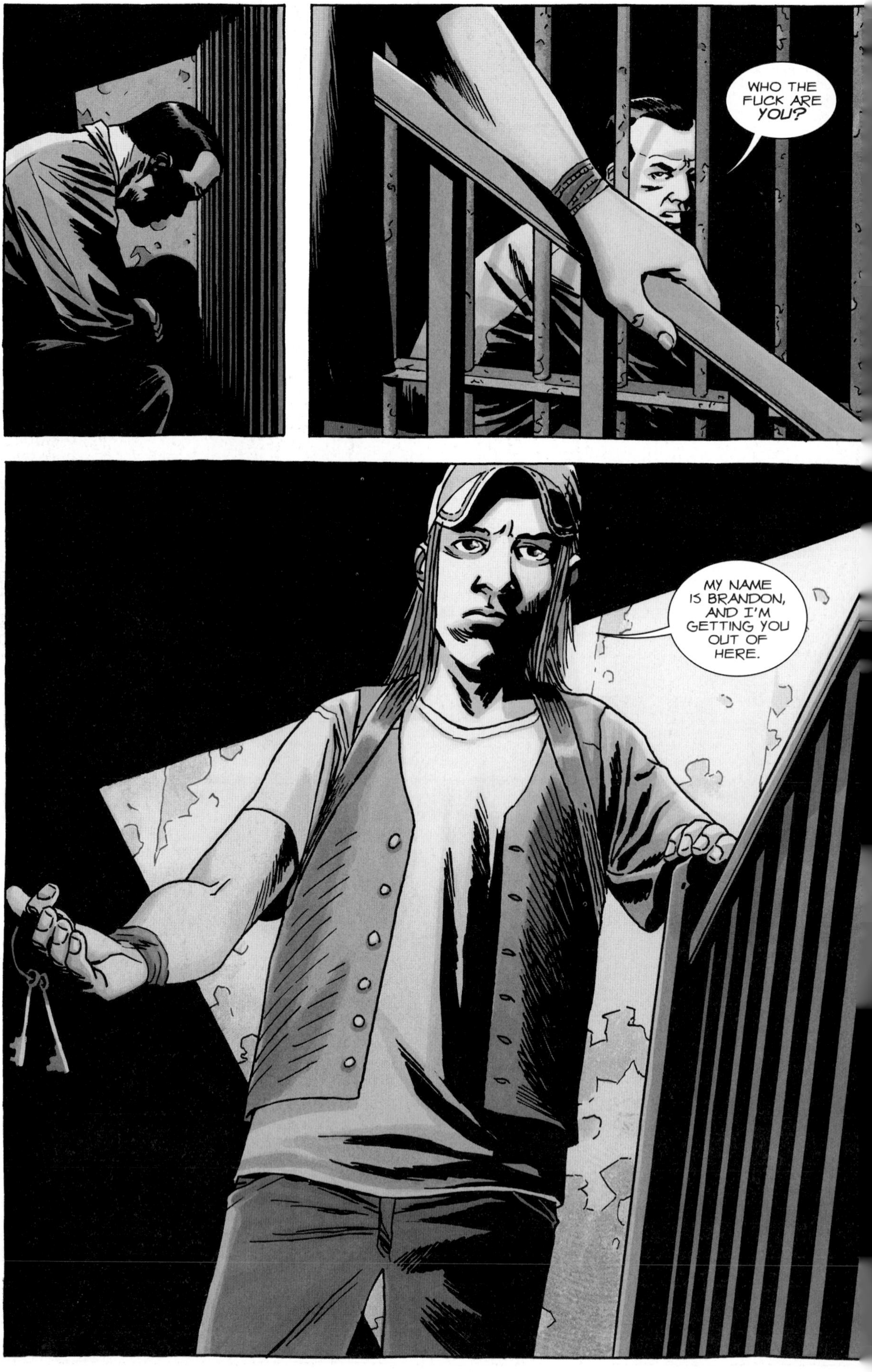
WHO THE FUCK ARE YOU?
MY NAME IS BRANDON, AND I'M GETTING YOU OUT OF HERE.

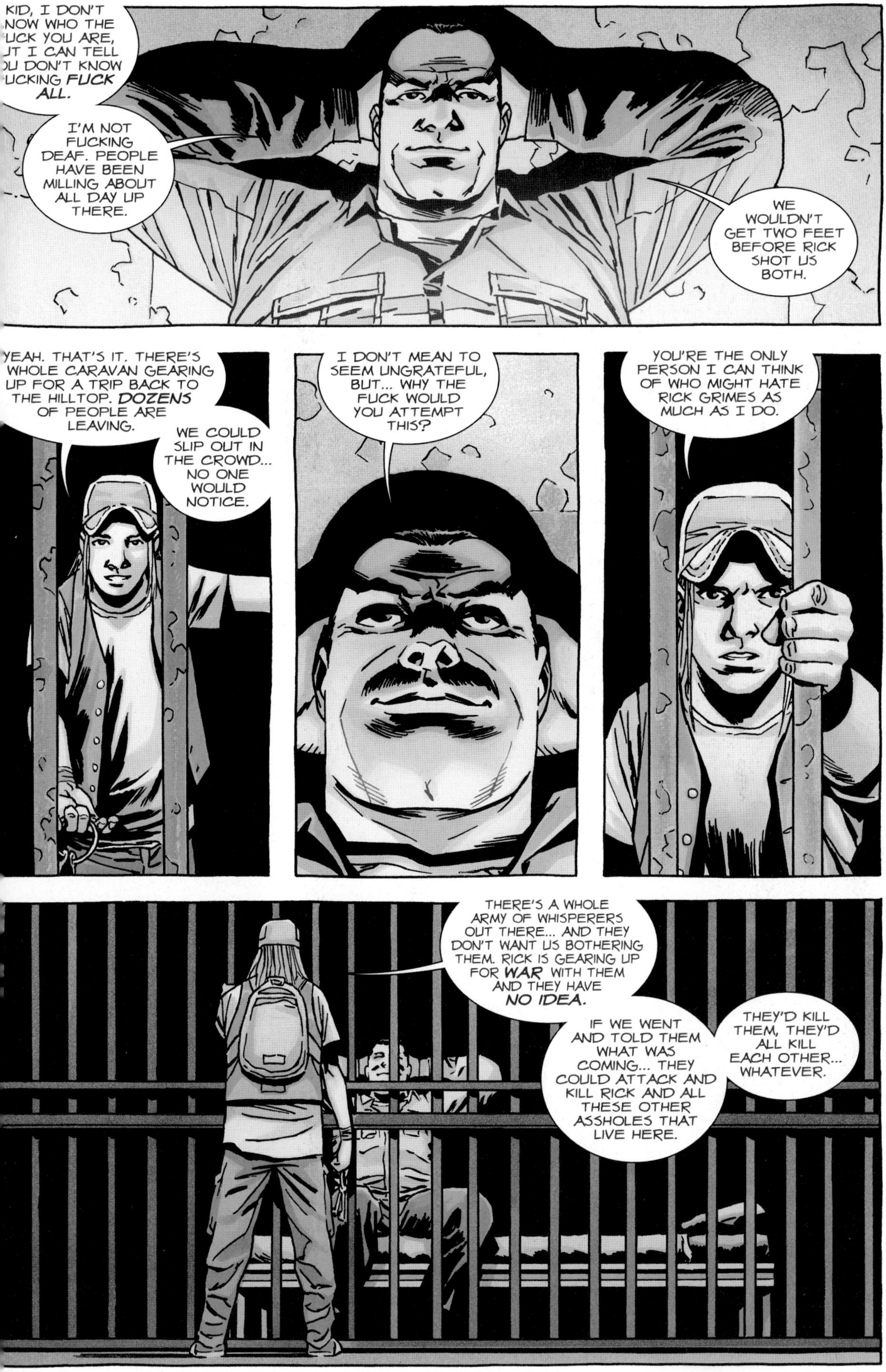
KID, I DON'T NOW WHO THE UCK YOU ARE, UT I CAN TELL OU DON'T KNOW UCKING FUCK ALL.
I'M NOT FUCKING DEAF. PEOPLE HAVE BEEN MILLING ABOUT ALL DAY UP THERE.
WE WOULDN'T GET TWO FEET BEFORE RICK SHOT US BOTH.
YEAH. THAT'S IT. THERE'S WHOLE CARAVAN GEARING UP FOR A TRIP BACK TO THE HILLTOP. DOZENS OF PEOPLE ARE LEAVING.
WE COULD SLIP OUT IN THE CROWD... NO ONE WOULD NOTICE.
I DON'T MEAN TO SEEM UNGRATEFUL, BUT... WHY THE FUCK WOULD YOU ATTEMPT THIS?
YOU'RE THE ONLY PERSON I CAN THINK OF WHO MIGHT HATE RICK GRIMES AS MUCH AS I DO.
THERE'S A WHOLE ARMY OF WHISPERERS OUT THERE... AND THEY DON'T WANT US BOTHERING THEM. RICK IS GEARING UP FOR WAR WITH THEM AND THEY HAVE NO IDEA.
IF WE WENT AND TOLD THEM WHAT WAS COMING... THEY COULD ATTACK AND KILL RICK AND ALL THESE OTHER ASSHOLES THAT LIVE HERE.
THEY'D KILL THEM, THEY'D ALL KILL EACH OTHER... WHATEVER.

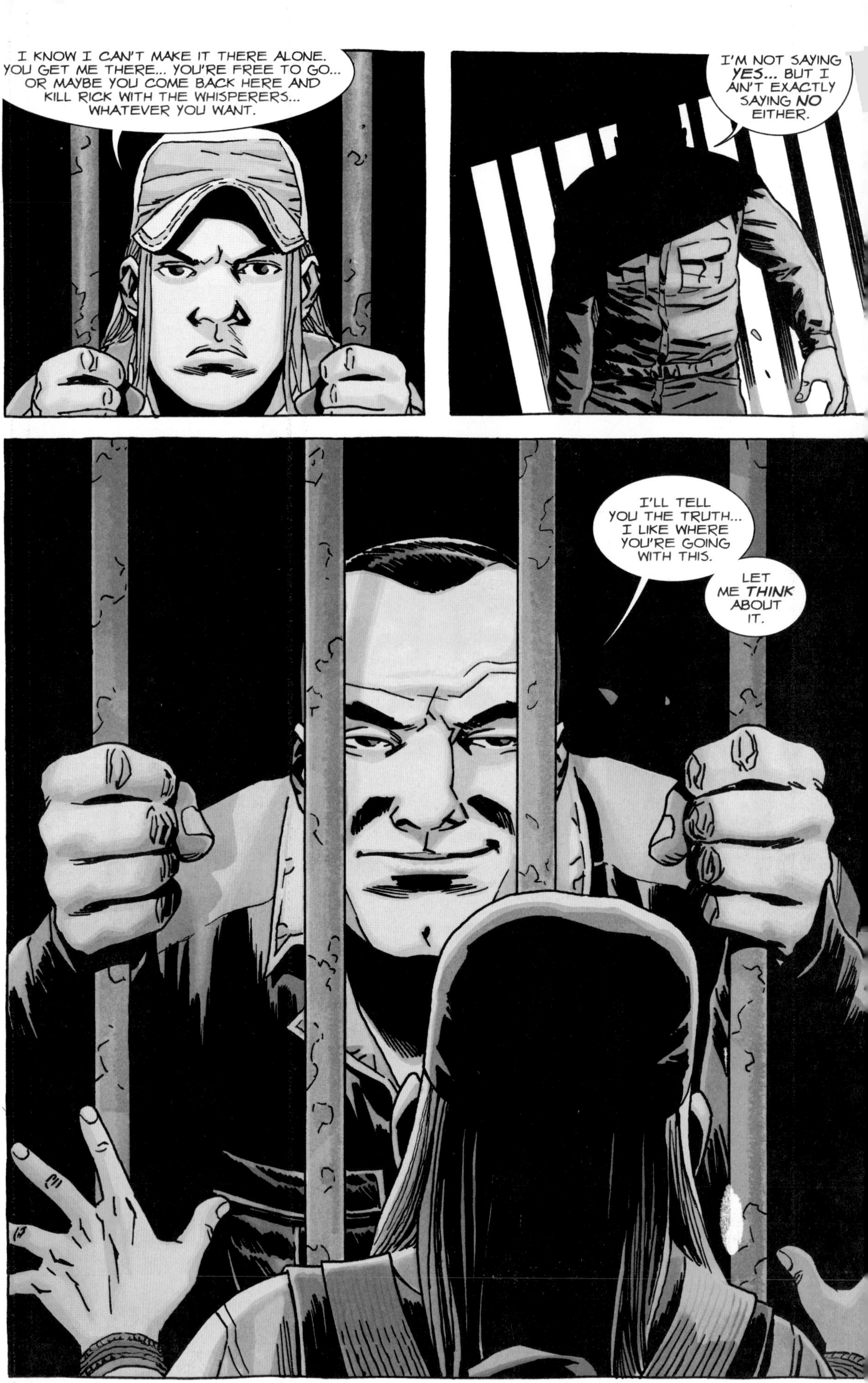

I KNOW I CAN'T MAKE IT THERE ALONE. YOU GET ME THERE... YOU'RE FREE TO GO... OR MAYBE YOU COME BACK HERE AND KILL RICK WITH THE WHISPERERS... WHATEVER YOU WANT.
I'M NOT SAYING YES... BUT I AIN'T EXACTLY SAYING NO EITHER.
I'LL TELL YOU THE TRUTH... I LIKE WHERE YOU'RE GOING WITH THIS.
LET ME THINK ABOUT IT.

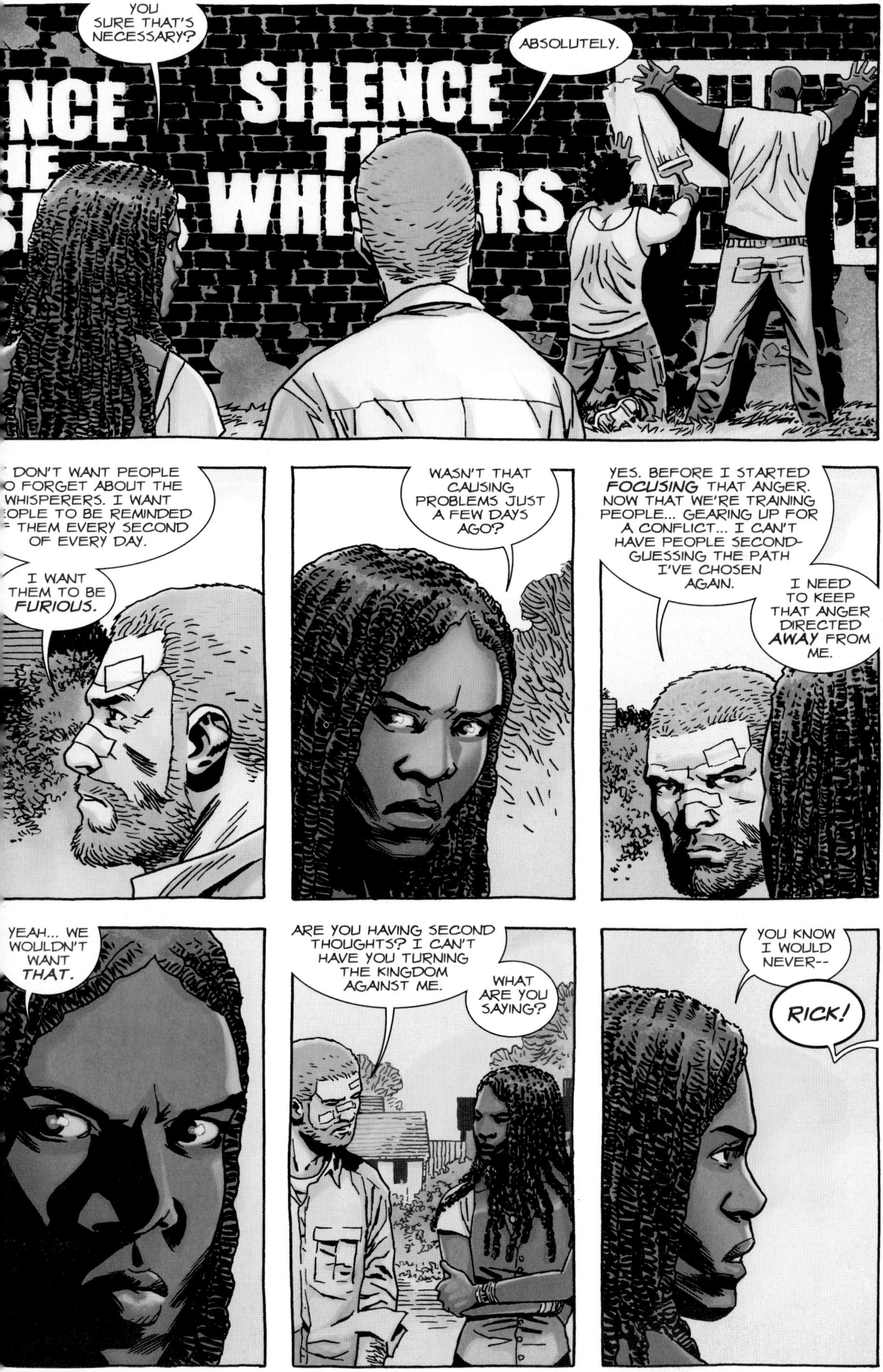
YOU SURE THAT'S NECESSARY?
ABSOLUTELY.
SILENCE THE WHISPERERS
I DON'T WANT PEOPLE TO FORGET ABOUT THE WHISPERERS. I WANT PEOPLE TO BE REMINDED OF THEM EVERY SECOND OF EVERY DAY.
I WANT THEM TO BE FURIOUS.
WASN'T THAT CAUSING PROBLEMS JUST A FEW DAYS AGO?
YES. BEFORE I STARTED FOCUSING THAT ANGER. NOW THAT WE'RE TRAINING PEOPLE... GEARING UP FOR A CONFLICT... I CAN'T HAVE PEOPLE SECOND-GUESSING THE PATH I'VE CHOSEN AGAIN.
I NEED TO KEEP THAT ANGER DIRECTED AWAY FROM ME.
YEAH... WE WOULDN'T WANT THAT.
ARE YOU HAVING SECOND THOUGHTS? I CAN'T HAVE YOU TURNING THE KINGDOM AGAINST ME.
WHAT ARE YOU SAYING?
YOU KNOW I WOULD NEVER--
RICK!

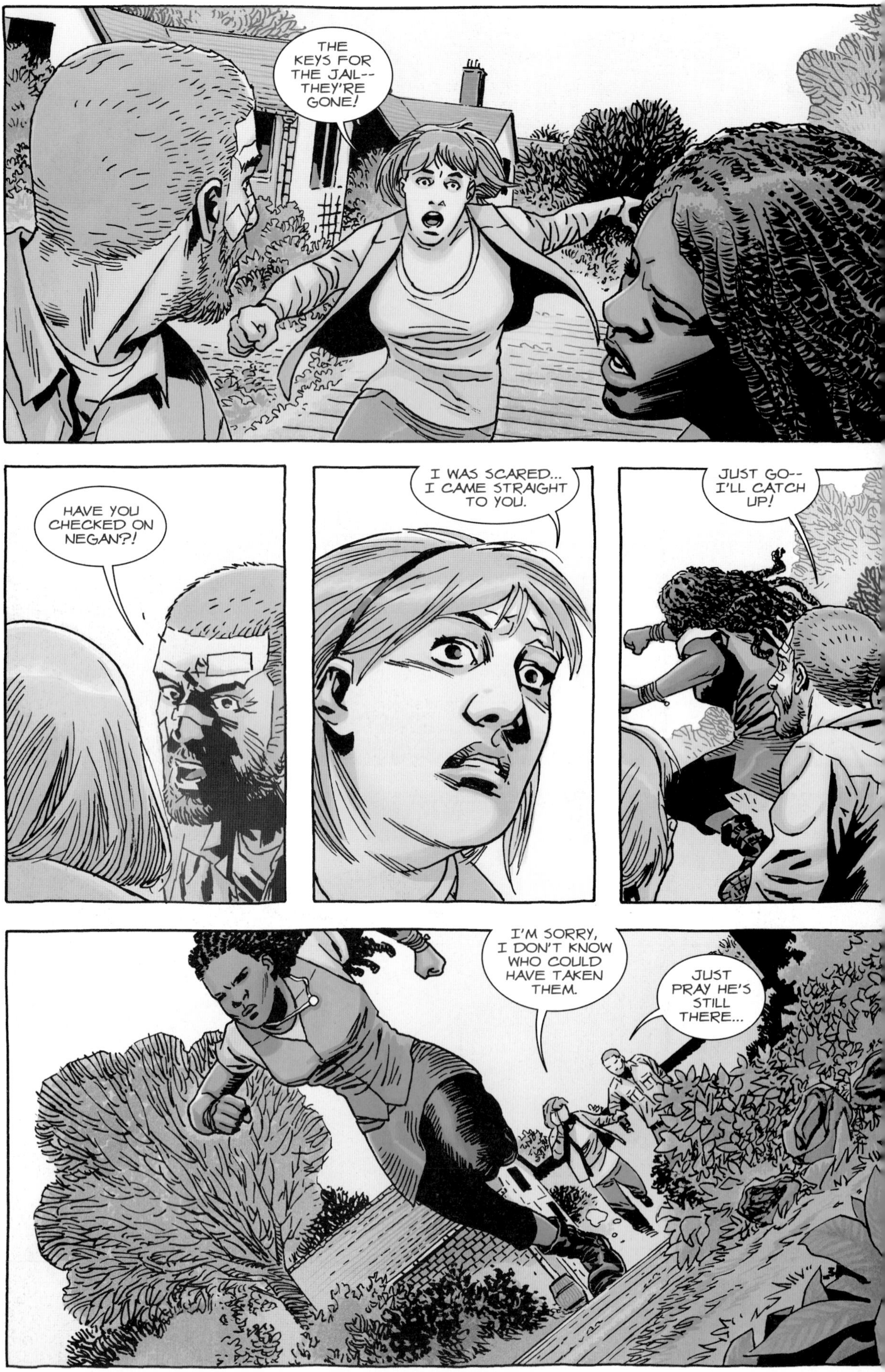
THE KEYS FOR THE JAIL-- THEY'RE GONE!
HAVE YOU CHECKED ON NEGAN?!
I WAS SCARED... I CAME STRAIGHT TO YOU.
JUST GO-- I'LL CATCH UP!
I'M SORRY, I DON'T KNOW WHO COULD HAVE TAKEN THEM.
JUST PRAY HE'S STILL THERE...

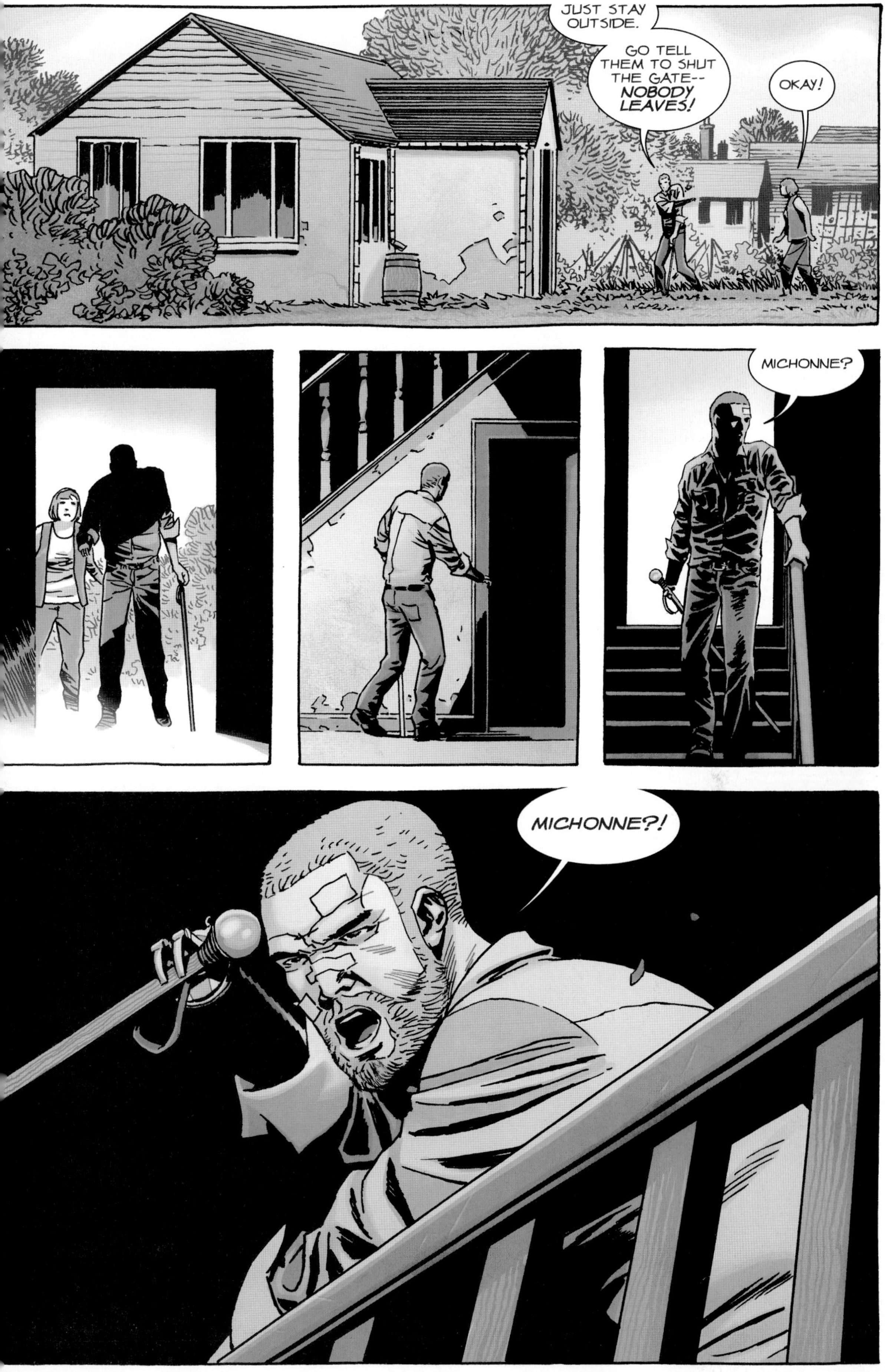
JUST STAY OUTSIDE.
GO TELL THEM TO SHUT THE GATE-- NOBODY LEAVES!
OKAY!
MICHONNE?
MICHONNE?!

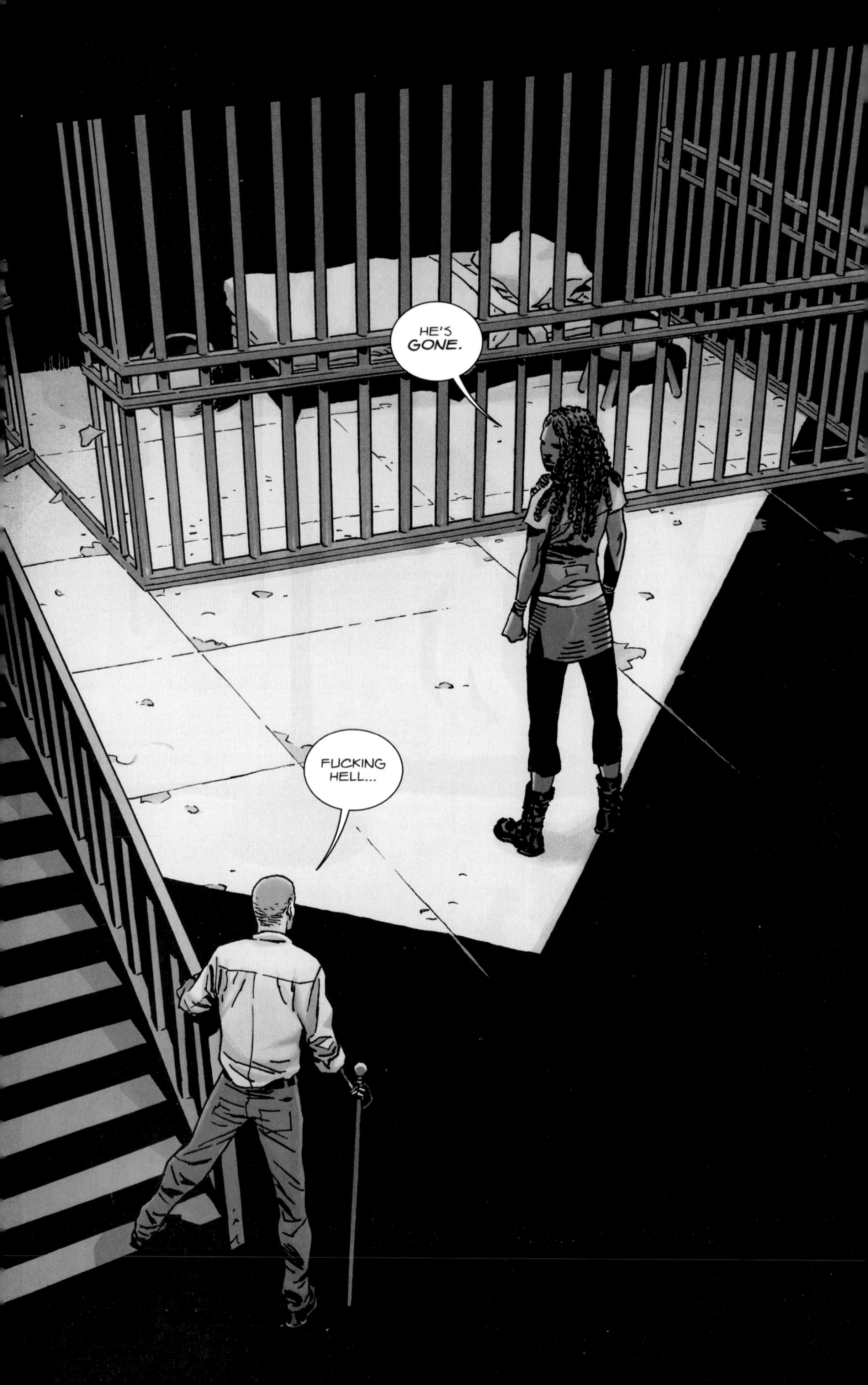
HE'S GONE.
FUCKING HELL...

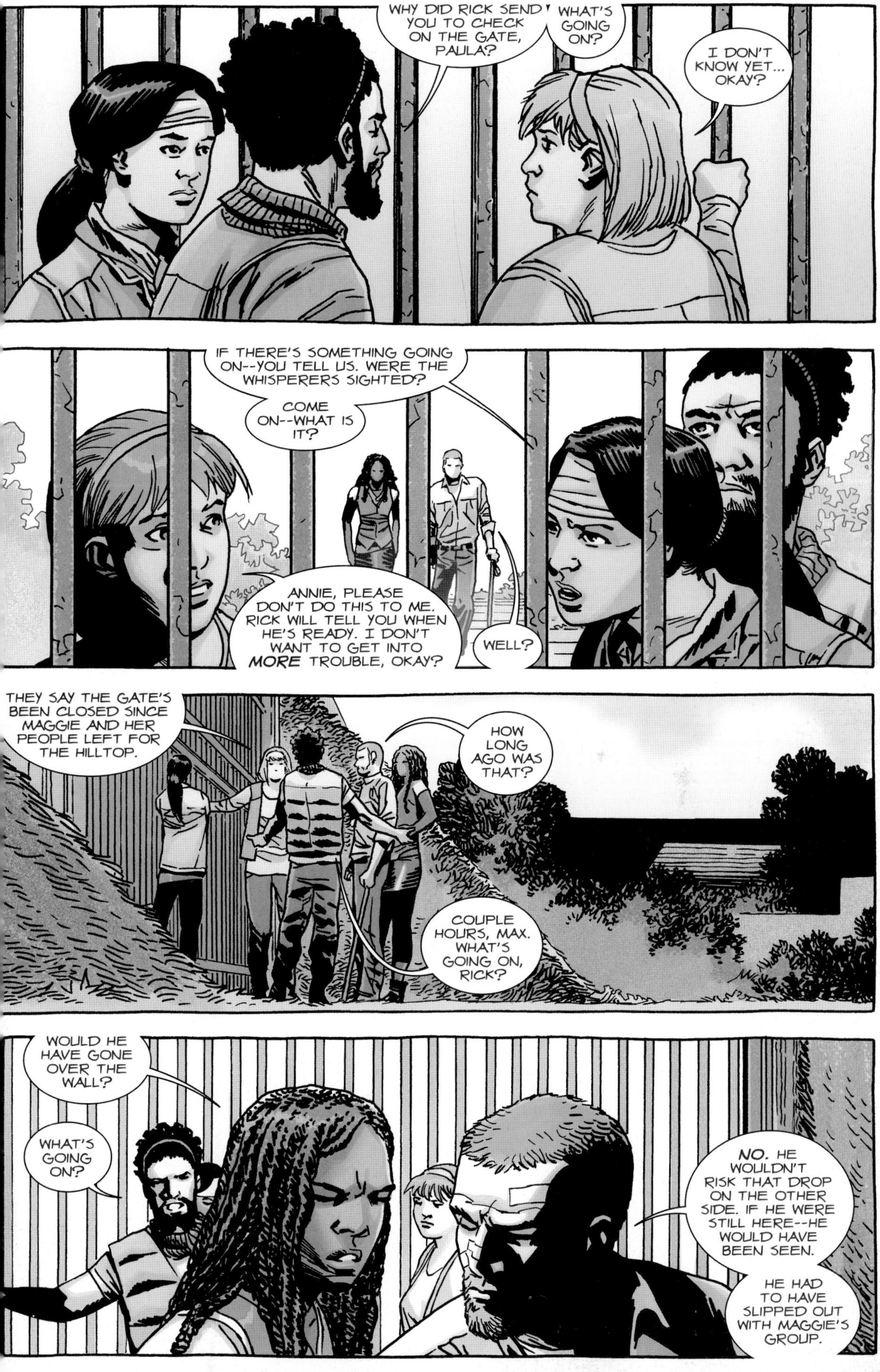
WHY DID RICK SEND YOU TO CHECK ON THE GATE, PAULA?
WHAT'S GOING ON?
I DON'T KNOW YET... OKAY?
IF THERE'S SOMETHING GOING ON--YOU TELL US. WERE THE WHISPERERS SIGHTED?
COME ON--WHAT IS IT?
ANNIE, PLEASE DON'T DO THIS TO ME. RICK WILL TELL YOU WHEN HE'S READY. I DON'T WANT TO GET INTO MORE TROUBLE, OKAY?
WELL?
THEY SAY THE GATE'S BEEN CLOSED SINCE MAGGIE AND HER PEOPLE LEFT FOR THE HILLTOP.
HOW LONG AGO WAS THAT?
COUPLE HOURS, MAX. WHAT'S GOING ON, RICK?
WOULD HE HAVE GONE OVER THE WALL?
WHAT'S GOING ON?
NO. HE WOULDN'T RISK THAT DROP ON THE OTHER SIDE. IF HE WERE STILL HERE--HE WOULD HAVE BEEN SEEN.
HE HAD TO HAVE SLIPPED OUT WITH MAGGIE'S GROUP.

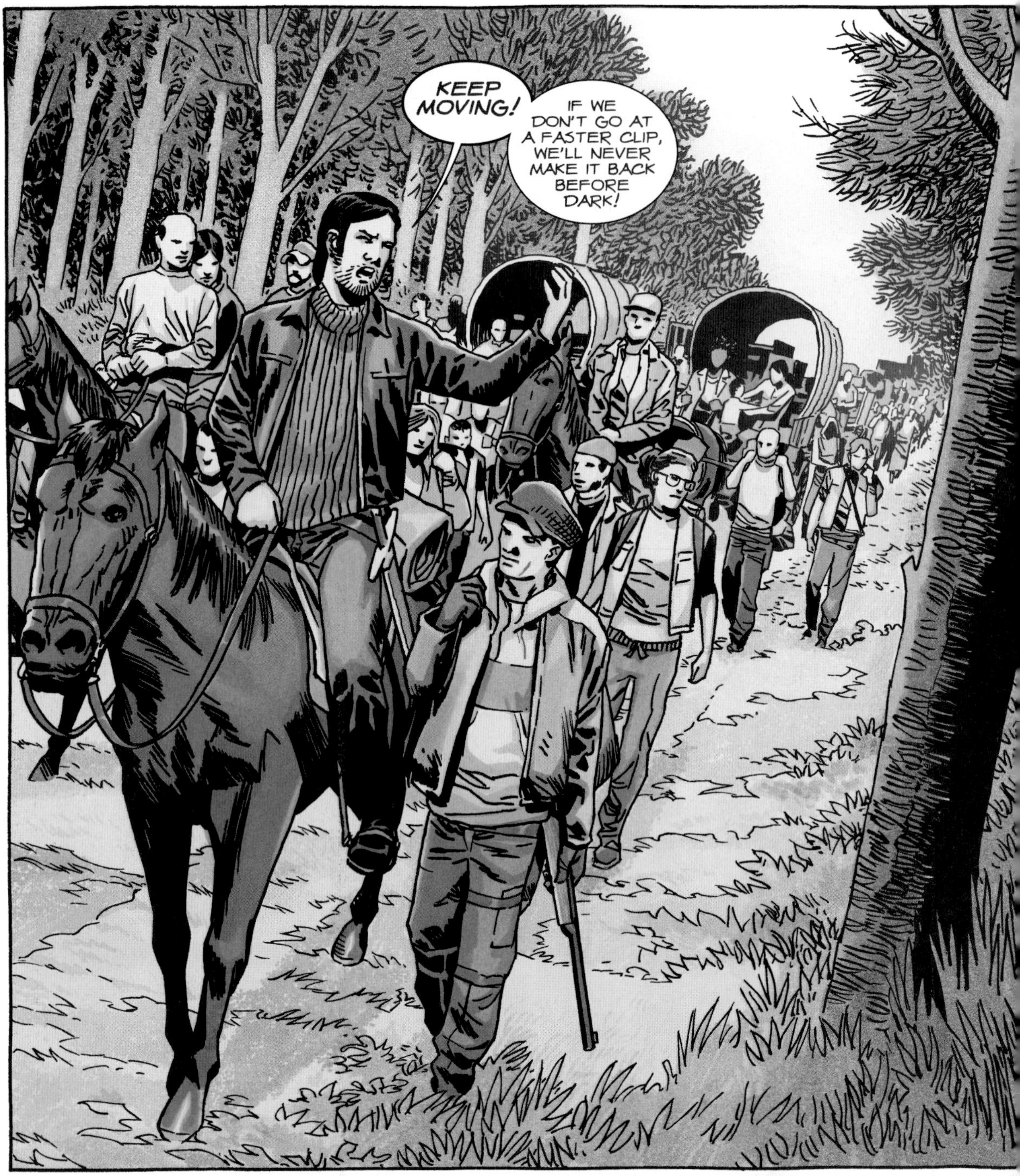
KEEP MOVING!
IF WE DON'T GO AT A FASTER CLIP, WE'LL NEVER MAKE IT BACK BEFORE DARK!

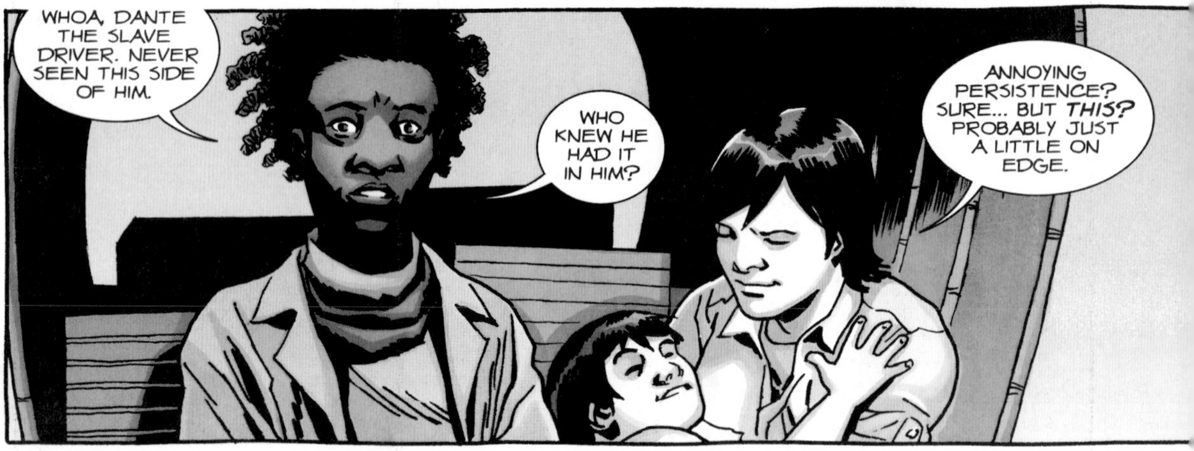
WHOA, DANTE THE SLAVE DRIVER. NEVER SEEN THIS SIDE OF HIM.
WHO KNEW HE HAD IT IN HIM?
ANNOYING PERSISTENCE? SURE... BUT THIS? PROBABLY JUST A LITTLE ON EDGE.

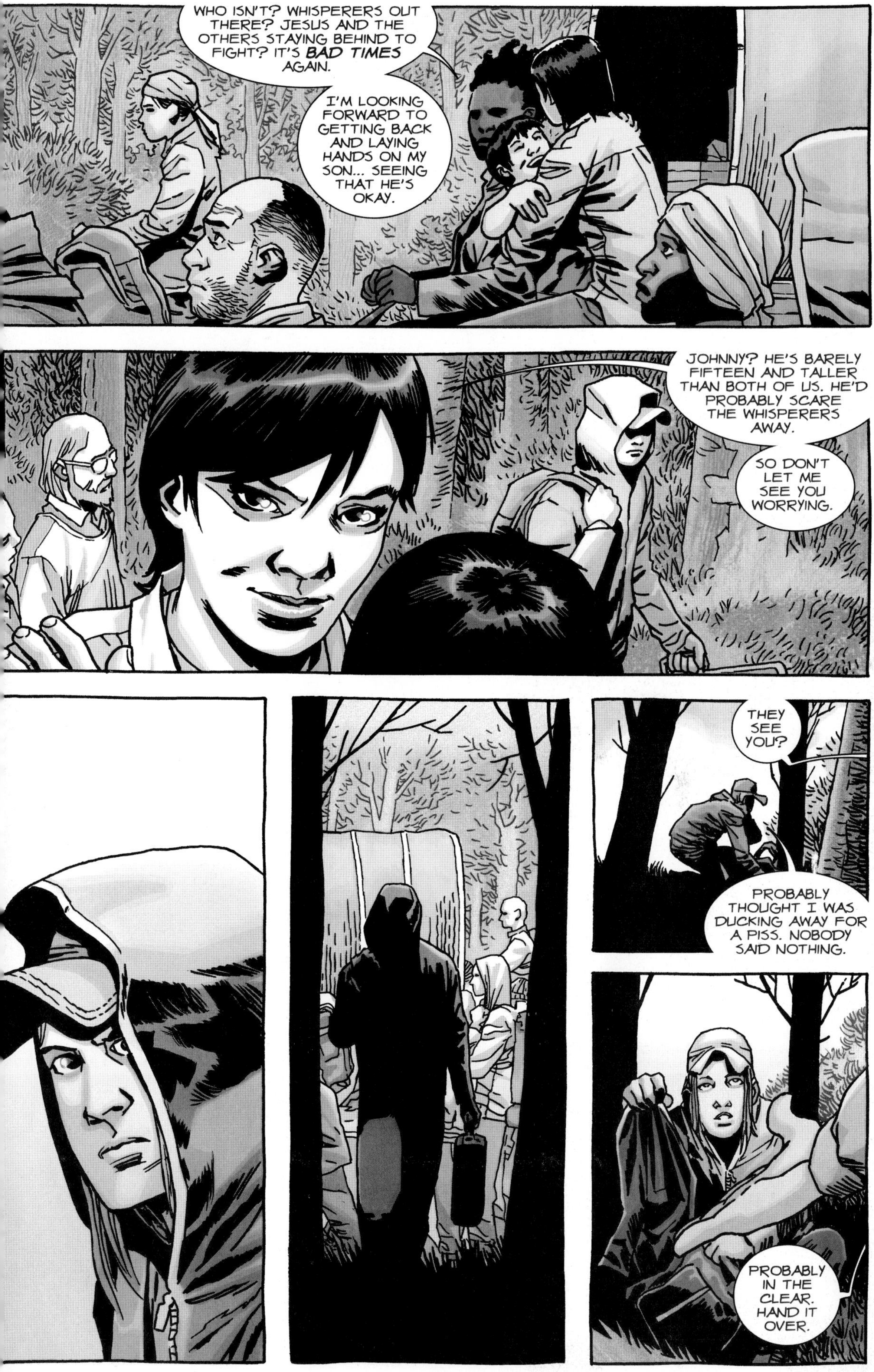
WHO ISN'T? WHISPERERS OUT THERE? JESUS AND THE OTHERS STAYING BEHIND TO FIGHT? IT'S BAD TIMES AGAIN.
I'M LOOKING FORWARD TO GETTING BACK AND LAYING HANDS ON MY SON... SEEING THAT HE'S OKAY.
JOHNNY? HE'S BARELY FIFTEEN AND TALLER THAN BOTH OF US. HE'D PROBABLY SCARE THE WHISPERERS AWAY.
SO DON'T LET ME SEE YOU WORRYING.
THEY SEE YOU?
PROBABLY THOUGHT I WAS DUCKING AWAY FOR A PISS. NOBODY SAID NOTHING.
PROBABLY IN THE CLEAR. HAND IT OVER.

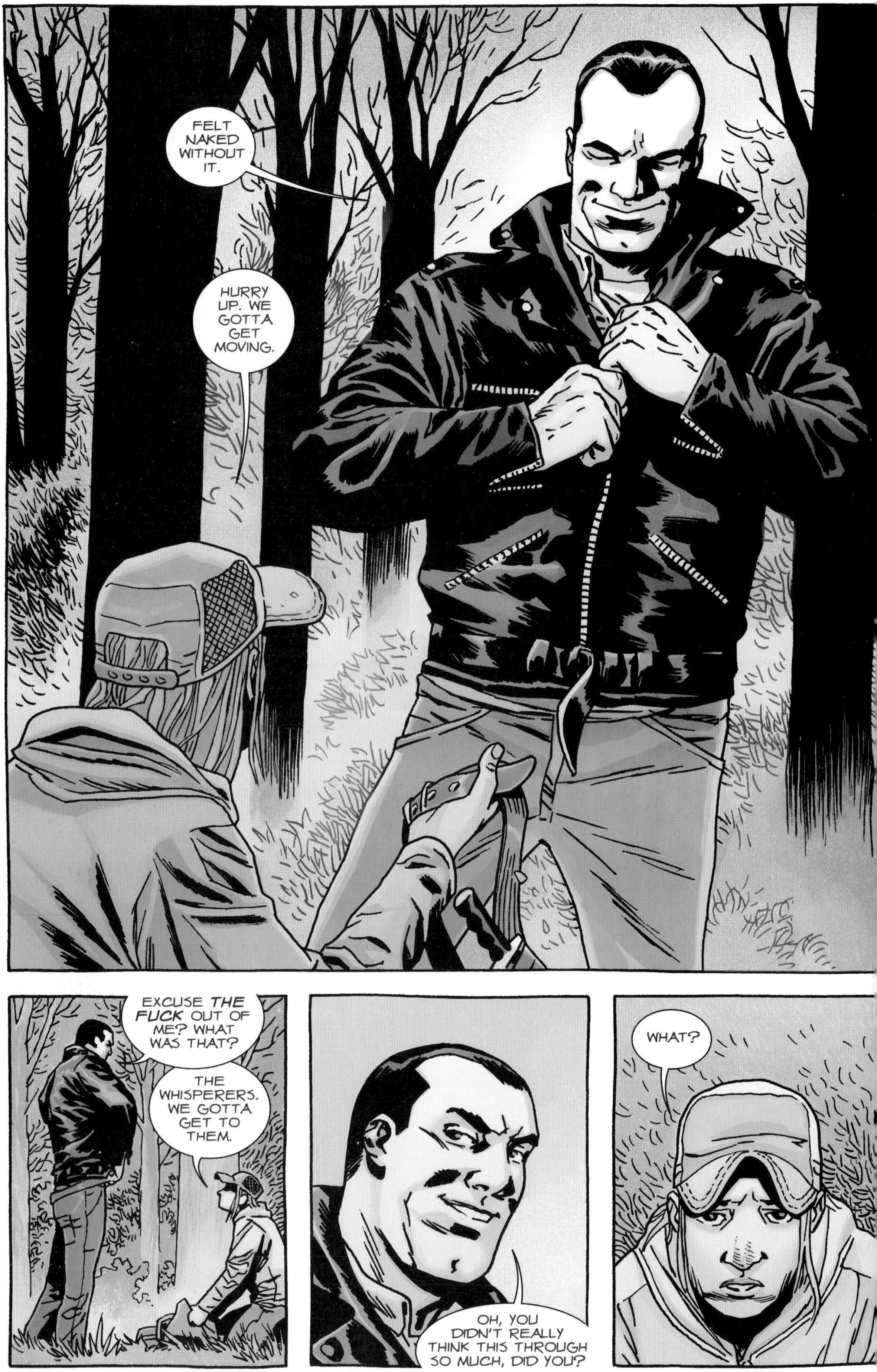
FELT NAKED WITHOUT IT.
HURRY UP. WE GOTTA GET MOVING.
EXCUSE THE FUCK OUT OF ME? WHAT WAS THAT?
THE WHISPERERS. WE GOTTA GET TO THEM.
OH, YOU DIDN'T REALLY THINK THIS THROUGH SO MUCH, DID YOU?
WHAT?

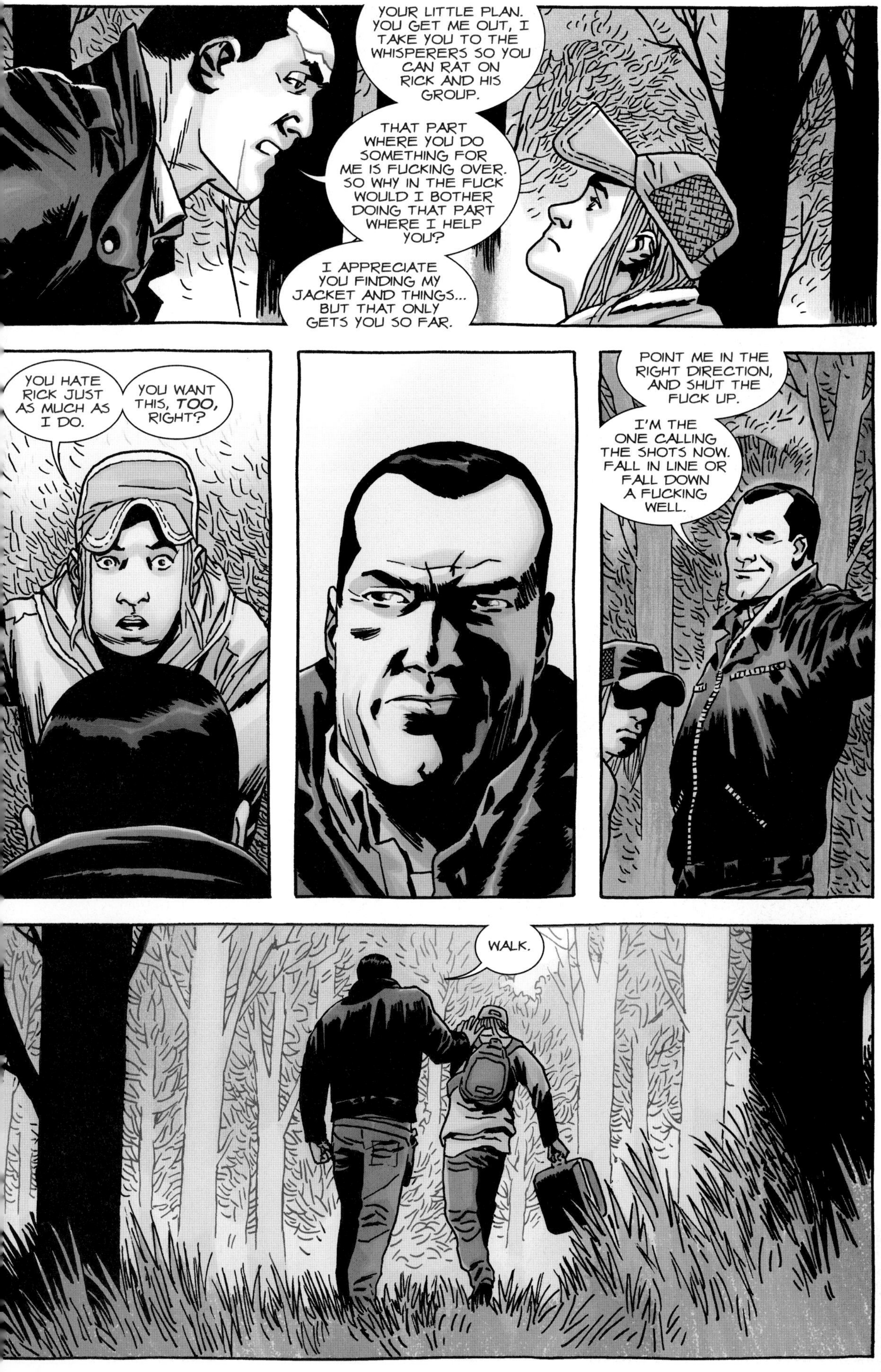
YOUR LITTLE PLAN. YOU GET ME OUT, I TAKE YOU TO THE WHISPERERS SO YOU CAN RAT ON RICK AND HIS GROUP.
THAT PART WHERE YOU DO SOMETHING FOR ME IS FUCKING OVER. SO WHY IN THE FUCK WOULD I BOTHER DOING THAT PART WHERE I HELP YOU?
I APPRECIATE YOU FINDING MY JACKET AND THINGS... BUT THAT ONLY GETS YOU SO FAR.
YOU HATE RICK JUST AS MUCH AS I DO.
YOU WANT THIS, *TOO,* RIGHT?
POINT ME IN THE RIGHT DIRECTION, AND SHUT THE FUCK UP.
I'M THE ONE CALLING THE SHOTS NOW. FALL IN LINE OR FALL DOWN A FUCKING WELL.
WALK.

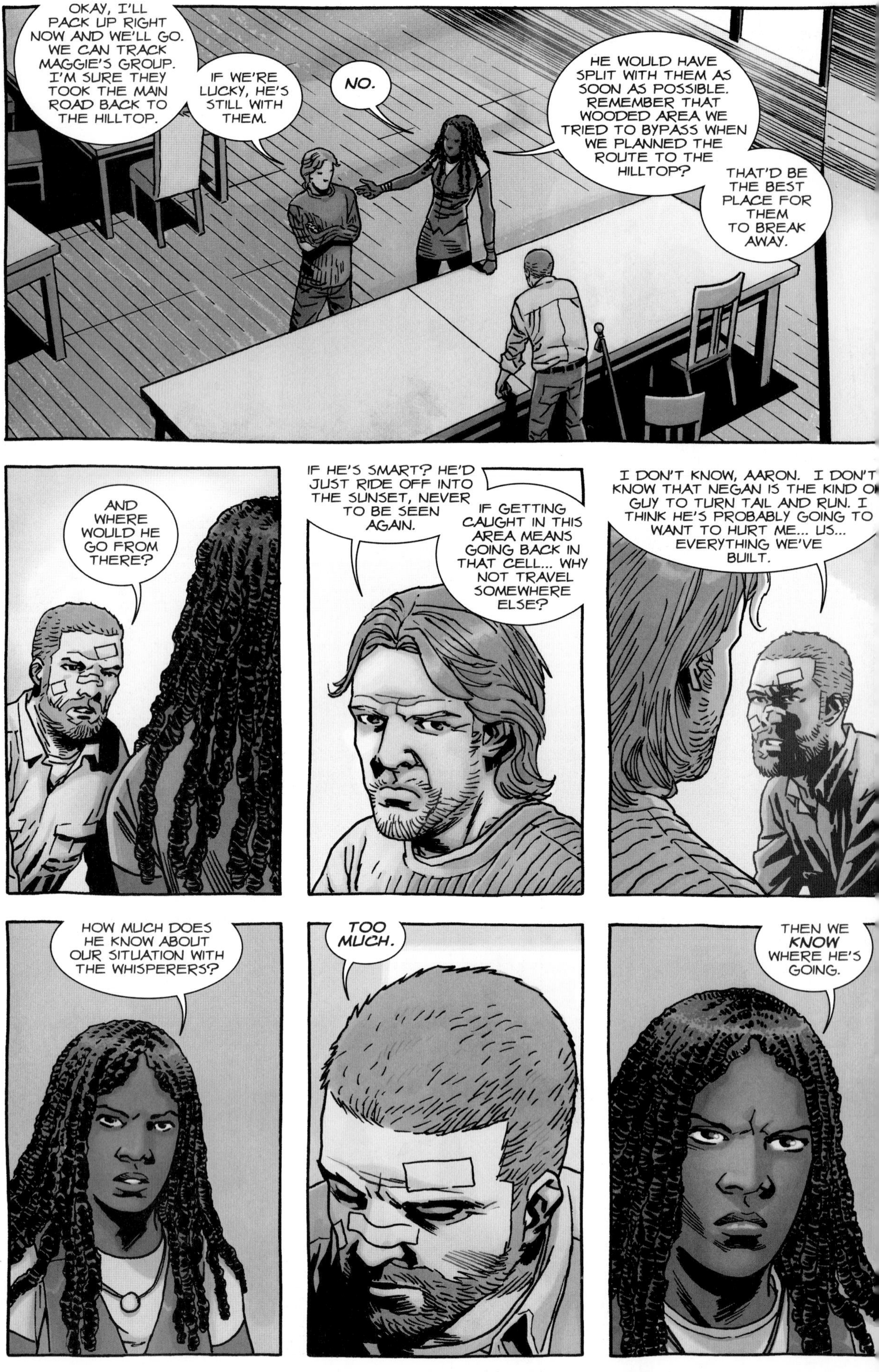
OKAY, I'LL PACK UP RIGHT NOW AND WE'LL GO. WE CAN TRACK MAGGIE'S GROUP. I'M SURE THEY TOOK THE MAIN ROAD BACK TO THE HILLTOP.
IF WE'RE LUCKY, HE'S STILL WITH THEM.
NO.
HE WOULD HAVE SPLIT WITH THEM AS SOON AS POSSIBLE. REMEMBER THAT WOODED AREA WE TRIED TO BYPASS WHEN WE PLANNED THE ROUTE TO THE HILLTOP?
THAT'D BE THE BEST PLACE FOR THEM TO BREAK AWAY.
AND WHERE WOULD HE GO FROM THERE?
IF HE'S SMART? HE'D JUST RIDE OFF INTO THE SUNSET, NEVER TO BE SEEN AGAIN.
IF GETTING CAUGHT IN THIS AREA MEANS GOING BACK IN THAT CELL... WHY NOT TRAVEL SOMEWHERE ELSE?
I DON'T KNOW, AARON. I DON'T KNOW THAT NEGAN IS THE KIND OF GUY TO TURN TAIL AND RUN. I THINK HE'S PROBABLY GOING TO WANT TO HURT ME... US... EVERYTHING WE'VE BUILT.
HOW MUCH DOES HE KNOW ABOUT OUR SITUATION WITH THE WHISPERERS?
TOO MUCH.
THEN WE KNOW WHERE HE'S GOING.

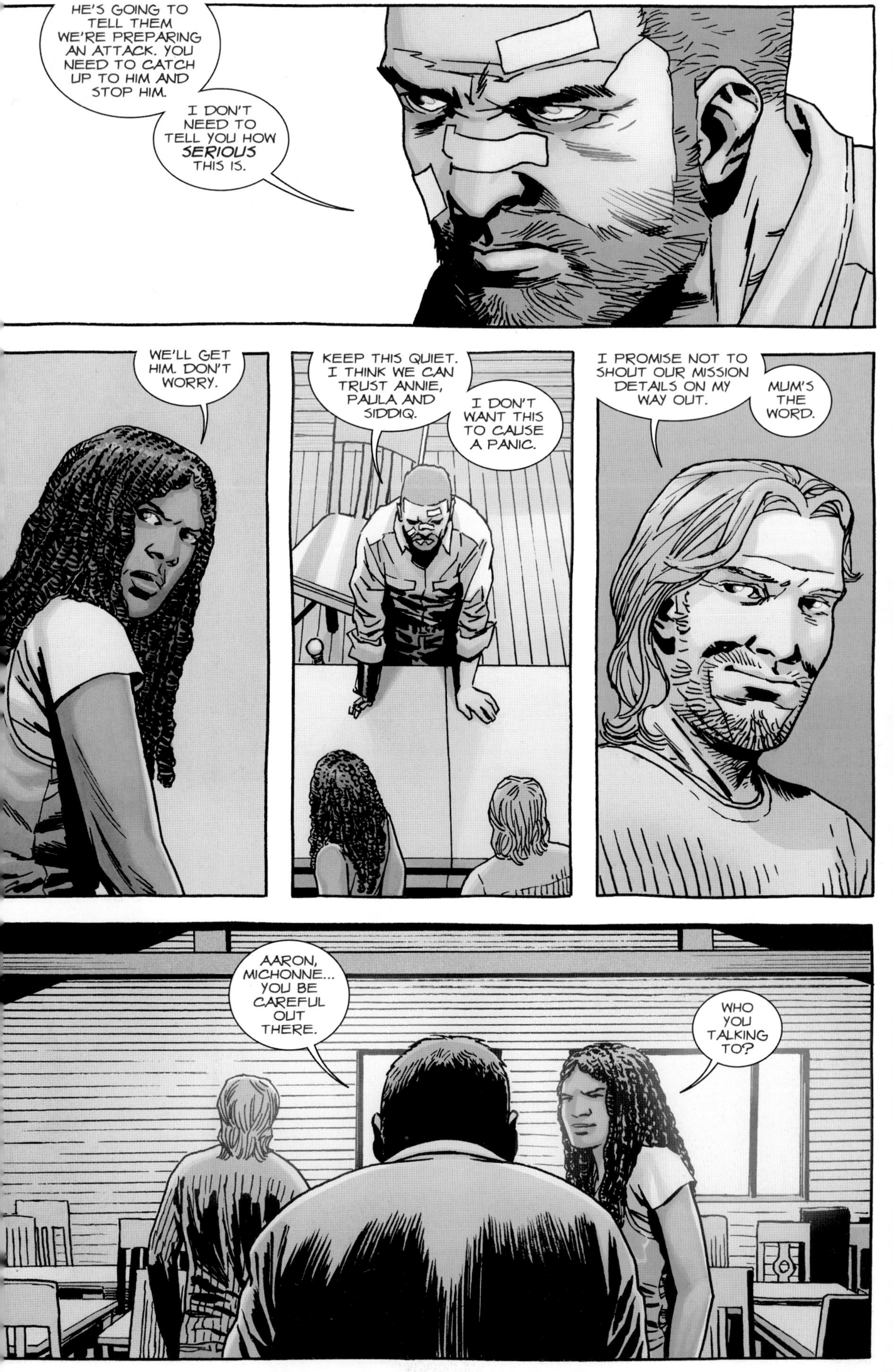
HE'S GOING TO TELL THEM WE'RE PREPARING AN ATTACK. YOU NEED TO CATCH UP TO HIM AND STOP HIM.
I DON'T NEED TO TELL YOU HOW SERIOUS THIS IS.
WE'LL GET HIM. DON'T WORRY.
KEEP THIS QUIET. I THINK WE CAN TRUST ANNIE, PAULA AND SIDDIQ.
I DON'T WANT THIS TO CAUSE A PANIC.
I PROMISE NOT TO SHOUT OUR MISSION DETAILS ON MY WAY OUT.
MUM'S THE WORD.
AARON, MICHONNE... YOU BE CAREFUL OUT THERE.
WHO YOU TALKING TO?

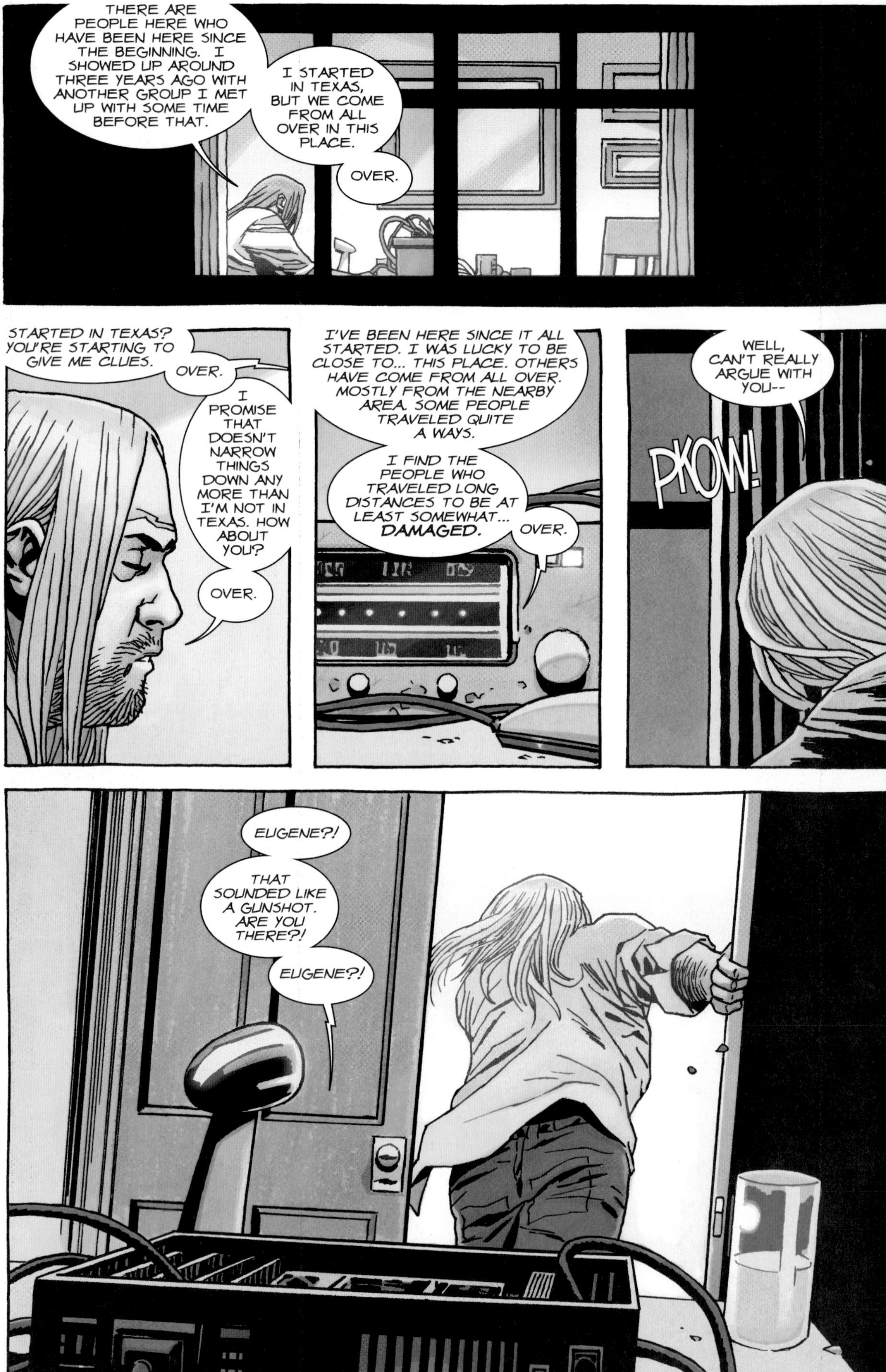
THERE ARE PEOPLE HERE WHO HAVE BEEN HERE SINCE THE BEGINNING. I SHOWED UP AROUND THREE YEARS AGO WITH ANOTHER GROUP I MET UP WITH SOME TIME BEFORE THAT.
I STARTED IN TEXAS, BUT WE COME FROM ALL OVER IN THIS PLACE.
OVER.
STARTED IN TEXAS? YOU'RE STARTING TO GIVE ME CLUES.
OVER.
I PROMISE THAT DOESN'T NARROW THINGS DOWN ANY MORE THAN I'M NOT IN TEXAS. HOW ABOUT YOU?
OVER.
I'VE BEEN HERE SINCE IT ALL STARTED. I WAS LUCKY TO BE CLOSE TO... THIS PLACE. OTHERS HAVE COME FROM ALL OVER. MOSTLY FROM THE NEARBY AREA. SOME PEOPLE TRAVELED QUITE A WAYS.
I FIND THE PEOPLE WHO TRAVELED LONG DISTANCES TO BE AT LEAST SOMEWHAT... **DAMAGED.**
OVER.
WELL, CAN'T REALLY ARGUE WITH YOU--
PKOW!
EUGENE?!
THAT SOUNDED LIKE A GUNSHOT. ARE YOU THERE?!
EUGENE?!

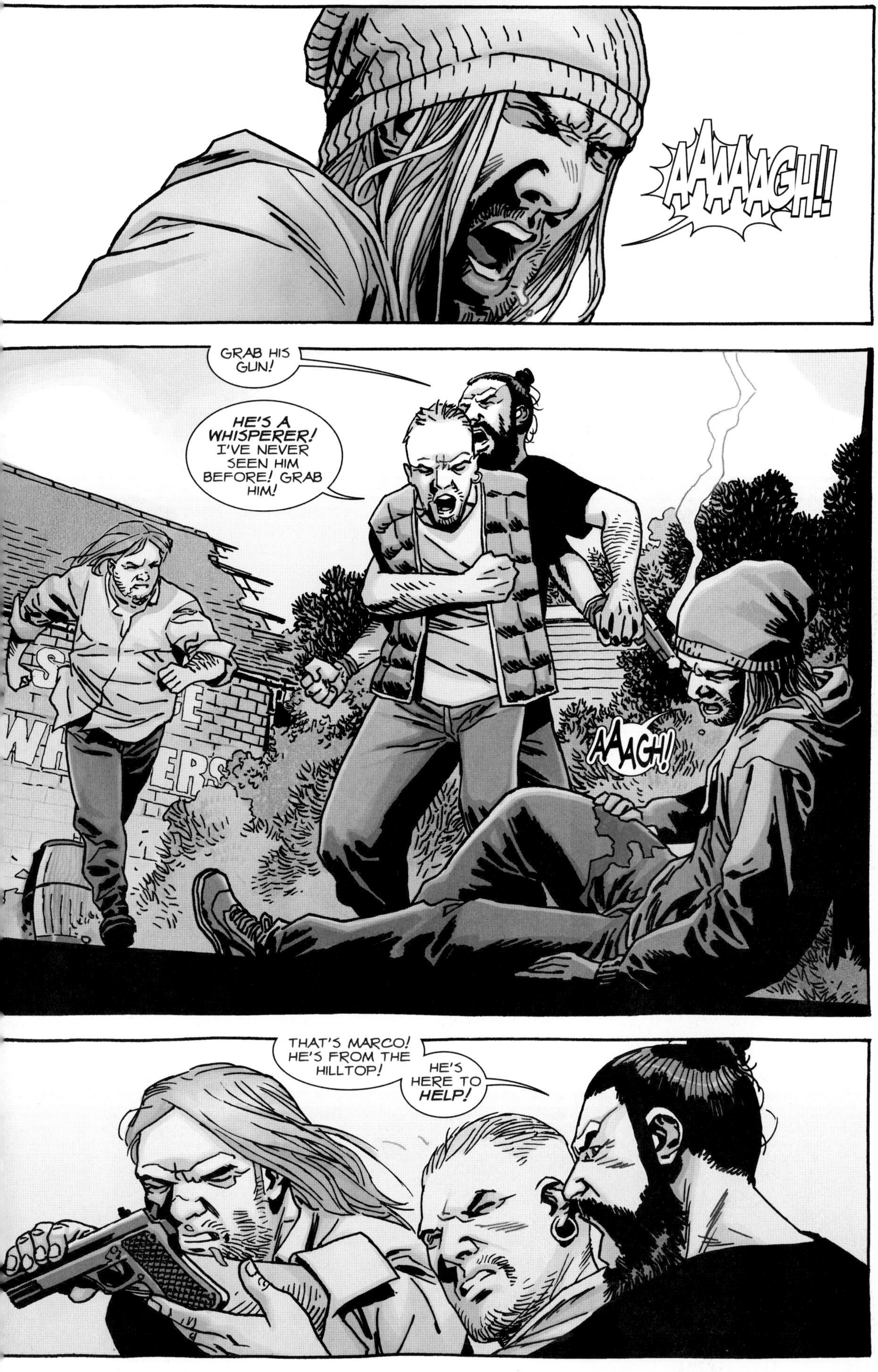
AAAAAGH!!
GRAB HIS GUN!
HE'S A WHISPERER! I'VE NEVER SEEN HIM BEFORE! GRAB HIM!
AAAGH!
THAT'S MARCO! HE'S FROM THE HILLTOP!
HE'S HERE TO HELP!

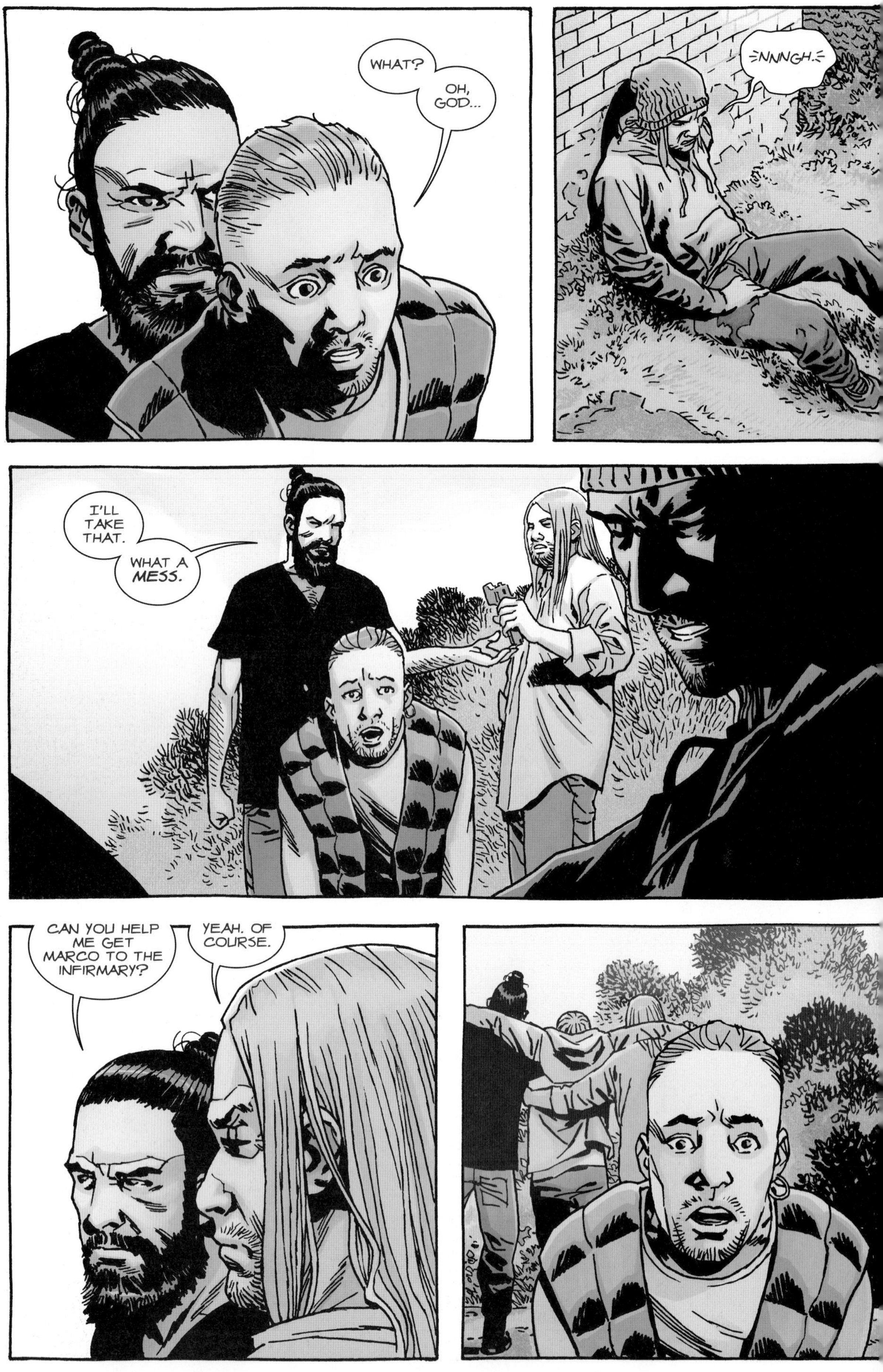
WHAT?
OH, GOD...
NNNGH.
I'LL TAKE THAT.
WHAT A MESS.
CAN YOU HELP ME GET MARCO TO THE INFIRMARY?
YEAH. OF COURSE.

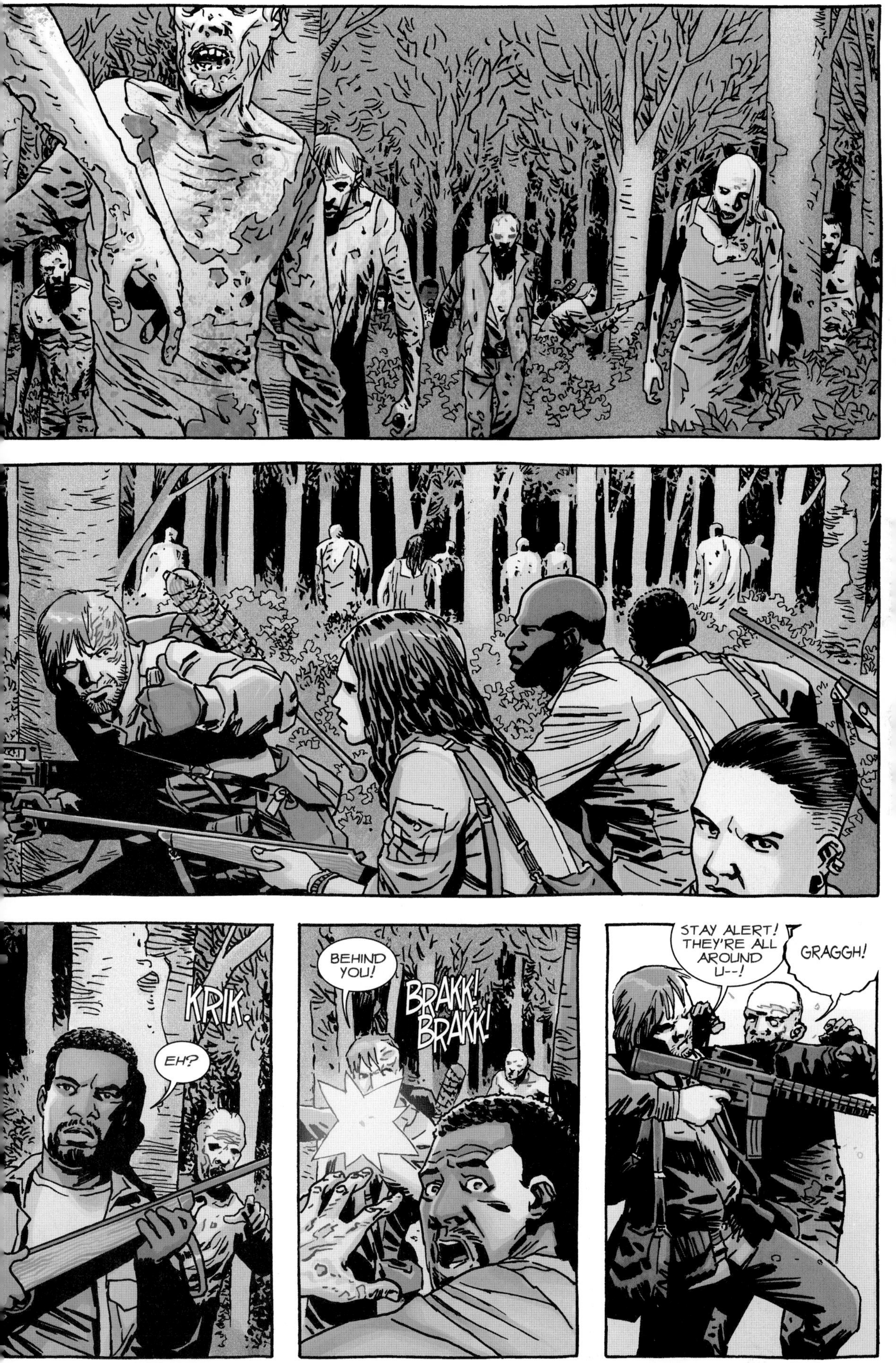
KRIK.
EH?
BEHIND YOU!
BRAKK! BRAKK!
STAY ALERT! THEY'RE ALL AROUND U--!
GRAGGH!

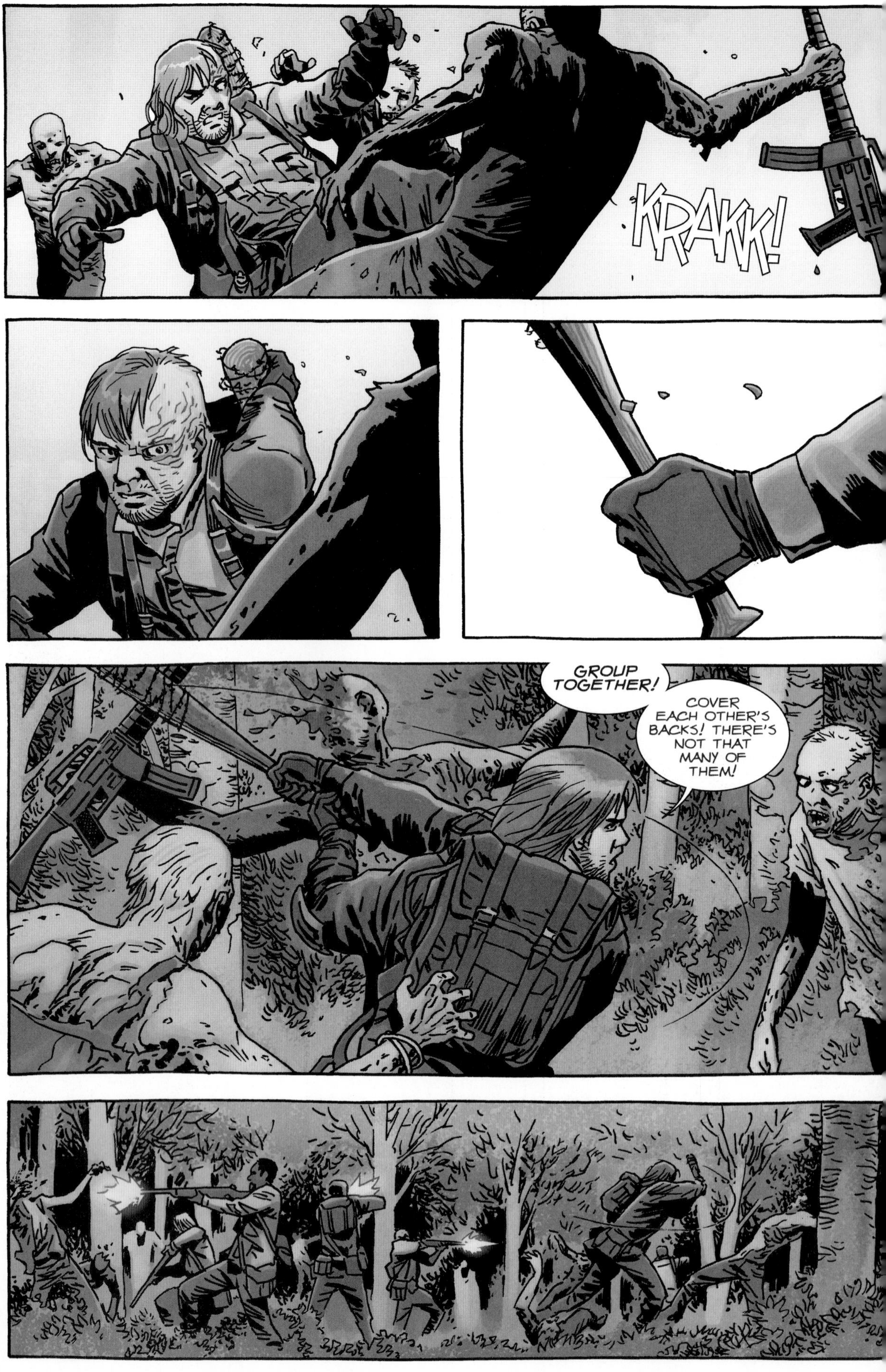
KRAKK!
GROUP TOGETHER!
COVER EACH OTHER'S BACKS! THERE'S NOT THAT MANY OF THEM!

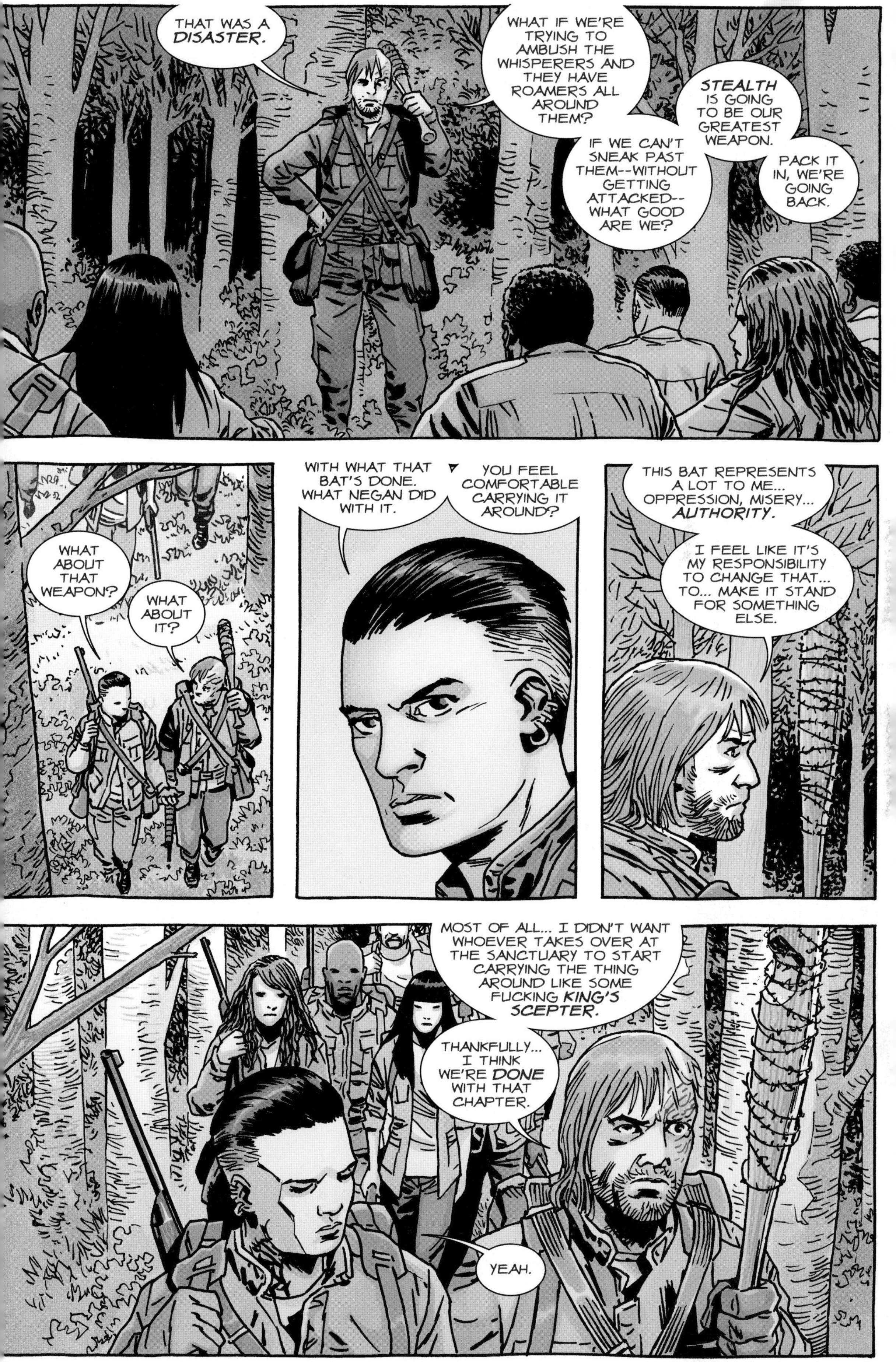
THAT WAS A *DISASTER.*
WHAT IF WE'RE TRYING TO AMBUSH THE WHISPERERS AND THEY HAVE ROAMERS ALL AROUND THEM?
IF WE CAN'T SNEAK PAST THEM--WITHOUT GETTING ATTACKED--WHAT GOOD ARE WE?
STEALTH IS GOING TO BE OUR GREATEST WEAPON.
PACK IT IN, WE'RE GOING BACK.
WHAT ABOUT THAT WEAPON?
WHAT ABOUT IT?
WITH WHAT THAT BAT'S DONE. WHAT NEGAN DID WITH IT.
YOU FEEL COMFORTABLE CARRYING IT AROUND?
THIS BAT REPRESENTS A LOT TO ME... OPPRESSION, MISERY... ***AUTHORITY.***
I FEEL LIKE IT'S MY RESPONSIBILITY TO CHANGE THAT... TO... MAKE IT STAND FOR SOMETHING ELSE.
MOST OF ALL... I DIDN'T WANT WHOEVER TAKES OVER AT THE SANCTUARY TO START CARRYING THE THING AROUND LIKE SOME FUCKING ***KING'S SCEPTER.***
THANKFULLY... I THINK WE'RE ***DONE*** WITH THAT CHAPTER.
YEAH.

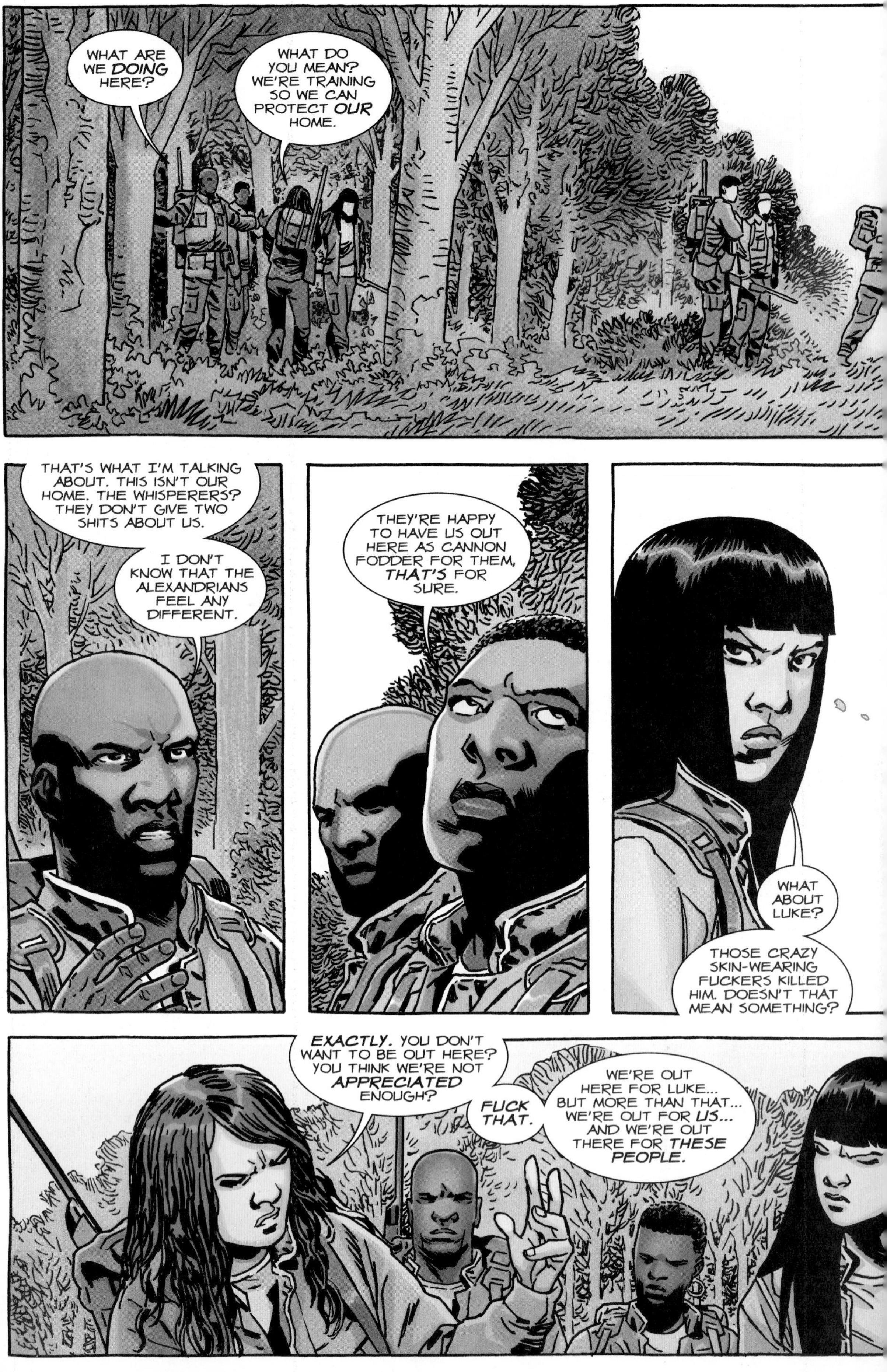
WHAT ARE WE *DOING* HERE?
WHAT DO YOU MEAN? WE'RE TRAINING SO WE CAN PROTECT *OUR* HOME.
THAT'S WHAT I'M TALKING ABOUT. THIS ISN'T OUR HOME. THE WHISPERERS? THEY DON'T GIVE TWO SHITS ABOUT US.
I DON'T KNOW THAT THE ALEXANDRIANS FEEL ANY DIFFERENT.
THEY'RE HAPPY TO HAVE US OUT HERE AS CANNON FODDER FOR THEM, *THAT'S* FOR SURE.
WHAT ABOUT LUKE?
THOSE CRAZY SKIN-WEARING FUCKERS KILLED HIM. DOESN'T THAT MEAN SOMETHING?
EXACTLY. YOU DON'T WANT TO BE OUT HERE? YOU THINK WE'RE NOT *APPRECIATED* ENOUGH?
FUCK THAT.
WE'RE OUT HERE FOR LUKE... BUT MORE THAN THAT... WE'RE OUT FOR *US*... AND WE'RE OUT THERE FOR *THESE PEOPLE.*

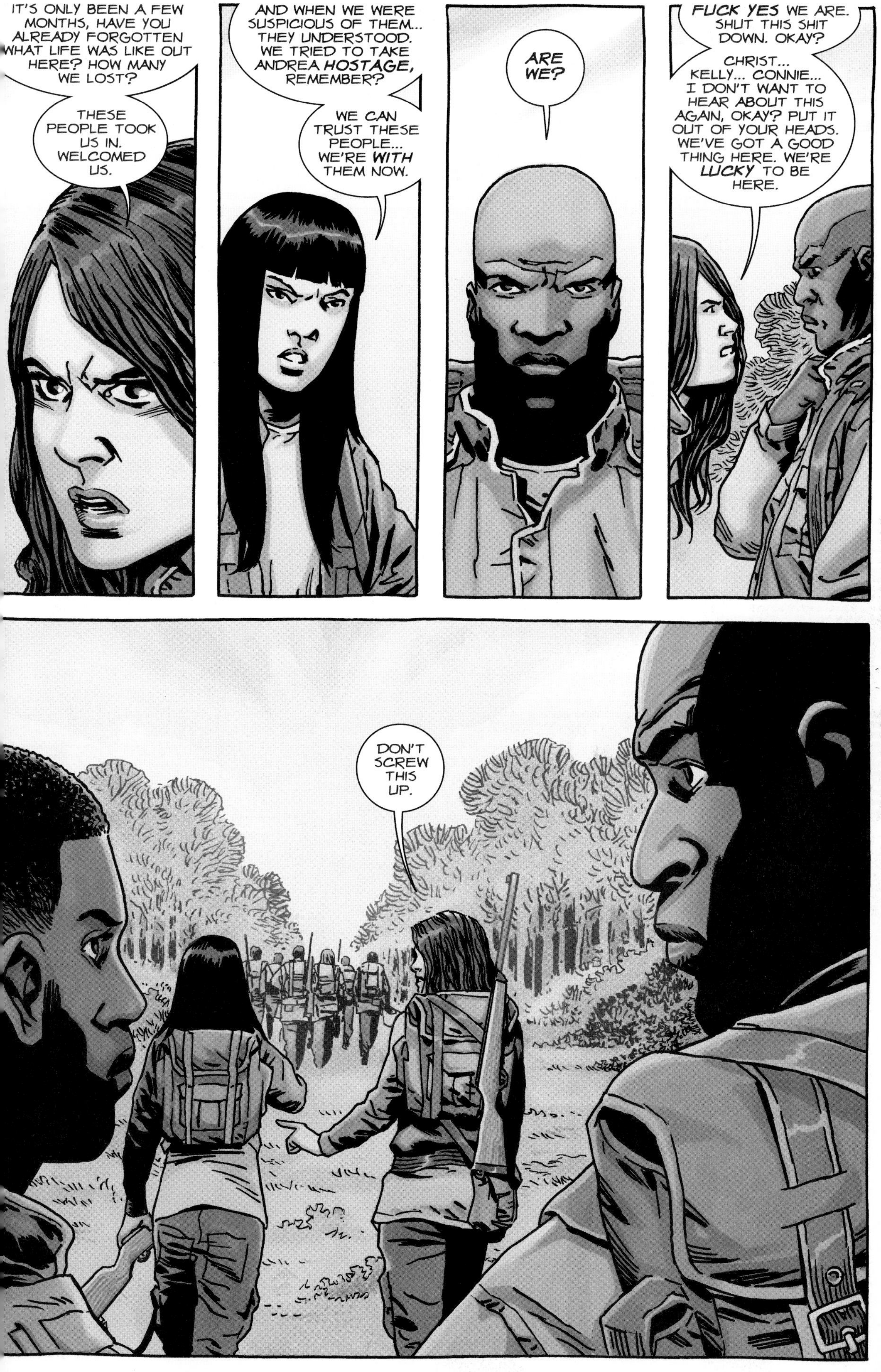
IT'S ONLY BEEN A FEW MONTHS, HAVE YOU ALREADY FORGOTTEN WHAT LIFE WAS LIKE OUT HERE? HOW MANY WE LOST?
THESE PEOPLE TOOK US IN. WELCOMED US.
AND WHEN WE WERE SUSPICIOUS OF THEM... THEY UNDERSTOOD. WE TRIED TO TAKE ANDREA HOSTAGE, REMEMBER?
WE CAN TRUST THESE PEOPLE... WE'RE WITH THEM NOW.
ARE WE?
FUCK YES WE ARE. SHUT THIS SHIT DOWN. OKAY?
CHRIST... KELLY... CONNIE... I DON'T WANT TO HEAR ABOUT THIS AGAIN, OKAY? PUT IT OUT OF YOUR HEADS. WE'VE GOT A GOOD THING HERE. WE'RE LUCKY TO BE HERE.
DON'T SCREW THIS UP.

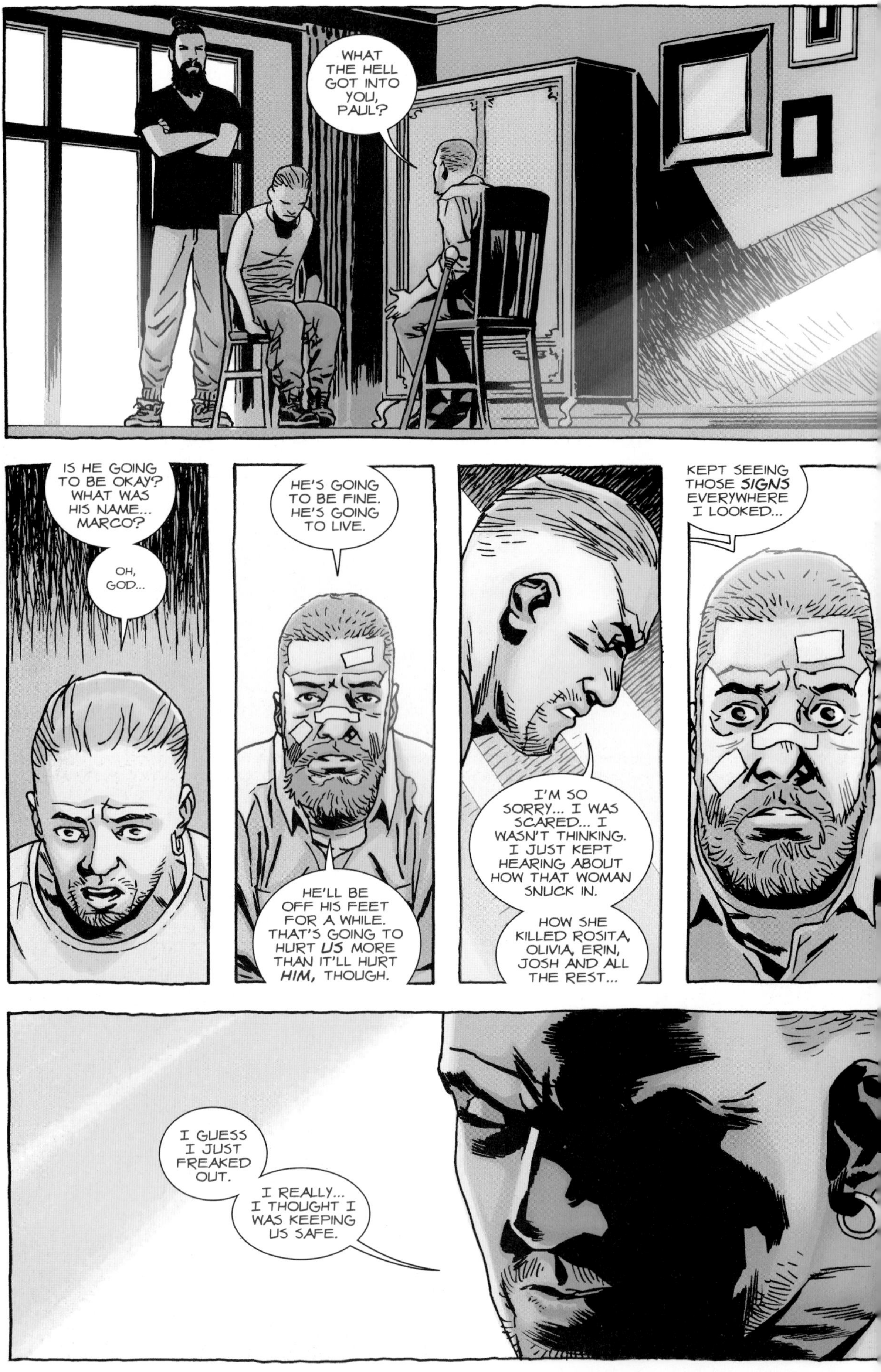
WHAT THE HELL GOT INTO YOU, PAUL?
IS HE GOING TO BE OKAY? WHAT WAS HIS NAME... MARCO?
OH, GOD...
HE'S GOING TO BE FINE. HE'S GOING TO LIVE.
HE'LL BE OFF HIS FEET FOR A WHILE. THAT'S GOING TO HURT US MORE THAN IT'LL HURT HIM, THOUGH.
I'M SO SORRY... I WAS SCARED... I WASN'T THINKING. I JUST KEPT HEARING ABOUT HOW THAT WOMAN SNUCK IN.
HOW SHE KILLED ROSITA, OLIVIA, ERIN, JOSH AND ALL THE REST...
KEPT SEEING THOSE SIGNS EVERYWHERE I LOOKED...
I GUESS I JUST FREAKED OUT.
I REALLY... I THOUGHT I WAS KEEPING US SAFE.

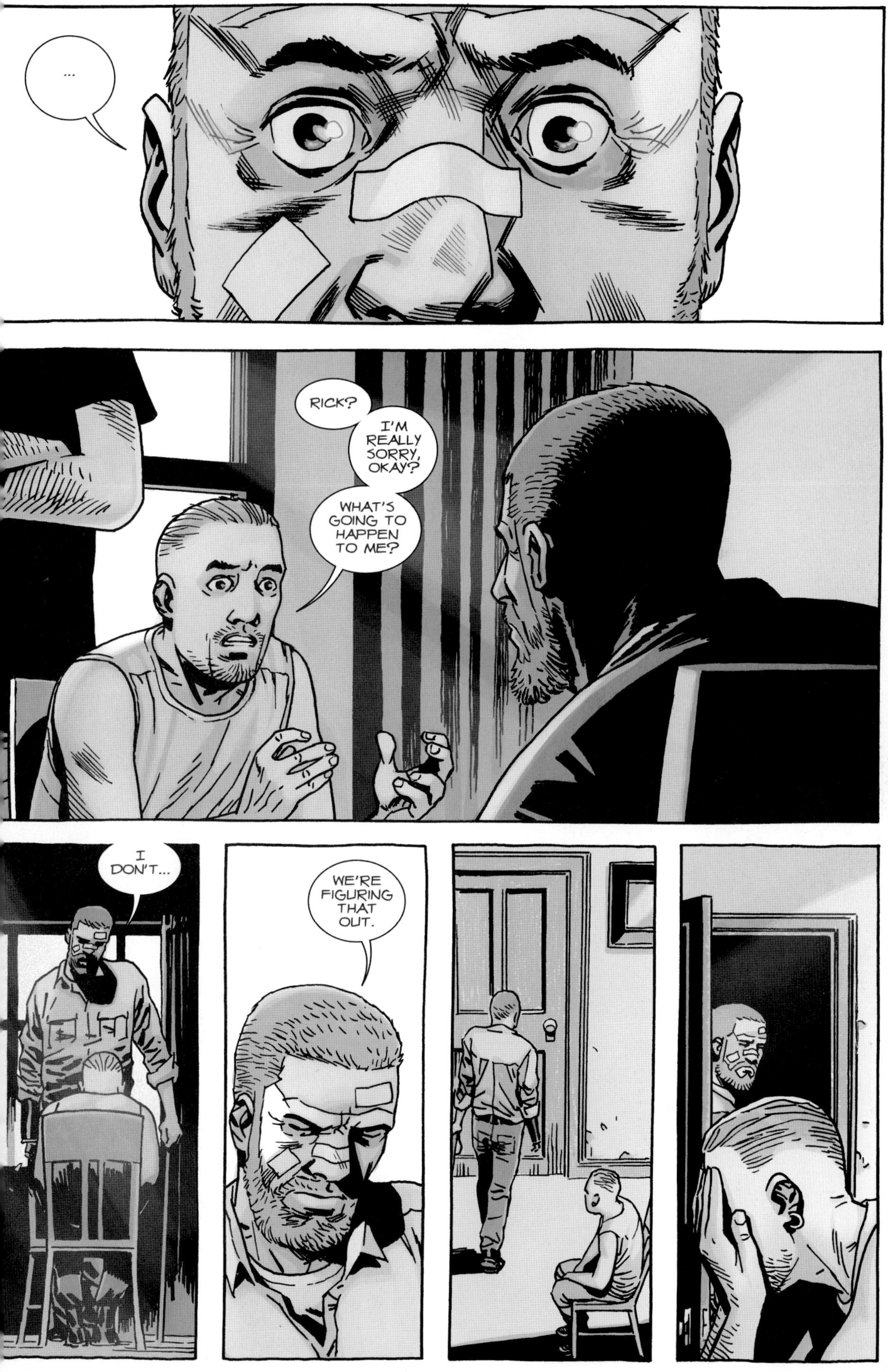
...
RICK?
I'M REALLY SORRY, OKAY?
WHAT'S GOING TO HAPPEN TO ME?
I DON'T...
WE'RE FIGURING THAT OUT.

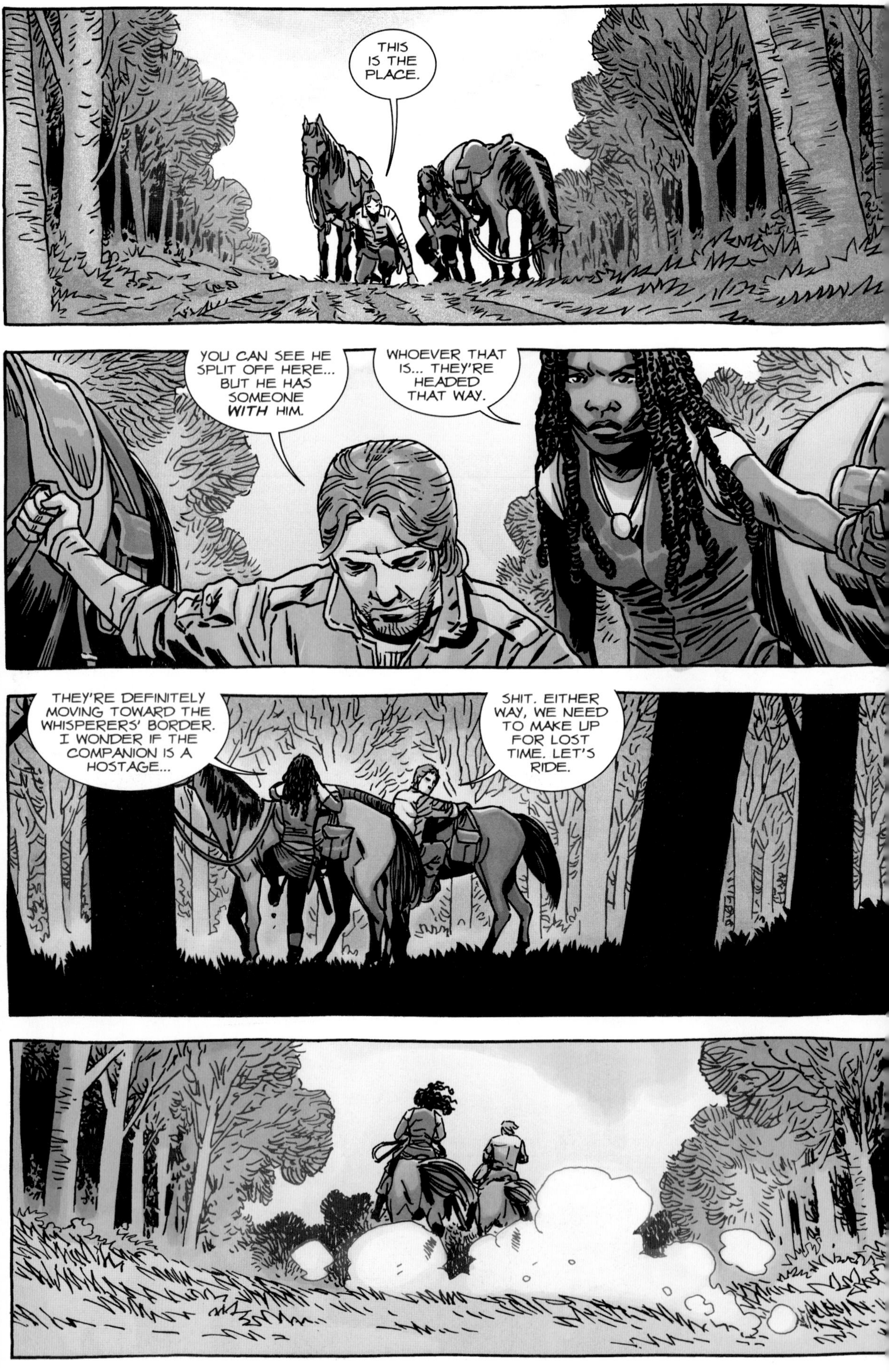
THIS IS THE PLACE.
YOU CAN SEE HE SPLIT OFF HERE... BUT HE HAS SOMEONE WITH HIM.
WHOEVER THAT IS... THEY'RE HEADED THAT WAY.
THEY'RE DEFINITELY MOVING TOWARD THE WHISPERERS' BORDER. I WONDER IF THE COMPANION IS A HOSTAGE...
SHIT. EITHER WAY, WE NEED TO MAKE UP FOR LOST TIME. LET'S RIDE.

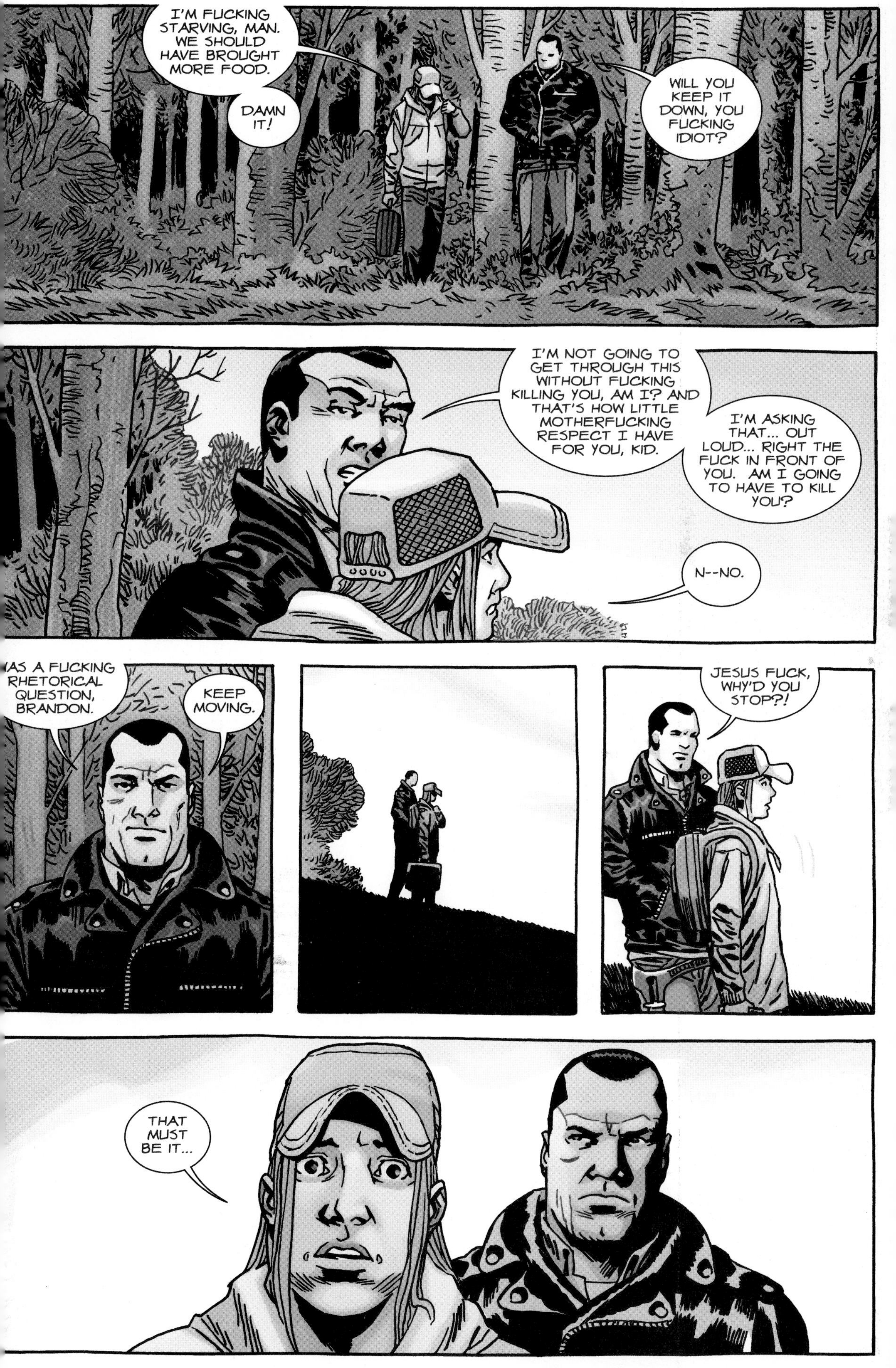
I'M FUCKING STARVING, MAN. WE SHOULD HAVE BROUGHT MORE FOOD.
DAMN IT!
WILL YOU KEEP IT DOWN, YOU FUCKING IDIOT?
I'M NOT GOING TO GET THROUGH THIS WITHOUT FUCKING KILLING YOU, AM I? AND THAT'S HOW LITTLE MOTHERFUCKING RESPECT I HAVE FOR YOU, KID.
I'M ASKING THAT... OUT LOUD... RIGHT THE FUCK IN FRONT OF YOU. AM I GOING TO HAVE TO KILL YOU?
N--NO.
AS A FUCKING RHETORICAL QUESTION, BRANDON.
KEEP MOVING.
JESUS FUCK, WHY'D YOU STOP?!
THAT MUST BE IT...

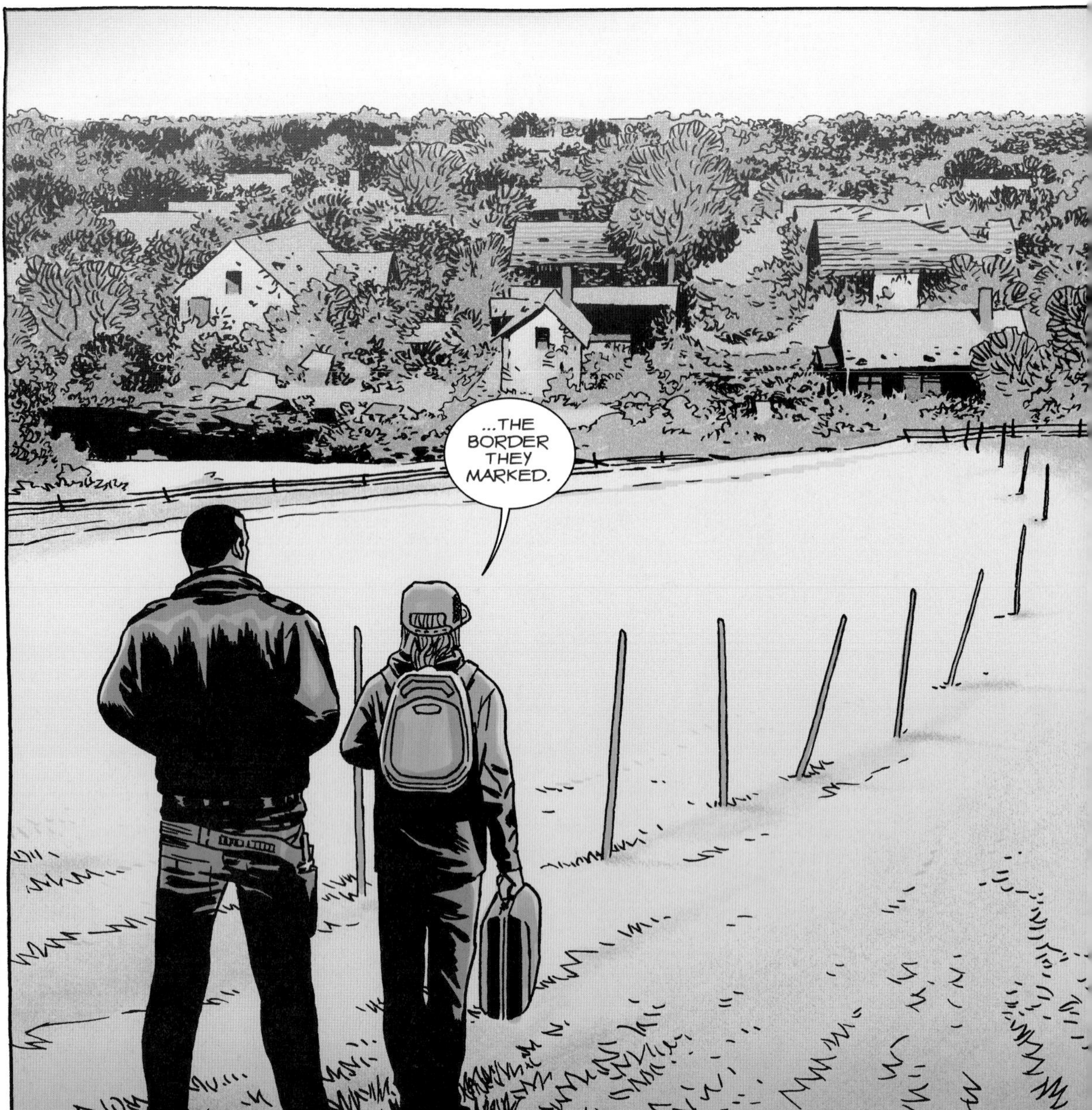
...THE BORDER THEY MARKED.

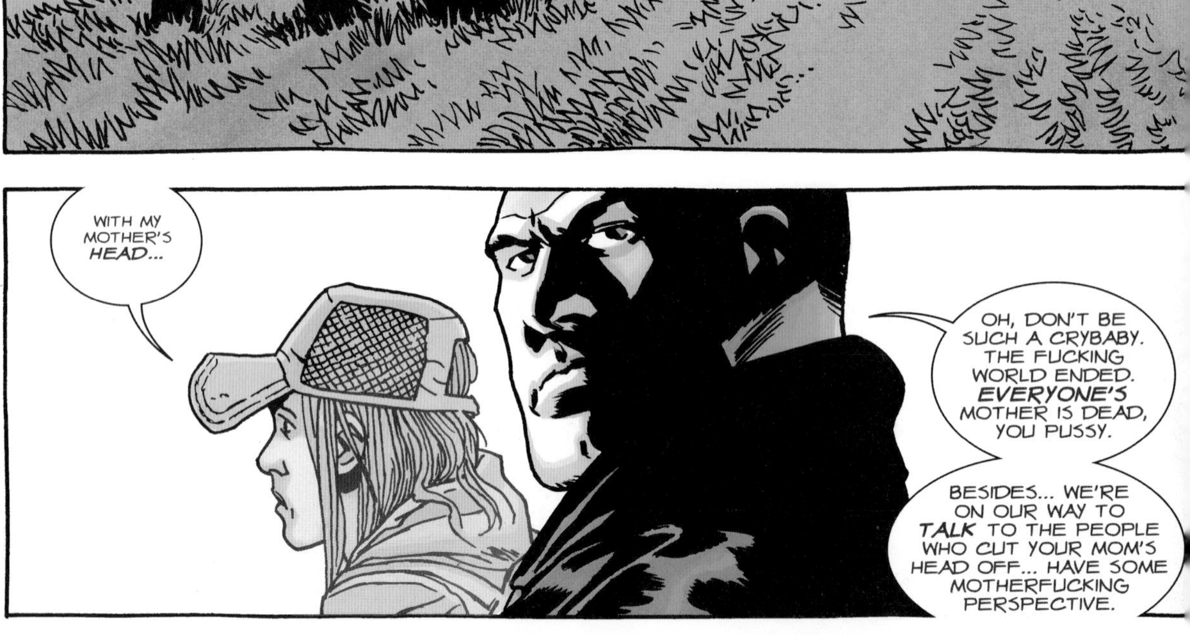
WITH MY MOTHER'S *HEAD*...
OH, DON'T BE SUCH A CRYBABY. THE FUCKING WORLD ENDED. *EVERYONE'S* MOTHER IS DEAD, YOU PUSSY.
BESIDES... WE'RE ON OUR WAY TO *TALK* TO THE PEOPLE WHO CUT YOUR MOM'S HEAD OFF... HAVE SOME MOTHERFUCKING PERSPECTIVE.

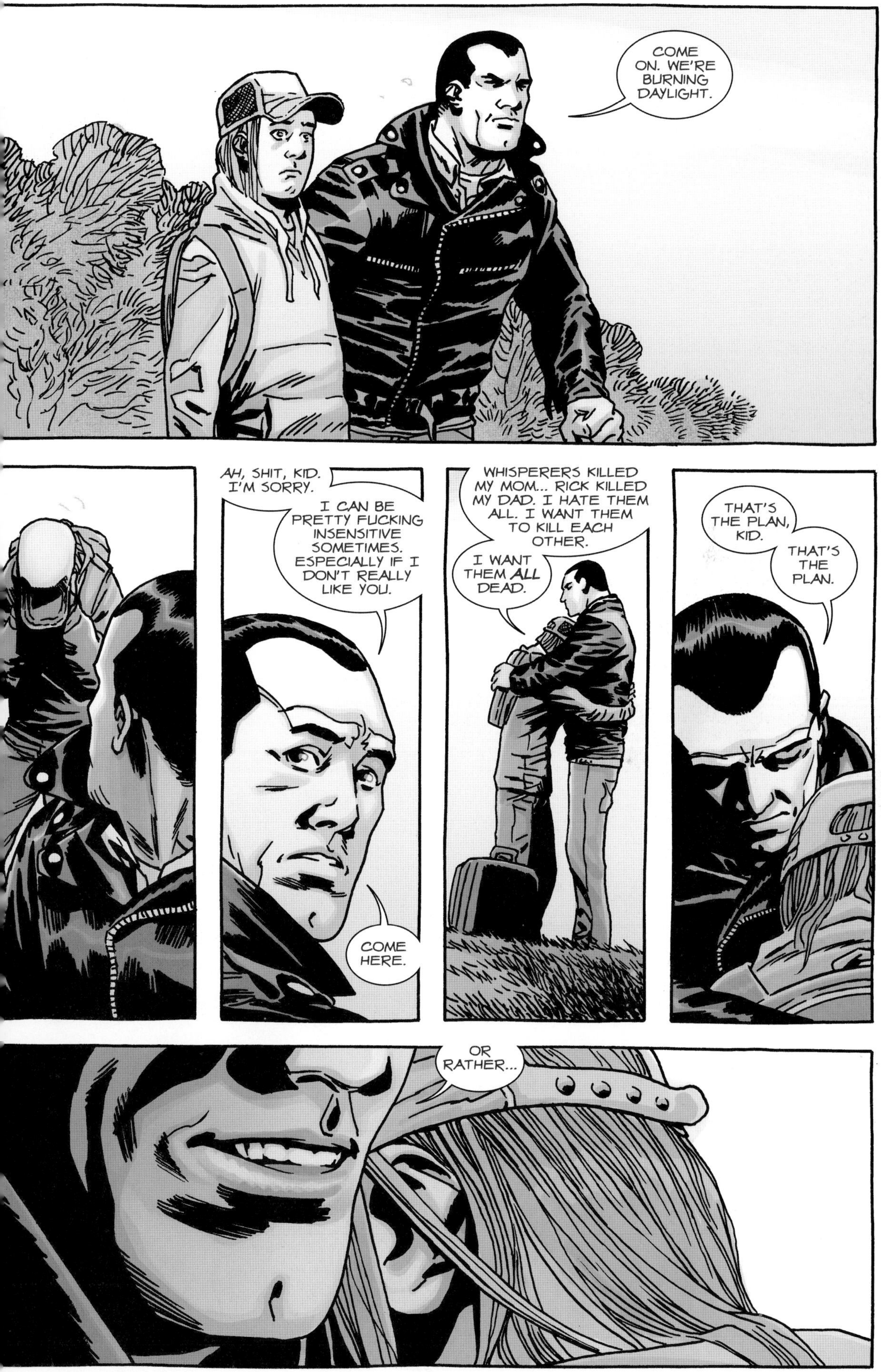
COME ON. WE'RE BURNING DAYLIGHT.
AH, SHIT, KID. I'M SORRY.
I CAN BE PRETTY FUCKING INSENSITIVE SOMETIMES. ESPECIALLY IF I DON'T REALLY LIKE YOU.
COME HERE.
WHISPERERS KILLED MY MOM... RICK KILLED MY DAD. I HATE THEM ALL. I WANT THEM TO KILL EACH OTHER.
I WANT THEM ALL DEAD.
THAT'S THE PLAN, KID.
THAT'S THE PLAN.
OR RATHER...

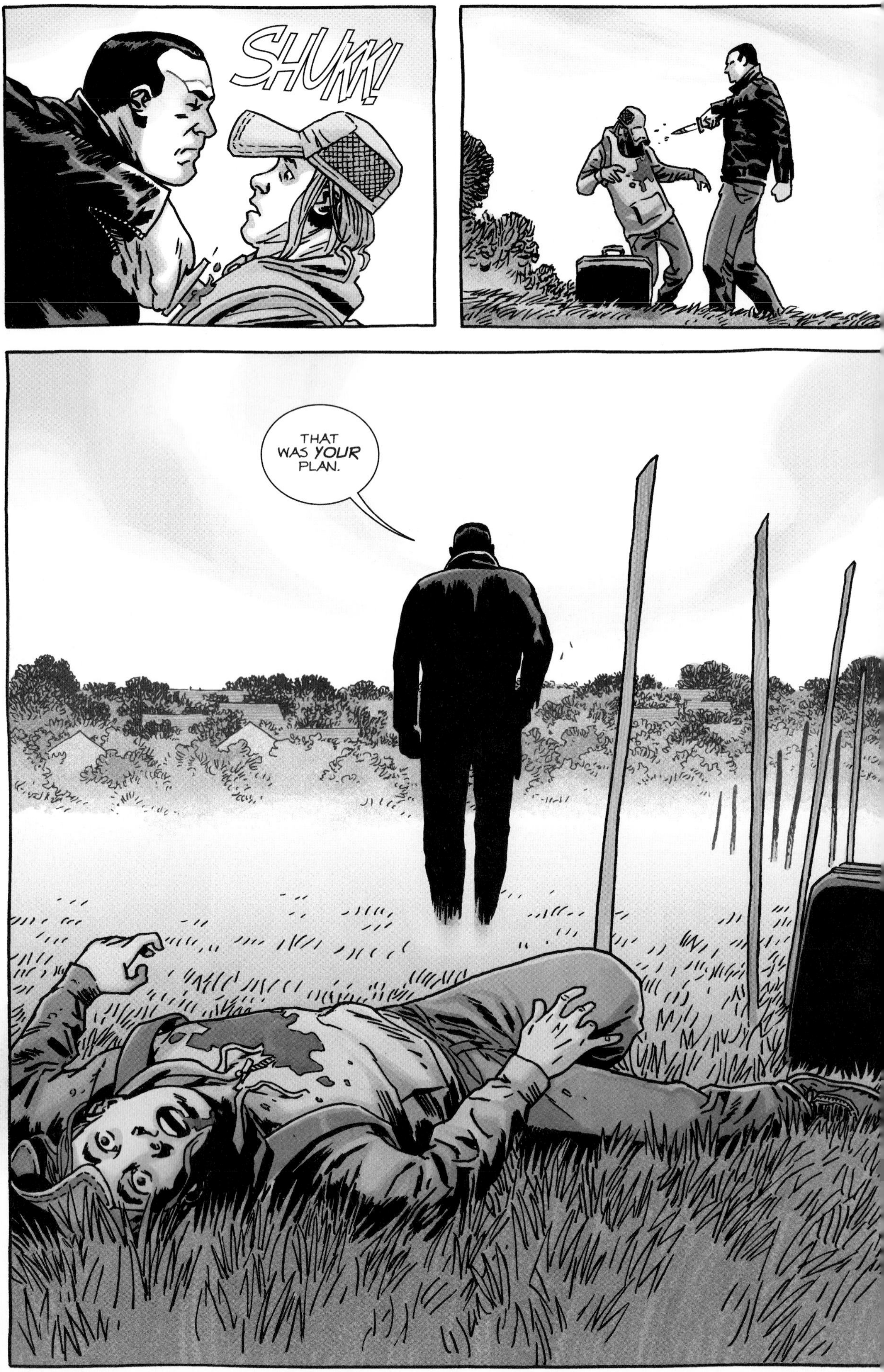
SHUKK!
THAT WAS *YOUR* PLAN.

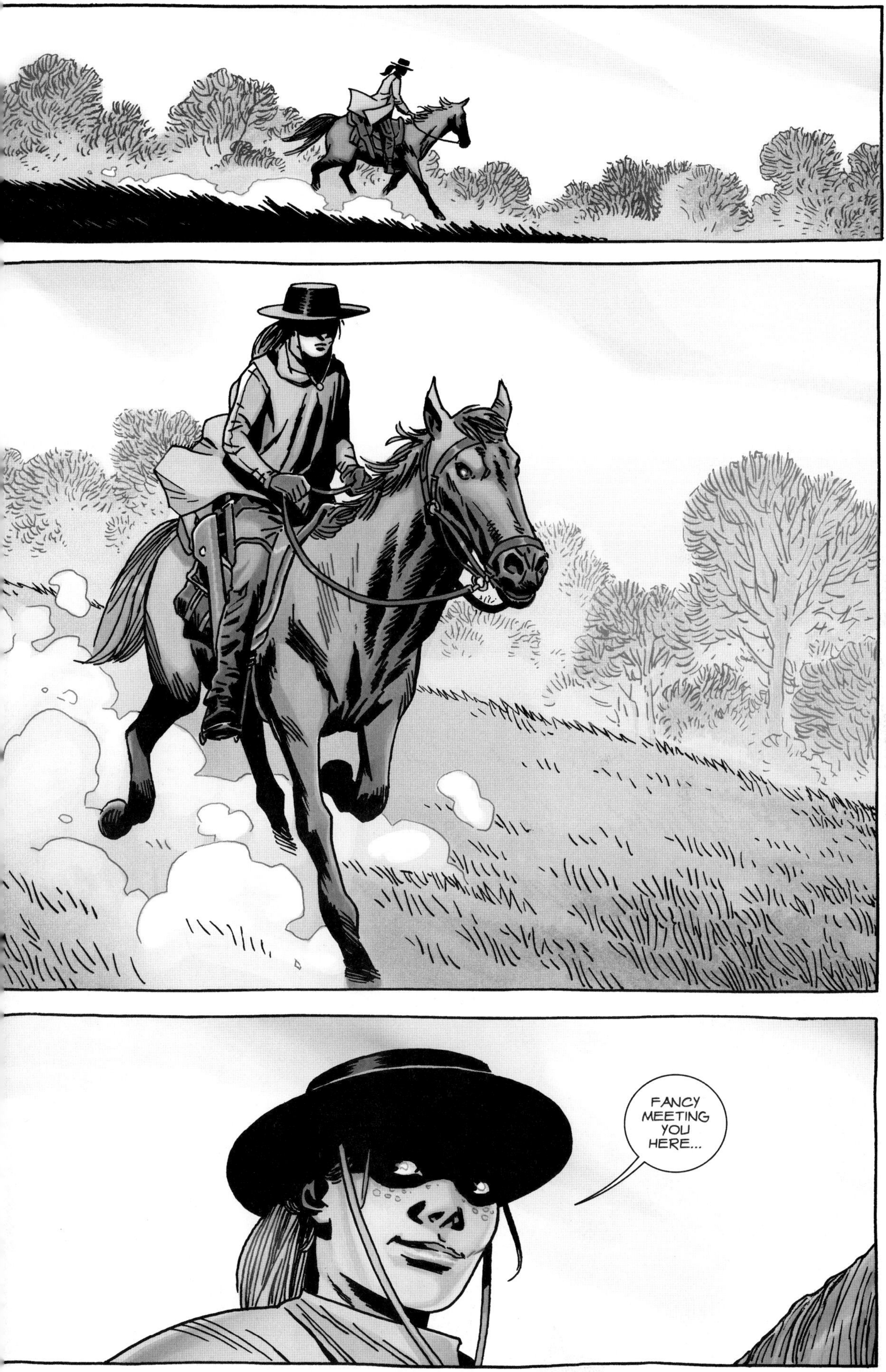
FANCY MEETING YOU HERE...

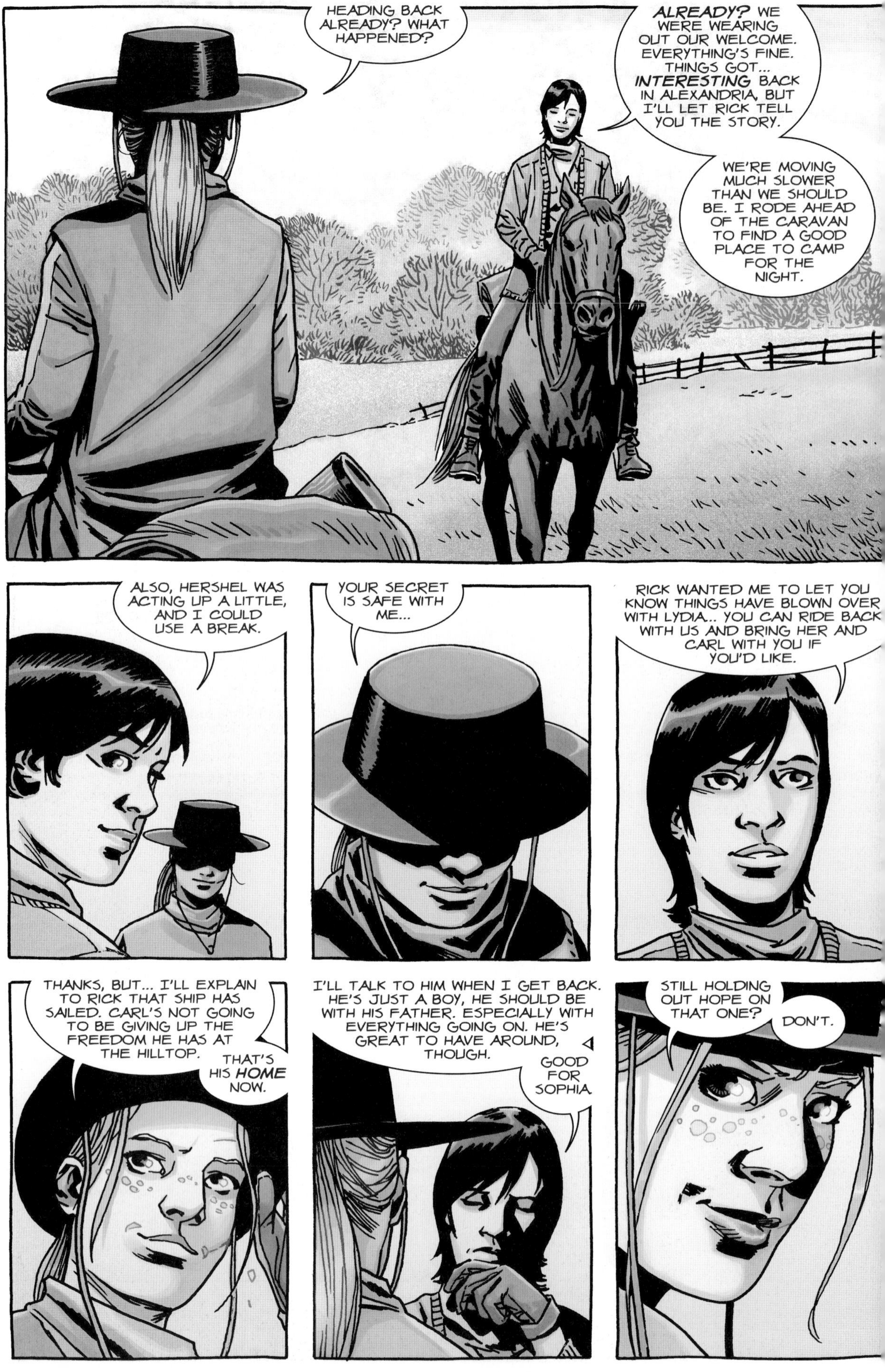
HEADING BACK ALREADY? WHAT HAPPENED?
ALREADY? WE WERE WEARING OUT OUR WELCOME. EVERYTHING'S FINE. THINGS GOT... INTERESTING BACK IN ALEXANDRIA, BUT I'LL LET RICK TELL YOU THE STORY.
WE'RE MOVING MUCH SLOWER THAN WE SHOULD BE. I RODE AHEAD OF THE CARAVAN TO FIND A GOOD PLACE TO CAMP FOR THE NIGHT.
ALSO, HERSHEL WAS ACTING UP A LITTLE, AND I COULD USE A BREAK.
YOUR SECRET IS SAFE WITH ME...
RICK WANTED ME TO LET YOU KNOW THINGS HAVE BLOWN OVER WITH LYDIA... YOU CAN RIDE BACK WITH US AND BRING HER AND CARL WITH YOU IF YOU'D LIKE.
THANKS, BUT... I'LL EXPLAIN TO RICK THAT SHIP HAS SAILED. CARL'S NOT GOING TO BE GIVING UP THE FREEDOM HE HAS AT THE HILLTOP.
THAT'S HIS HOME NOW.
I'LL TALK TO HIM WHEN I GET BACK. HE'S JUST A BOY, HE SHOULD BE WITH HIS FATHER. ESPECIALLY WITH EVERYTHING GOING ON. HE'S GREAT TO HAVE AROUND, THOUGH.
GOOD FOR SOPHIA
STILL HOLDING OUT HOPE ON THAT ONE?
DON'T.

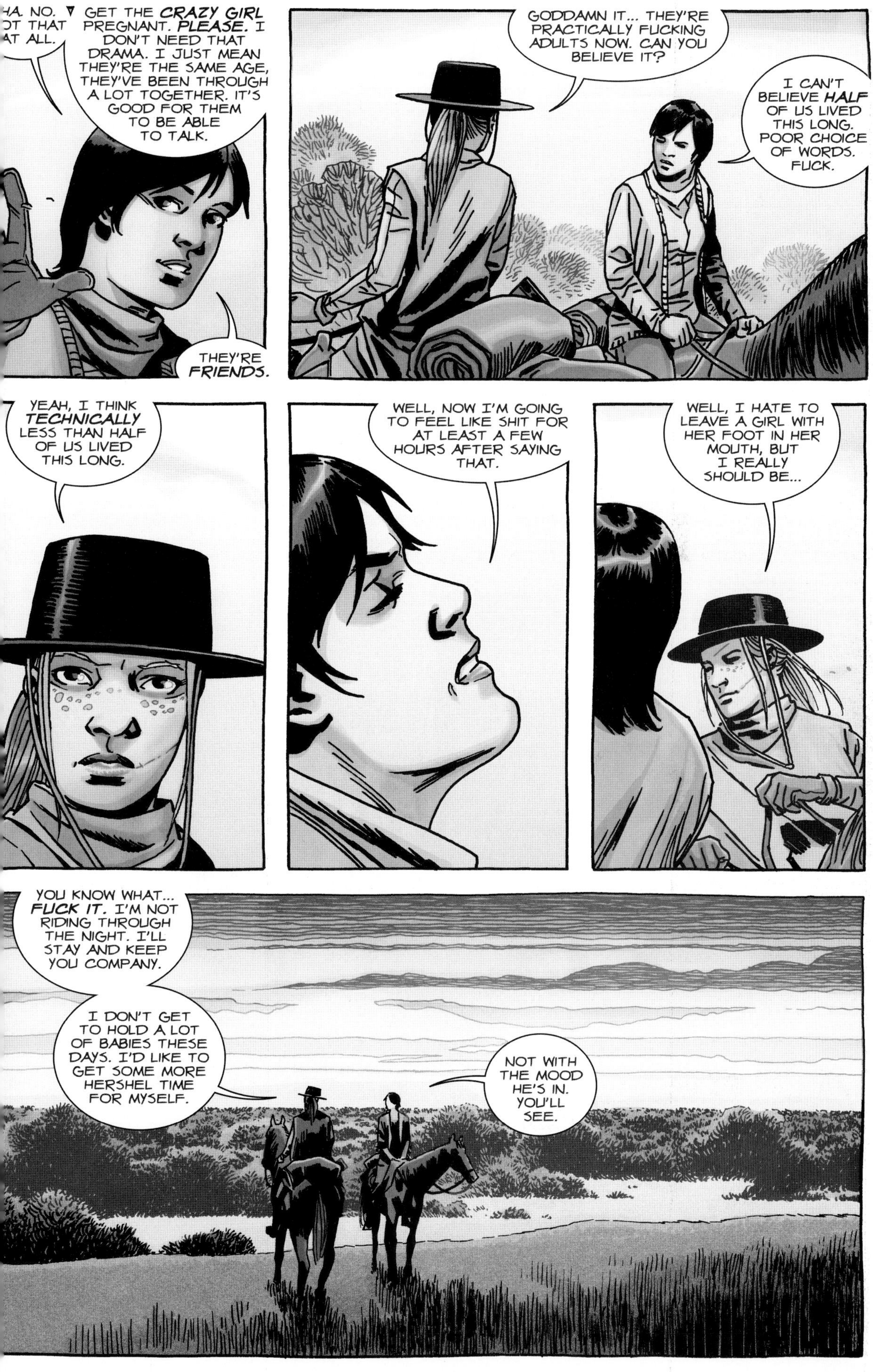
HA. NO. NOT THAT AT ALL.
GET THE CRAZY GIRL PREGNANT. PLEASE. I DON'T NEED THAT DRAMA. I JUST MEAN THEY'RE THE SAME AGE, THEY'VE BEEN THROUGH A LOT TOGETHER. IT'S GOOD FOR THEM TO BE ABLE TO TALK.
THEY'RE FRIENDS.
GODDAMN IT... THEY'RE PRACTICALLY FUCKING ADULTS NOW. CAN YOU BELIEVE IT?
I CAN'T BELIEVE HALF OF US LIVED THIS LONG. POOR CHOICE OF WORDS. FUCK.
YEAH, I THINK TECHNICALLY LESS THAN HALF OF US LIVED THIS LONG.
WELL, NOW I'M GOING TO FEEL LIKE SHIT FOR AT LEAST A FEW HOURS AFTER SAYING THAT.
WELL, I HATE TO LEAVE A GIRL WITH HER FOOT IN HER MOUTH, BUT I REALLY SHOULD BE...
YOU KNOW WHAT... FUCK IT. I'M NOT RIDING THROUGH THE NIGHT. I'LL STAY AND KEEP YOU COMPANY.
I DON'T GET TO HOLD A LOT OF BABIES THESE DAYS. I'D LIKE TO GET SOME MORE HERSHEL TIME FOR MYSELF.
NOT WITH THE MOOD HE'S IN. YOU'LL SEE.

SHIT. DO YOU KNOW WHO THIS IS?
YEAH... THIS IS BRANDON. HE ATTACKED RICK YESTERDAY. SO... NOW WE KNOW HOW NEGAN GOT OUT.
HE HASN'T TURNED YET.
I'LL TAKE CARE OF IT. DO WE BURY HIM?
NO TIME. NEGAN SHOULDN'T HAVE MADE IT THIS FAR. AND IF HE KILLED BRANDON... AND HE HASN'T TURNED YET... HE COULD BE CLOSE.
THIS IS NOT GOOD. IT'S GETTING DARK. WE NEED TO HURRY
WE'LL WORRY ABOUT HIM ON THE WAY BACK...

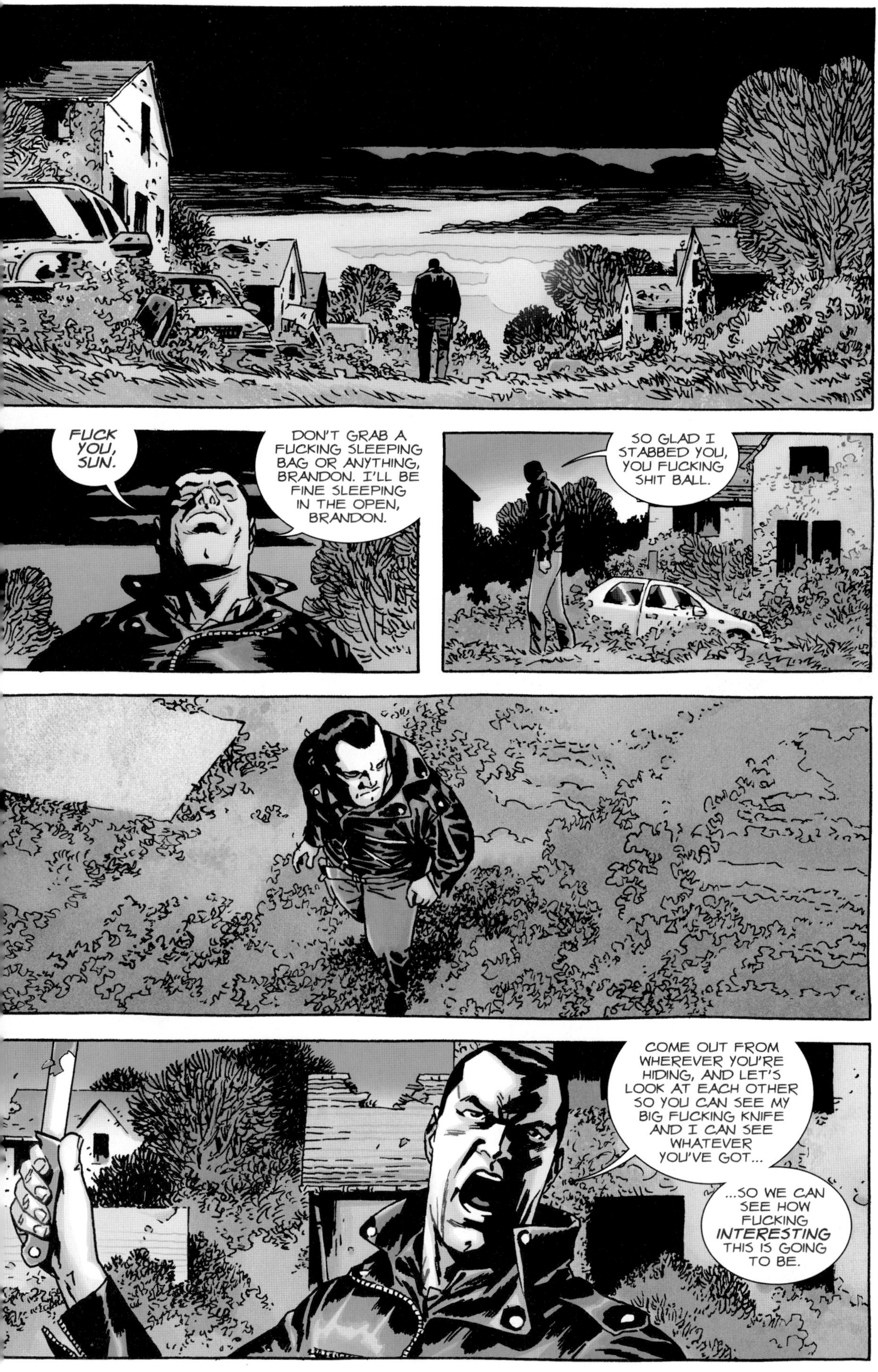
FUCK YOU, SUN.
DON'T GRAB A FUCKING SLEEPING BAG OR ANYTHING, BRANDON. I'LL BE FINE SLEEPING IN THE OPEN, BRANDON.
SO GLAD I STABBED YOU, YOU FUCKING SHIT BALL.
COME OUT FROM WHEREVER YOU'RE HIDING, AND LET'S LOOK AT EACH OTHER SO YOU CAN SEE MY BIG FUCKING KNIFE AND I CAN SEE WHATEVER YOU'VE GOT...
...SO WE CAN SEE HOW FUCKING *INTERESTING* THIS IS GOING TO BE.

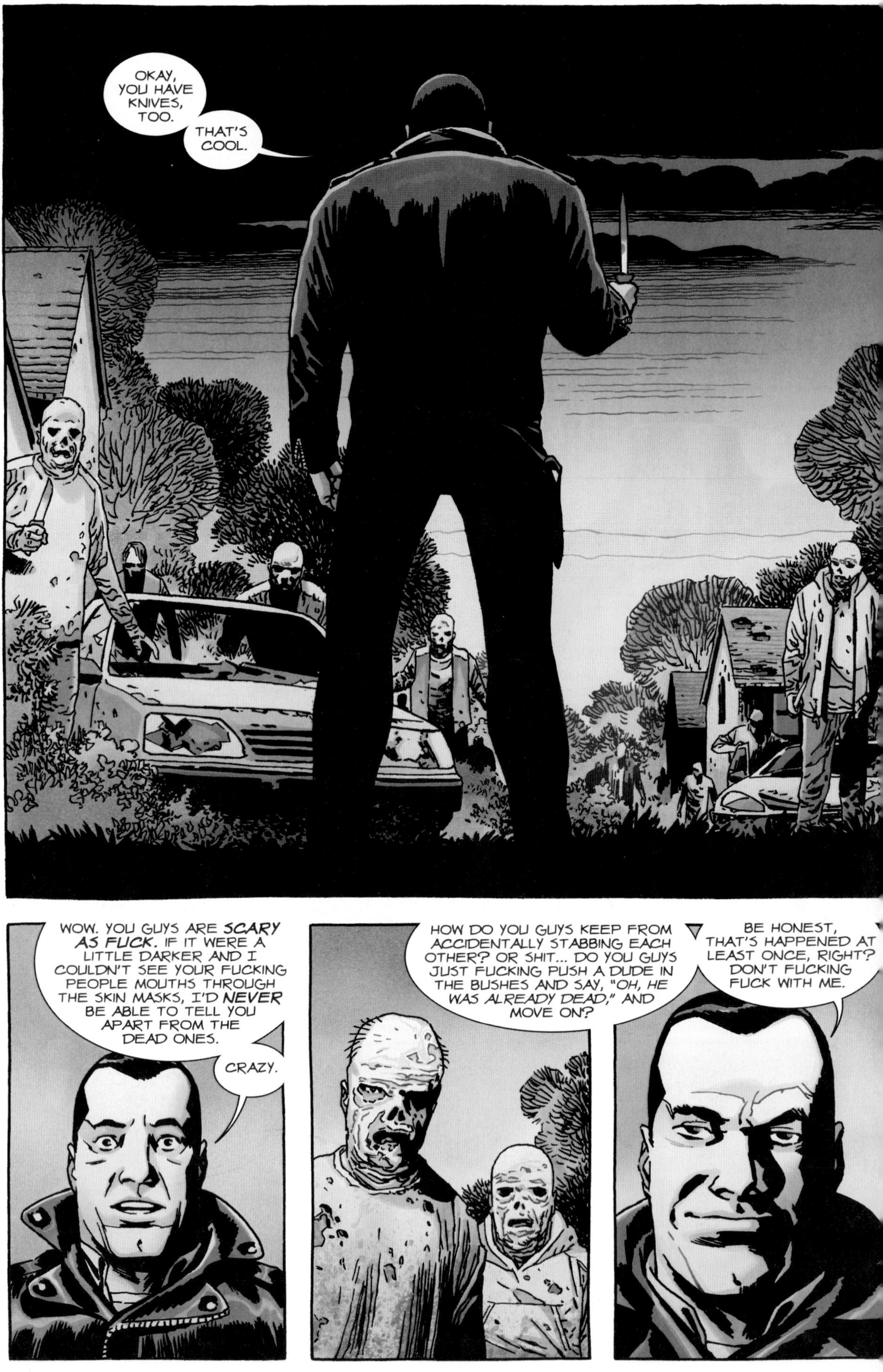
OKAY, YOU HAVE KNIVES, TOO.
THAT'S COOL.
WOW. YOU GUYS ARE SCARY AS FUCK. IF IT WERE A LITTLE DARKER AND I COULDN'T SEE YOUR FUCKING PEOPLE MOUTHS THROUGH THE SKIN MASKS, I'D NEVER BE ABLE TO TELL YOU APART FROM THE DEAD ONES.
CRAZY.
HOW DO YOU GUYS KEEP FROM ACCIDENTALLY STABBING EACH OTHER? OR SHIT... DO YOU GUYS JUST FUCKING PUSH A DUDE IN THE BUSHES AND SAY, "OH, HE WAS ALREADY DEAD," AND MOVE ON?
BE HONEST, THAT'S HAPPENED AT LEAST ONCE, RIGHT? DON'T FUCKING FUCK WITH ME.

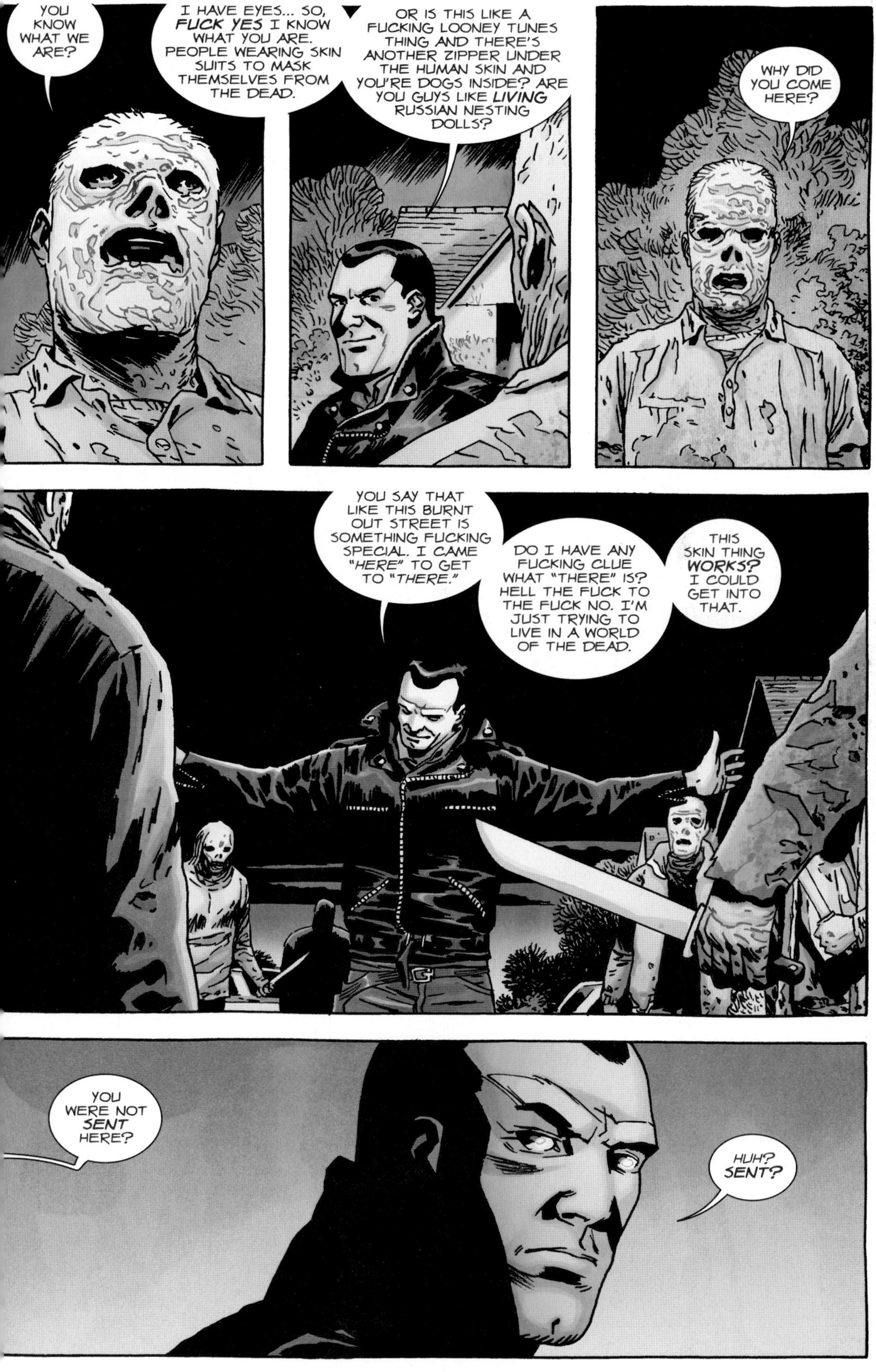

YOU KNOW WHAT WE ARE?
I HAVE EYES... SO, FUCK YES I KNOW WHAT YOU ARE. PEOPLE WEARING SKIN SUITS TO MASK THEMSELVES FROM THE DEAD.
OR IS THIS LIKE A FUCKING LOONEY TUNES THING AND THERE'S ANOTHER ZIPPER UNDER THE HUMAN SKIN AND YOU'RE DOGS INSIDE? ARE YOU GUYS LIKE LIVING RUSSIAN NESTING DOLLS?
WHY DID YOU COME HERE?
YOU SAY THAT LIKE THIS BURNT OUT STREET IS SOMETHING FUCKING SPECIAL. I CAME "HERE" TO GET TO "THERE."
DO I HAVE ANY FUCKING CLUE WHAT "THERE" IS? HELL THE FUCK TO THE FUCK NO. I'M JUST TRYING TO LIVE IN A WORLD OF THE DEAD.
THIS SKIN THING WORKS? I COULD GET INTO THAT.
YOU WERE NOT SENT HERE?
HUH? SENT?

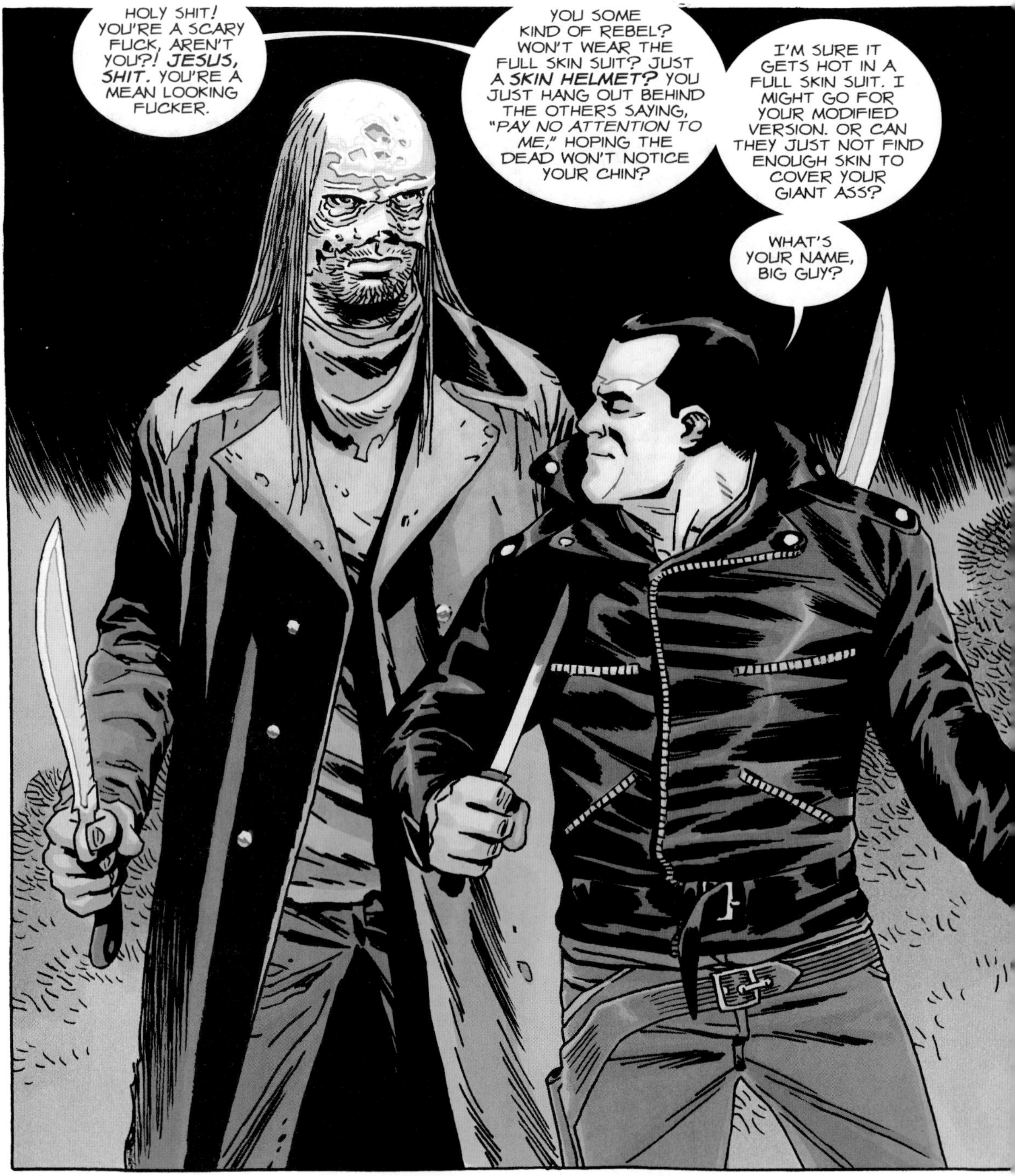
HOLY SHIT! YOU'RE A SCARY FUCK, AREN'T YOU?! JESUS, SHIT. YOU'RE A MEAN LOOKING FUCKER.
YOU SOME KIND OF REBEL? WON'T WEAR THE FULL SKIN SUIT? JUST A SKIN HELMET? YOU JUST HANG OUT BEHIND THE OTHERS SAYING, "PAY NO ATTENTION TO ME," HOPING THE DEAD WON'T NOTICE YOUR CHIN?
I'M SURE IT GETS HOT IN A FULL SKIN SUIT. I MIGHT GO FOR YOUR MODIFIED VERSION. OR CAN THEY JUST NOT FIND ENOUGH SKIN TO COVER YOUR GIANT ASS?
WHAT'S YOUR NAME, BIG GUY?

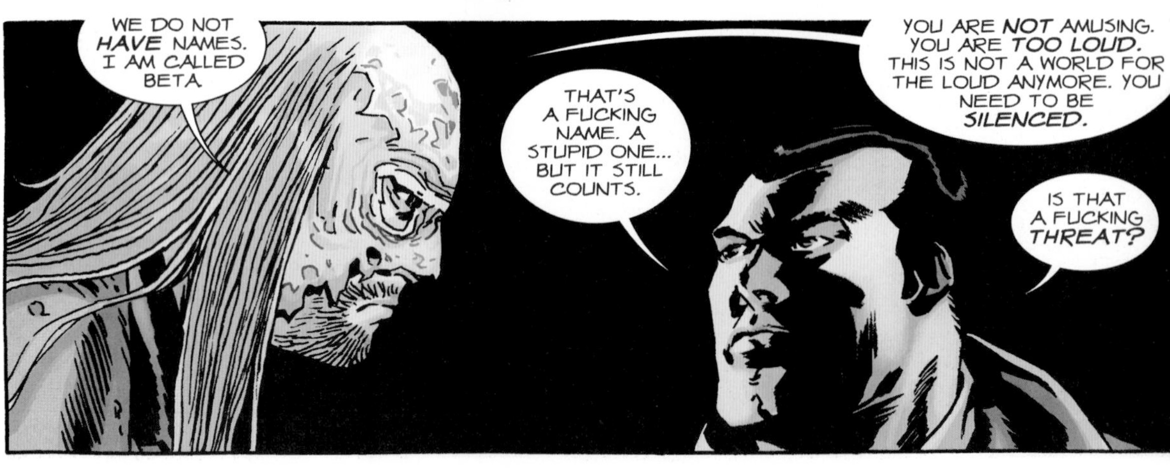
WE DO NOT HAVE NAMES. I AM CALLED BETA.
THAT'S A FUCKING NAME. A STUPID ONE... BUT IT STILL COUNTS.
YOU ARE NOT AMUSING. YOU ARE TOO LOUD. THIS IS NOT A WORLD FOR THE LOUD ANYMORE. YOU NEED TO BE SILENCED.
IS THAT A FUCKING THREAT?

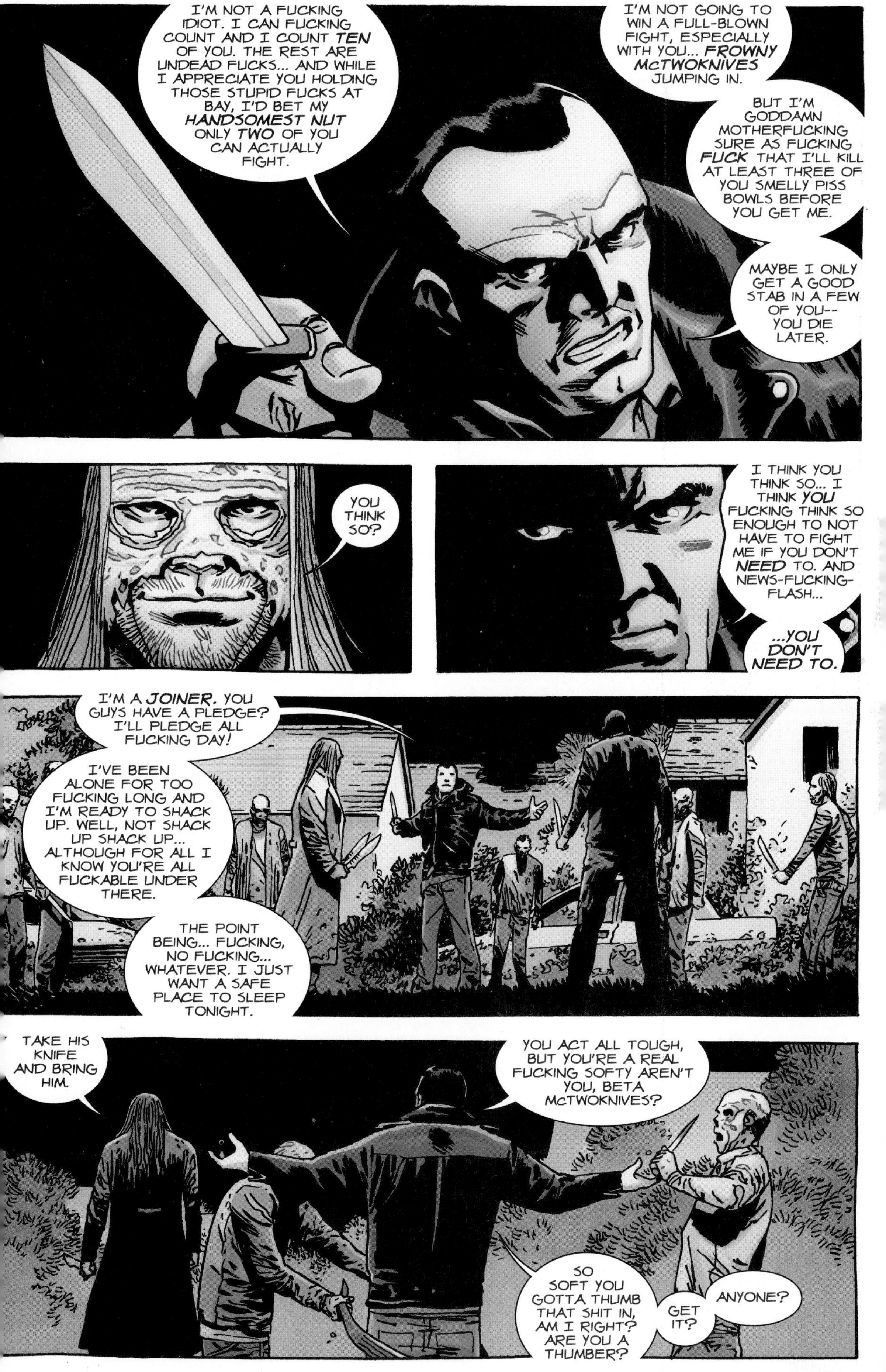
I'M NOT A FUCKING IDIOT. I CAN FUCKING COUNT AND I COUNT TEN OF YOU. THE REST ARE UNDEAD FUCKS... AND WHILE I APPRECIATE YOU HOLDING THOSE STUPID FUCKS AT BAY, I'D BET MY HANDSOMEST NUT ONLY TWO OF YOU CAN ACTUALLY FIGHT.
I'M NOT GOING TO WIN A FULL-BLOWN FIGHT, ESPECIALLY WITH YOU... FROWNY McTWOKNIVES JUMPING IN.
BUT I'M GODDAMN MOTHERFUCKING SURE AS FUCKING FUCK THAT I'LL KILL AT LEAST THREE OF YOU SMELLY PISS BOWLS BEFORE YOU GET ME.
MAYBE I ONLY GET A GOOD STAB IN A FEW OF YOU-- YOU DIE LATER.
YOU THINK SO?
I THINK YOU THINK SO... I THINK YOU FUCKING THINK SO ENOUGH TO NOT HAVE TO FIGHT ME IF YOU DON'T NEED TO. AND NEWS-FUCKING-FLASH...
...YOU DON'T NEED TO.
I'M A JOINER. YOU GUYS HAVE A PLEDGE? I'LL PLEDGE ALL FUCKING DAY!
I'VE BEEN ALONE FOR TOO FUCKING LONG AND I'M READY TO SHACK UP. WELL, NOT SHACK UP SHACK UP... ALTHOUGH FOR ALL I KNOW YOU'RE ALL FUCKABLE UNDER THERE.
THE POINT BEING... FUCKING, NO FUCKING... WHATEVER. I JUST WANT A SAFE PLACE TO SLEEP TONIGHT.
TAKE HIS KNIFE AND BRING HIM.
YOU ACT ALL TOUGH, BUT YOU'RE A REAL FUCKING SOFTY AREN'T YOU, BETA McTWOKNIVES?
SO SOFT YOU GOTTA THUMB THAT SHIT IN, AM I RIGHT? ARE YOU A THUMBER?
GET IT?
ANYONE?

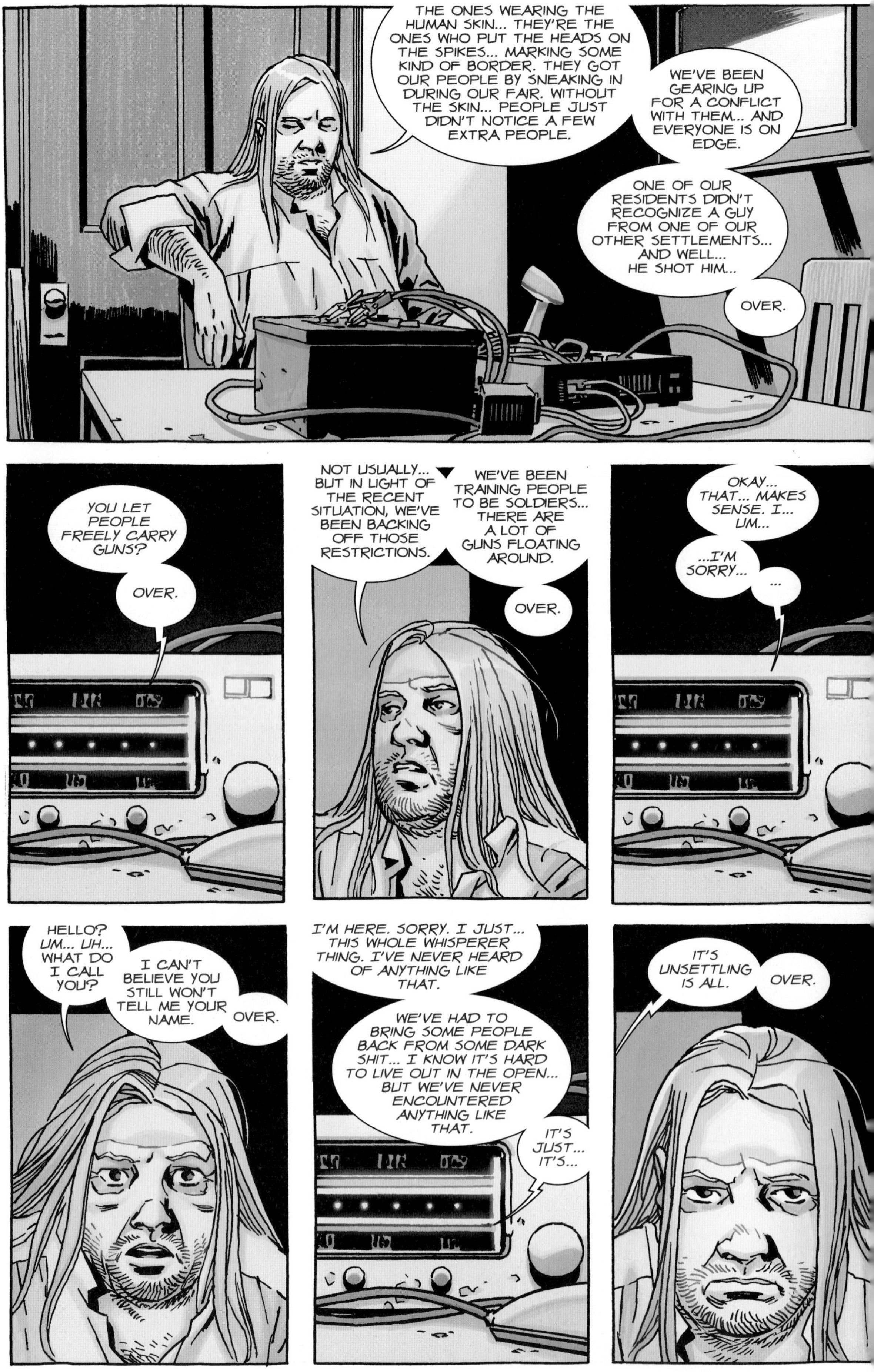
THE ONES WEARING THE HUMAN SKIN... THEY'RE THE ONES WHO PUT THE HEADS ON THE SPIKES... MARKING SOME KIND OF BORDER. THEY GOT OUR PEOPLE BY SNEAKING IN DURING OUR FAIR. WITHOUT THE SKIN... PEOPLE JUST DIDN'T NOTICE A FEW EXTRA PEOPLE.
WE'VE BEEN GEARING UP FOR A CONFLICT WITH THEM... AND EVERYONE IS ON EDGE.
ONE OF OUR RESIDENTS DIDN'T RECOGNIZE A GUY FROM ONE OF OUR OTHER SETTLEMENTS... AND WELL... HE SHOT HIM...
OVER.
YOU LET PEOPLE FREELY CARRY GUNS?
OVER.
NOT USUALLY... BUT IN LIGHT OF THE RECENT SITUATION, WE'VE BEEN BACKING OFF THOSE RESTRICTIONS.
WE'VE BEEN TRAINING PEOPLE TO BE SOLDIERS... THERE ARE A LOT OF GUNS FLOATING AROUND.
OVER.
OKAY... THAT... MAKES SENSE. I... UM...
...I'M SORRY...
...
HELLO? UM... UH... WHAT DO I CALL YOU?
I CAN'T BELIEVE YOU STILL WON'T TELL ME YOUR NAME.
OVER.
I'M HERE. SORRY. I JUST... THIS WHOLE WHISPERER THING. I'VE NEVER HEARD OF ANYTHING LIKE THAT.
WE'VE HAD TO BRING SOME PEOPLE BACK FROM SOME DARK SHIT... I KNOW IT'S HARD TO LIVE OUT IN THE OPEN... BUT WE'VE NEVER ENCOUNTERED ANYTHING LIKE THAT.
IT'S JUST... IT'S...
IT'S UNSETTLING IS ALL.
OVER.

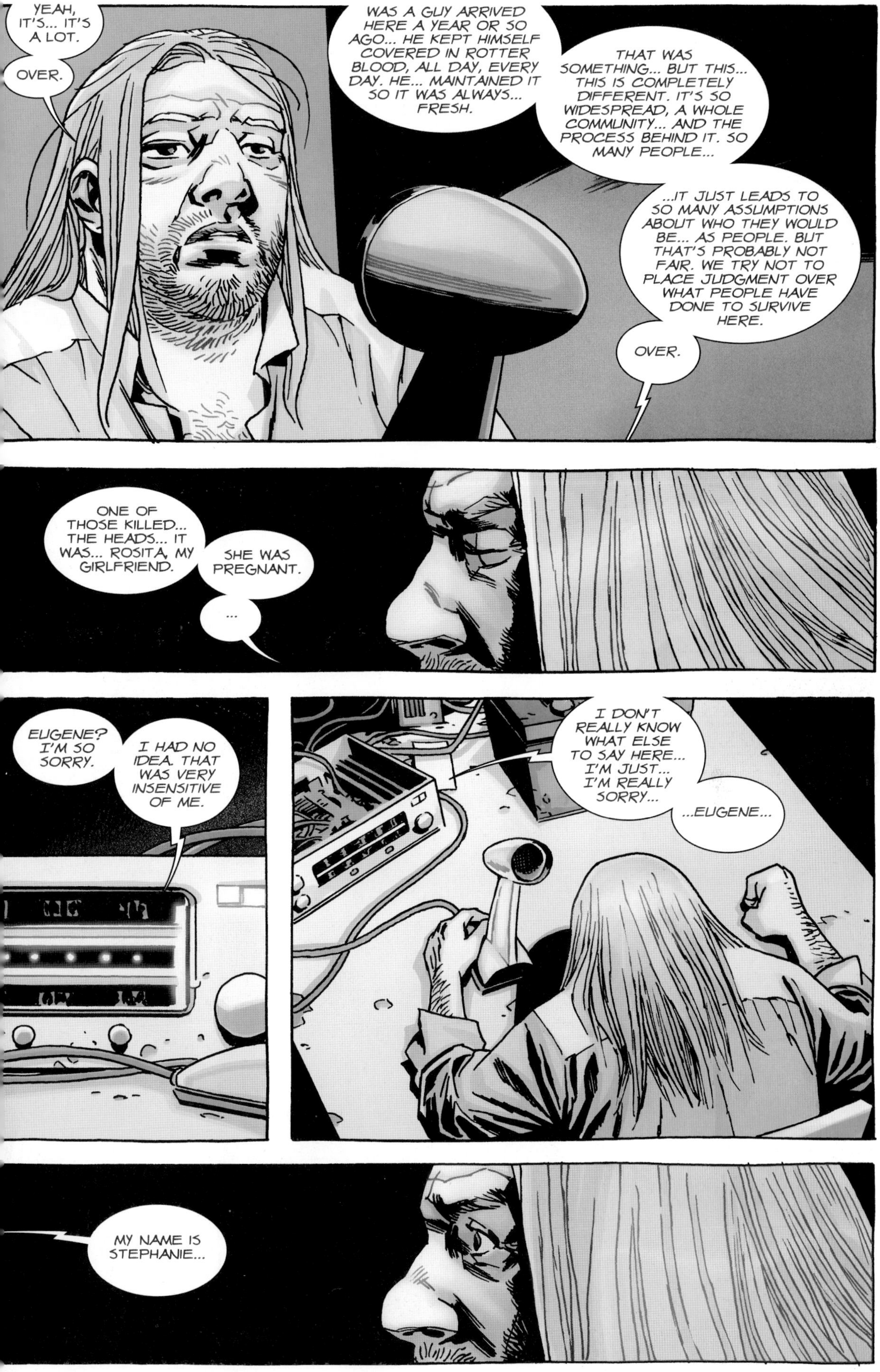
YEAH, IT'S... IT'S A LOT.
OVER.
WAS A GUY ARRIVED HERE A YEAR OR SO AGO... HE KEPT HIMSELF COVERED IN ROTTER BLOOD, ALL DAY, EVERY DAY. HE... MAINTAINED IT SO IT WAS ALWAYS... FRESH.
THAT WAS SOMETHING... BUT THIS... THIS IS COMPLETELY DIFFERENT. IT'S SO WIDESPREAD, A WHOLE COMMUNITY... AND THE PROCESS BEHIND IT. SO MANY PEOPLE...
...IT JUST LEADS TO SO MANY ASSUMPTIONS ABOUT WHO THEY WOULD BE... AS PEOPLE. BUT THAT'S PROBABLY NOT FAIR. WE TRY NOT TO PLACE JUDGMENT OVER WHAT PEOPLE HAVE DONE TO SURVIVE HERE.
OVER.
ONE OF THOSE KILLED... THE HEADS... IT WAS... ROSITA, MY GIRLFRIEND.
SHE WAS PREGNANT.
...
EUGENE? I'M SO SORRY.
I HAD NO IDEA. THAT WAS VERY INSENSITIVE OF ME.
I DON'T REALLY KNOW WHAT ELSE TO SAY HERE... I'M JUST... I'M REALLY SORRY...
...EUGENE...
MY NAME IS STEPHANIE...

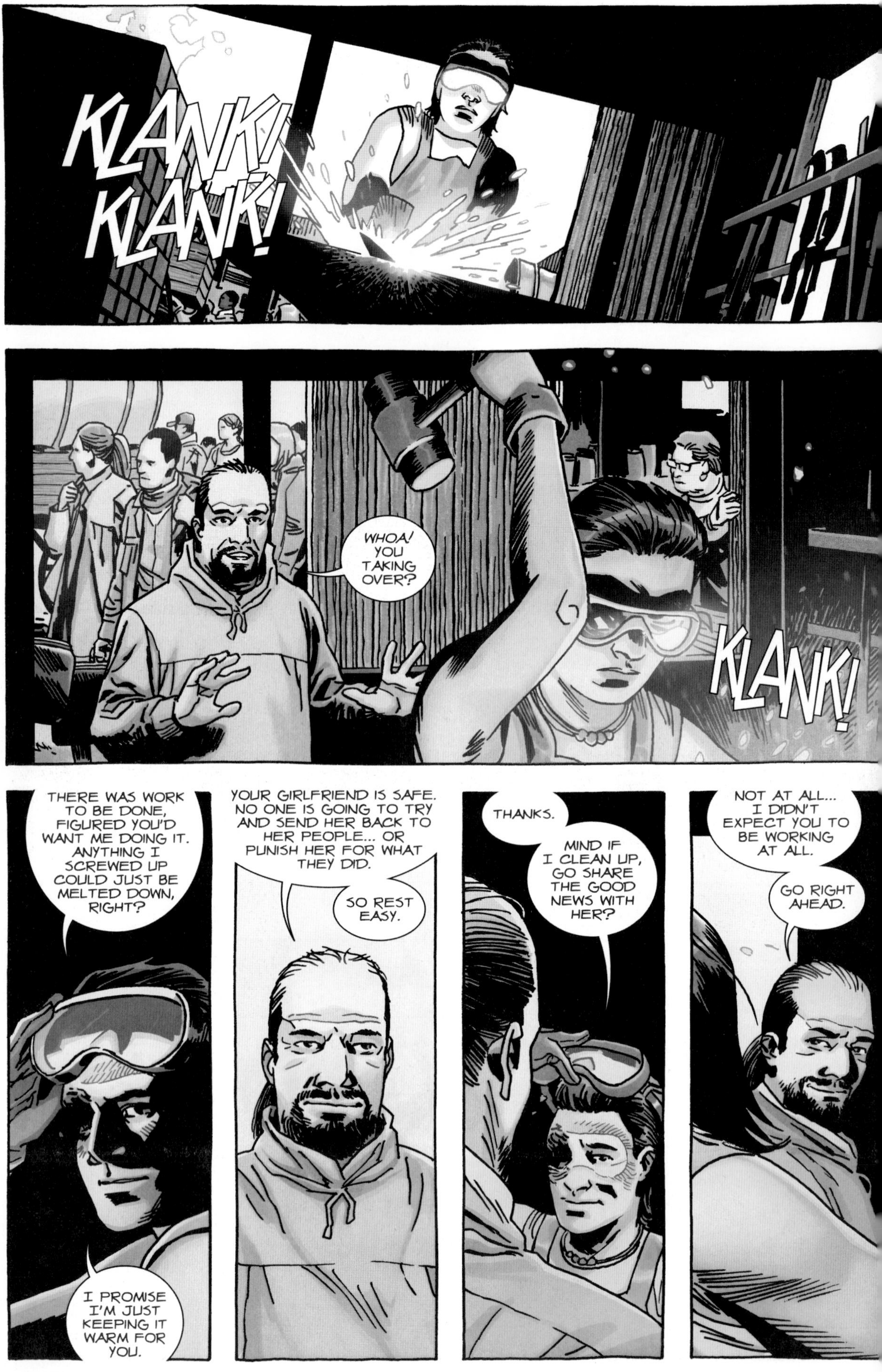
KLANK! KLANK!
WHOA! YOU TAKING OVER?
KLANK!
THERE WAS WORK TO BE DONE, FIGURED YOU'D WANT ME DOING IT. ANYTHING I SCREWED UP COULD JUST BE MELTED DOWN, RIGHT?
I PROMISE I'M JUST KEEPING IT WARM FOR YOU.
YOUR GIRLFRIEND IS SAFE. NO ONE IS GOING TO TRY AND SEND HER BACK TO HER PEOPLE... OR PUNISH HER FOR WHAT THEY DID.
SO REST EASY.
THANKS.
MIND IF I CLEAN UP, GO SHARE THE GOOD NEWS WITH HER?
NOT AT ALL... I DIDN'T EXPECT YOU TO BE WORKING AT ALL.
GO RIGHT AHEAD.

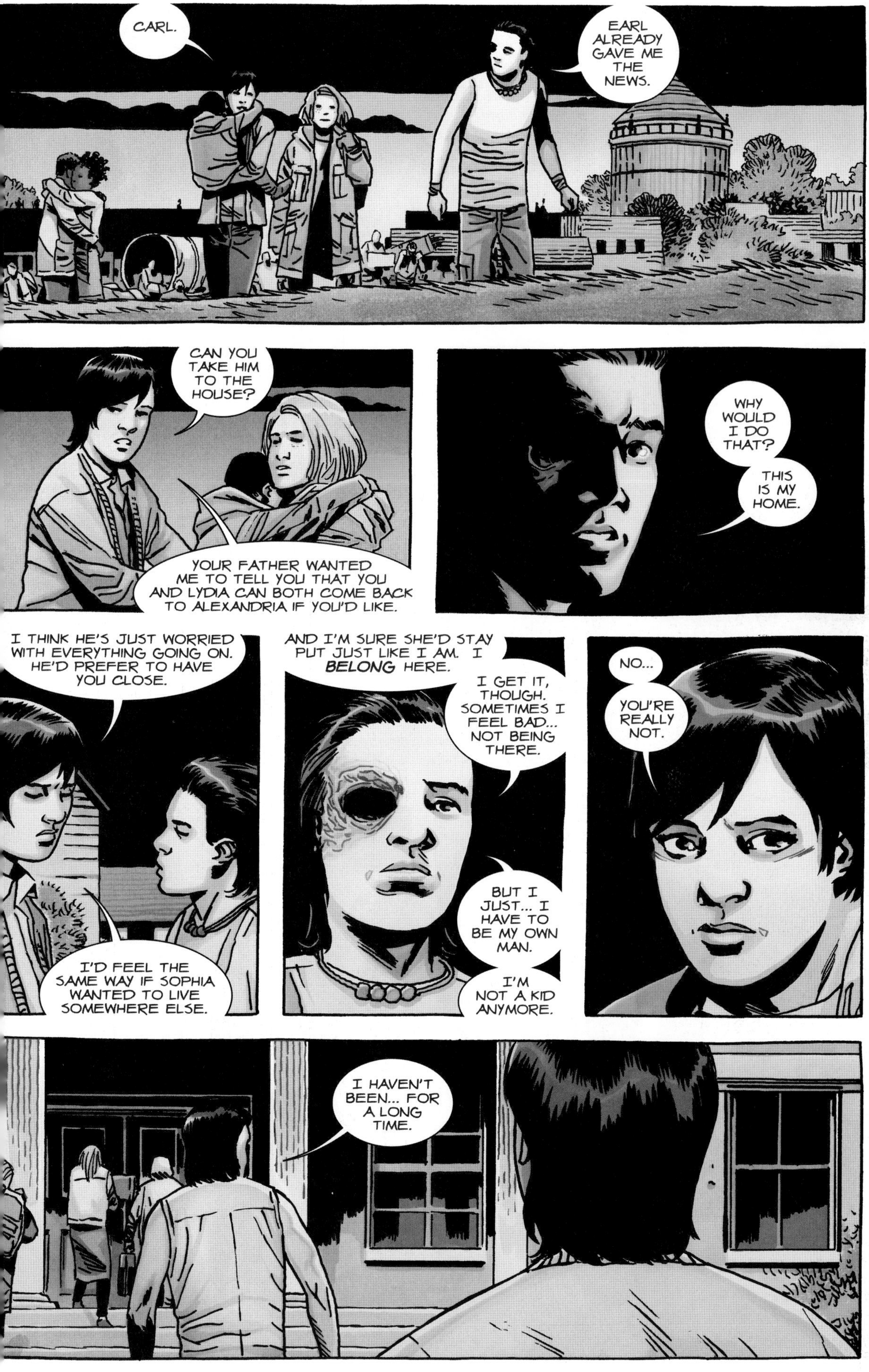

CARL.
EARL ALREADY GAVE ME THE NEWS.
CAN YOU TAKE HIM TO THE HOUSE?
YOUR FATHER WANTED ME TO TELL YOU THAT YOU AND LYDIA CAN BOTH COME BACK TO ALEXANDRIA IF YOU'D LIKE.
WHY WOULD I DO THAT?
THIS IS MY HOME.
I THINK HE'S JUST WORRIED WITH EVERYTHING GOING ON. HE'D PREFER TO HAVE YOU CLOSE.
I'D FEEL THE SAME WAY IF SOPHIA WANTED TO LIVE SOMEWHERE ELSE.
AND I'M SURE SHE'D STAY PUT JUST LIKE I AM. I *BELONG* HERE.
I GET IT, THOUGH. SOMETIMES I FEEL BAD... NOT BEING THERE.
BUT I JUST... I HAVE TO BE MY OWN MAN.
I'M NOT A KID ANYMORE.
NO...
YOU'RE REALLY NOT.
I HAVEN'T BEEN... FOR A LONG TIME.

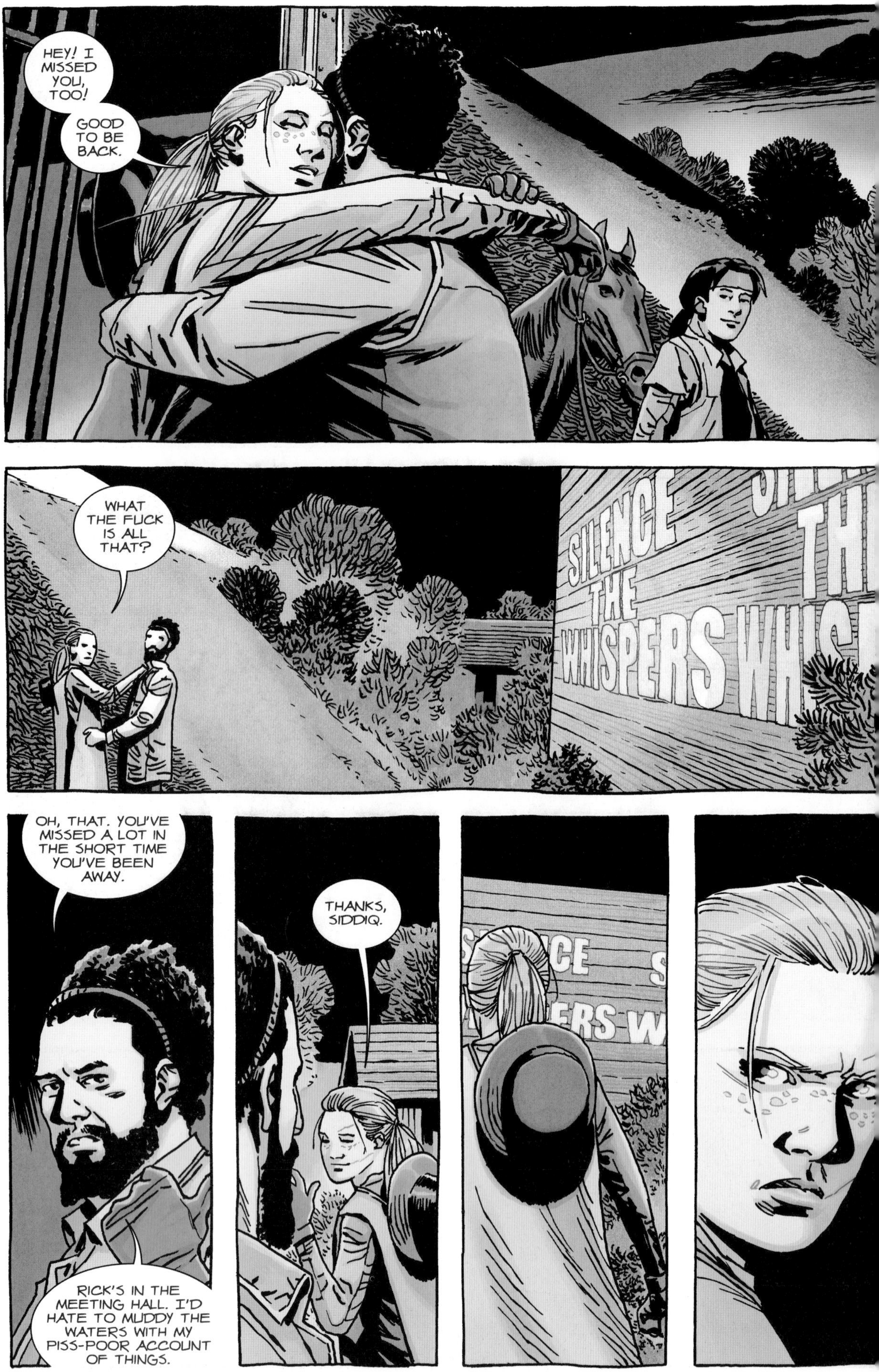
HEY! I MISSED YOU, TOO!
GOOD TO BE BACK.
WHAT THE FUCK IS ALL THAT?
SILENCE THE WHISPERS
OH, THAT. YOU'VE MISSED A LOT IN THE SHORT TIME YOU'VE BEEN AWAY.
RICK'S IN THE MEETING HALL. I'D HATE TO MUDDY THE WATERS WITH MY PISS-POOR ACCOUNT OF THINGS.
THANKS, SIDDIQ.

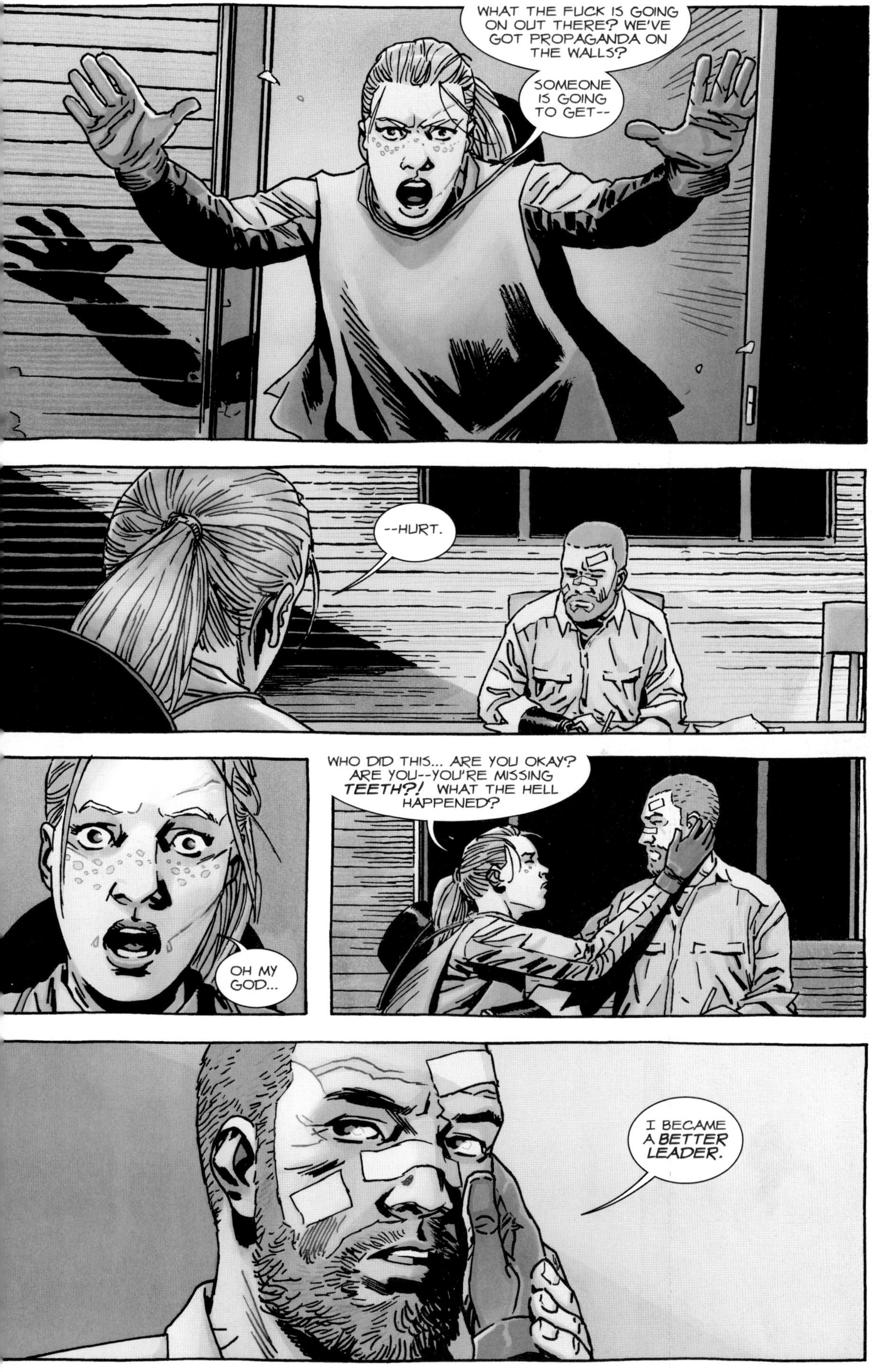
WHAT THE FUCK IS GOING ON OUT THERE? WE'VE GOT PROPAGANDA ON THE WALLS?
SOMEONE IS GOING TO GET--
--HURT.
OH MY GOD...
WHO DID THIS... ARE YOU OKAY? ARE YOU--YOU'RE MISSING TEETH?! WHAT THE HELL HAPPENED?
I BECAME A BETTER LEADER.

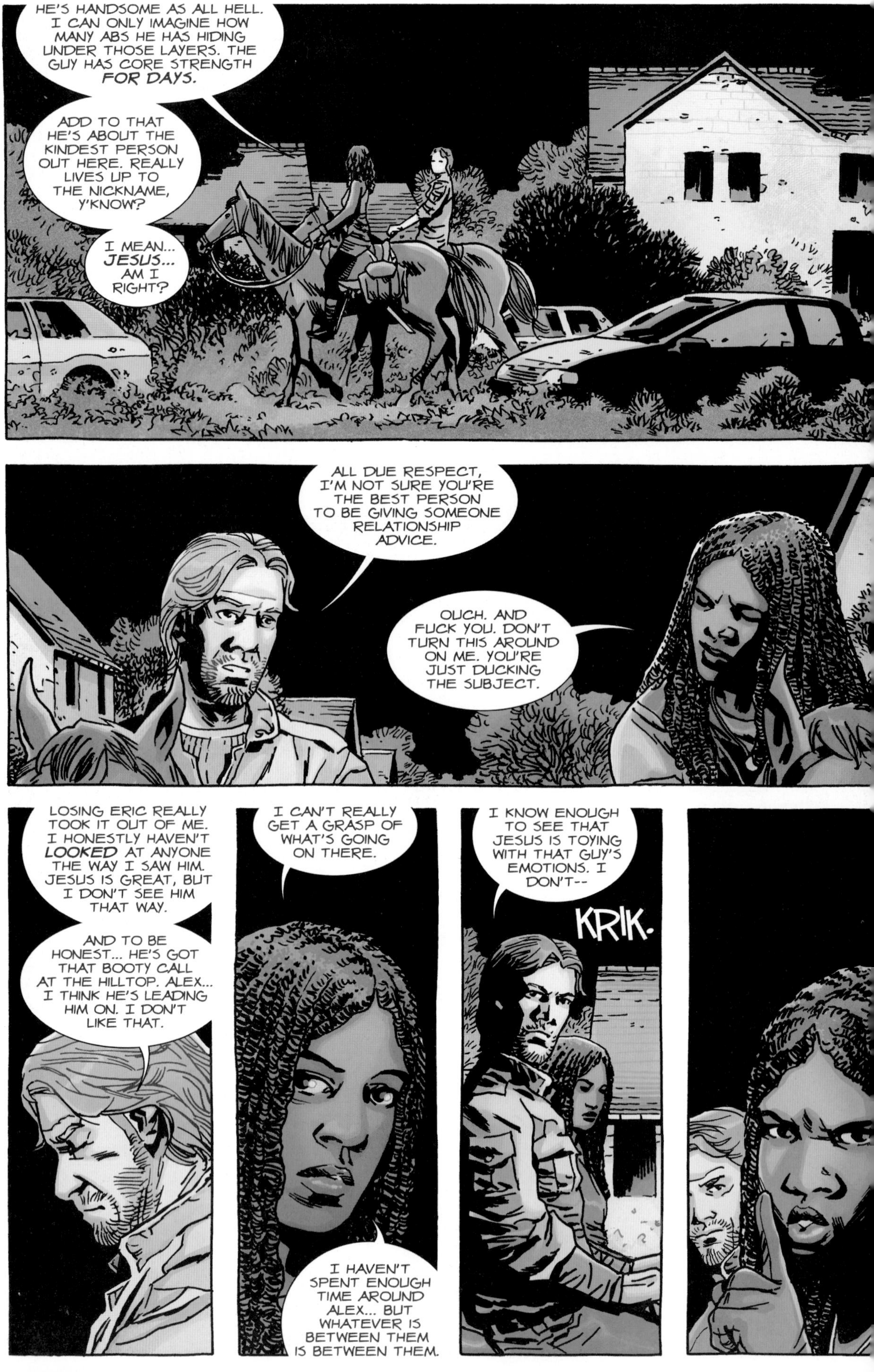
HE'S HANDSOME AS ALL HELL. I CAN ONLY IMAGINE HOW MANY ABS HE HAS HIDING UNDER THOSE LAYERS. THE GUY HAS CORE STRENGTH FOR DAYS.
ADD TO THAT HE'S ABOUT THE KINDEST PERSON OUT HERE. REALLY LIVES UP TO THE NICKNAME, Y'KNOW?
I MEAN... JESUS... AM I RIGHT?
ALL DUE RESPECT, I'M NOT SURE YOU'RE THE BEST PERSON TO BE GIVING SOMEONE RELATIONSHIP ADVICE.
OUCH. AND FUCK YOU. DON'T TURN THIS AROUND ON ME. YOU'RE JUST DUCKING THE SUBJECT.
LOSING ERIC REALLY TOOK IT OUT OF ME. I HONESTLY HAVEN'T LOOKED AT ANYONE THE WAY I SAW HIM. JESUS IS GREAT, BUT I DON'T SEE HIM THAT WAY.
AND TO BE HONEST... HE'S GOT THAT BOOTY CALL AT THE HILLTOP. ALEX... I THINK HE'S LEADING HIM ON. I DON'T LIKE THAT.
I CAN'T REALLY GET A GRASP OF WHAT'S GOING ON THERE.
I HAVEN'T SPENT ENOUGH TIME AROUND ALEX... BUT WHATEVER IS BETWEEN THEM IS BETWEEN THEM.
I KNOW ENOUGH TO SEE THAT JESUS IS TOYING WITH THAT GUY'S EMOTIONS. I DON'T--
KRIK.

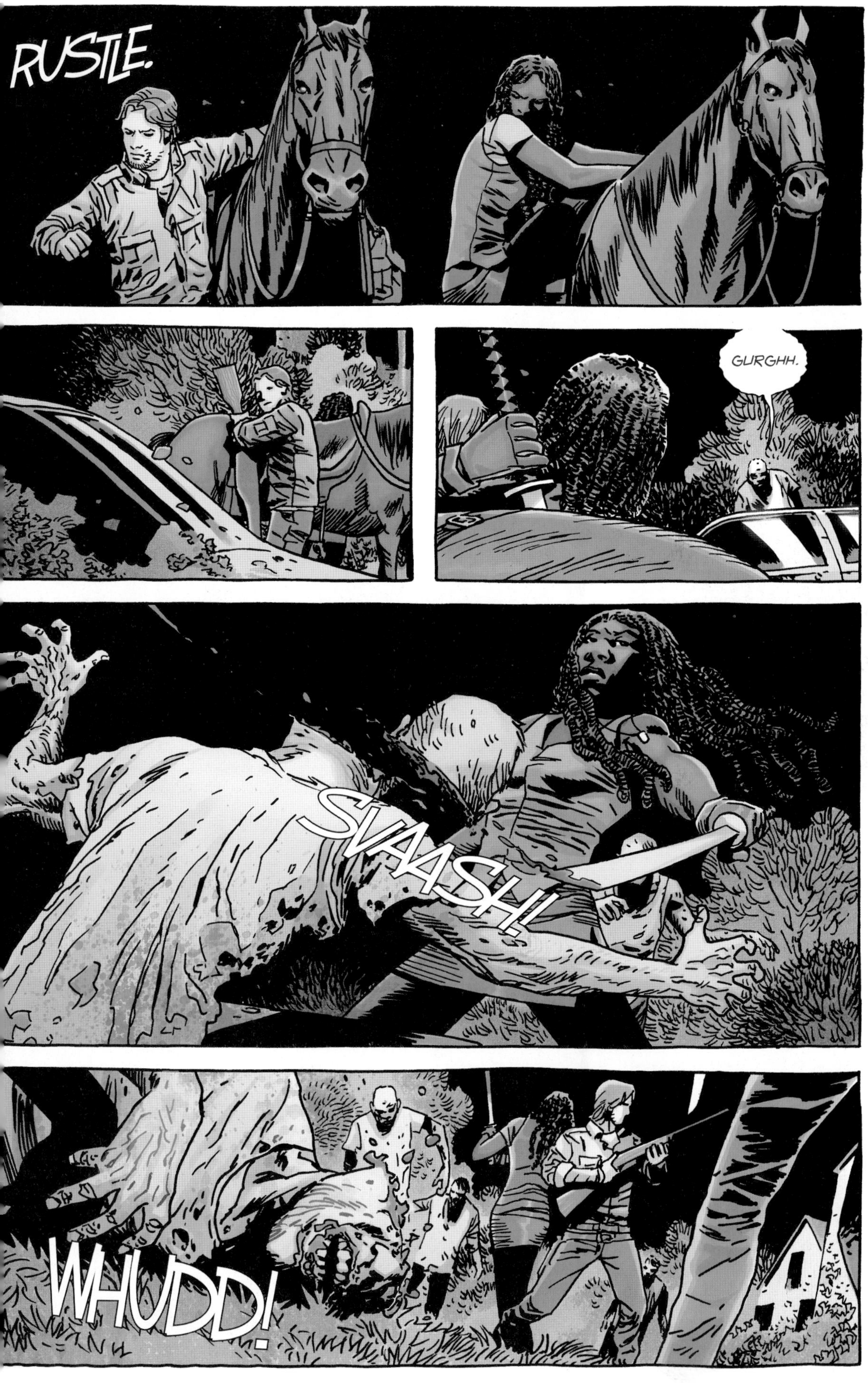
RUSTLE.
GURGHH.
SVAASH!
WHUDD!

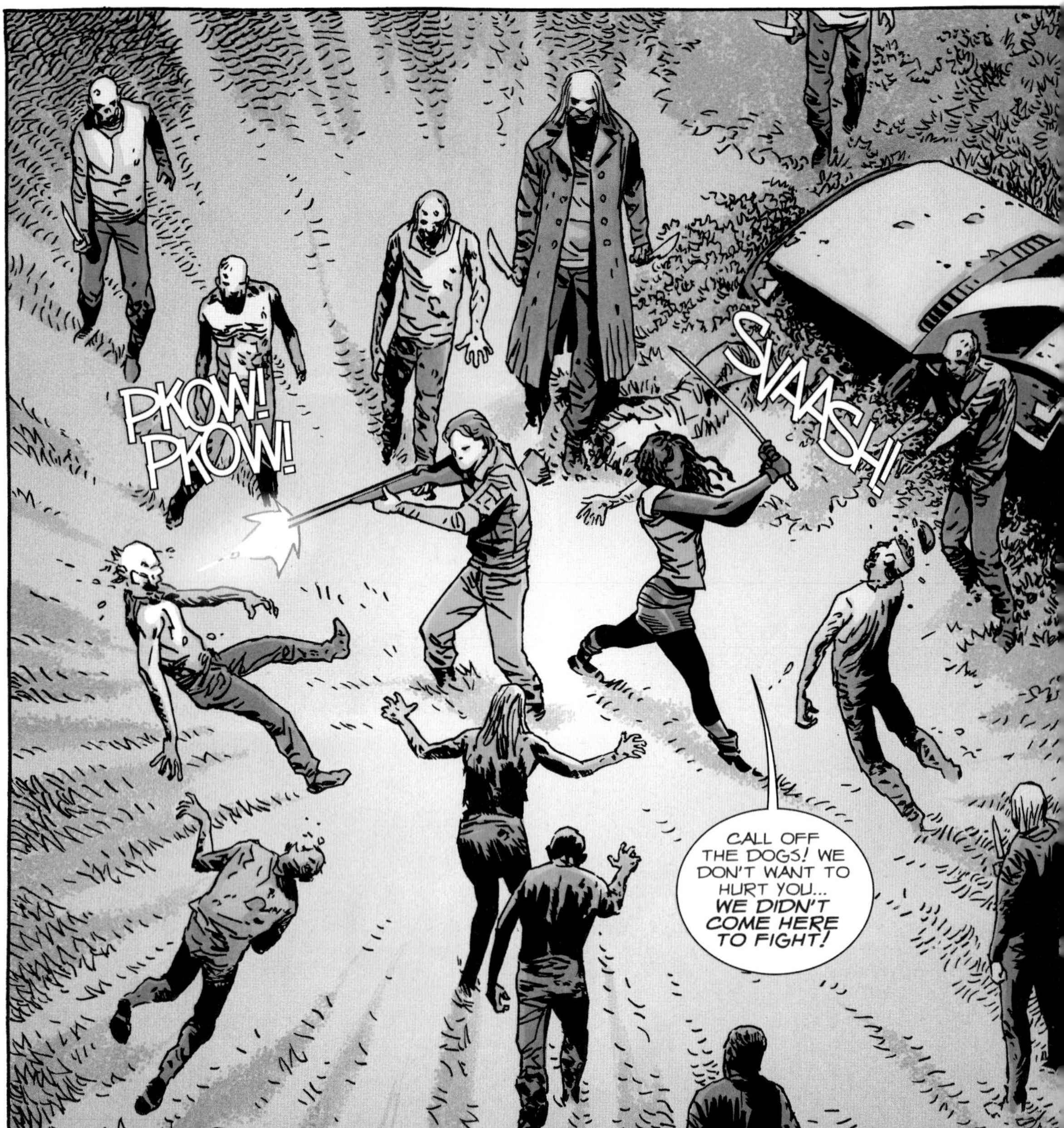
PKOW! PKOW!
SWAASH!
CALL OFF THE DOGS! WE DON'T WANT TO HURT YOU... WE DIDN'T COME HERE TO FIGHT!

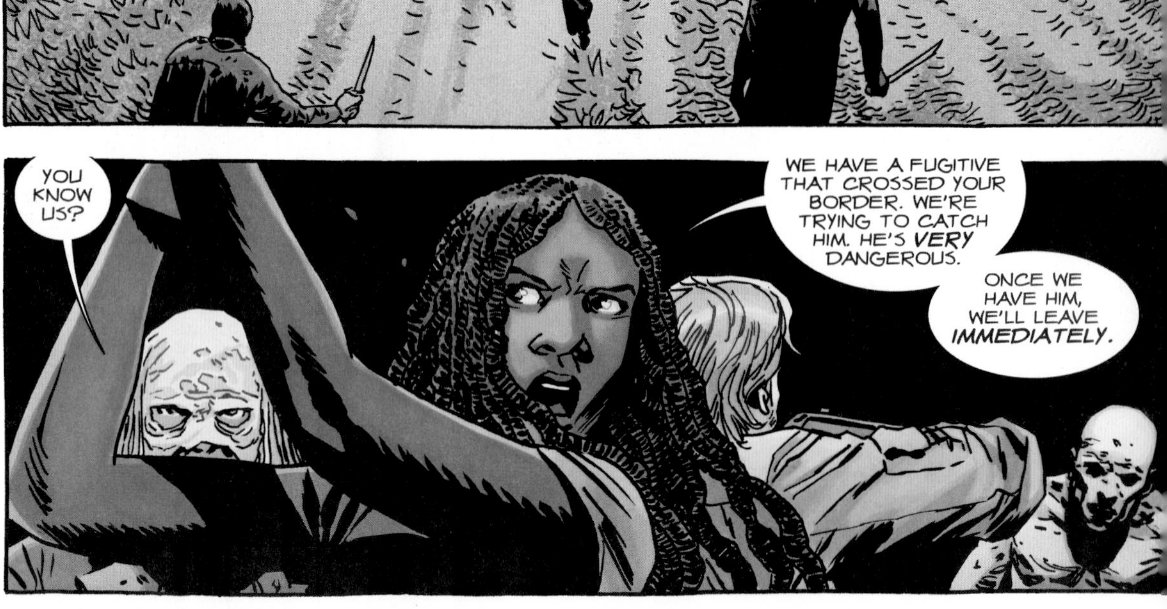
YOU KNOW US?
WE HAVE A FUGITIVE THAT CROSSED YOUR BORDER. WE'RE TRYING TO CATCH HIM. HE'S VERY DANGEROUS.
ONCE WE HAVE HIM, WE'LL LEAVE IMMEDIATELY.

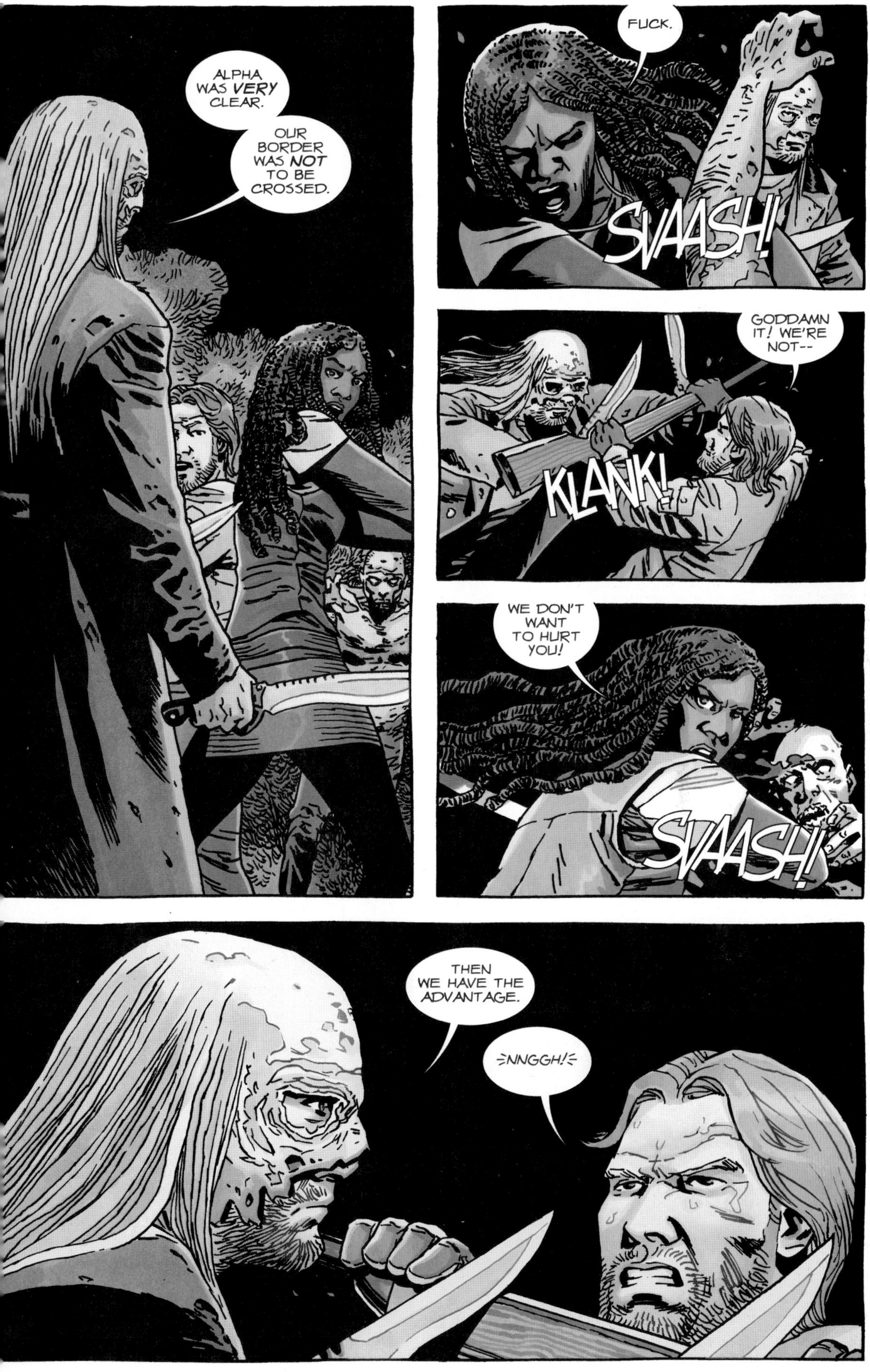
ALPHA WAS VERY CLEAR.
OUR BORDER WAS NOT TO BE CROSSED.
FUCK.
SVAASH!
GODDAMN IT! WE'RE NOT--
KLANK!
WE DON'T WANT TO HURT YOU!
SVAASH!
THEN WE HAVE THE ADVANTAGE.
NNGGH!

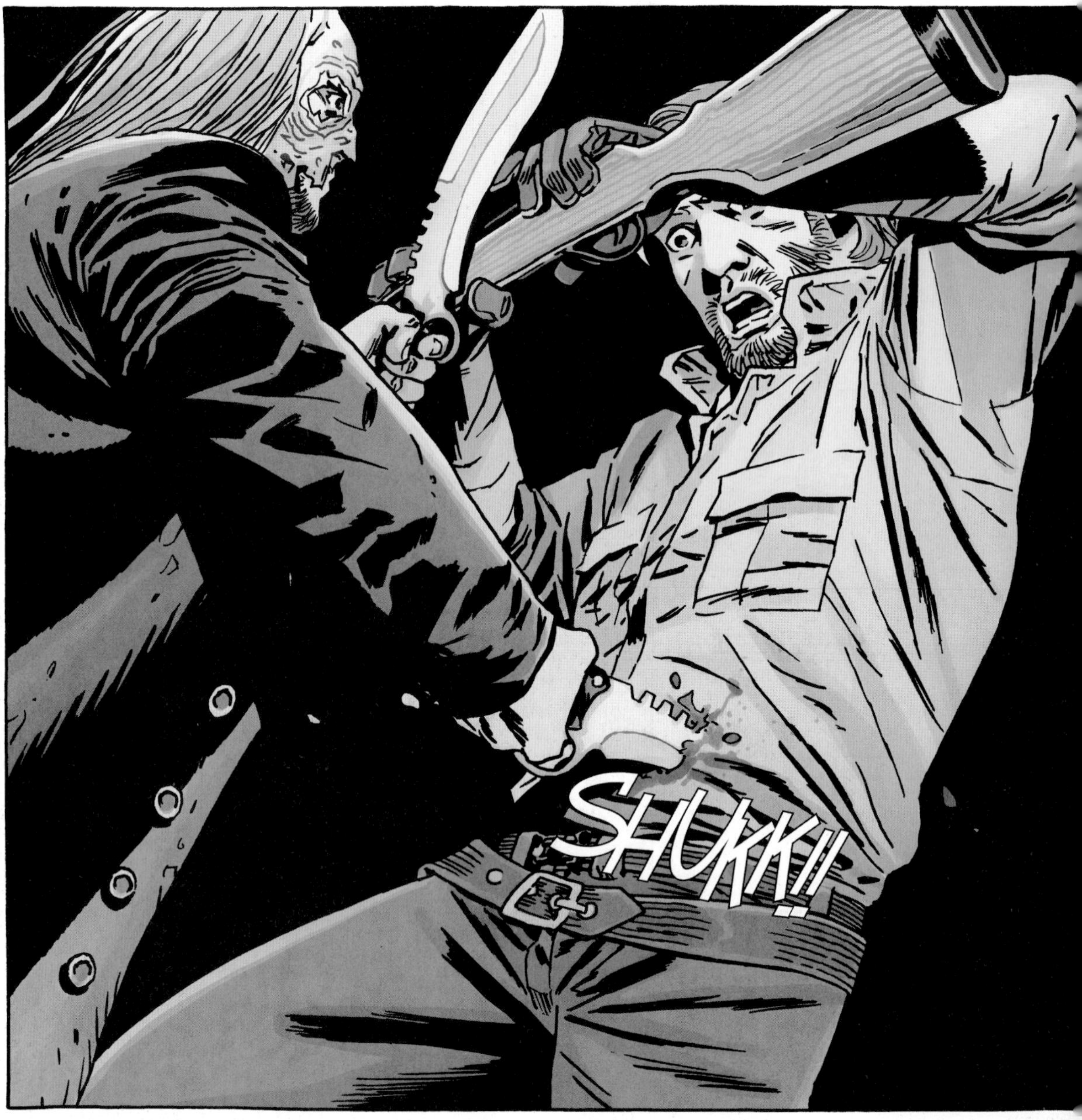
SHUKK!!

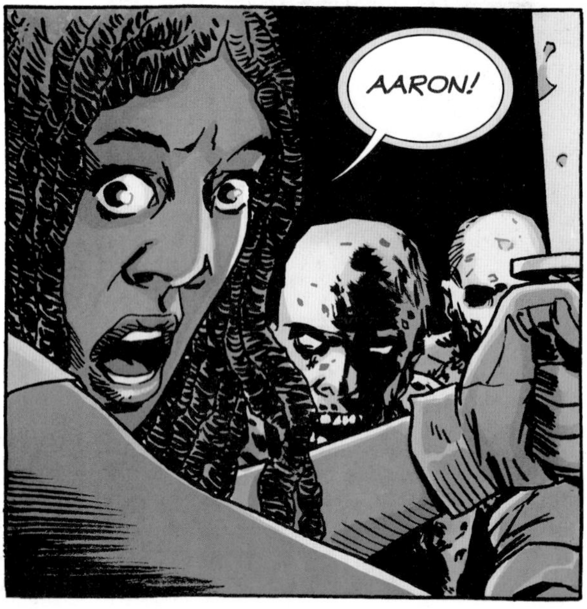
AARON!

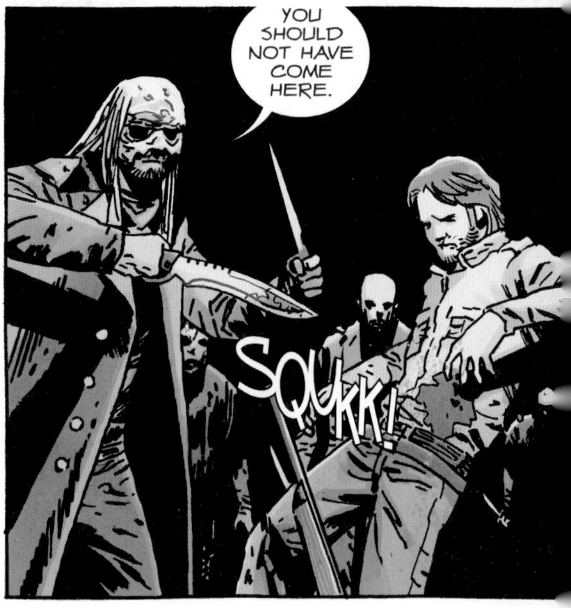
YOU SHOULD NOT HAVE COME HERE.
SQUKK!

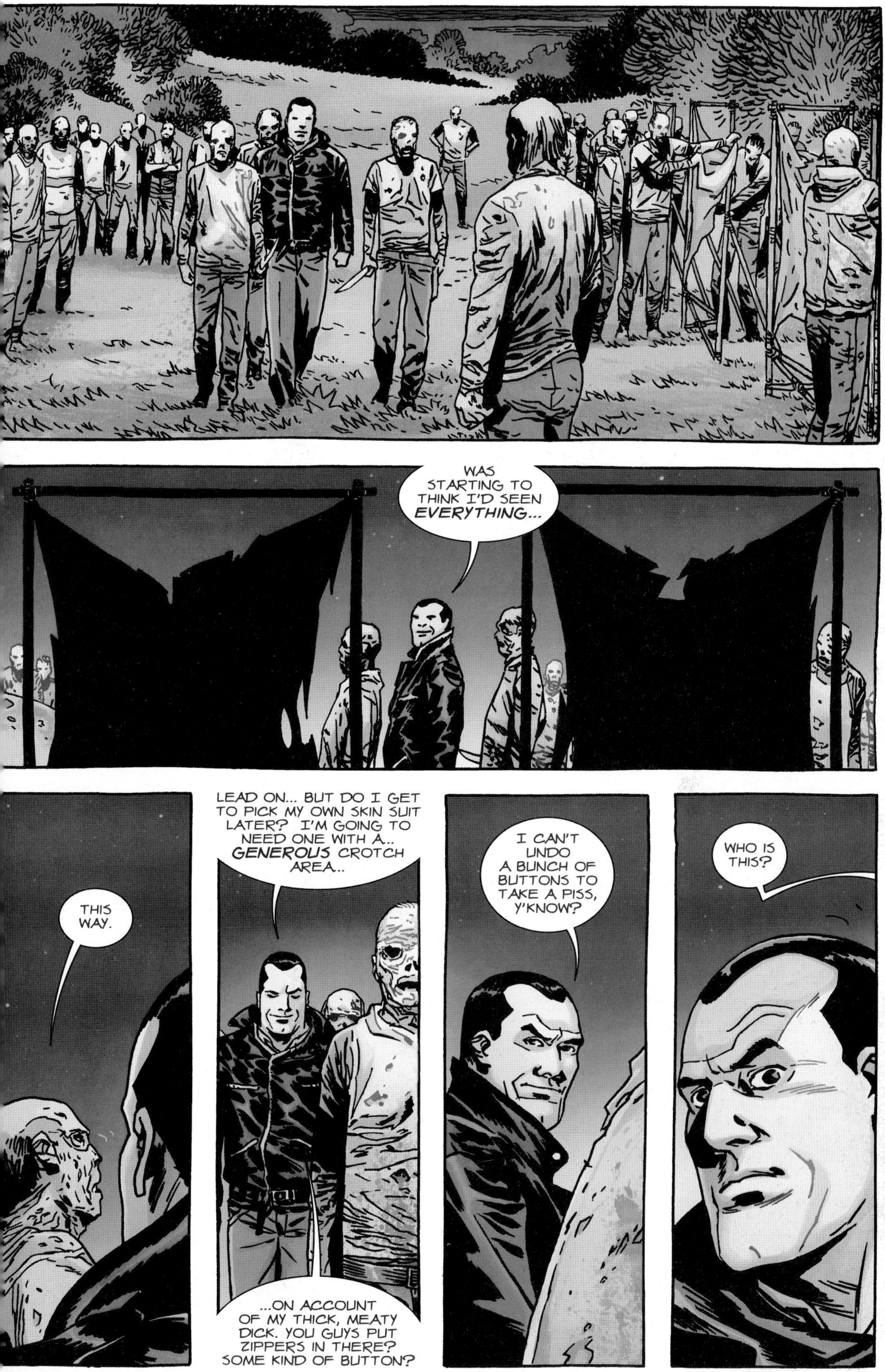

WAS STARTING TO THINK I'D SEEN EVERYTHING...
THIS WAY.
LEAD ON... BUT DO I GET TO PICK MY OWN SKIN SUIT LATER? I'M GOING TO NEED ONE WITH A... GENEROUS CROTCH AREA..
...ON ACCOUNT OF MY THICK, MEATY DICK. YOU GUYS PUT ZIPPERS IN THERE? SOME KIND OF BUTTON?
I CAN'T UNDO A BUNCH OF BUTTONS TO TAKE A PISS, Y'KNOW?
WHO IS THIS?

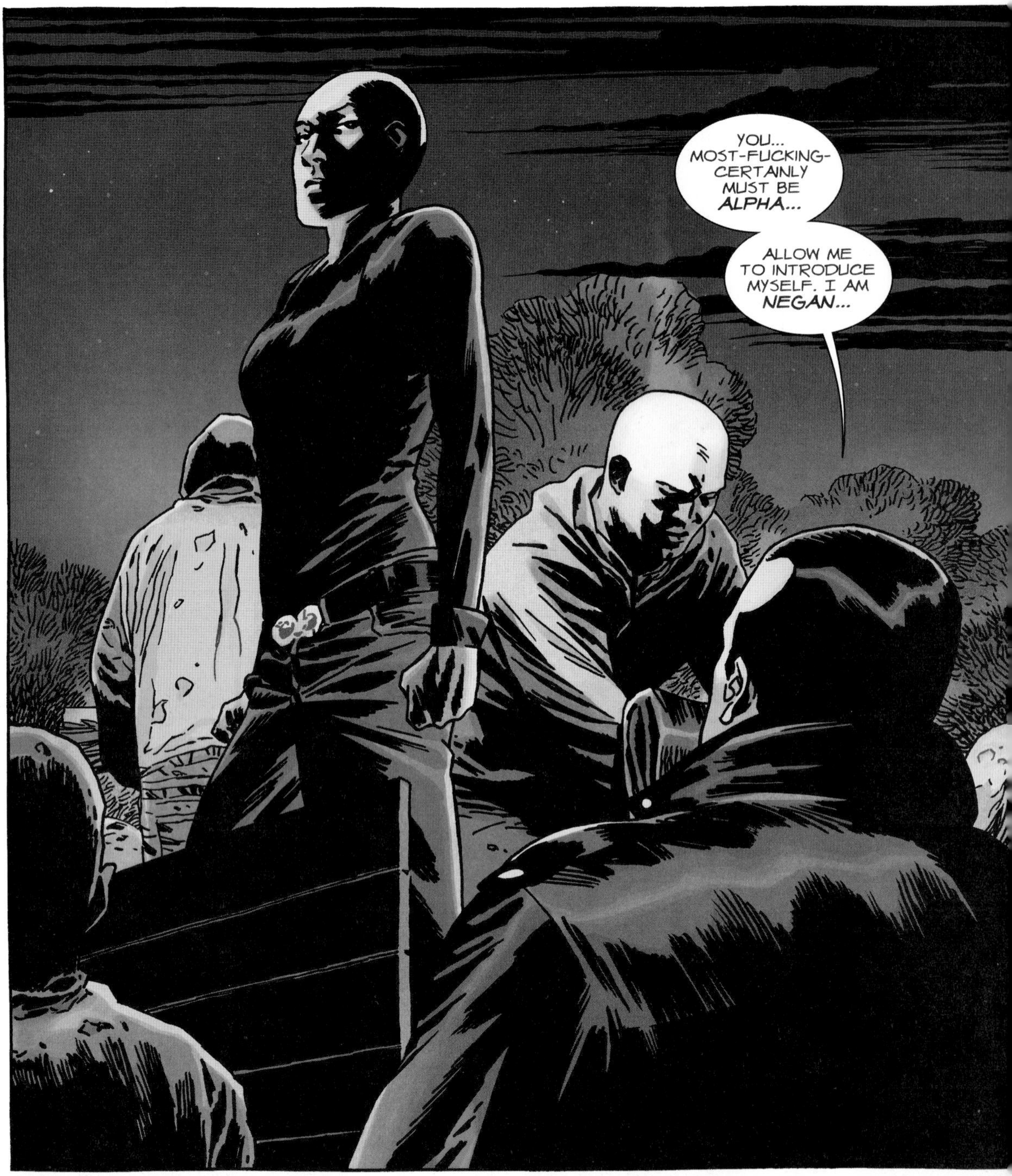
YOU... MOST-FUCKING-CERTAINLY MUST BE ALPHA...
ALLOW ME TO INTRODUCE MYSELF. I AM NEGAN...
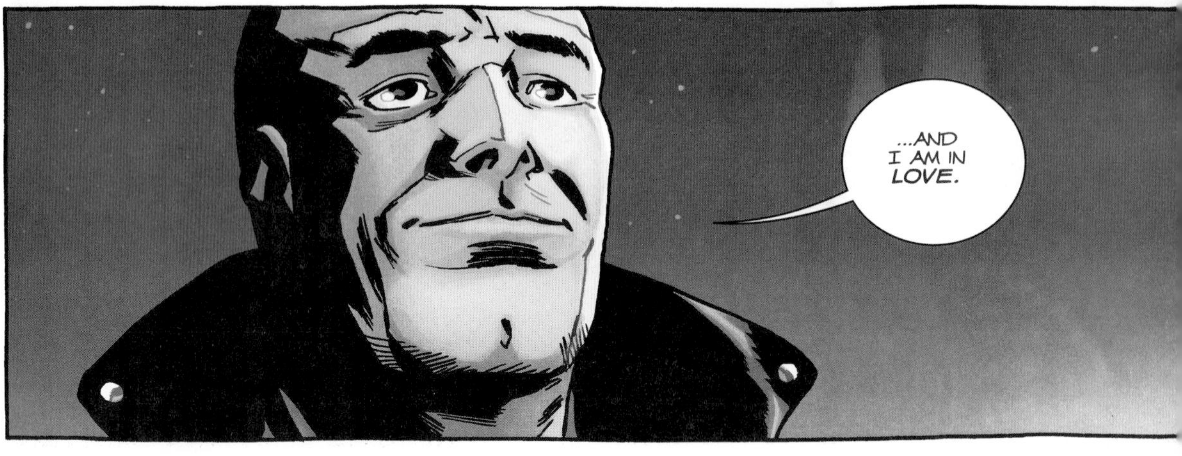
...AND I AM IN LOVE.

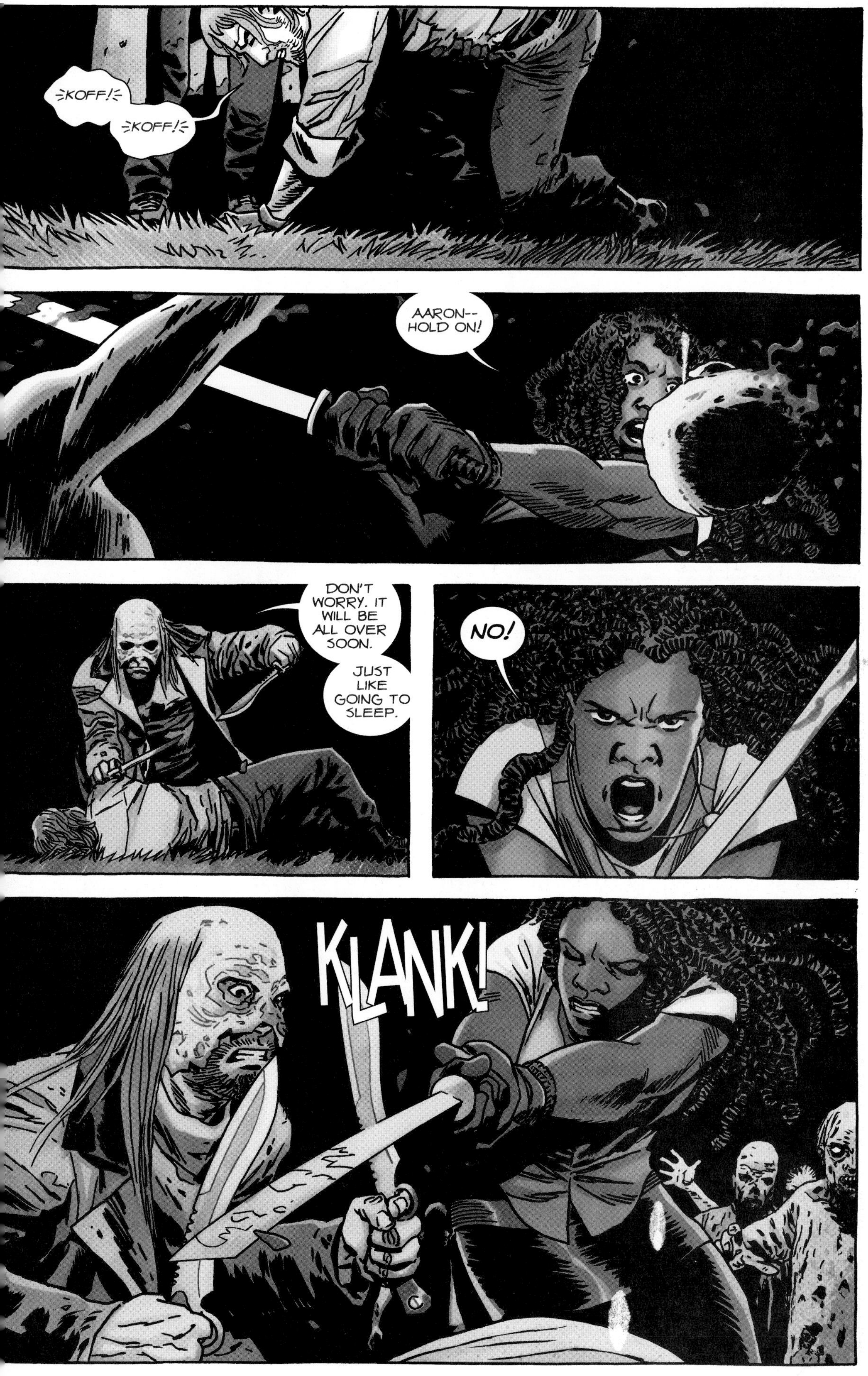

KOFF!
KOFF!
AARON-- HOLD ON!
DON'T WORRY. IT WILL BE ALL OVER SOON.
JUST LIKE GOING TO SLEEP.
NO!
KLANK!

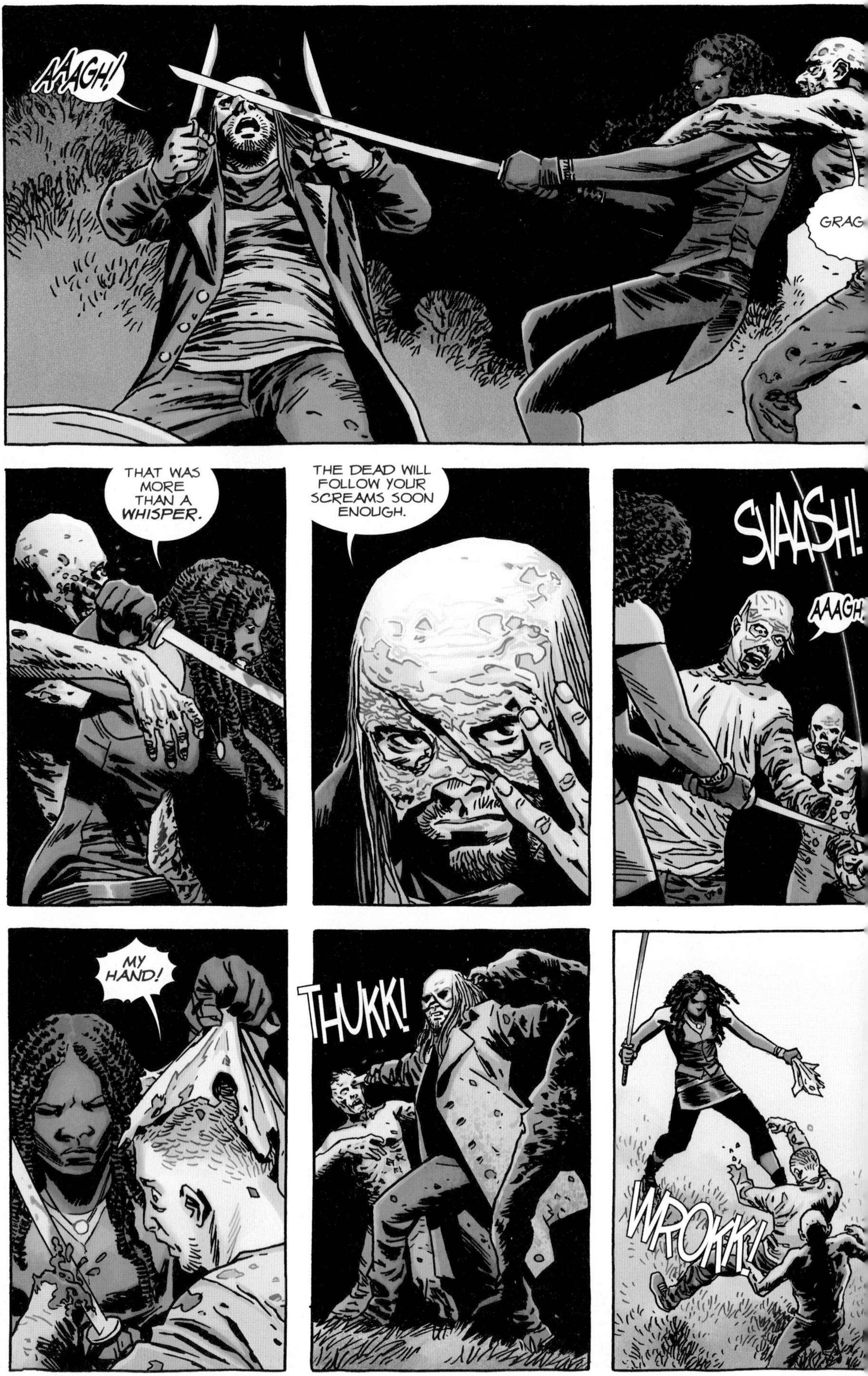
AAAGH!
GRAG
THAT WAS MORE THAN A WHISPER.
THE DEAD WILL FOLLOW YOUR SCREAMS SOON ENOUGH.
SVAASH!
AAAGH
MY HAND!
THUKK!
WROKK!

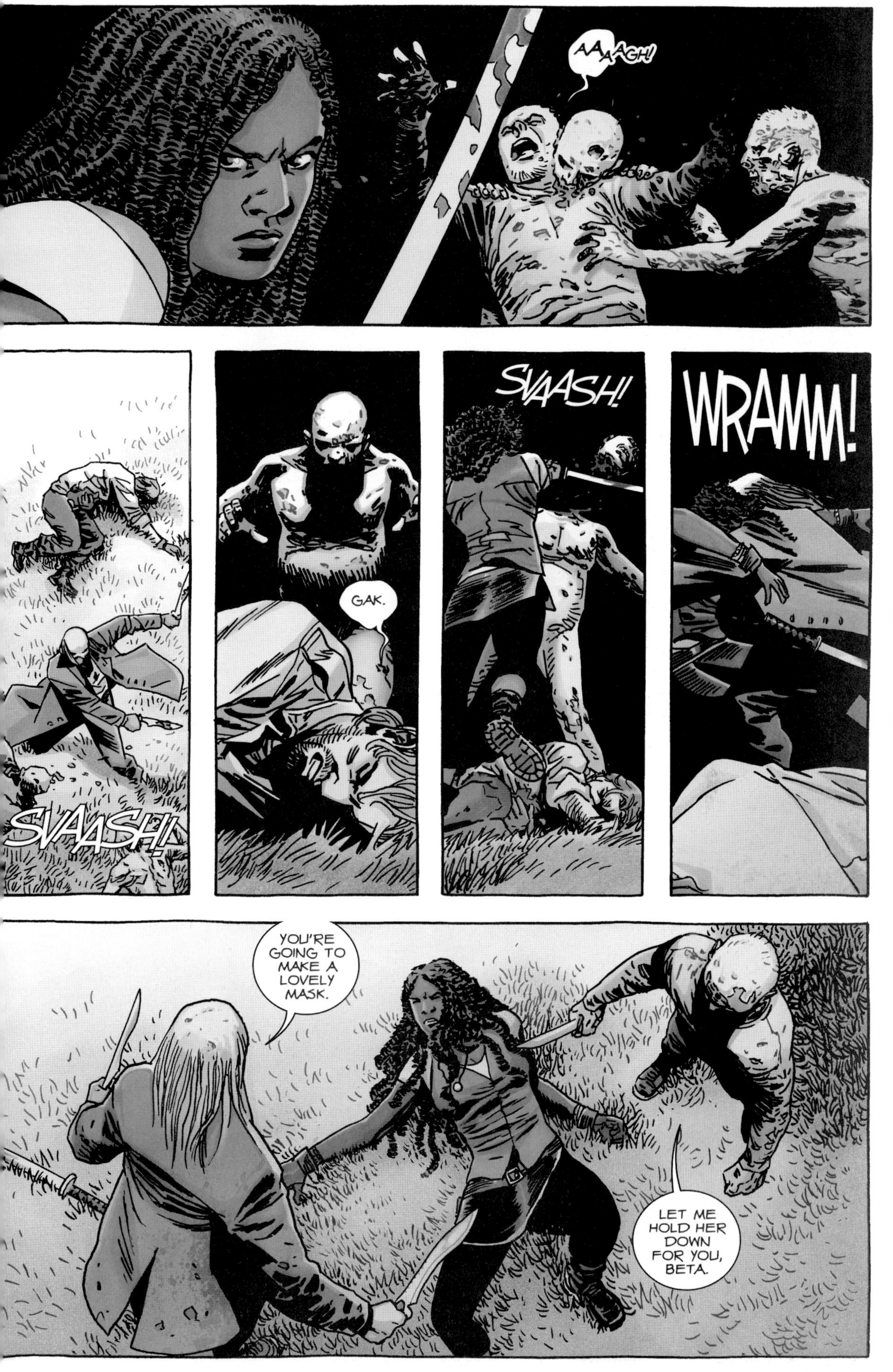
AAAAAGH!
SVAASH!
GAK.
SVAASH!
WRAMM!
YOU'RE GOING TO MAKE A LOVELY MASK.
LET ME HOLD HER DOWN FOR YOU, BETA.

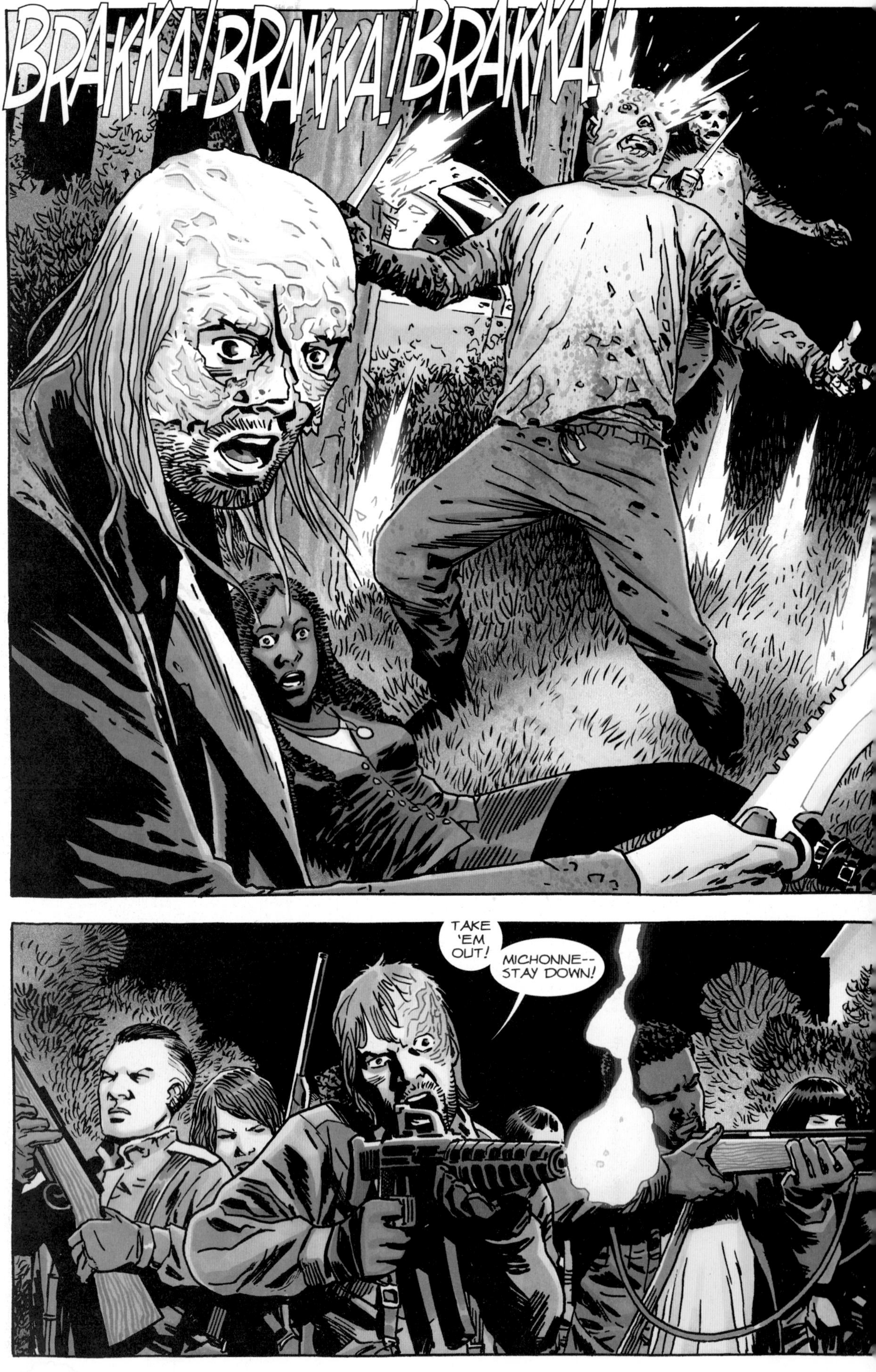
BRAKKA! BRAKKA! BRAKKA!
TAKE 'EM OUT!
MICHONNE-- STAY DOWN!

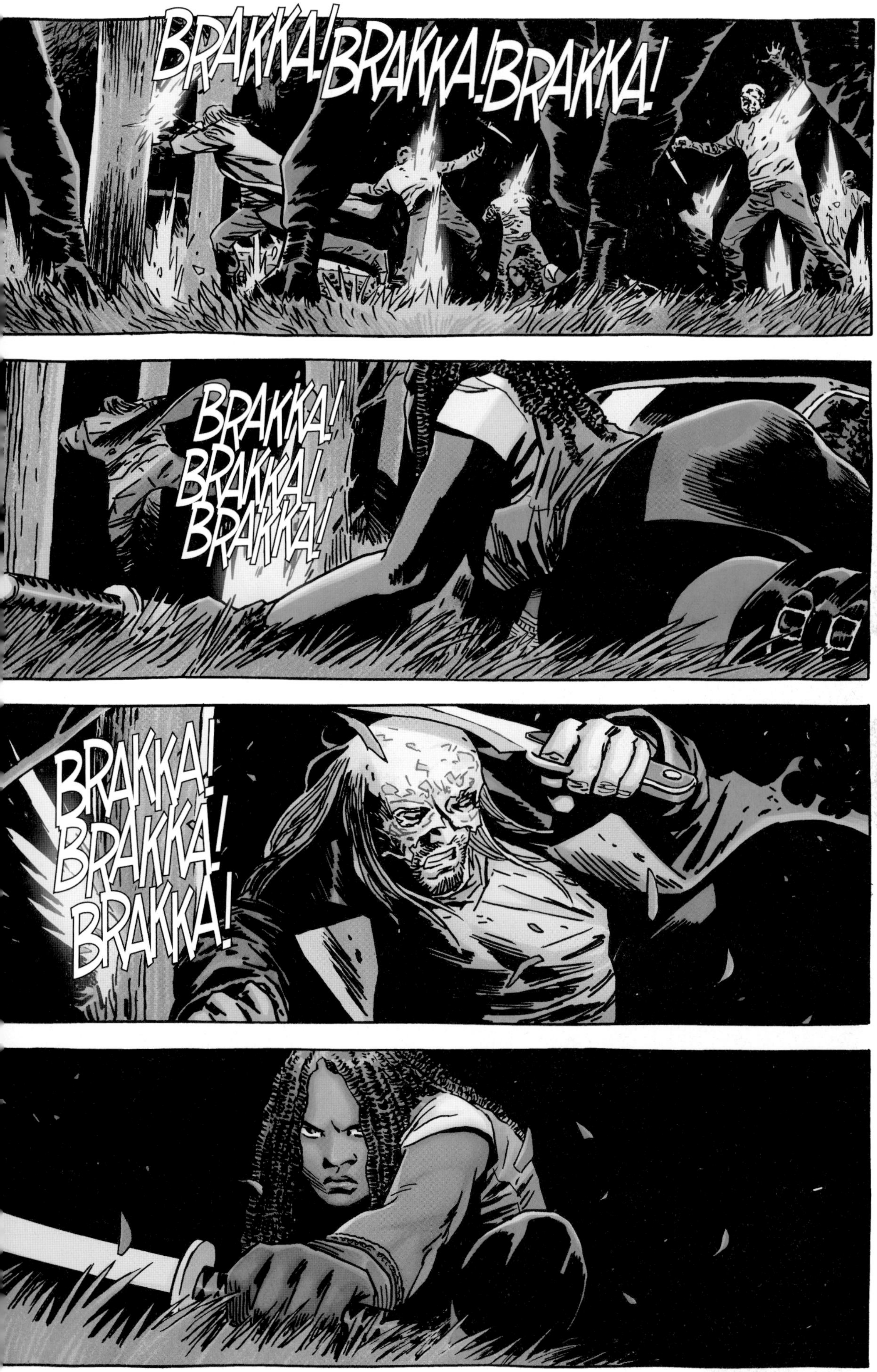
BRAKKA! BRAKKA! BRAKKA!
BRAKKA! BRAKKA! BRAKKA!
BRAKKA! BRAKKA! BRAKKA!

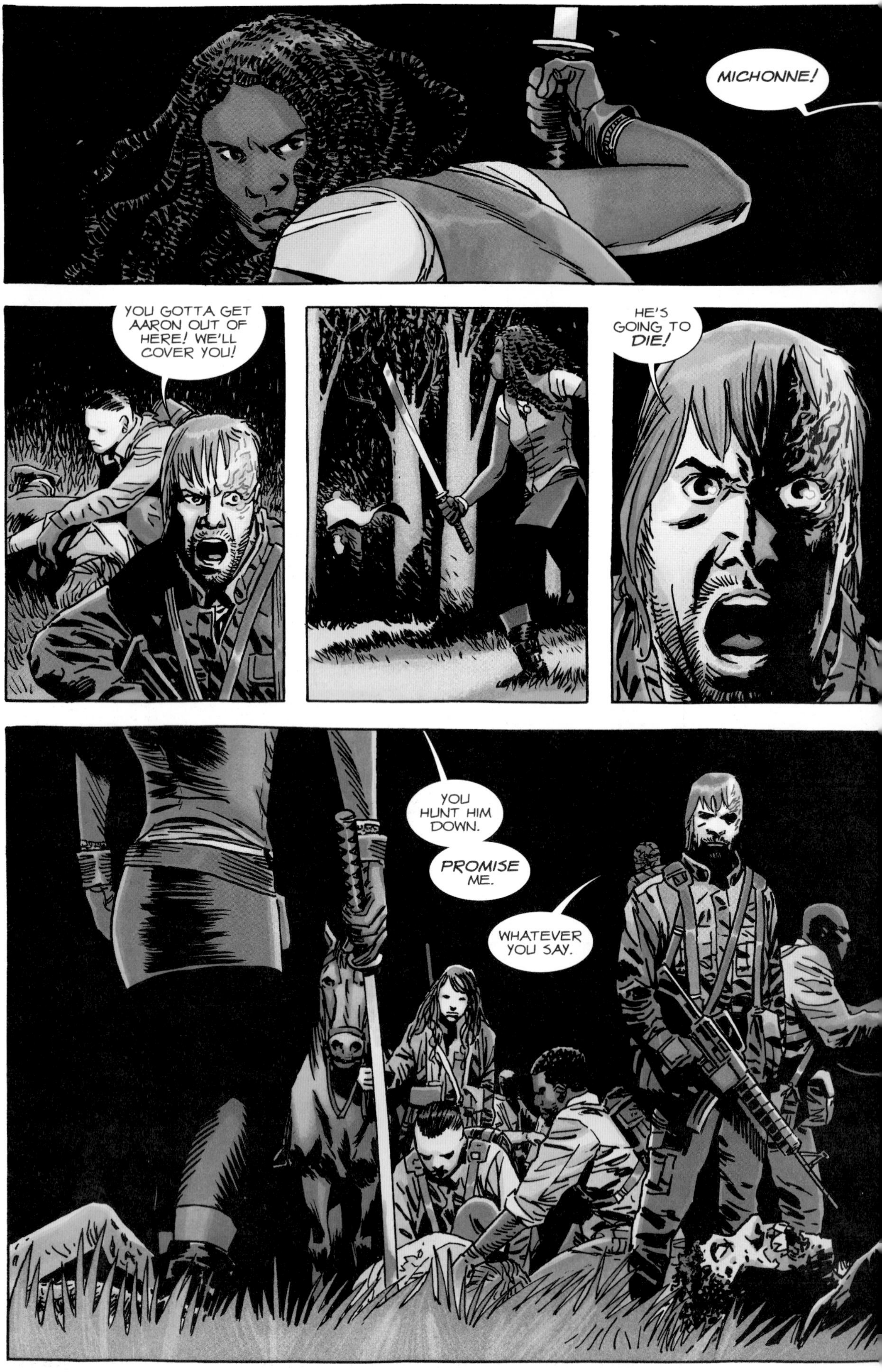
MICHONNE!
YOU GOTTA GET AARON OUT OF HERE! WE'LL COVER YOU!
HE'S GOING TO DIE!
YOU HUNT HIM DOWN.
PROMISE ME.
WHATEVER YOU SAY.

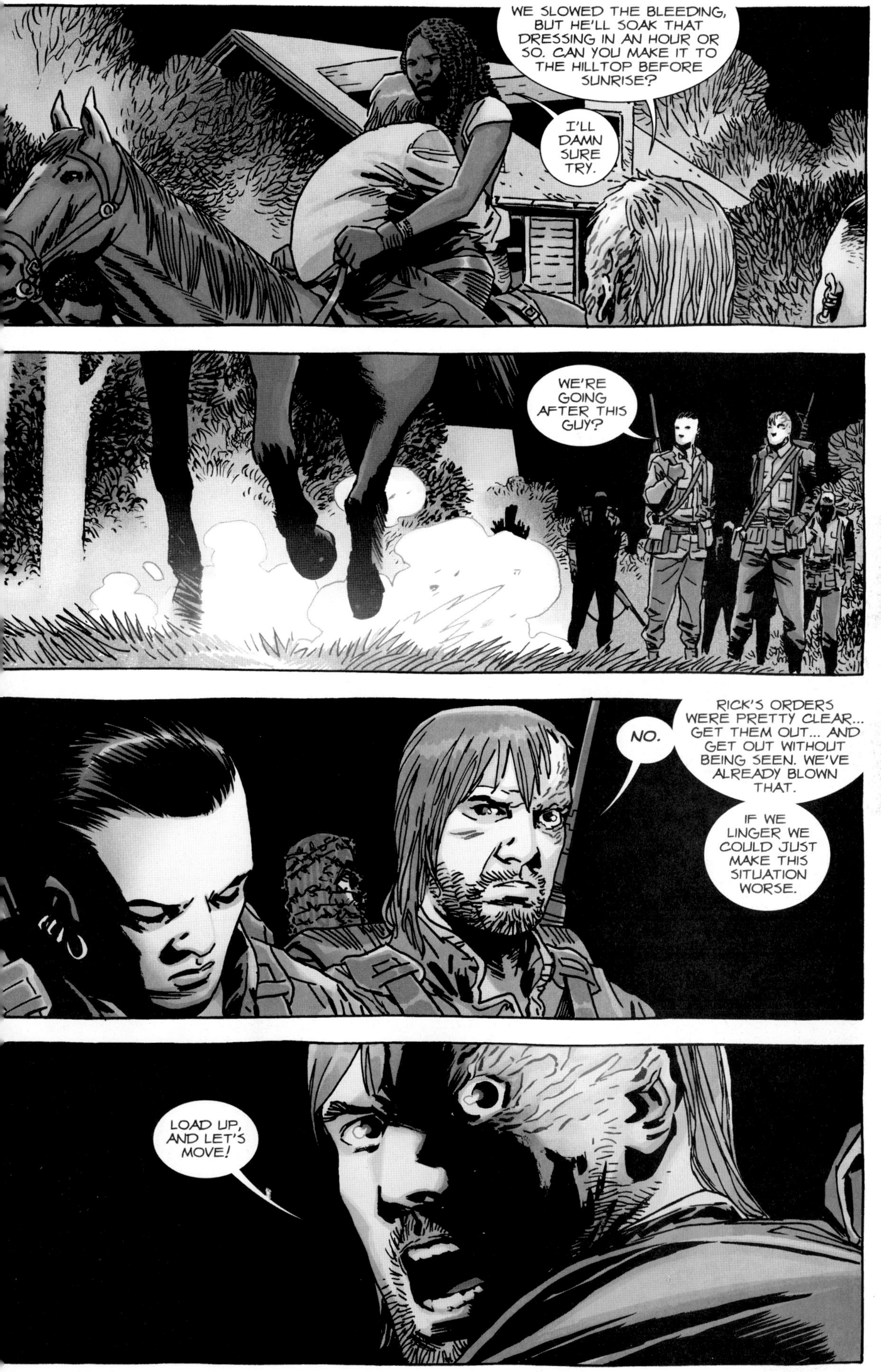
WE SLOWED THE BLEEDING, BUT HE'LL SOAK THAT DRESSING IN AN HOUR OR SO. CAN YOU MAKE IT TO THE HILLTOP BEFORE SUNRISE?
I'LL DAMN SURE TRY.
WE'RE GOING AFTER THIS GUY?
NO.
RICK'S ORDERS WERE PRETTY CLEAR... GET THEM OUT... AND GET OUT WITHOUT BEING SEEN. WE'VE ALREADY BLOWN THAT.
IF WE LINGER WE COULD JUST MAKE THIS SITUATION WORSE.
LOAD UP, AND LET'S MOVE!

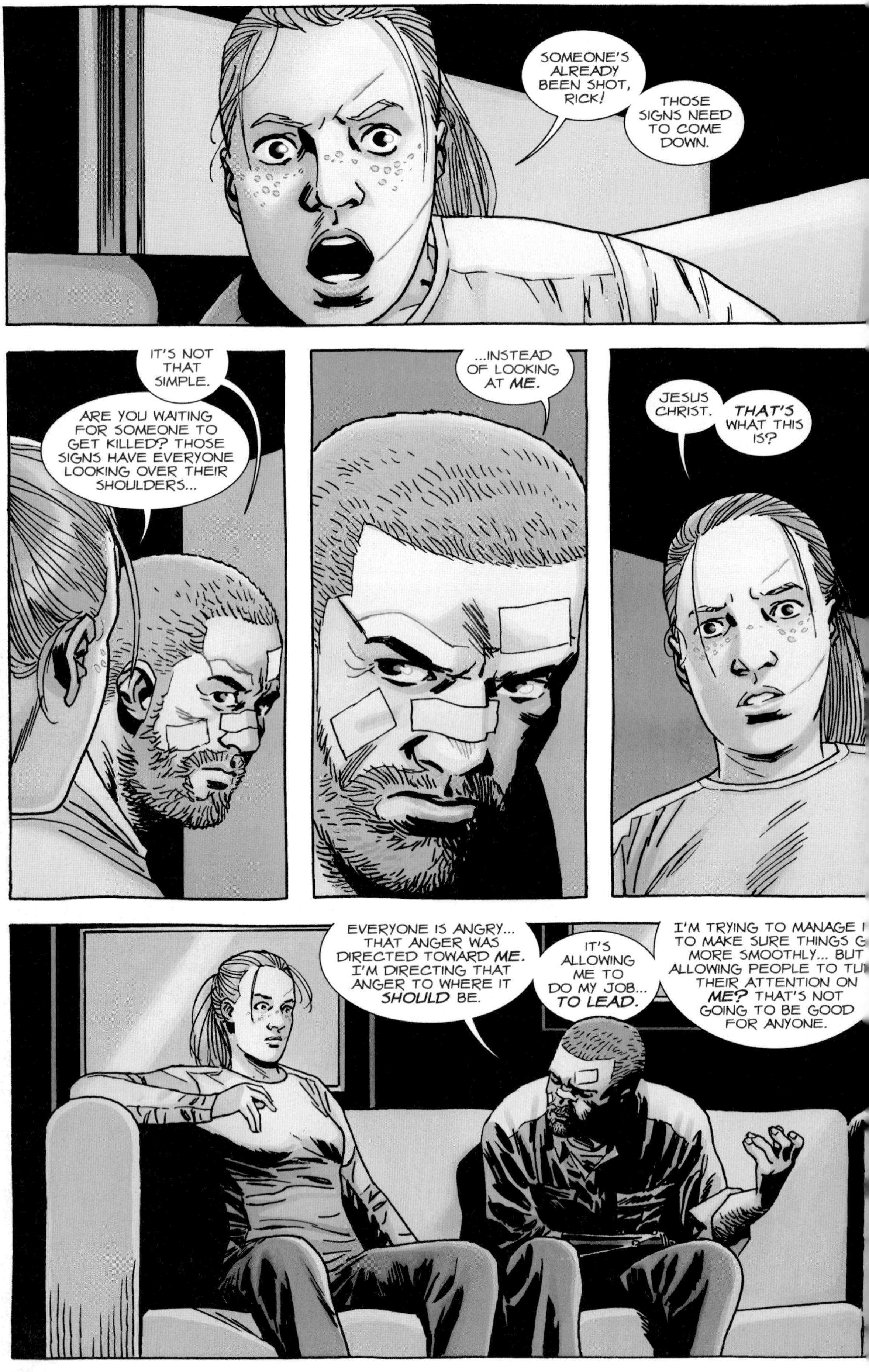

SOMEONE'S ALREADY BEEN SHOT, RICK!
THOSE SIGNS NEED TO COME DOWN.
IT'S NOT THAT SIMPLE.
ARE YOU WAITING FOR SOMEONE TO GET KILLED? THOSE SIGNS HAVE EVERYONE LOOKING OVER THEIR SHOULDERS...
...INSTEAD OF LOOKING AT ME.
JESUS CHRIST.
THAT'S WHAT THIS IS?
EVERYONE IS ANGRY... THAT ANGER WAS DIRECTED TOWARD ME. I'M DIRECTING THAT ANGER TO WHERE IT SHOULD BE.
IT'S ALLOWING ME TO DO MY JOB... TO LEAD.
I'M TRYING TO MANAGE I TO MAKE SURE THINGS G MORE SMOOTHLY... BUT ALLOWING PEOPLE TO TU THEIR ATTENTION ON ME? THAT'S NOT GOING TO BE GOOD FOR ANYONE.

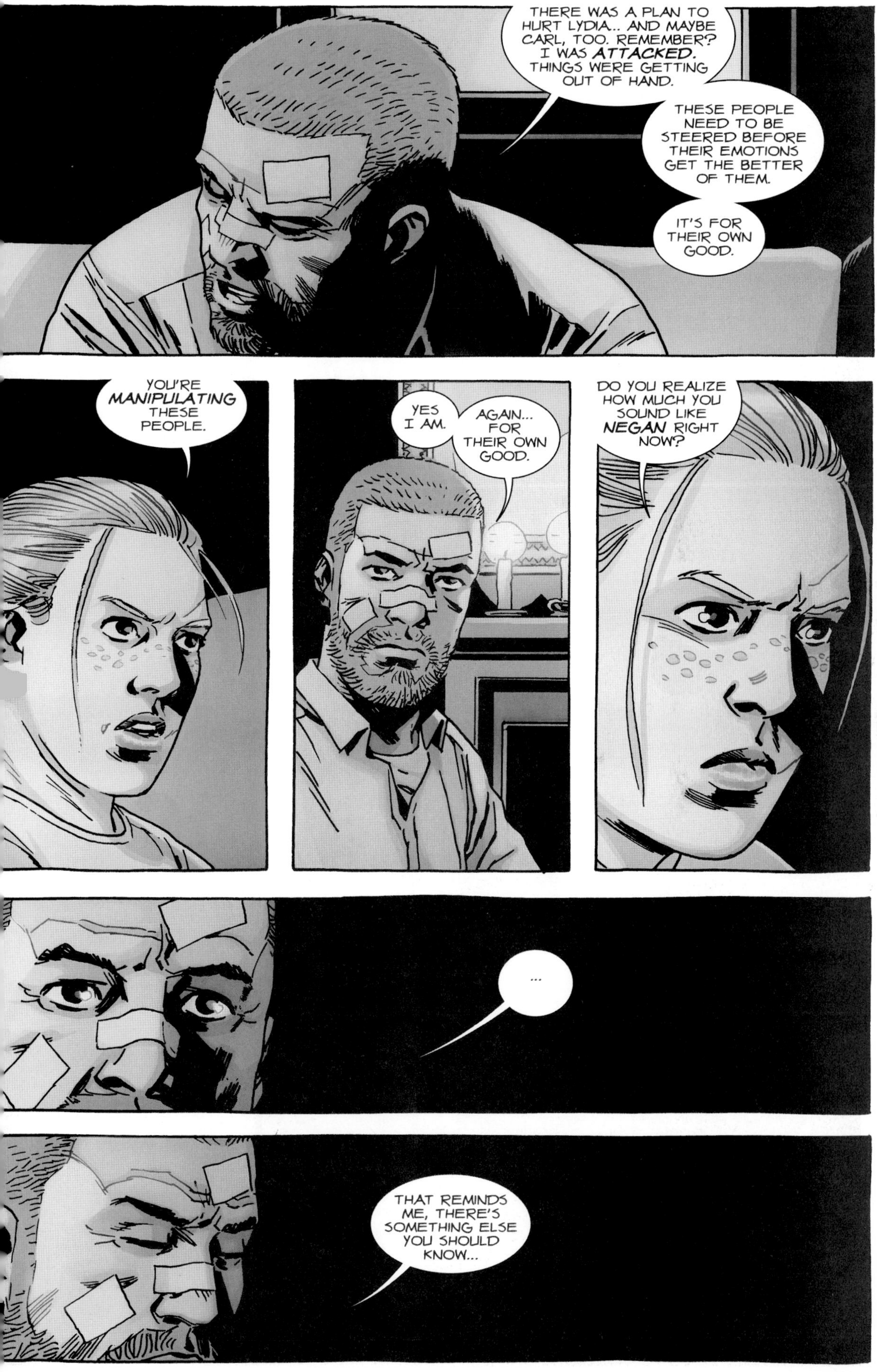
THERE WAS A PLAN TO HURT LYDIA.. AND MAYBE CARL, TOO. REMEMBER? I WAS **ATTACKED.** THINGS WERE GETTING OUT OF HAND.
THESE PEOPLE NEED TO BE STEERED BEFORE THEIR EMOTIONS GET THE BETTER OF THEM.
IT'S FOR THEIR OWN GOOD.
YOU'RE ***MANIPULATING*** THESE PEOPLE.
YES I AM.
AGAIN... FOR THEIR OWN GOOD.
DO YOU REALIZE HOW MUCH YOU SOUND LIKE ***NEGAN*** RIGHT NOW?
...
THAT REMINDS ME, THERE'S SOMETHING ELSE YOU SHOULD KNOW...

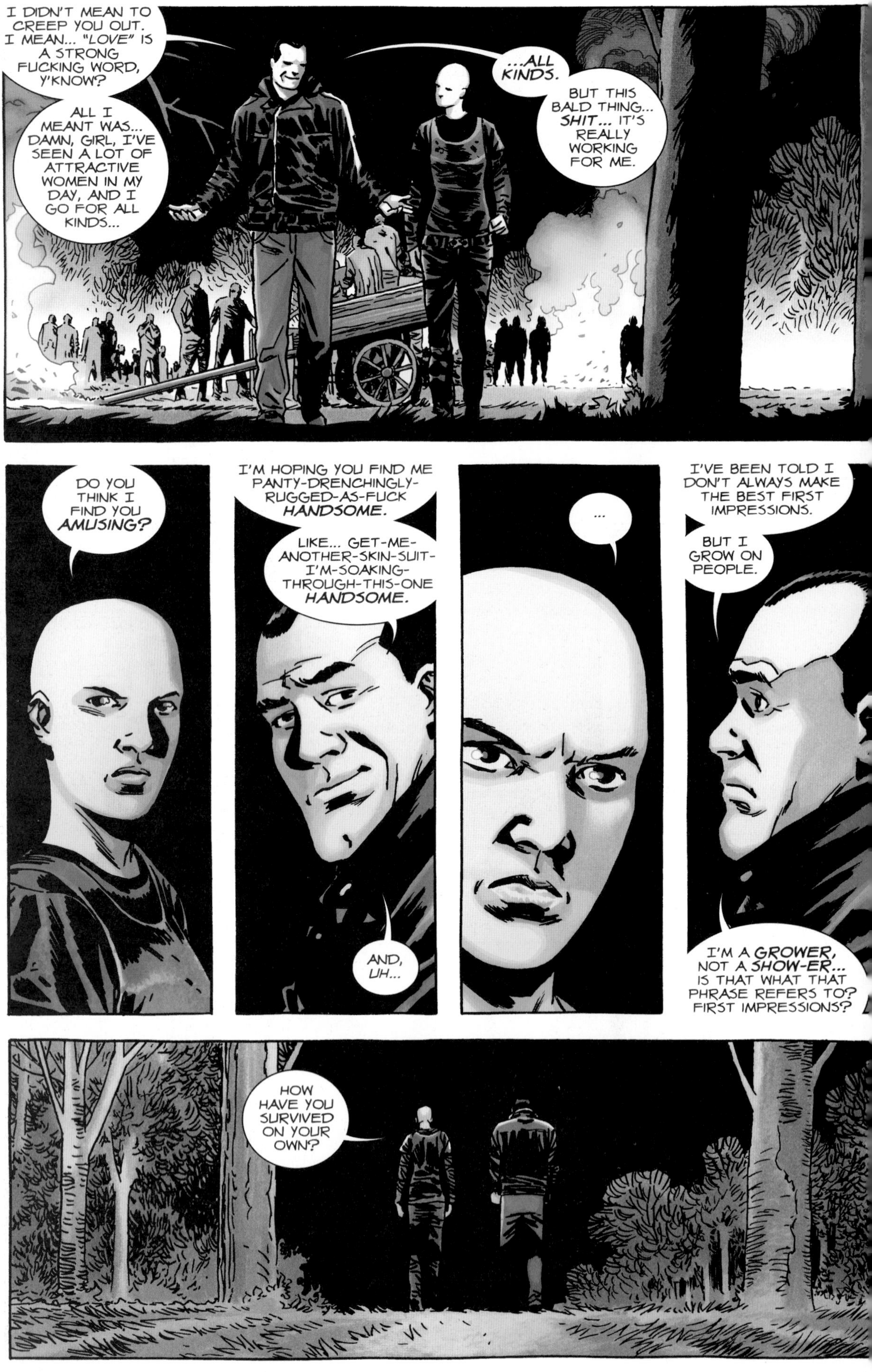

I DIDN'T MEAN TO CREEP YOU OUT. I MEAN... "LOVE" IS A STRONG FUCKING WORD, Y'KNOW?
ALL I MEANT WAS... DAMN, GIRL, I'VE SEEN A LOT OF ATTRACTIVE WOMEN IN MY DAY, AND I GO FOR ALL KINDS...
...ALL KINDS.
BUT THIS BALD THING... SHIT... IT'S REALLY WORKING FOR ME.
DO YOU THINK I FIND YOU AMUSING?
I'M HOPING YOU FIND ME PANTY-DRENCHINGLY-RUGGED-AS-FUCK HANDSOME.
LIKE... GET-ME-ANOTHER-SKIN-SUIT-I'M-SOAKING-THROUGH-THIS-ONE HANDSOME.
AND, UH...
...
I'VE BEEN TOLD I DON'T ALWAYS MAKE THE BEST FIRST IMPRESSIONS.
BUT I GROW ON PEOPLE.
I'M A GROWER, NOT A SHOW-ER... IS THAT WHAT THAT PHRASE REFERS TO? FIRST IMPRESSIONS?
HOW HAVE YOU SURVIVED ON YOUR OWN?

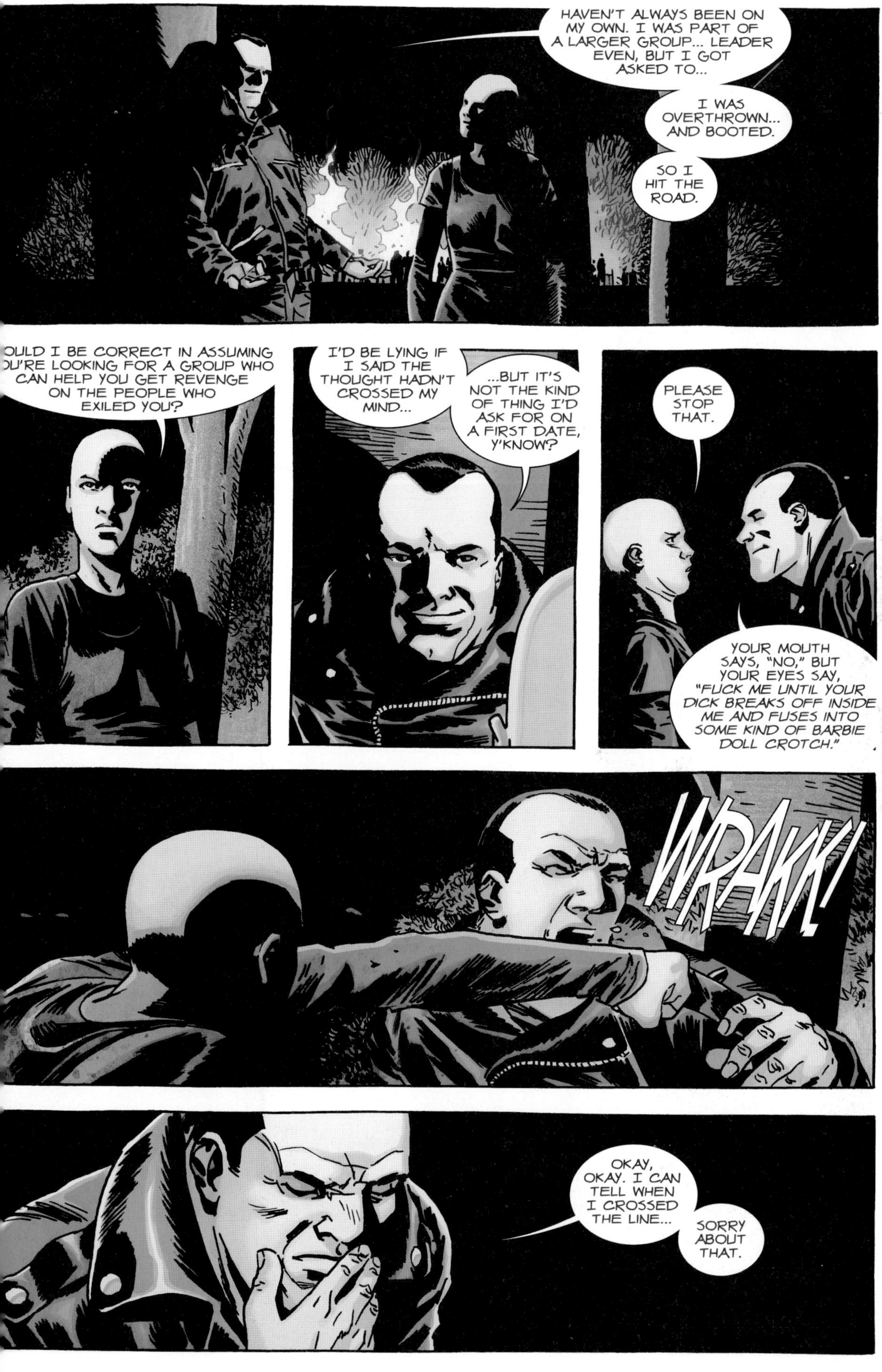
HAVEN'T ALWAYS BEEN ON MY OWN. I WAS PART OF A LARGER GROUP... LEADER EVEN, BUT I GOT ASKED TO...
I WAS OVERTHROWN... AND BOOTED.
SO I HIT THE ROAD.
OULD I BE CORRECT IN ASSUMING OU'RE LOOKING FOR A GROUP WHO CAN HELP YOU GET REVENGE ON THE PEOPLE WHO EXILED YOU?
I'D BE LYING IF I SAID THE THOUGHT HADN'T CROSSED MY MIND...
...BUT IT'S NOT THE KIND OF THING I'D ASK FOR ON A FIRST DATE, Y'KNOW?
PLEASE STOP THAT.
YOUR MOUTH SAYS, "NO," BUT YOUR EYES SAY, "FUCK ME UNTIL YOUR DICK BREAKS OFF INSIDE ME AND FUSES INTO SOME KIND OF BARBIE DOLL CROTCH."
WRAKK!
OKAY, OKAY. I CAN TELL WHEN I CROSSED THE LINE...
SORRY ABOUT THAT.

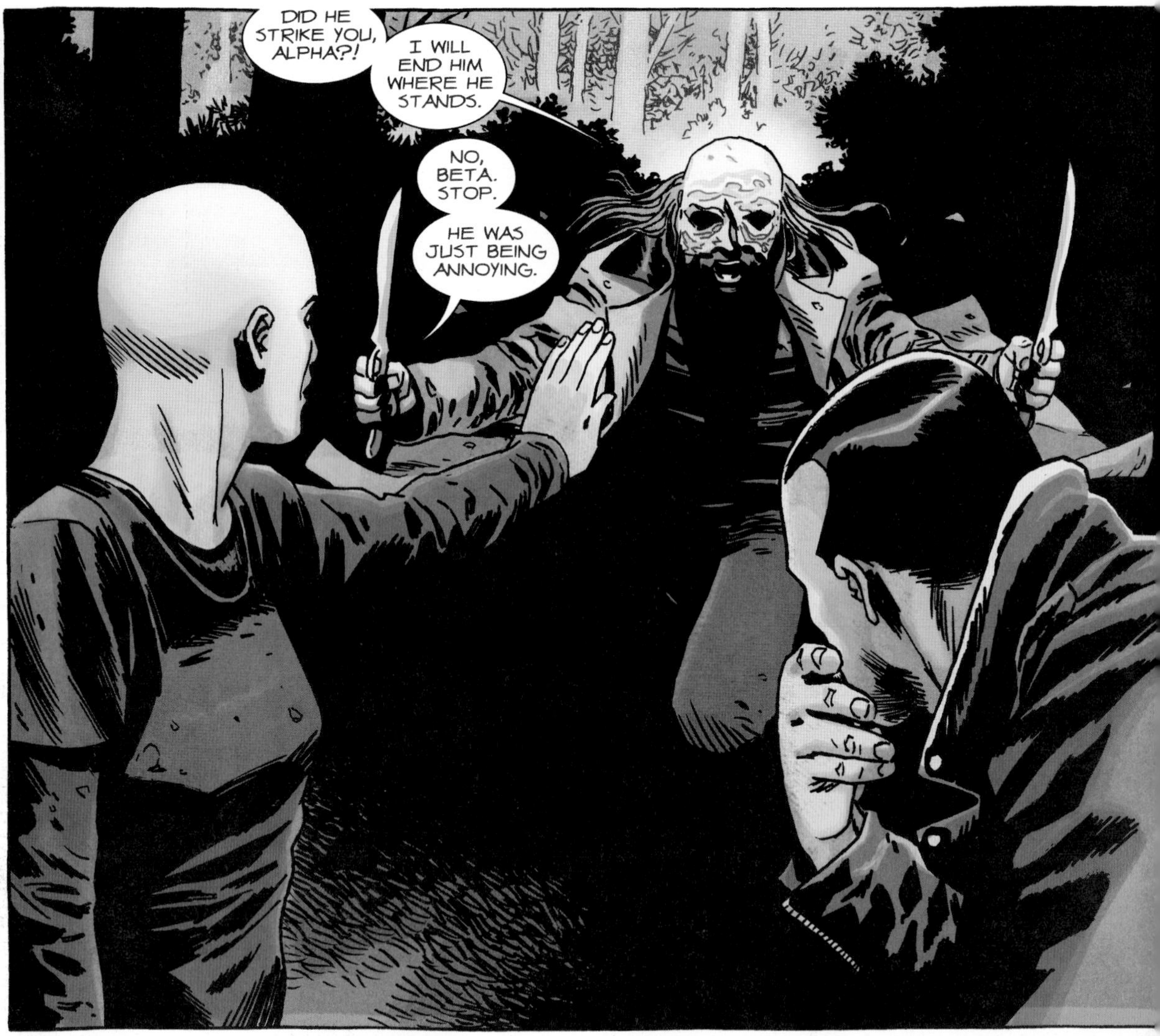
DID HE STRIKE YOU, ALPHA?!
I WILL END HIM WHERE HE STANDS.
NO, BETA. STOP.
HE WAS JUST BEING ANNOYING.

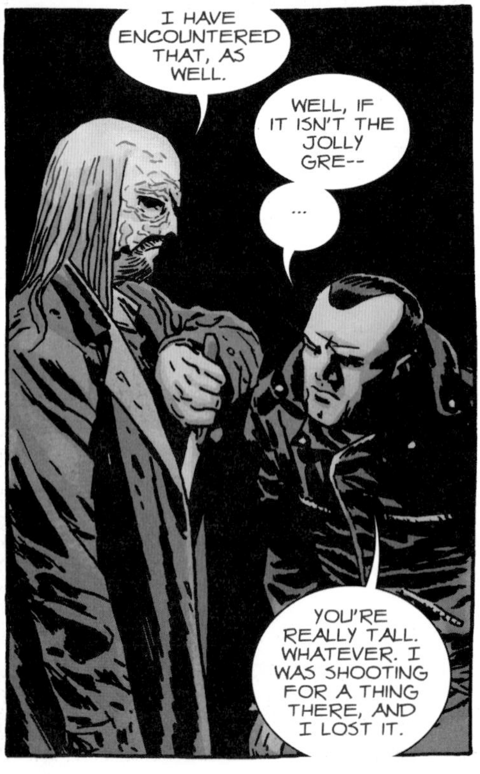
I HAVE ENCOUNTERED THAT, AS WELL.
WELL, IF IT ISN'T THE JOLLY GRE--
...
YOU'RE REALLY TALL. WHATEVER. I WAS SHOOTING FOR A THING THERE, AND I LOST IT.

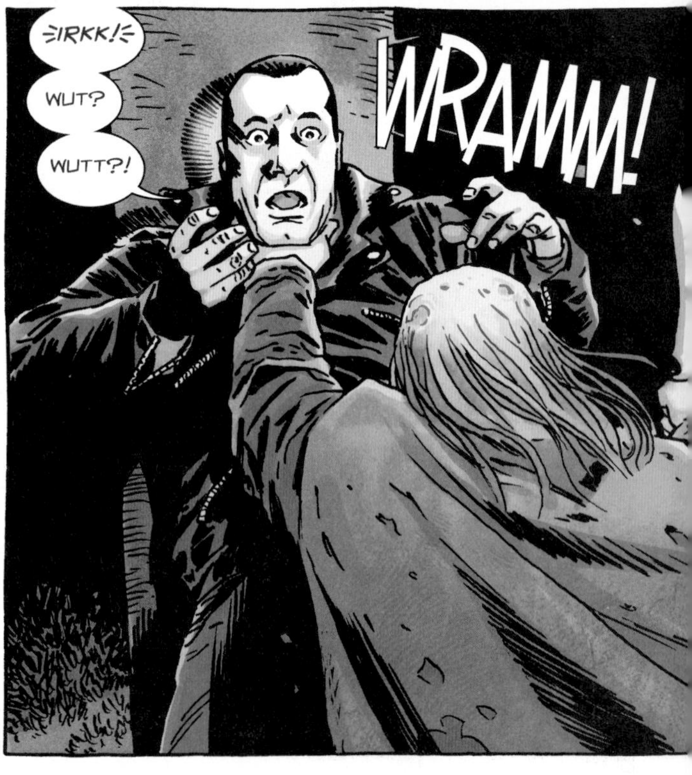
IRKK!
WUT?
WUTT?!
WRAMM!

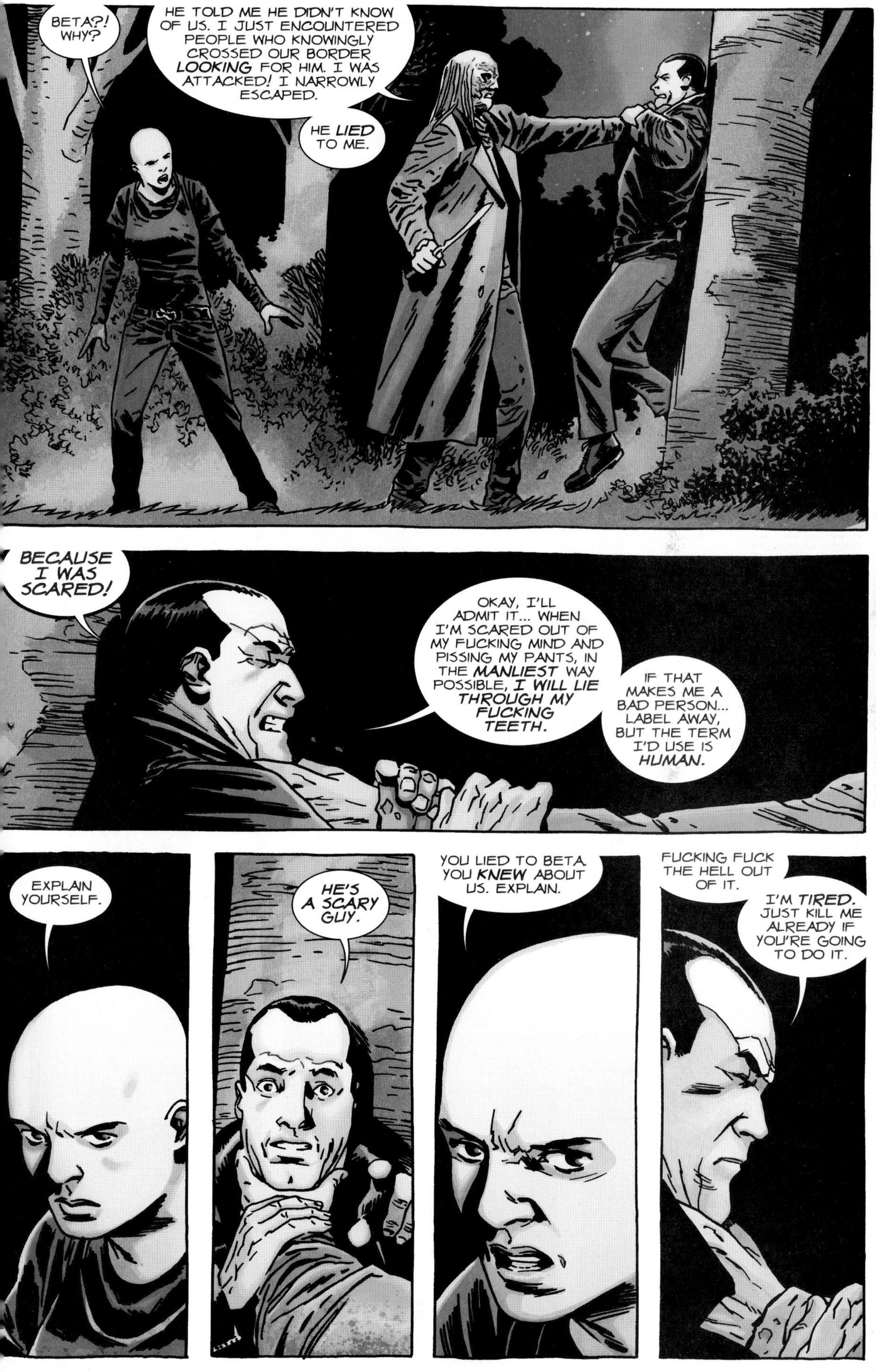
BETA?! WHY?
HE TOLD ME HE DIDN'T KNOW OF US. I JUST ENCOUNTERED PEOPLE WHO KNOWINGLY CROSSED OUR BORDER LOOKING FOR HIM. I WAS ATTACKED! I NARROWLY ESCAPED.
HE LIED TO ME.
BECAUSE I WAS SCARED!
OKAY, I'LL ADMIT IT... WHEN I'M SCARED OUT OF MY FUCKING MIND AND PISSING MY PANTS, IN THE MANLIEST WAY POSSIBLE, I WILL LIE THROUGH MY FUCKING TEETH.
IF THAT MAKES ME A BAD PERSON... LABEL AWAY, BUT THE TERM I'D USE IS HUMAN.
EXPLAIN YOURSELF.
HE'S A SCARY GUY.
YOU LIED TO BETA. YOU KNEW ABOUT US. EXPLAIN.
FUCKING FUCK THE HELL OUT OF IT.
I'M TIRED. JUST KILL ME ALREADY IF YOU'RE GOING TO DO IT.

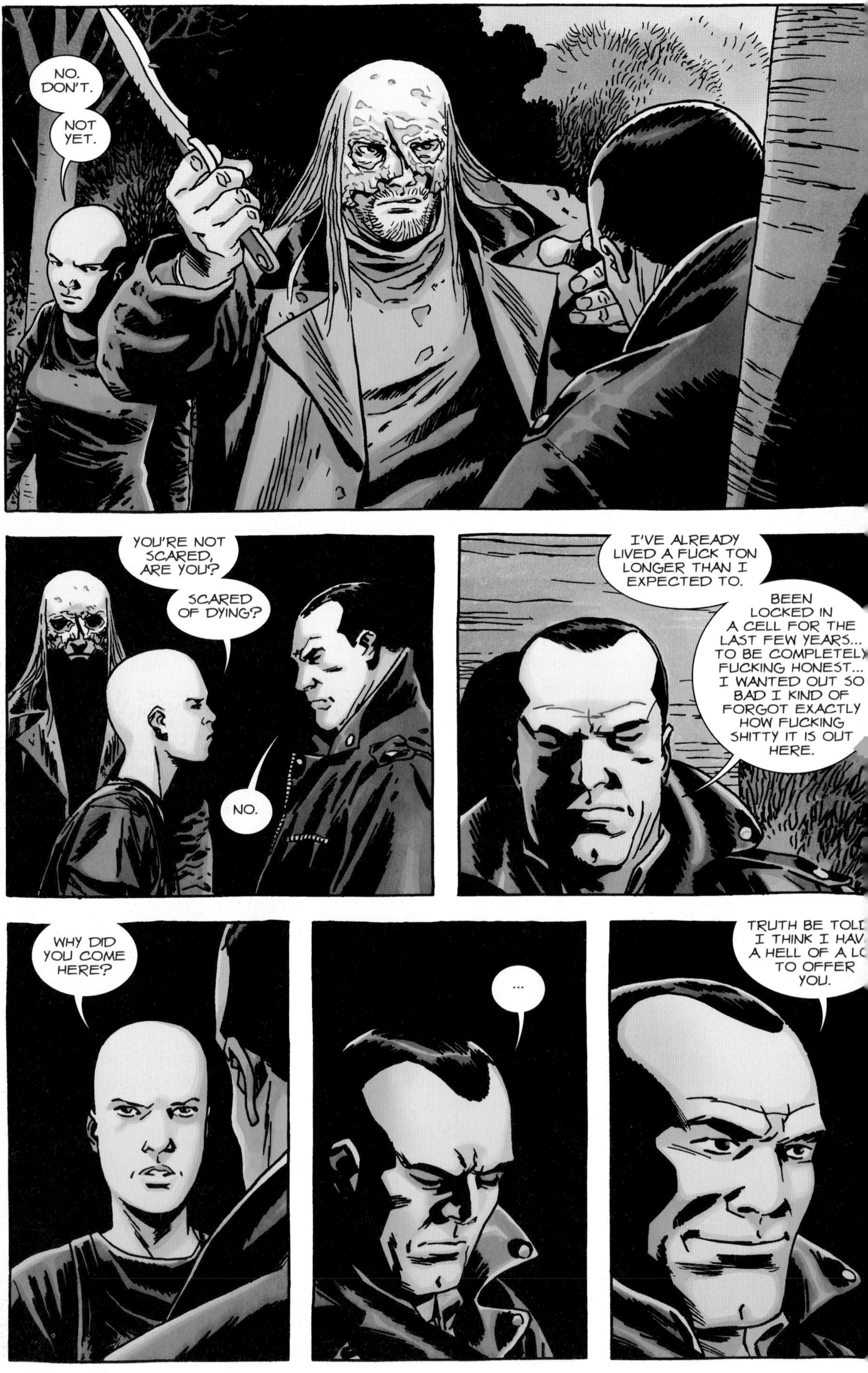
NO. DON'T.
NOT YET.
YOU'RE NOT SCARED, ARE YOU?
SCARED OF DYING?
NO.
I'VE ALREADY LIVED A FUCK TON LONGER THAN I EXPECTED TO.
BEEN LOCKED IN A CELL FOR THE LAST FEW YEARS... TO BE COMPLETELY FUCKING HONEST... I WANTED OUT SO BAD I KIND OF FORGOT EXACTLY HOW FUCKING SHITTY IT IS OUT HERE.
WHY DID YOU COME HERE?
...
TRUTH BE TOL I THINK I HAV A HELL OF A L TO OFFER YOU.

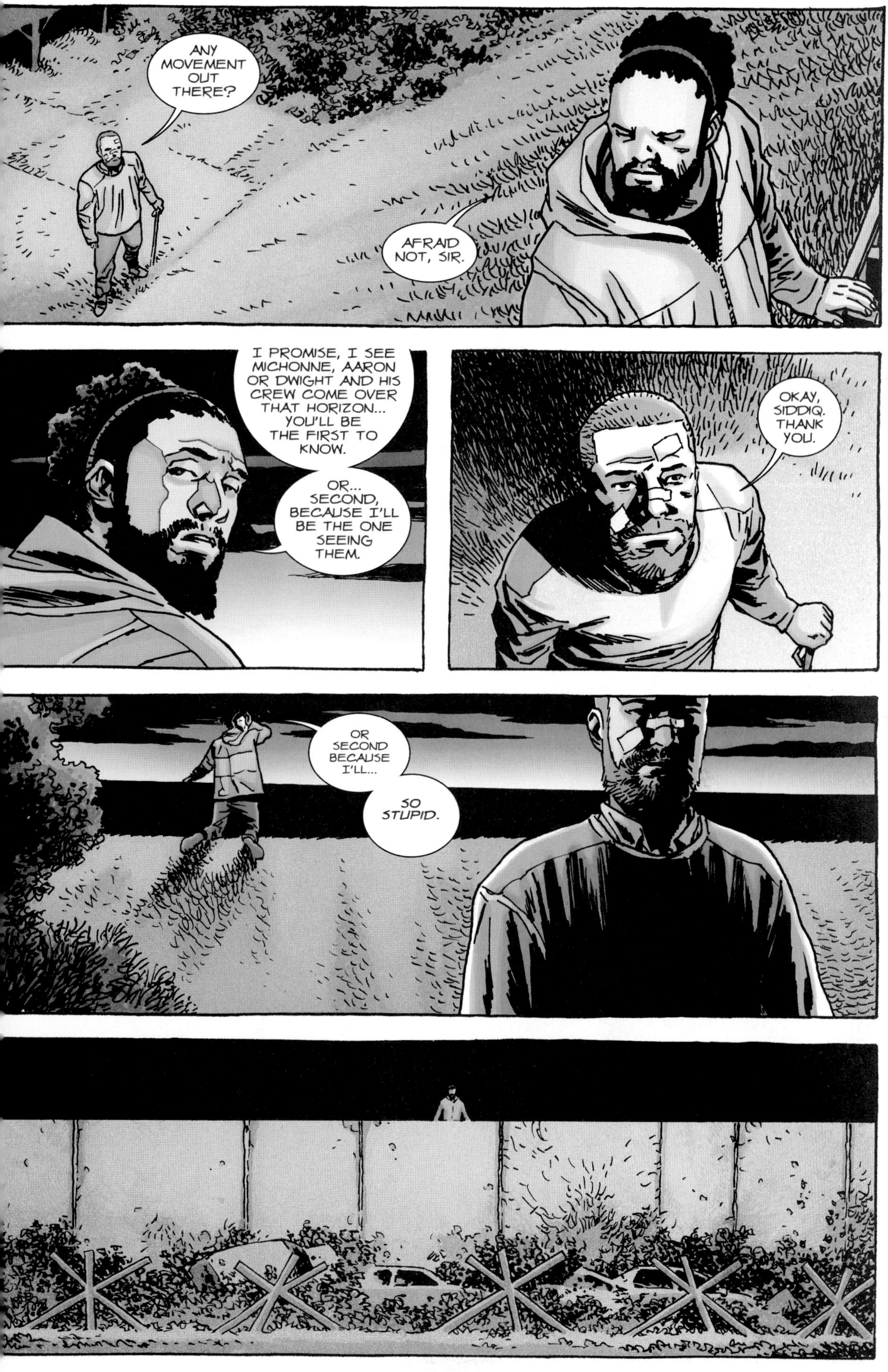
ANY MOVEMENT OUT THERE?
AFRAID NOT, SIR.
I PROMISE, I SEE MICHONNE, AARON OR DWIGHT AND HIS CREW COME OVER THAT HORIZON... YOU'LL BE THE FIRST TO KNOW.
OR... SECOND, BECAUSE I'LL BE THE ONE SEEING THEM.
OKAY, SIDDIQ. THANK YOU.
OR SECOND BECAUSE I'LL...
SO STUPID.

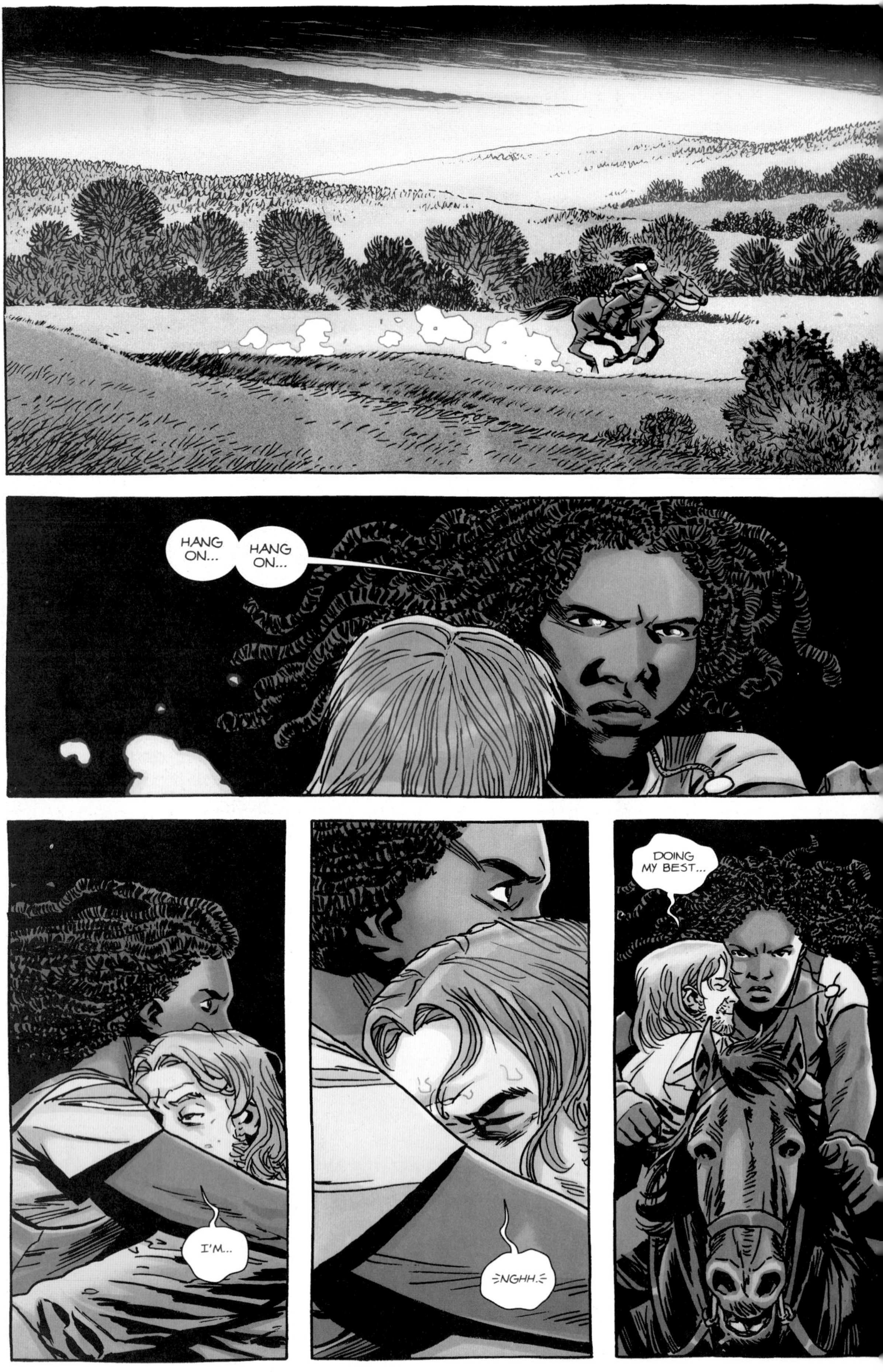
HANG ON...
HANG ON...
I'M...
NGHH.
DOING MY BEST...

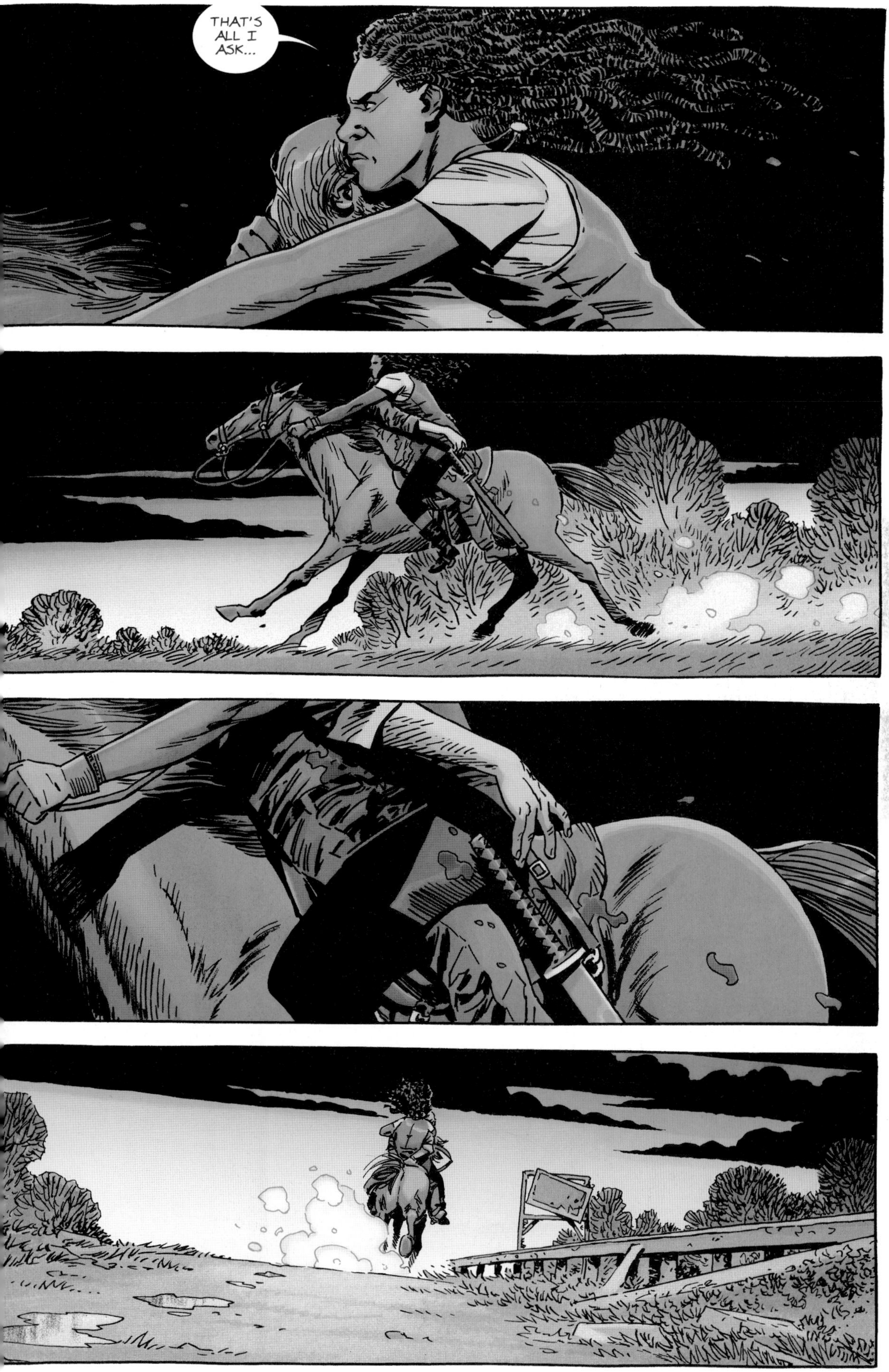
THAT'S ALL I ASK...

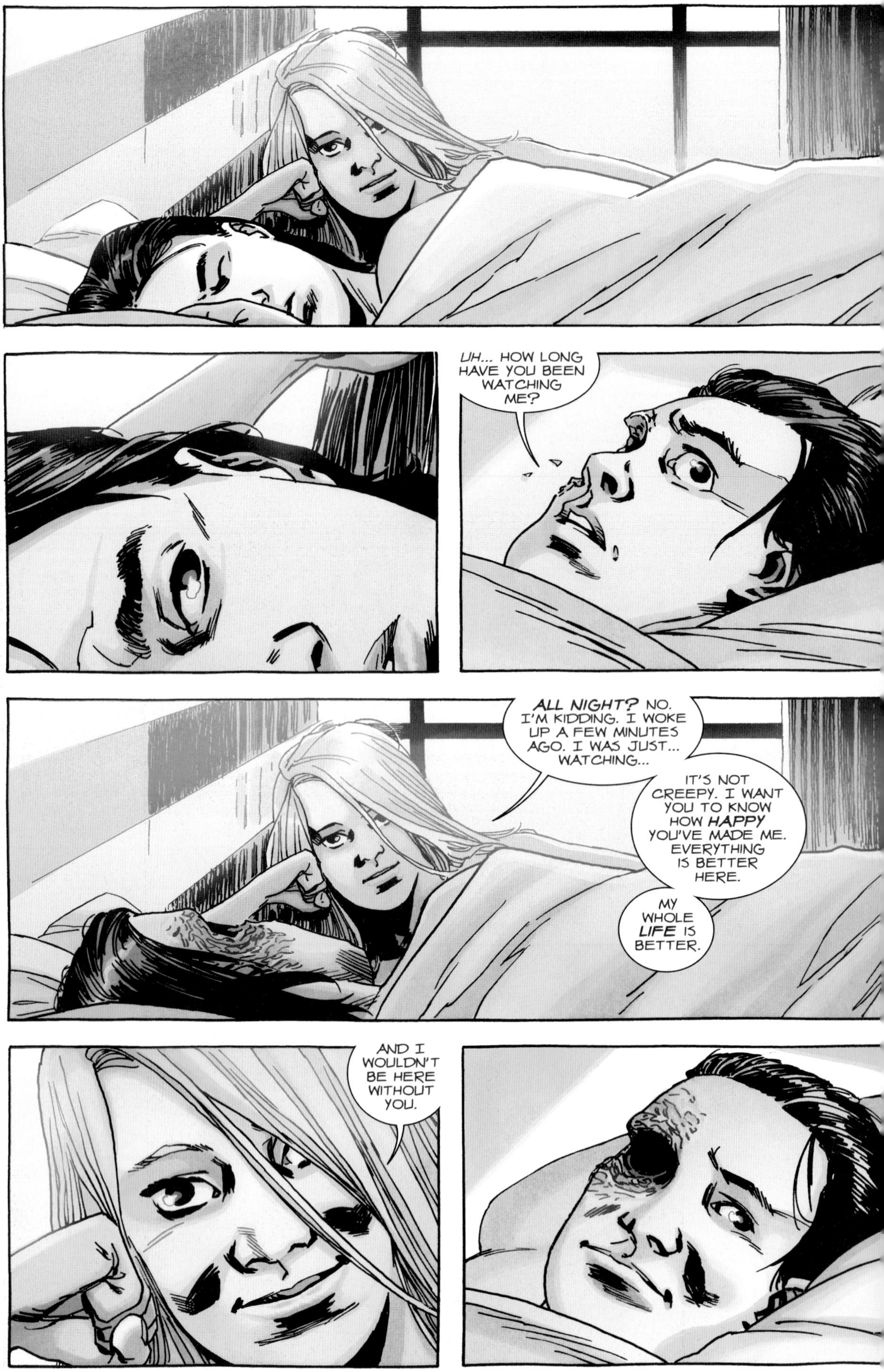
UH... HOW LONG HAVE YOU BEEN WATCHING ME?
ALL NIGHT? NO. I'M KIDDING. I WOKE UP A FEW MINUTES AGO. I WAS JUST... WATCHING...
IT'S NOT CREEPY. I WANT YOU TO KNOW HOW HAPPY YOU'VE MADE ME. EVERYTHING IS BETTER HERE.
MY WHOLE LIFE IS BETTER.
AND I WOULDN'T BE HERE WITHOUT YOU.

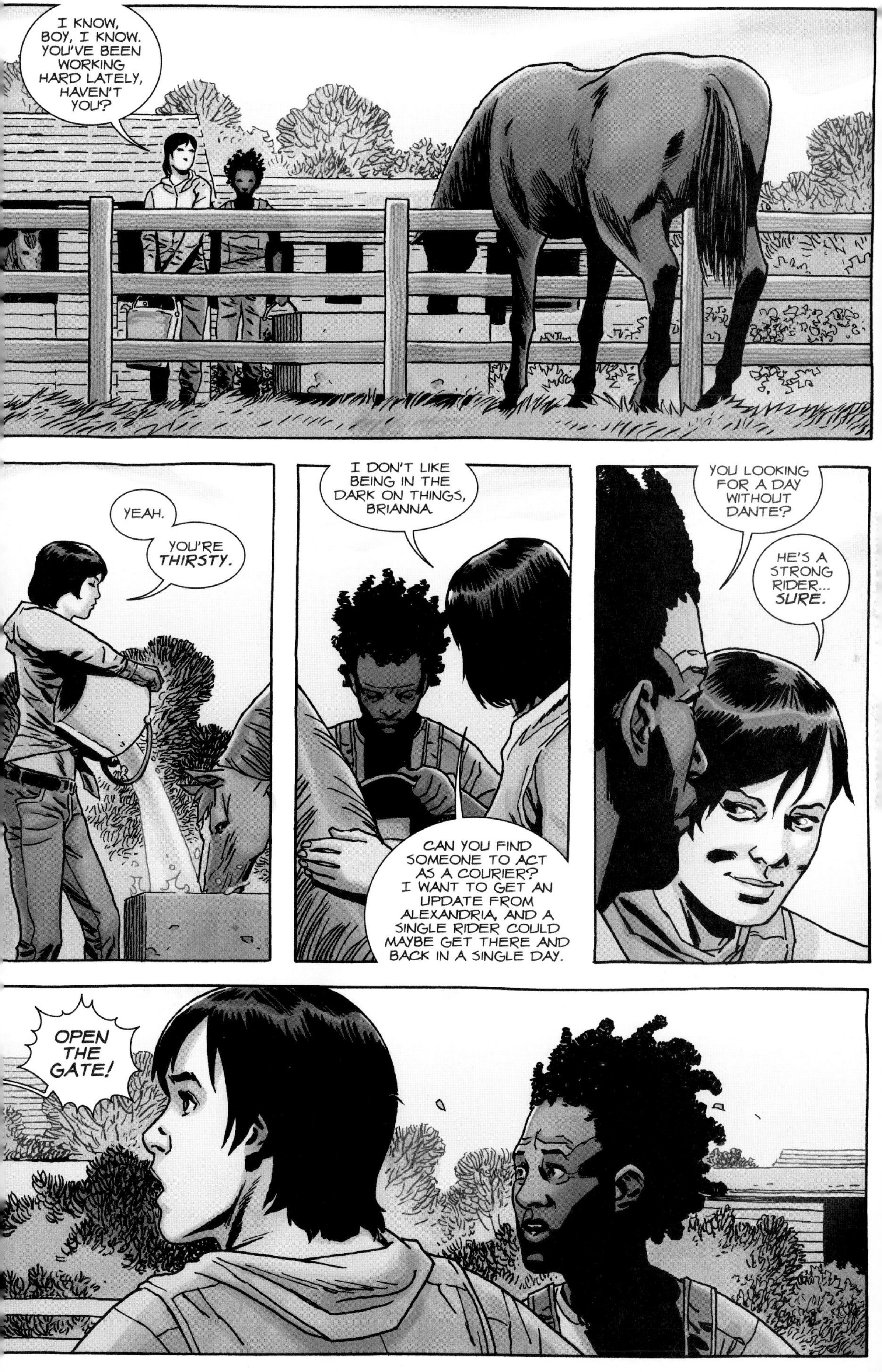
I KNOW, BOY, I KNOW. YOU'VE BEEN WORKING HARD LATELY, HAVEN'T YOU?
YEAH.
YOU'RE THIRSTY.
I DON'T LIKE BEING IN THE DARK ON THINGS, BRIANNA.
CAN YOU FIND SOMEONE TO ACT AS A COURIER? I WANT TO GET AN UPDATE FROM ALEXANDRIA, AND A SINGLE RIDER COULD MAYBE GET THERE AND BACK IN A SINGLE DAY.
YOU LOOKING FOR A DAY WITHOUT DANTE?
HE'S A STRONG RIDER... SURE.
OPEN THE GATE!

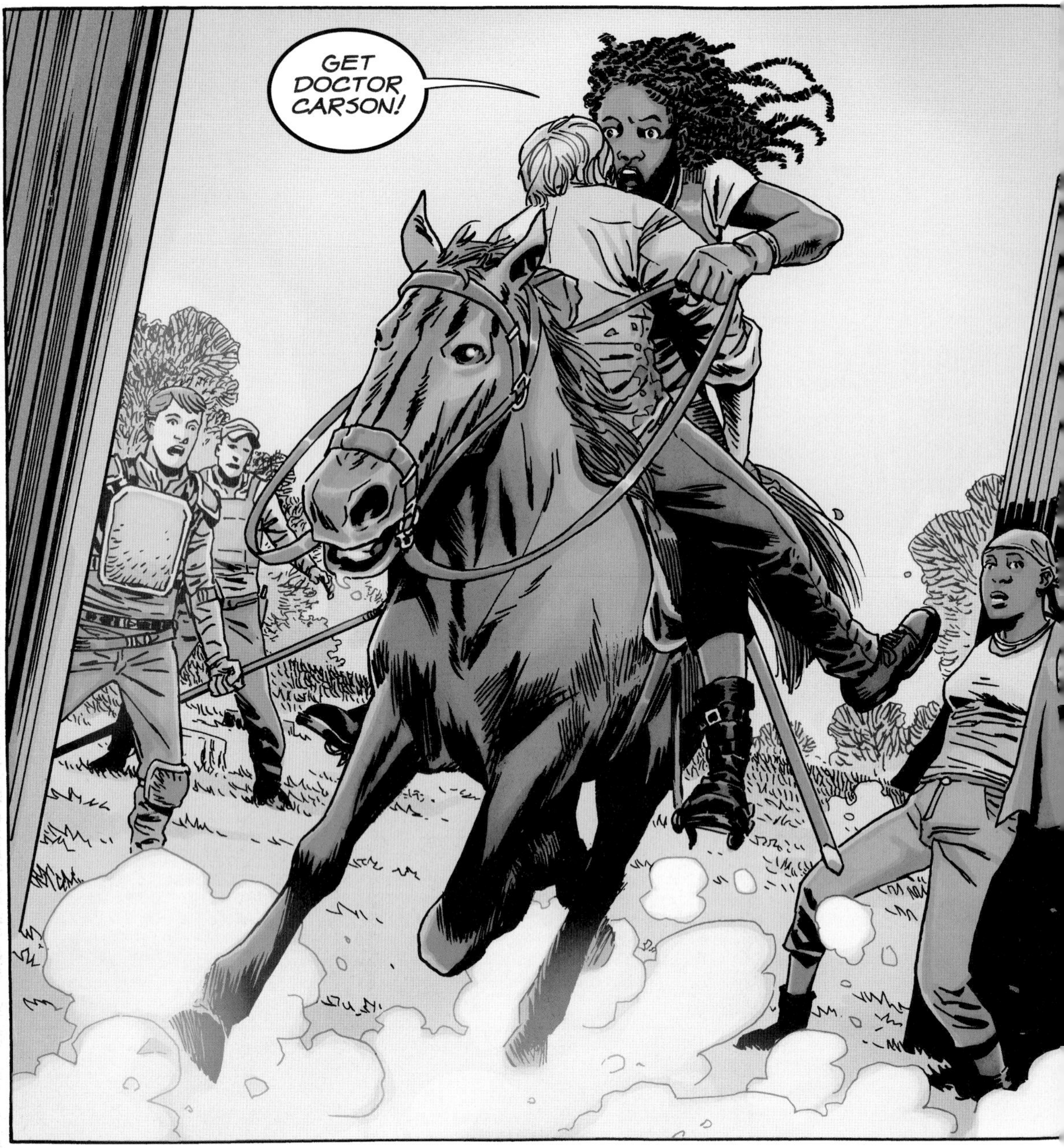
GET DOCTOR CARSON!

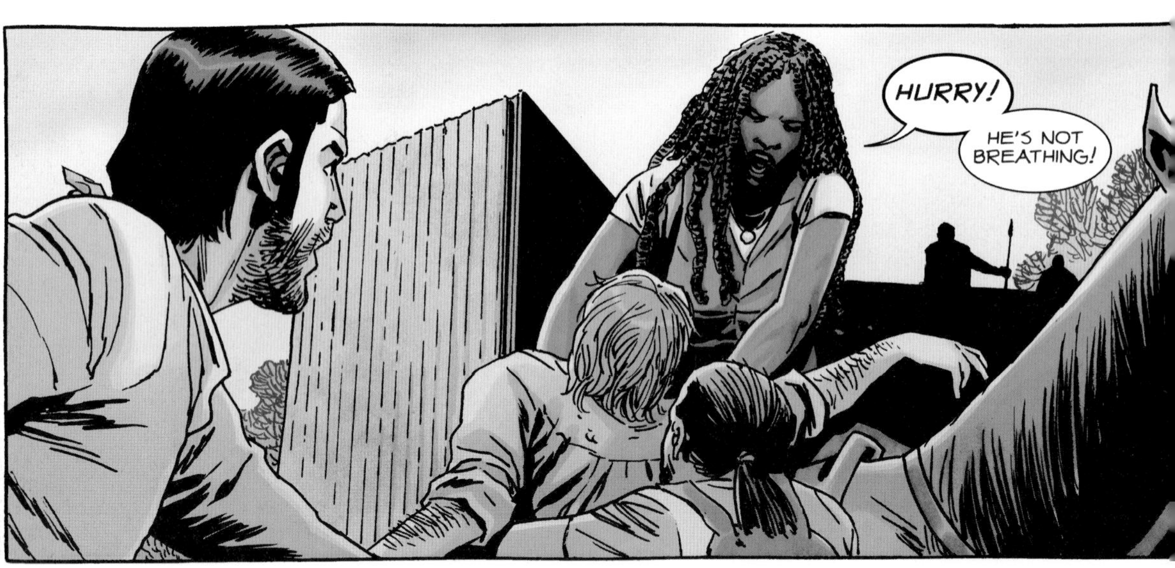
HURRY!
HE'S NOT BREATHING!

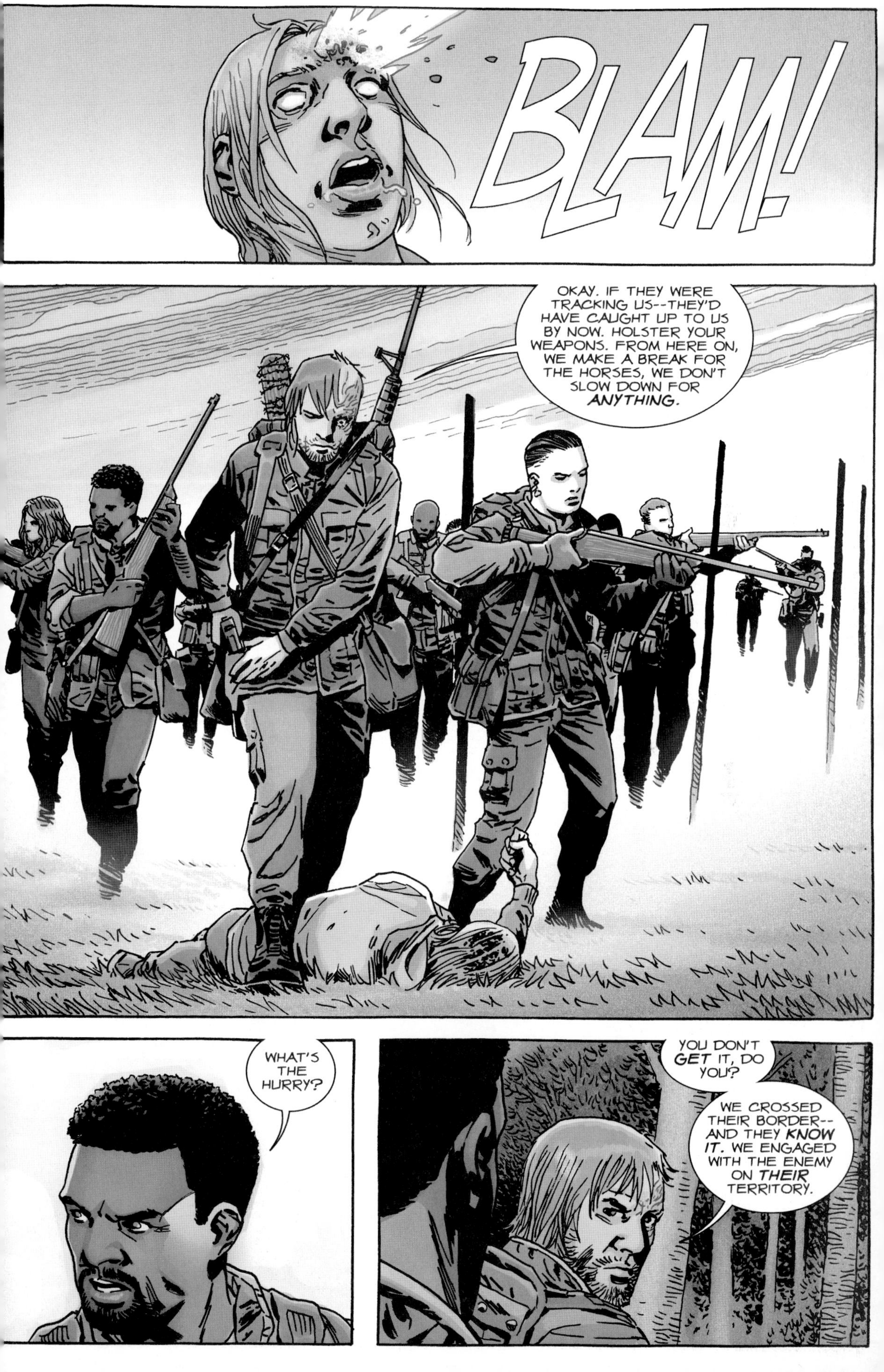
BLAM!
OKAY. IF THEY WERE TRACKING US--THEY'D HAVE CAUGHT UP TO US BY NOW. HOLSTER YOUR WEAPONS. FROM HERE ON, WE MAKE A BREAK FOR THE HORSES, WE DON'T SLOW DOWN FOR ANYTHING.
WHAT'S THE HURRY?
YOU DON'T GET IT, DO YOU?
WE CROSSED THEIR BORDER-- AND THEY KNOW IT. WE ENGAGED WITH THE ENEMY ON THEIR TERRITORY.

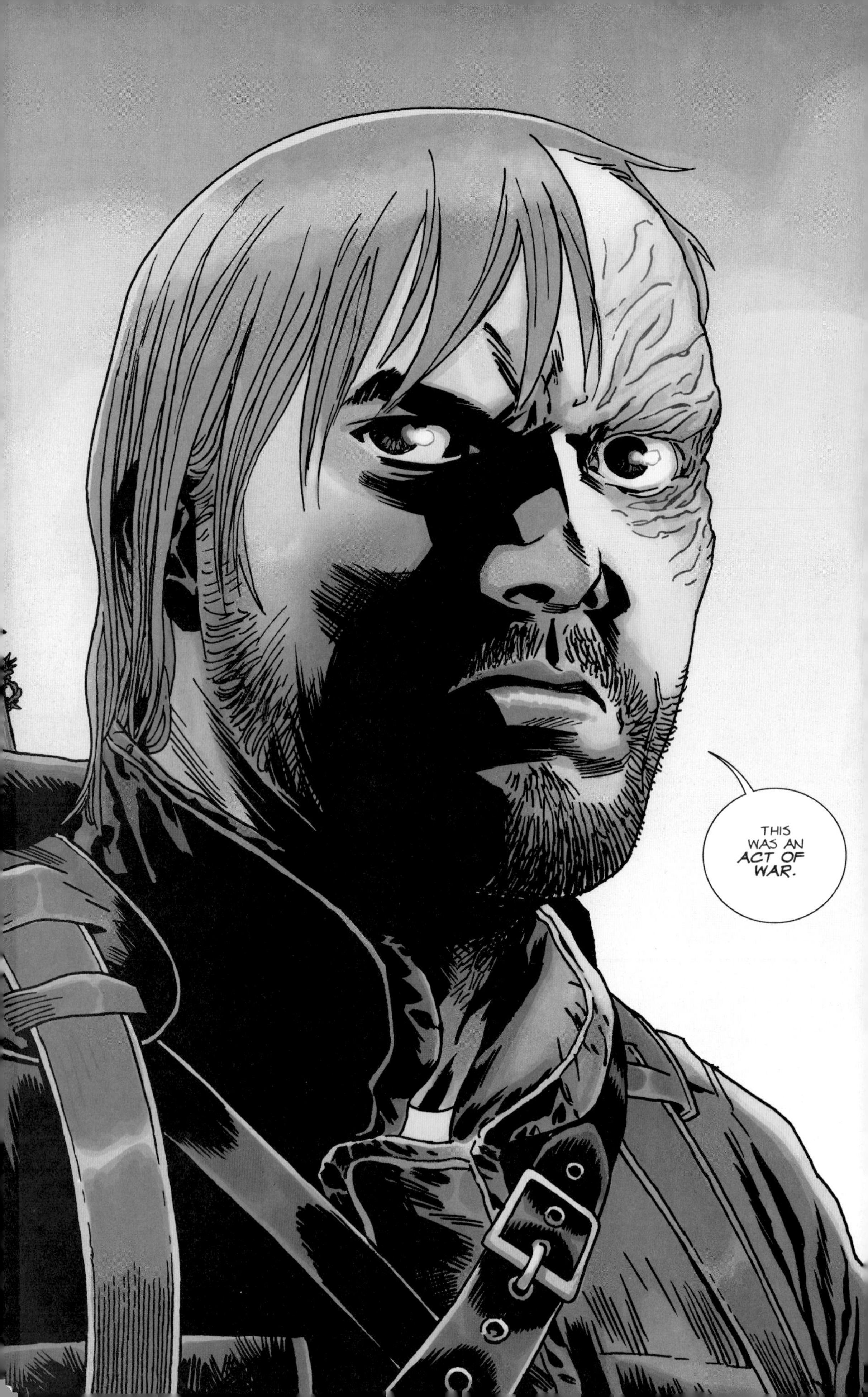
THIS WAS AN ACT OF WAR.

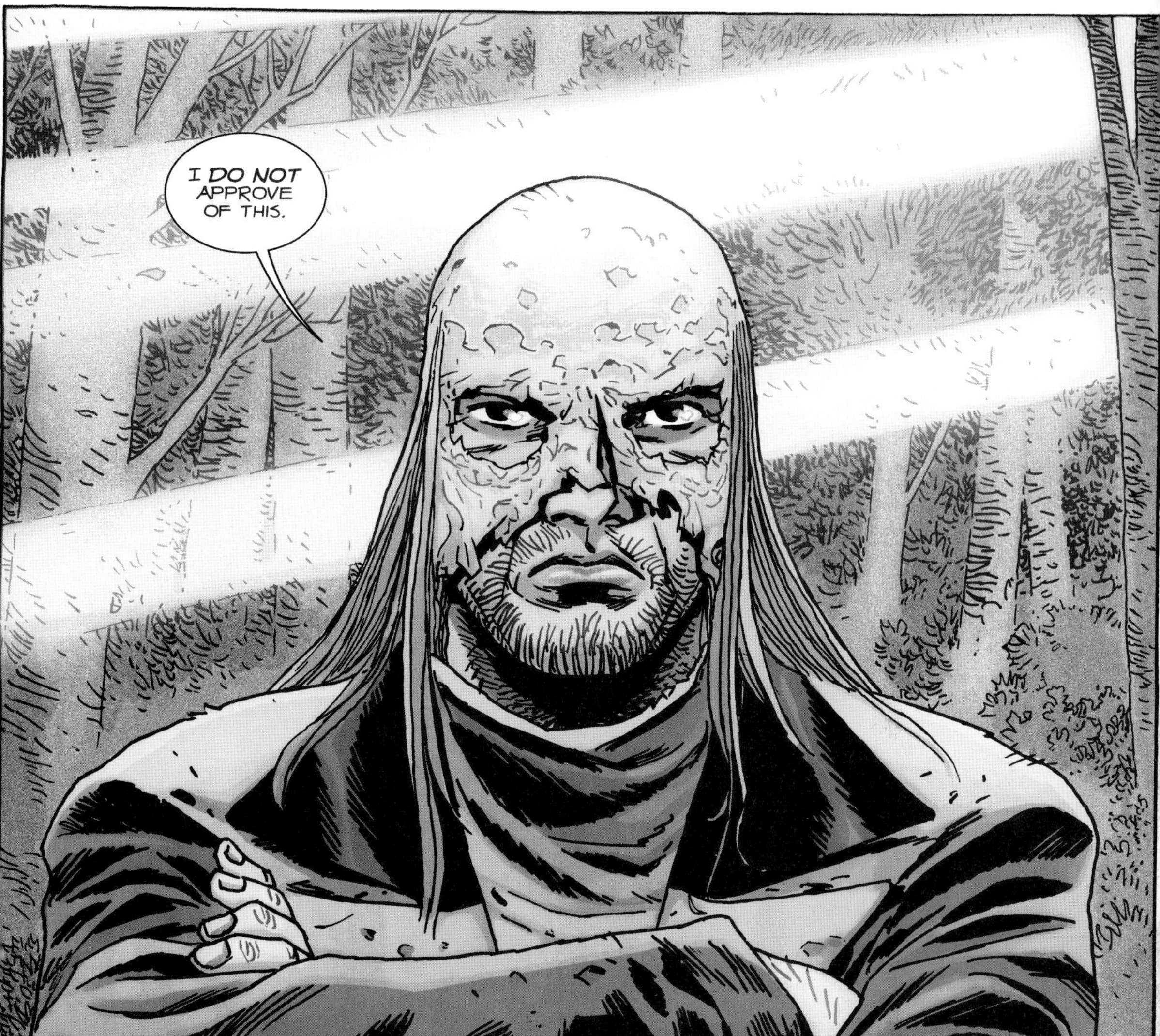
I DO NOT APPROVE OF THIS.

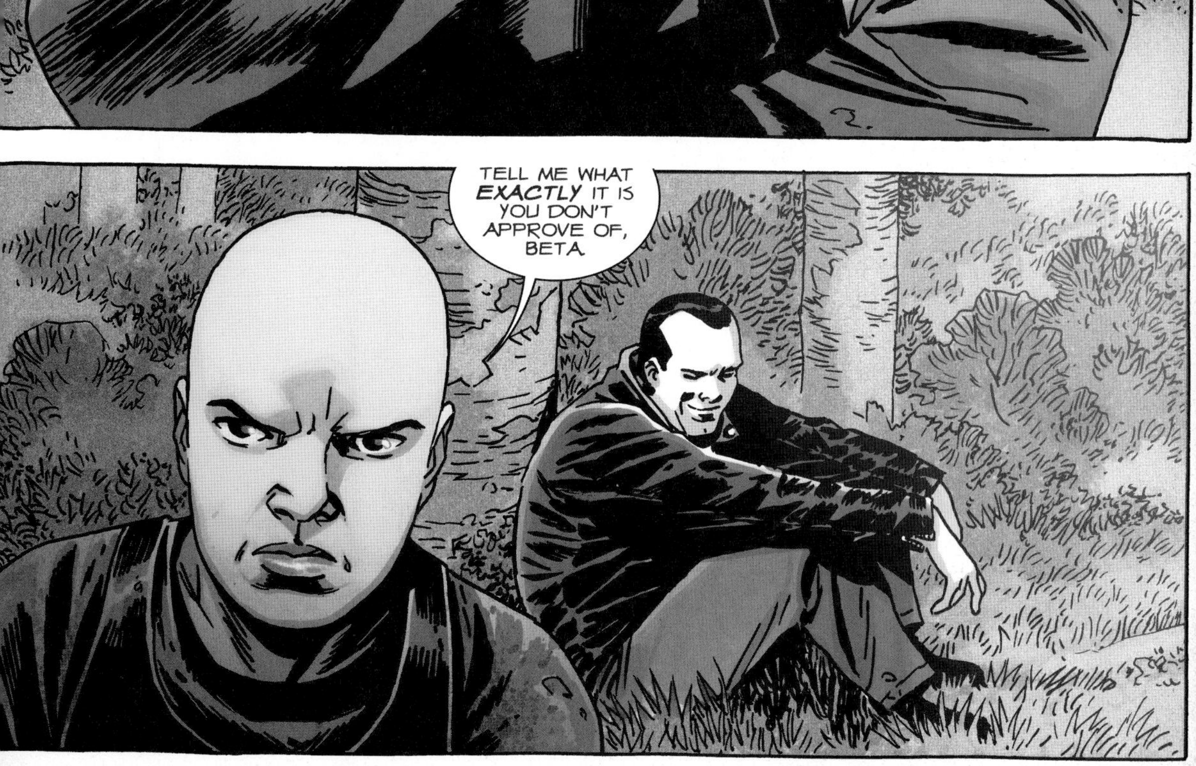
TELL ME WHAT EXACTLY IT IS YOU DON'T APPROVE OF, BETA.

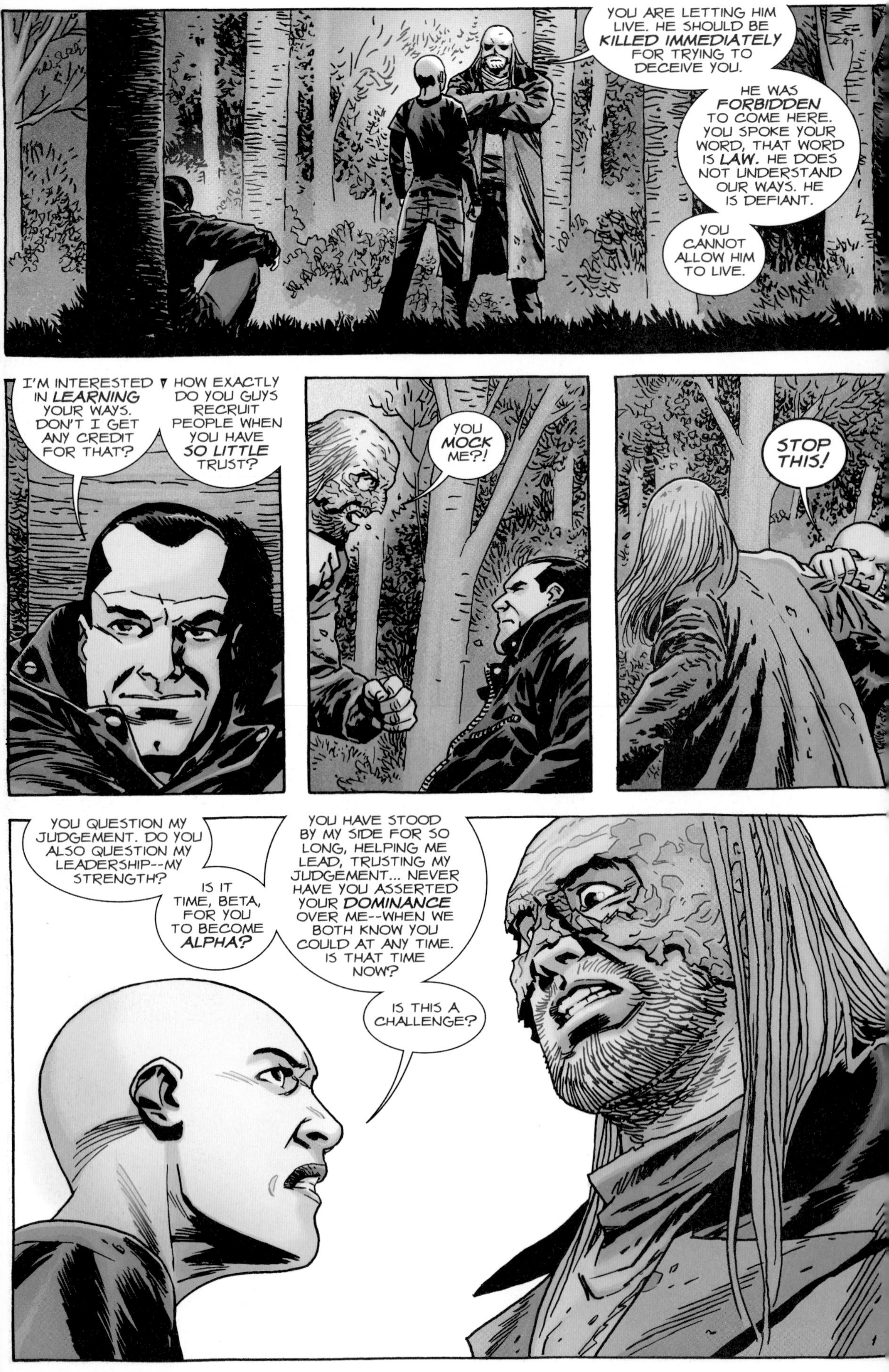
YOU ARE LETTING HIM LIVE. HE SHOULD BE KILLED IMMEDIATELY FOR TRYING TO DECEIVE YOU.
HE WAS FORBIDDEN TO COME HERE. YOU SPOKE YOUR WORD, THAT WORD IS LAW. HE DOES NOT UNDERSTAND OUR WAYS. HE IS DEFIANT.
YOU CANNOT ALLOW HIM TO LIVE.
I'M INTERESTED IN LEARNING YOUR WAYS. DON'T I GET ANY CREDIT FOR THAT?
HOW EXACTLY DO YOU GUYS RECRUIT PEOPLE WHEN YOU HAVE SO LITTLE TRUST?
YOU MOCK ME?!
STOP THIS!
YOU QUESTION MY JUDGEMENT. DO YOU ALSO QUESTION MY LEADERSHIP--MY STRENGTH?
IS IT TIME, BETA, FOR YOU TO BECOME ALPHA?
YOU HAVE STOOD BY MY SIDE FOR SO LONG, HELPING ME LEAD, TRUSTING MY JUDGEMENT... NEVER HAVE YOU ASSERTED YOUR DOMINANCE OVER ME--WHEN WE BOTH KNOW YOU COULD AT ANY TIME. IS THAT TIME NOW?
IS THIS A CHALLENGE?

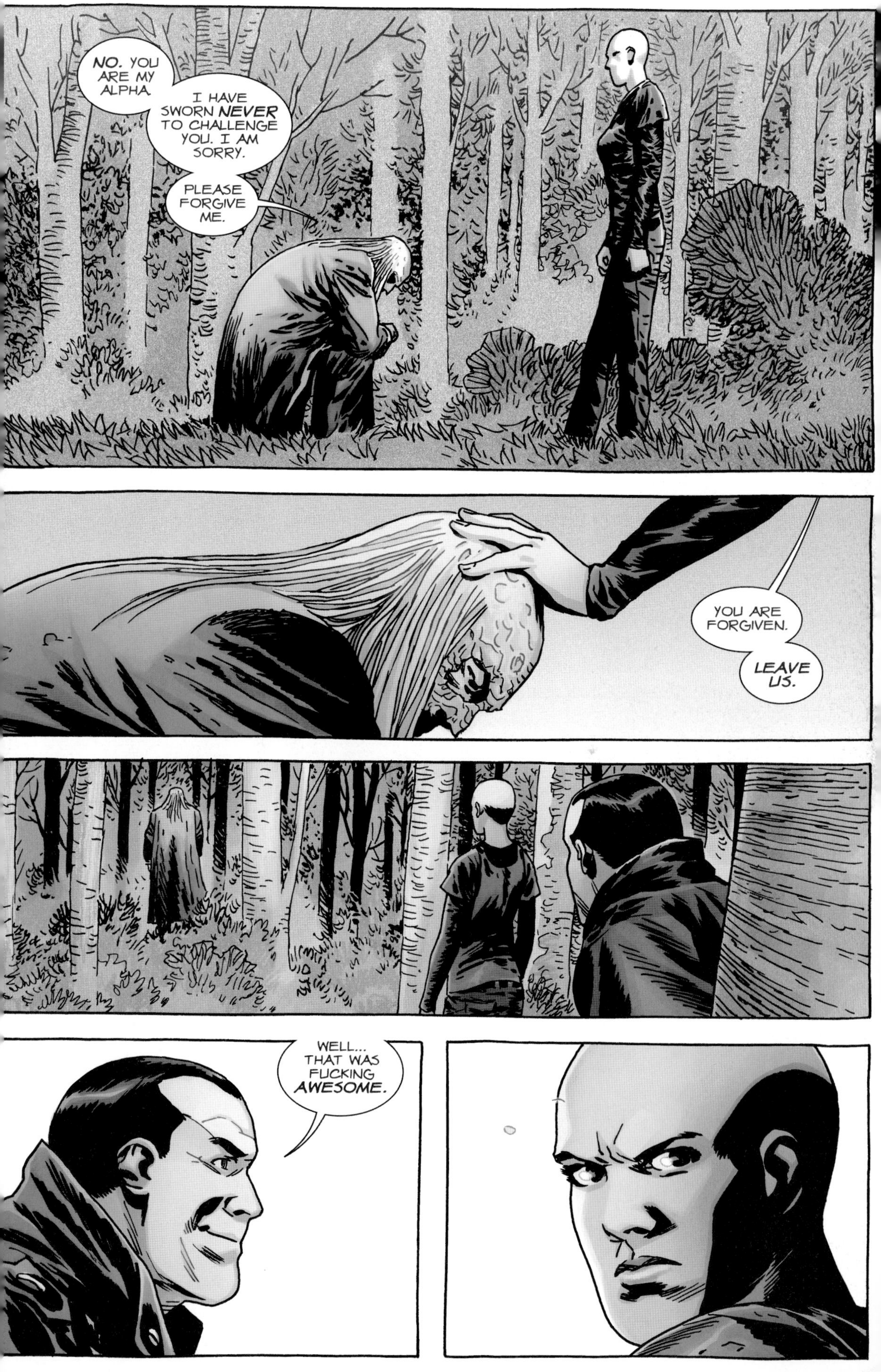
NO. YOU ARE MY ALPHA.
I HAVE SWORN NEVER TO CHALLENGE YOU. I AM SORRY.
PLEASE FORGIVE ME.
YOU ARE FORGIVEN.
LEAVE US.
WELL... THAT WAS FUCKING AWESOME.

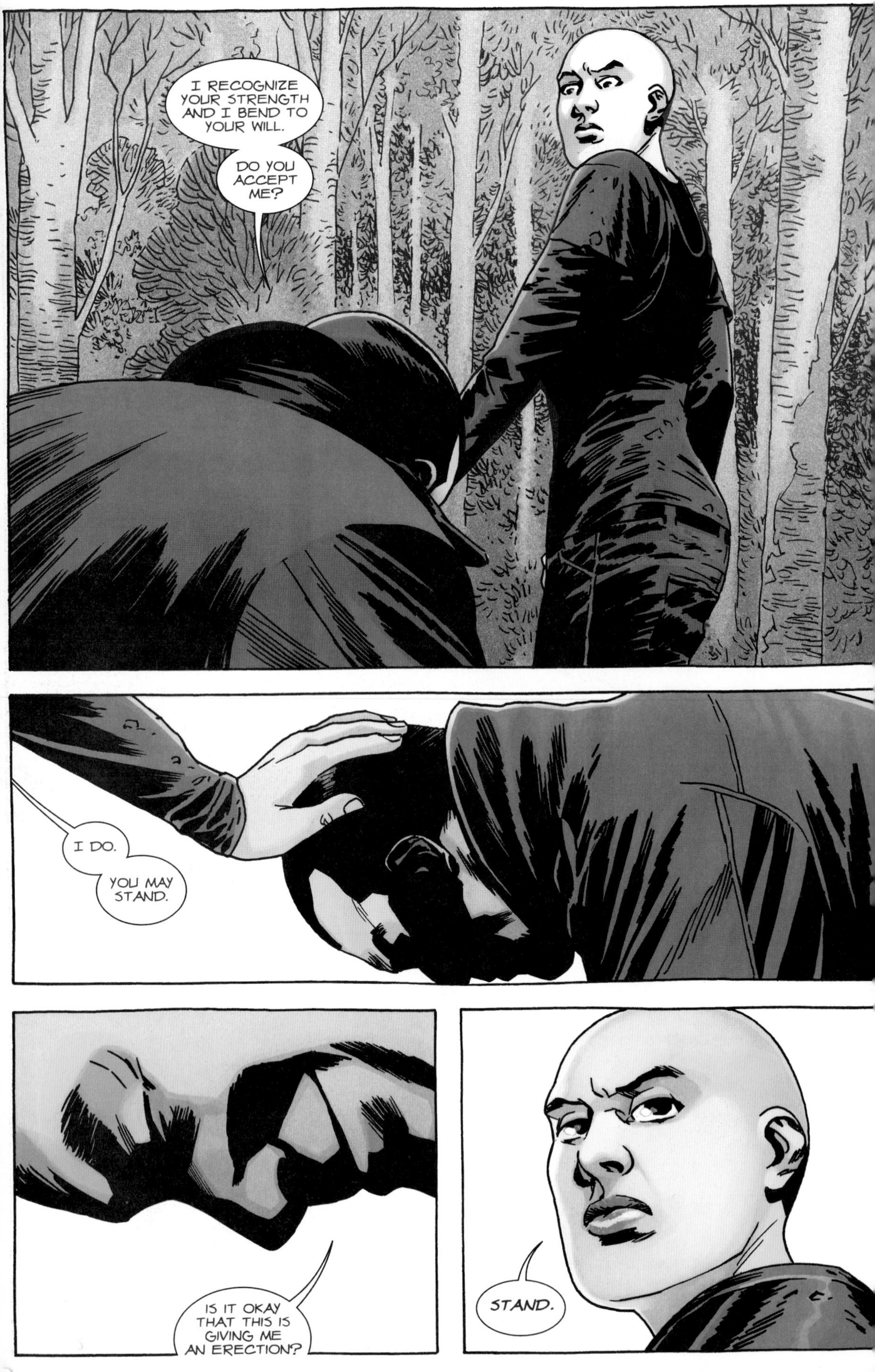
I RECOGNIZE YOUR STRENGTH AND I BEND TO YOUR WILL.
DO YOU ACCEPT ME?
I DO.
YOU MAY STAND.
IS IT OKAY THAT THIS IS GIVING ME AN ERECTION?
STAND.

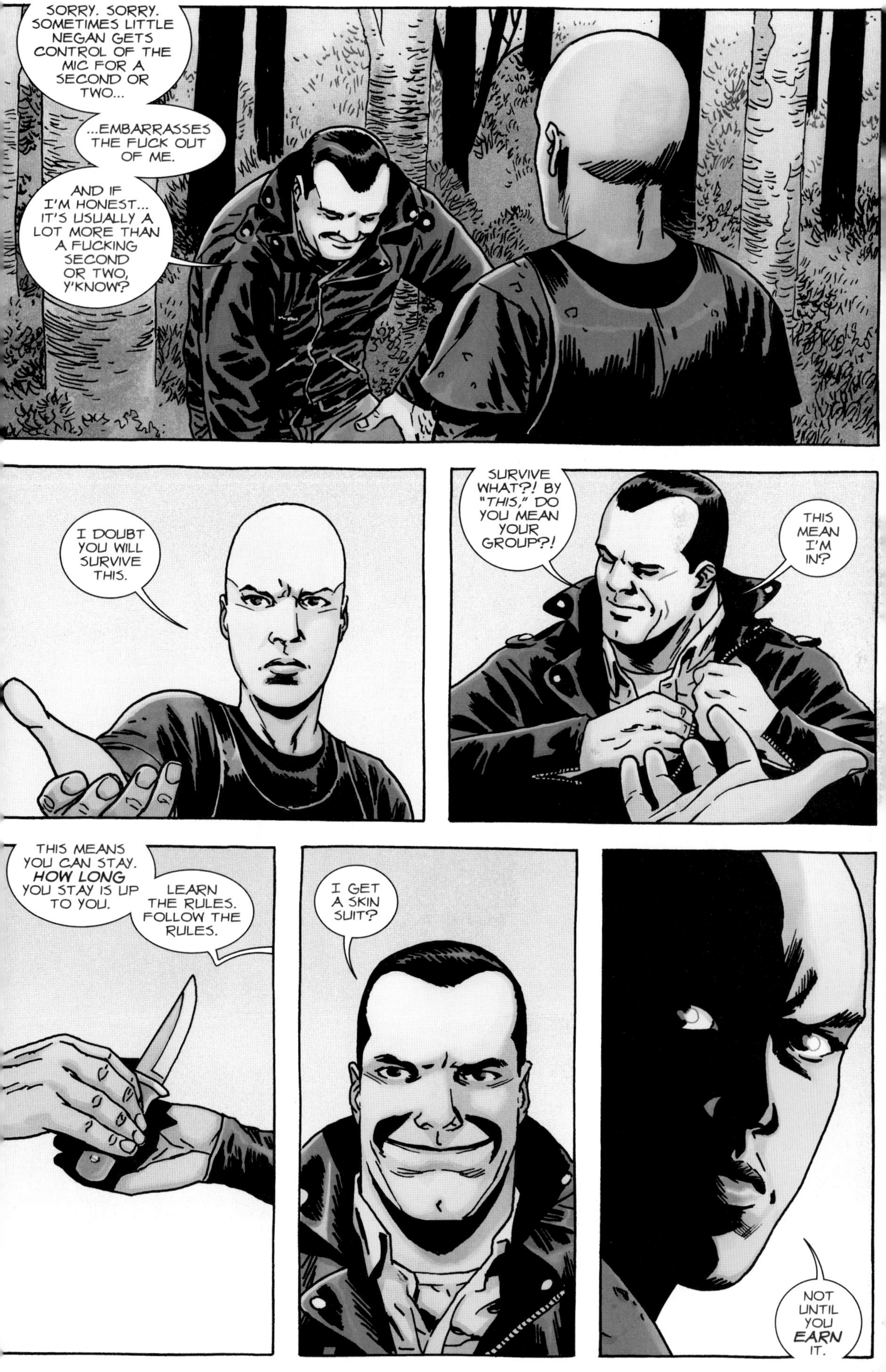
SORRY. SORRY. SOMETIMES LITTLE NEGAN GETS CONTROL OF THE MIC FOR A SECOND OR TWO...
...EMBARRASSES THE FUCK OUT OF ME.
AND IF I'M HONEST... IT'S USUALLY A LOT MORE THAN A FUCKING SECOND OR TWO, Y'KNOW?
I DOUBT YOU WILL SURVIVE THIS.
SURVIVE WHAT?! BY "THIS," DO YOU MEAN YOUR GROUP?!
THIS MEAN I'M IN?
THIS MEANS YOU CAN STAY. HOW LONG YOU STAY IS UP TO YOU.
LEARN THE RULES. FOLLOW THE RULES.
I GET A SKIN SUIT?
NOT UNTIL YOU EARN IT.

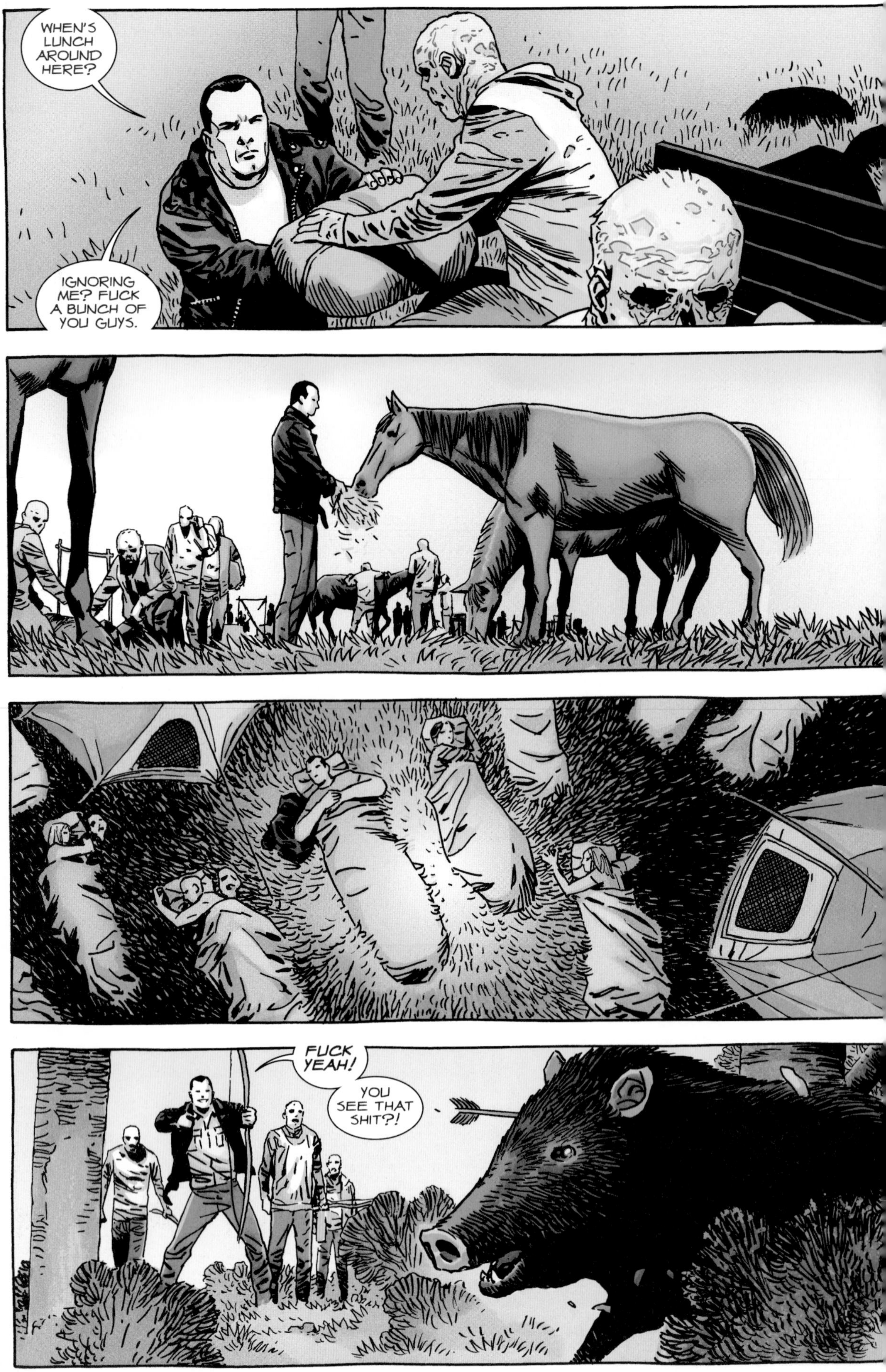
WHEN'S LUNCH AROUND HERE?
IGNORING ME? FUCK A BUNCH OF YOU GUYS.
FUCK YEAH!
YOU SEE THAT SHIT?!

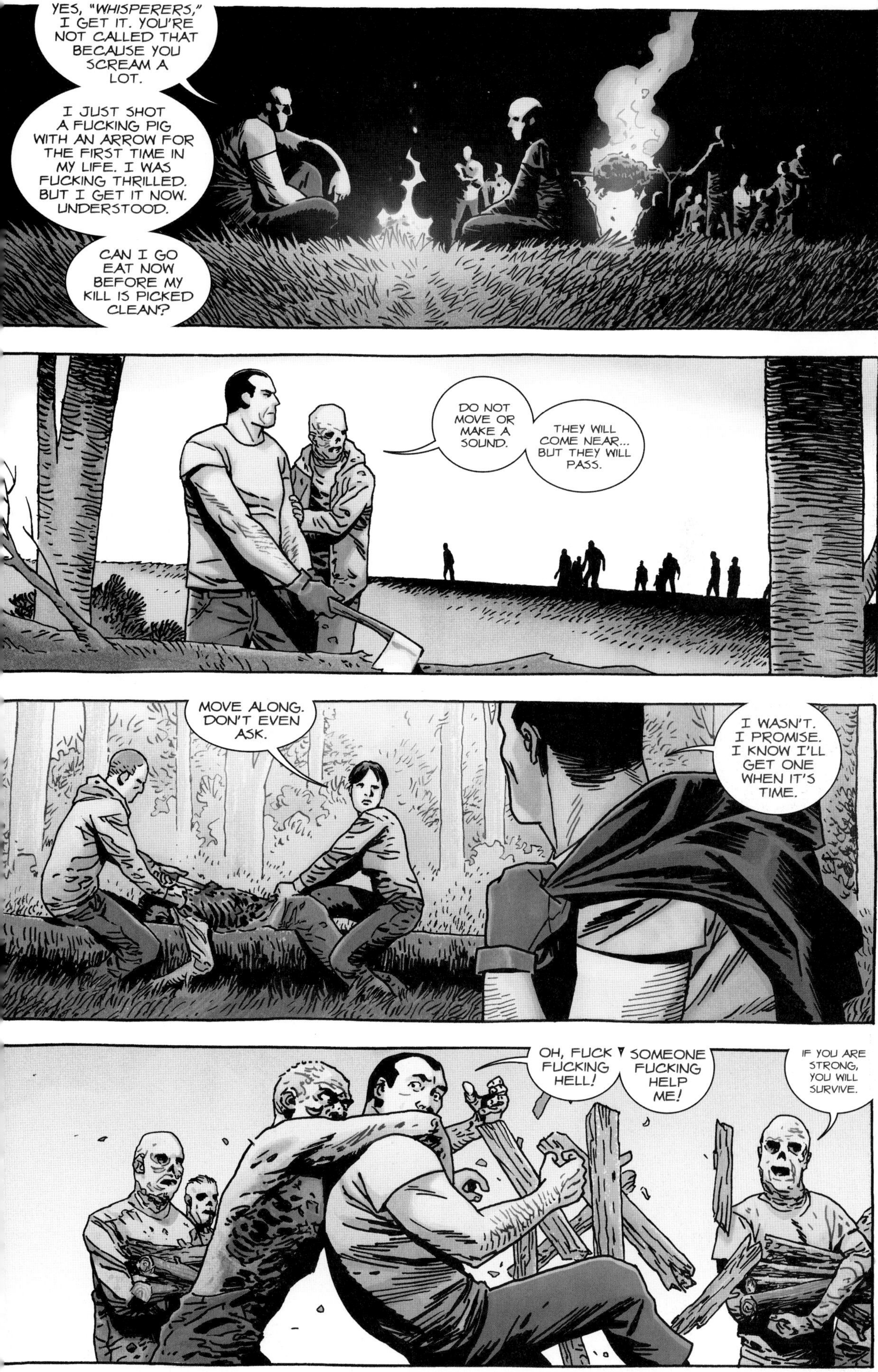
YES, "WHISPERERS," I GET IT. YOU'RE NOT CALLED THAT BECAUSE YOU SCREAM A LOT.
I JUST SHOT A FUCKING PIG WITH AN ARROW FOR THE FIRST TIME IN MY LIFE. I WAS FUCKING THRILLED. BUT I GET IT NOW. UNDERSTOOD.
CAN I GO EAT NOW BEFORE MY KILL IS PICKED CLEAN?
DO NOT MOVE OR MAKE A SOUND.
THEY WILL COME NEAR... BUT THEY WILL PASS.
MOVE ALONG. DON'T EVEN ASK.
I WASN'T. I PROMISE. I KNOW I'LL GET ONE WHEN IT'S TIME.
OH, FUCK FUCKING HELL!
SOMEONE FUCKING HELP ME!
IF YOU ARE STRONG, YOU WILL SURVIVE.

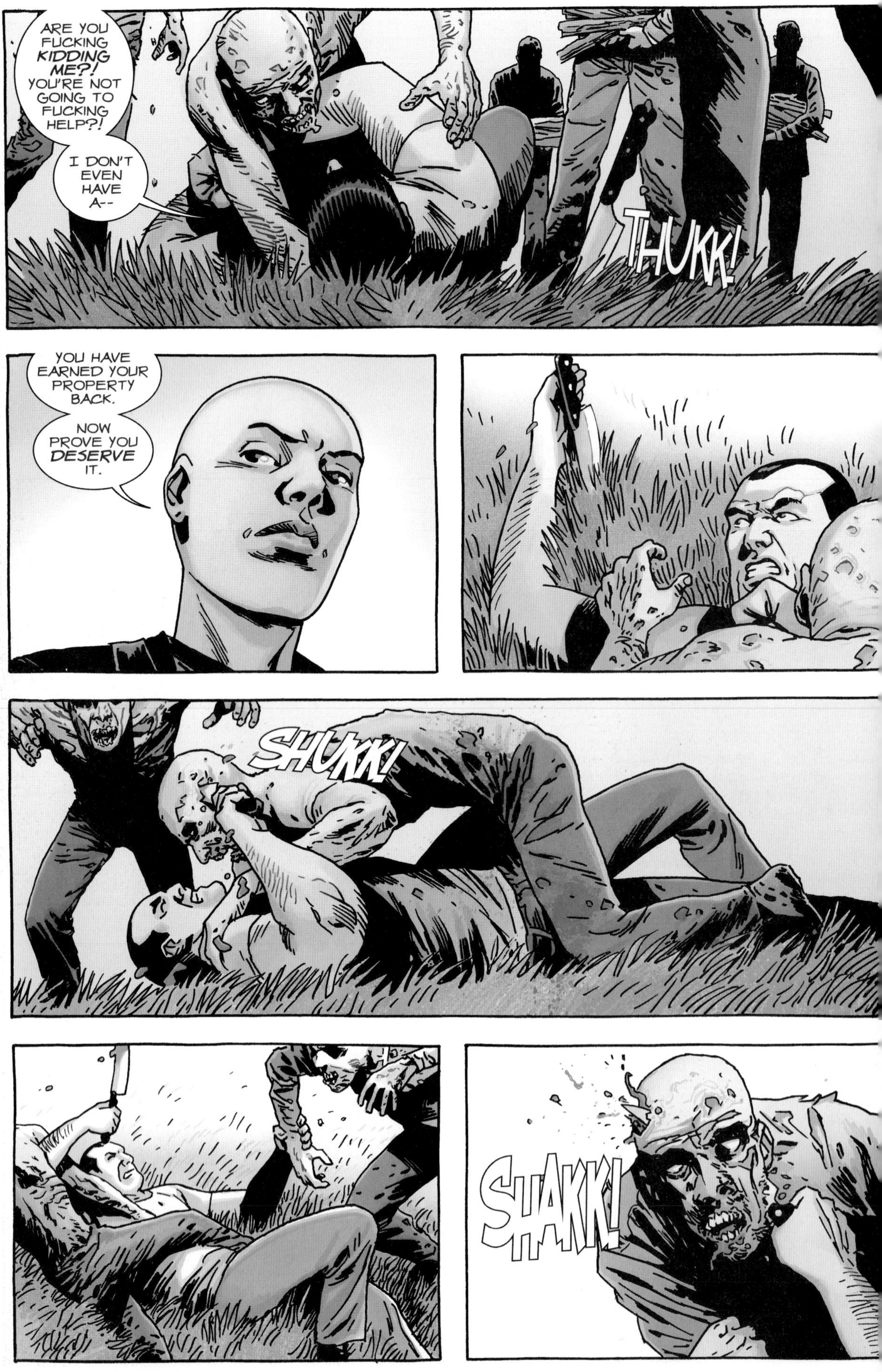
ARE YOU FUCKING KIDDING ME?! YOU'RE NOT GOING TO FUCKING HELP?!
I DON'T EVEN HAVE A--
THUKK!
YOU HAVE EARNED YOUR PROPERTY BACK.
NOW PROVE YOU DESERVE IT.
SHUKK!
SHAKK!

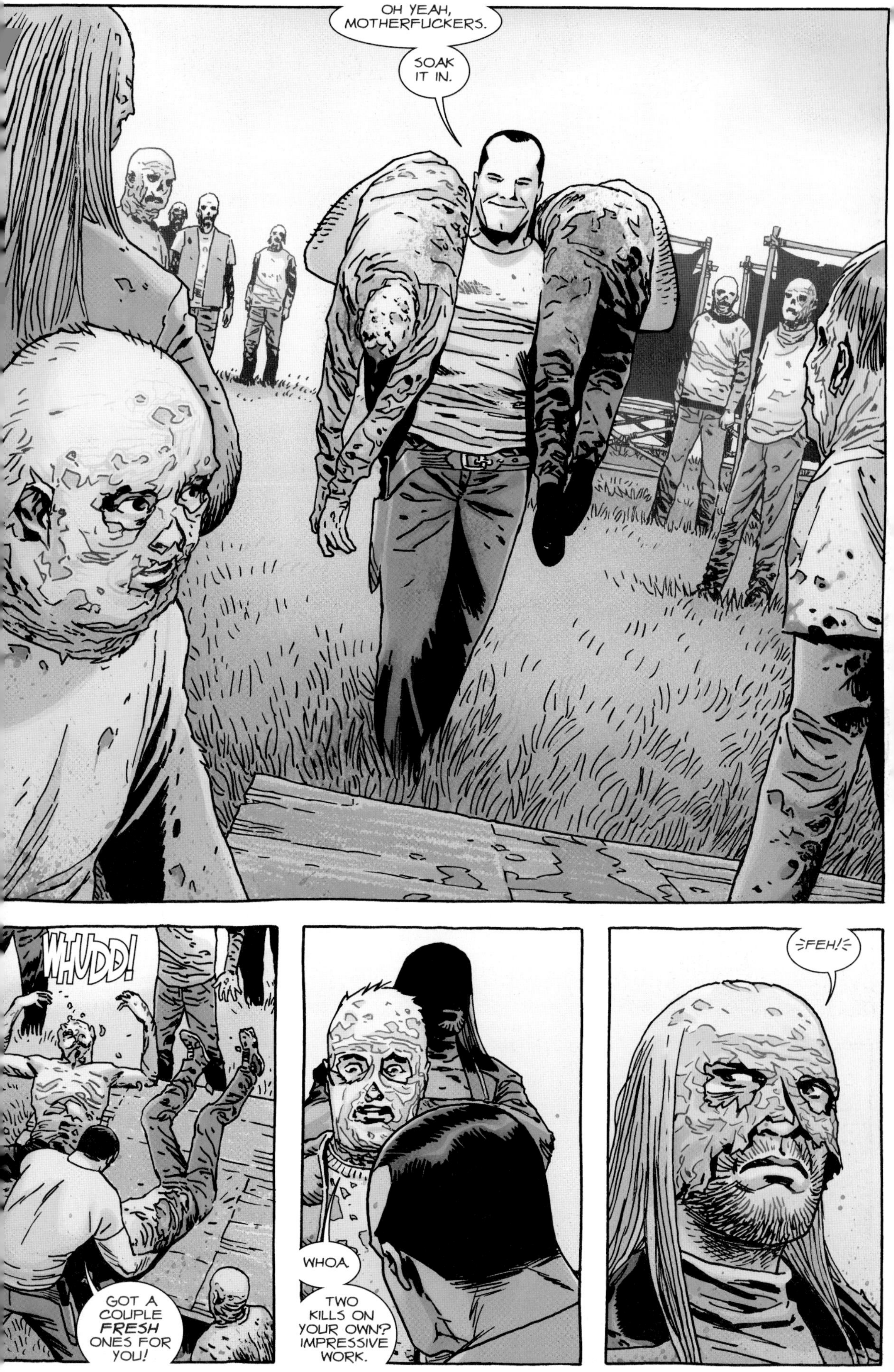
OH YEAH, MOTHERFUCKERS.
SOAK IT IN.
WHUDD!
GOT A COUPLE *FRESH* ONES FOR YOU!
WHOA.
TWO KILLS ON YOUR OWN? IMPRESSIVE WORK.
FEH!

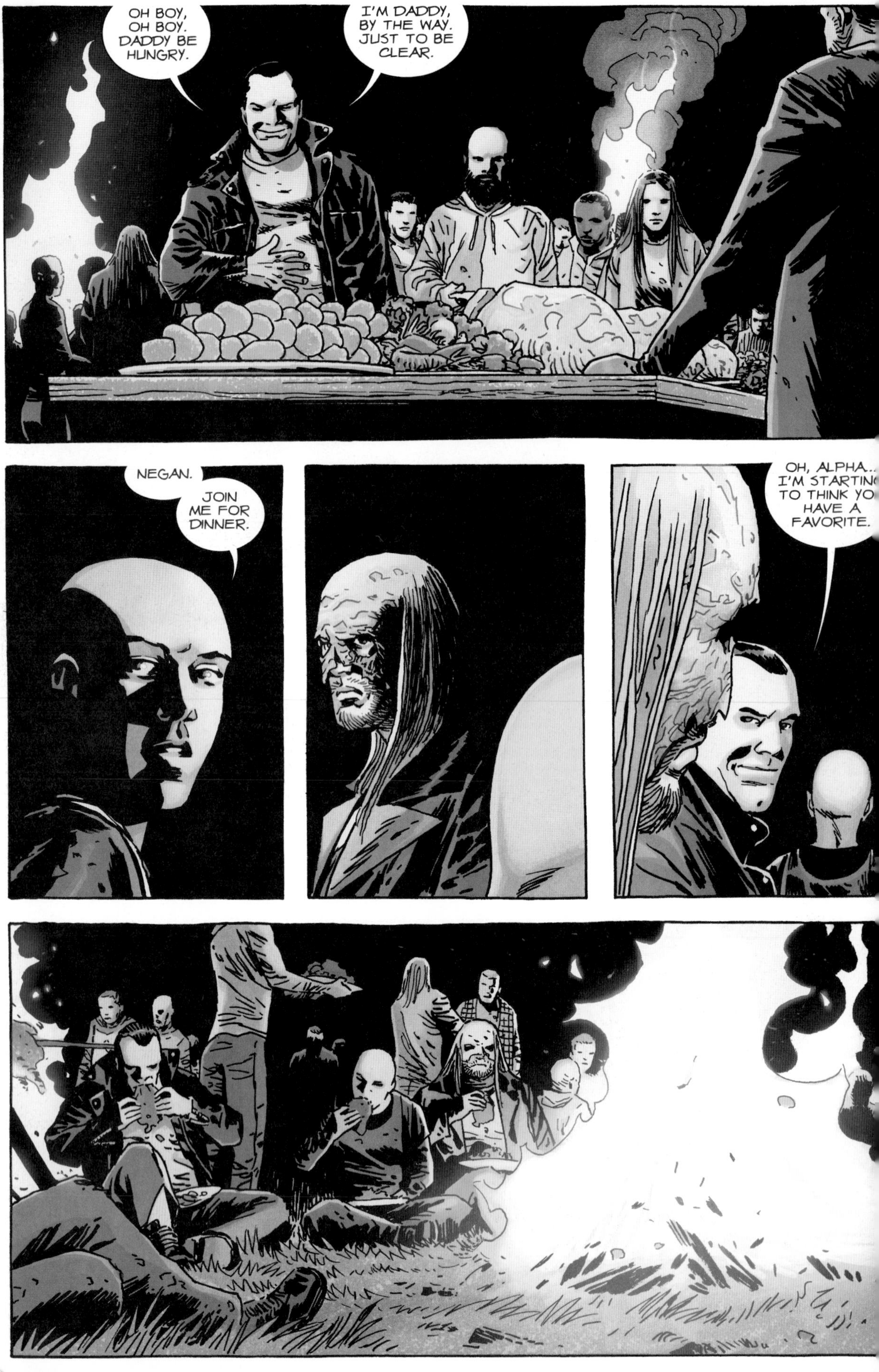
OH BOY, OH BOY. DADDY BE HUNGRY.
I'M DADDY, BY THE WAY. JUST TO BE CLEAR.
NEGAN.
JOIN ME FOR DINNER.
OH, ALPHA.. I'M STARTIN TO THINK YO HAVE A FAVORITE.

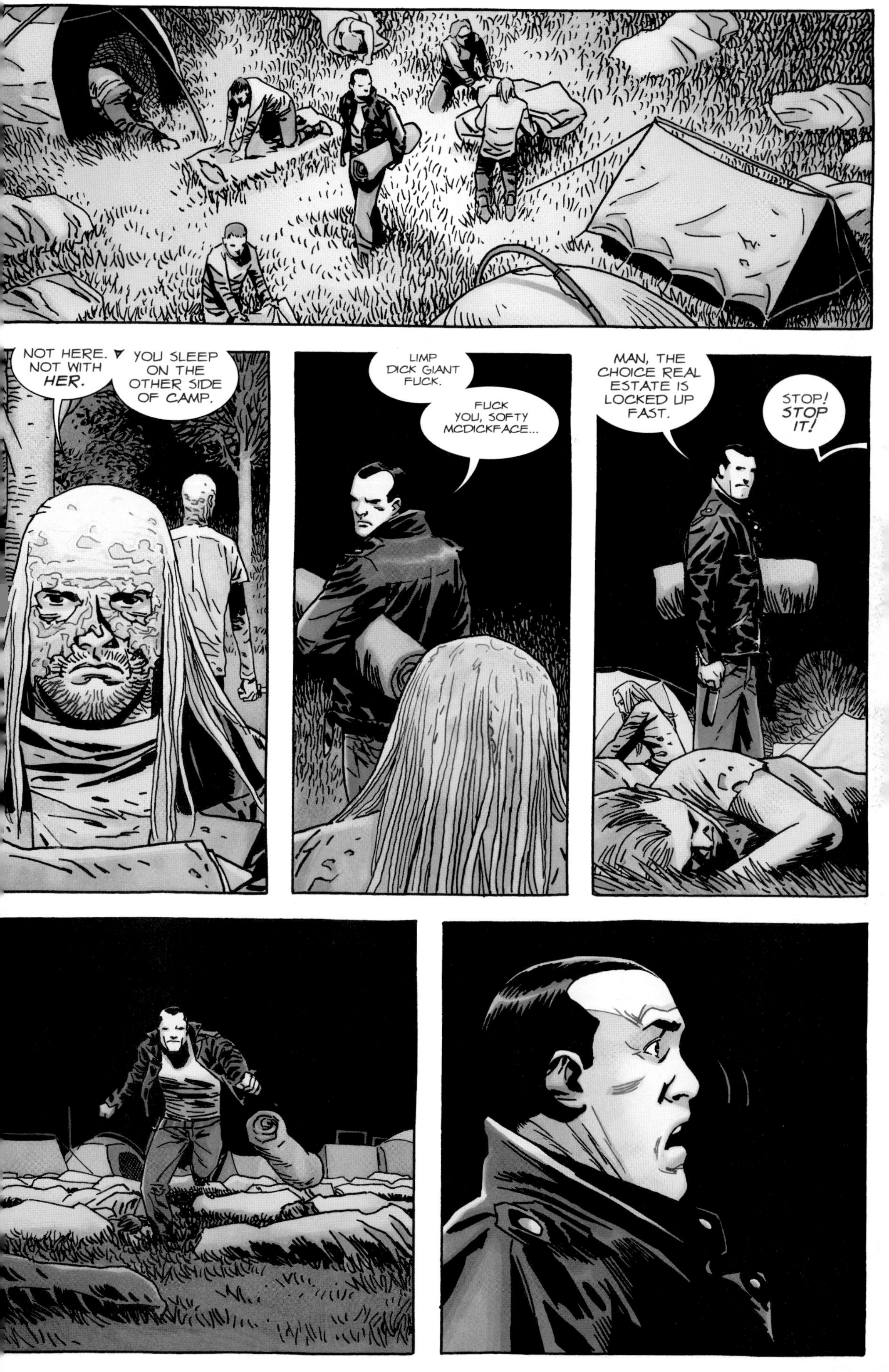
NOT HERE. NOT WITH HER.
YOU SLEEP ON THE OTHER SIDE OF CAMP.
LIMP DICK GIANT FUCK.
FUCK YOU, SOFTY MCDICKFACE...
MAN, THE CHOICE REAL ESTATE IS LOCKED UP FAST.
STOP! STOP IT!

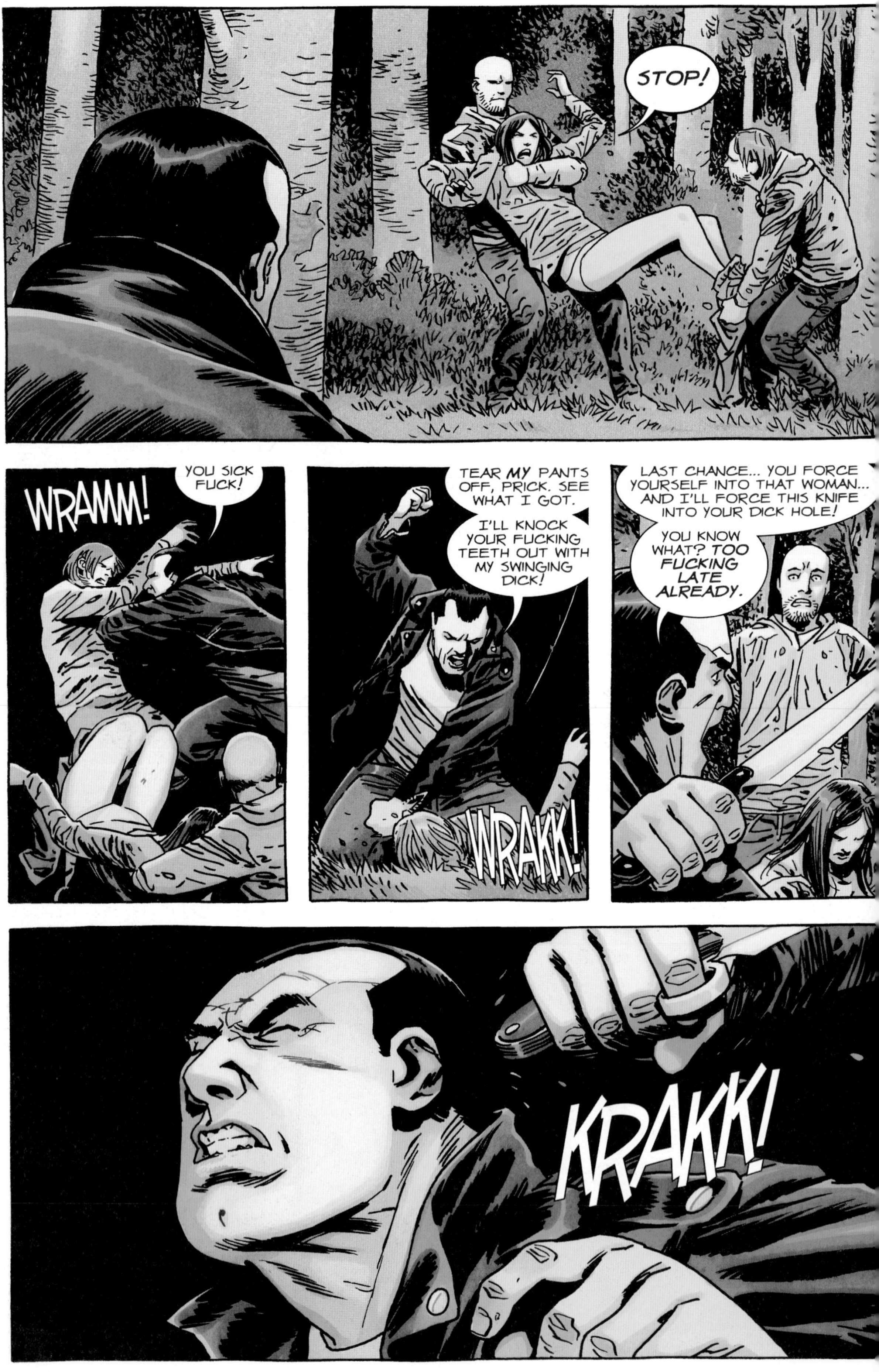
STOP!
WRAMM!
YOU SICK FUCK!
TEAR MY PANTS OFF, PRICK. SEE WHAT I GOT.
I'LL KNOCK YOUR FUCKING TEETH OUT WITH MY SWINGING DICK!
WRAKK!
LAST CHANCE... YOU FORCE YOURSELF INTO THAT WOMAN... AND I'LL FORCE THIS KNIFE INTO YOUR DICK HOLE!
YOU KNOW WHAT? TOO FUCKING LATE ALREADY.
KRAKK!

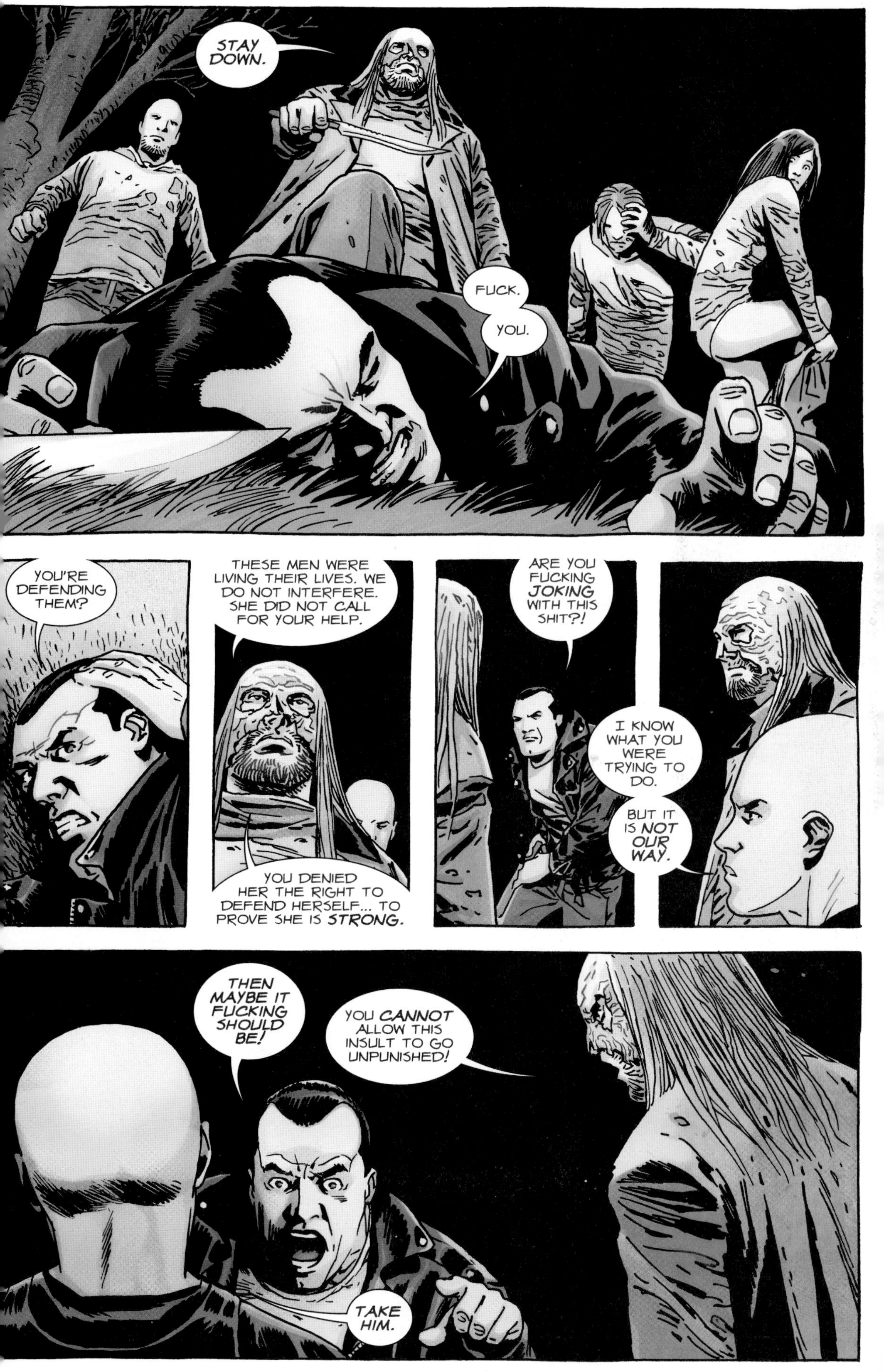
STAY DOWN.
FUCK.
YOU.
YOU'RE DEFENDING THEM?
THESE MEN WERE LIVING THEIR LIVES. WE DO NOT INTERFERE. SHE DID NOT CALL FOR YOUR HELP.
YOU DENIED HER THE RIGHT TO DEFEND HERSELF... TO PROVE SHE IS STRONG.
ARE YOU FUCKING JOKING WITH THIS SHIT?!
I KNOW WHAT YOU WERE TRYING TO DO.
BUT IT IS NOT OUR WAY.
THEN MAYBE IT FUCKING SHOULD BE!
YOU CANNOT ALLOW THIS INSULT TO GO UNPUNISHED!
TAKE HIM.

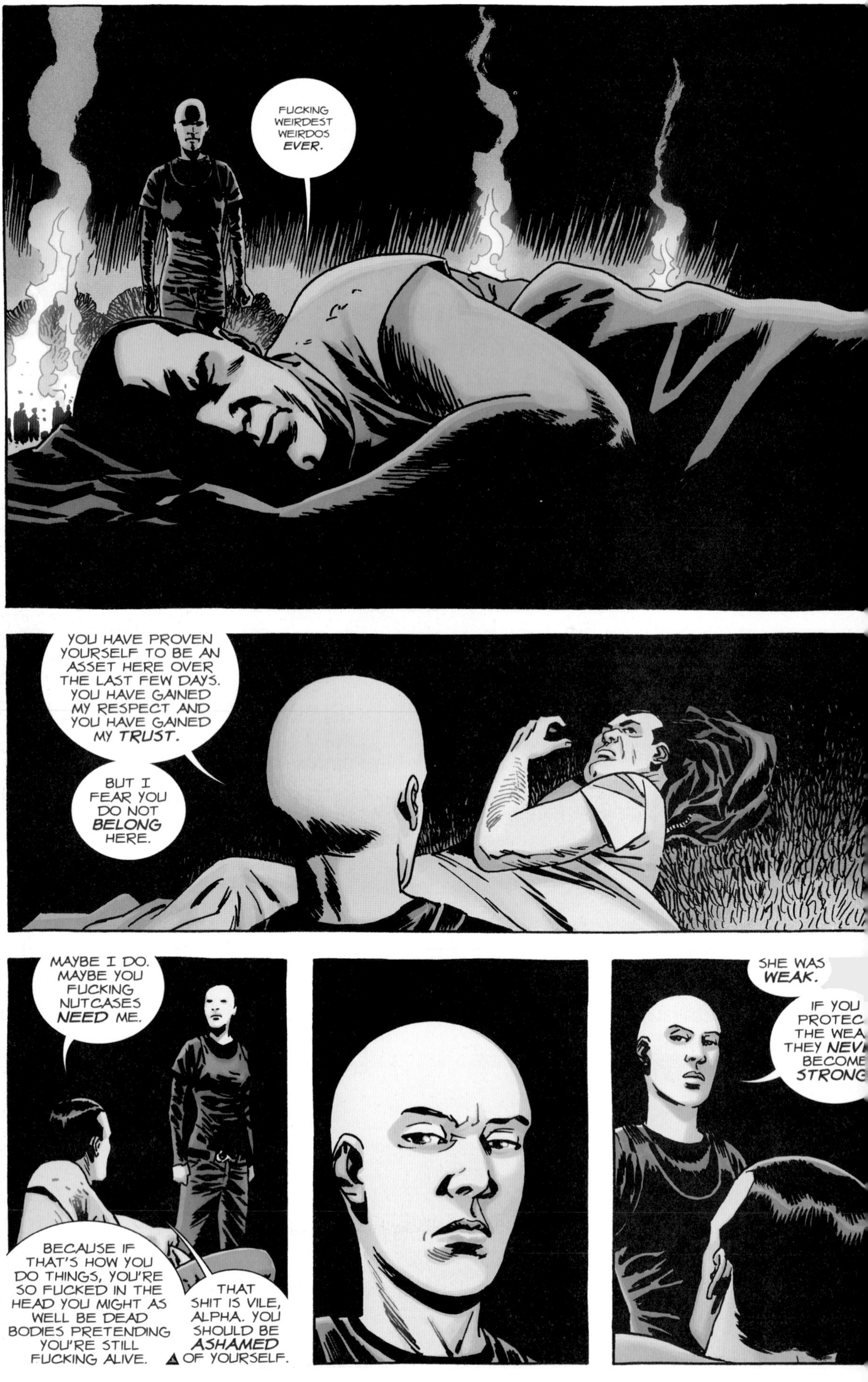
FUCKING WEIRDEST WEIRDOS EVER.
YOU HAVE PROVEN YOURSELF TO BE AN ASSET HERE OVER THE LAST FEW DAYS. YOU HAVE GAINED MY RESPECT AND YOU HAVE GAINED MY TRUST.
BUT I FEAR YOU DO NOT BELONG HERE.
MAYBE I DO. MAYBE YOU FUCKING NUTCASES NEED ME.
BECAUSE IF THAT'S HOW YOU DO THINGS, YOU'RE SO FUCKED IN THE HEAD YOU MIGHT AS WELL BE DEAD BODIES PRETENDING YOU'RE STILL FUCKING ALIVE.
THAT SHIT IS VILE, ALPHA. YOU SHOULD BE ASHAMED OF YOURSELF.
SHE WAS WEAK.
IF YOU PROTEC THE WEA THEY NEV BECOME STRONG

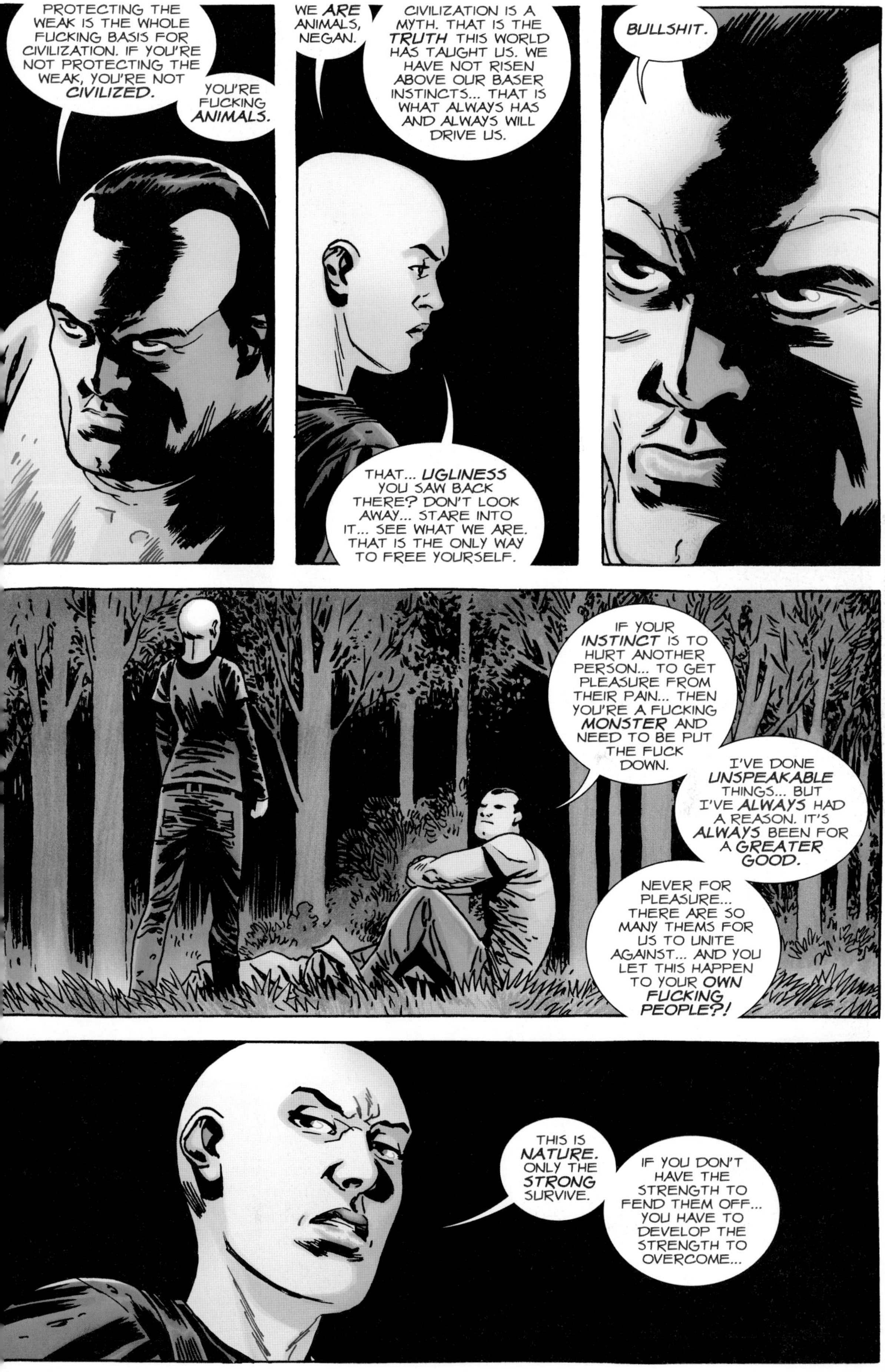
PROTECTING THE WEAK IS THE WHOLE FUCKING BASIS FOR CIVILIZATION. IF YOU'RE NOT PROTECTING THE WEAK, YOU'RE NOT CIVILIZED.
YOU'RE FUCKING ANIMALS.
WE ARE ANIMALS, NEGAN.
CIVILIZATION IS A MYTH. THAT IS THE TRUTH THIS WORLD HAS TAUGHT US. WE HAVE NOT RISEN ABOVE OUR BASER INSTINCTS... THAT IS WHAT ALWAYS HAS AND ALWAYS WILL DRIVE US.
THAT... UGLINESS YOU SAW BACK THERE? DON'T LOOK AWAY... STARE INTO IT... SEE WHAT WE ARE. THAT IS THE ONLY WAY TO FREE YOURSELF.
BULLSHIT.
IF YOUR INSTINCT IS TO HURT ANOTHER PERSON... TO GET PLEASURE FROM THEIR PAIN... THEN YOU'RE A FUCKING MONSTER AND NEED TO BE PUT THE FUCK DOWN.
I'VE DONE UNSPEAKABLE THINGS... BUT I'VE ALWAYS HAD A REASON. IT'S ALWAYS BEEN FOR A GREATER GOOD.
NEVER FOR PLEASURE... THERE ARE SO MANY THEMS FOR US TO UNITE AGAINST... AND YOU LET THIS HAPPEN TO YOUR OWN FUCKING PEOPLE?!
THIS IS NATURE. ONLY THE STRONG SURVIVE.
IF YOU DON'T HAVE THE STRENGTH TO FEND THEM OFF... YOU HAVE TO DEVELOP THE STRENGTH TO OVERCOME...

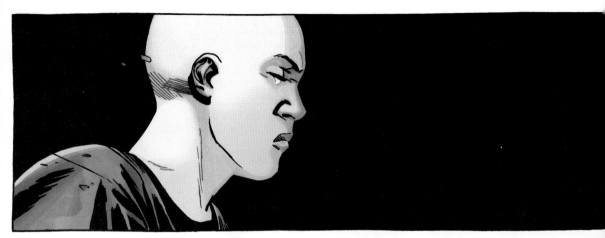

YOU ARE PUNISHED... YOU SLEEP ON YOUR OWN OUT HERE... WITH NO PROTECTION. YOU WON'T BE SEEN OR HEARD OUT HERE IN THE DARK.

IF YOU ARE STRONG... WE WILL SPEAK TOMORROW.

GET BACK HERE AND SIT THE FUCK DOWN.

TALK TO ME.

THERE IS NOTHING MORE TO TALK ABOUT.

I'M NOT THE THINNEST DICK AT THE ORGY. I SEE HOW THINGS WORK HERE. YOU'RE ALPHA UNTIL YOU'RE NOT. YOU SHOW WEAKNESS... IT'S OVER.

I DON'T WANT TO BE ALPHA... YOU DON'T HAVE TO WORRY ABOUT THAT.

I'M NEGAN... THAT'S BETTER.

YOU HAVE BETA PROTECTING YOU... IN TIME, I THINK YOU'LL SEE YOU HAVE ME PROTECTING YOU, TOO.

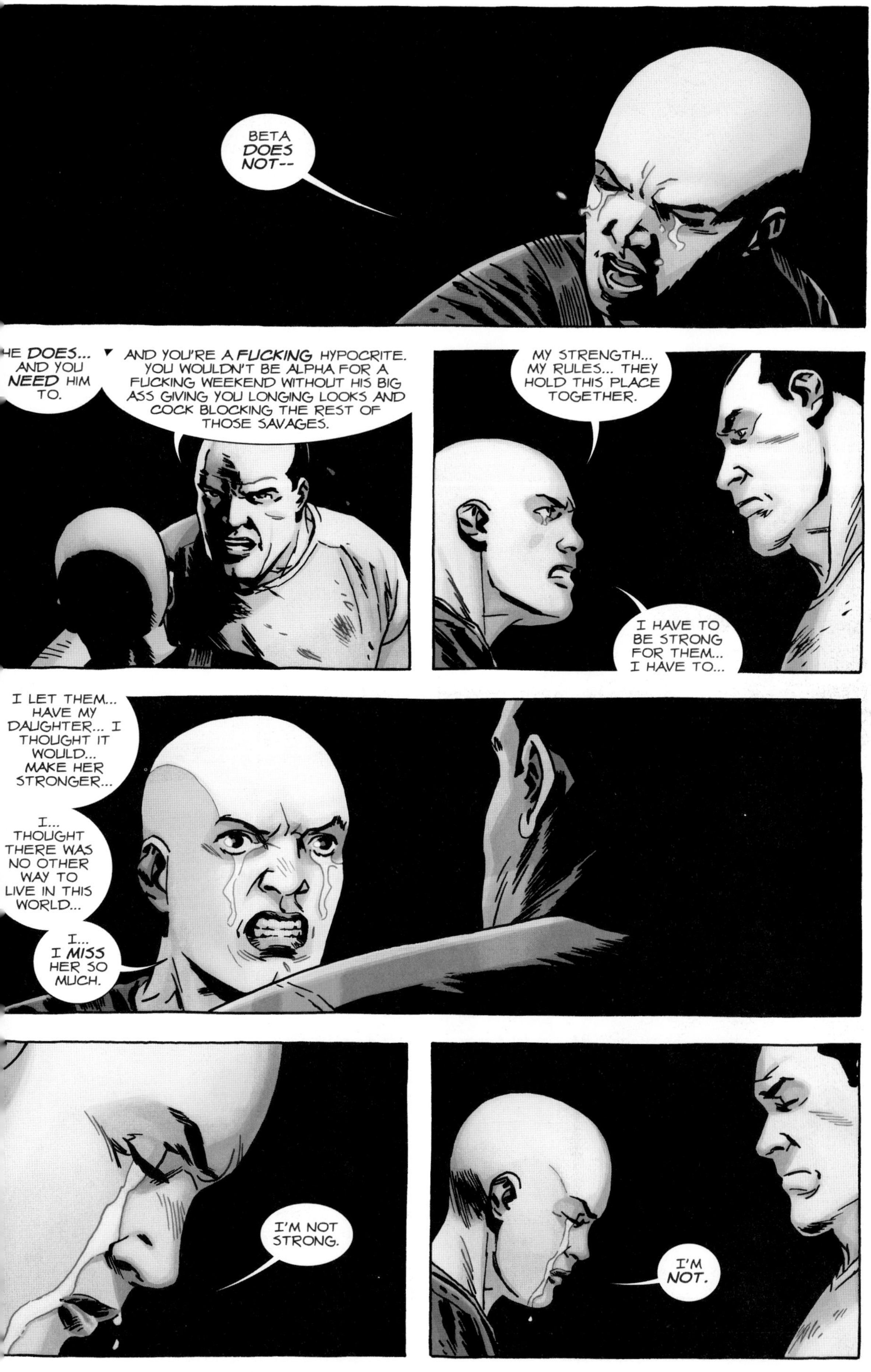
BETA DOES NOT--
HE DOES... AND YOU NEED HIM TO.
AND YOU'RE A FUCKING HYPOCRITE. YOU WOULDN'T BE ALPHA FOR A FUCKING WEEKEND WITHOUT HIS BIG ASS GIVING YOU LONGING LOOKS AND COCK BLOCKING THE REST OF THOSE SAVAGES.
MY STRENGTH... MY RULES... THEY HOLD THIS PLACE TOGETHER.
I HAVE TO BE STRONG FOR THEM... I HAVE TO...
I LET THEM... HAVE MY DAUGHTER... I THOUGHT IT WOULD... MAKE HER STRONGER...
I... THOUGHT THERE WAS NO OTHER WAY TO LIVE IN THIS WORLD...
I... I MISS HER SO MUCH.
I'M NOT STRONG.
I'M NOT.

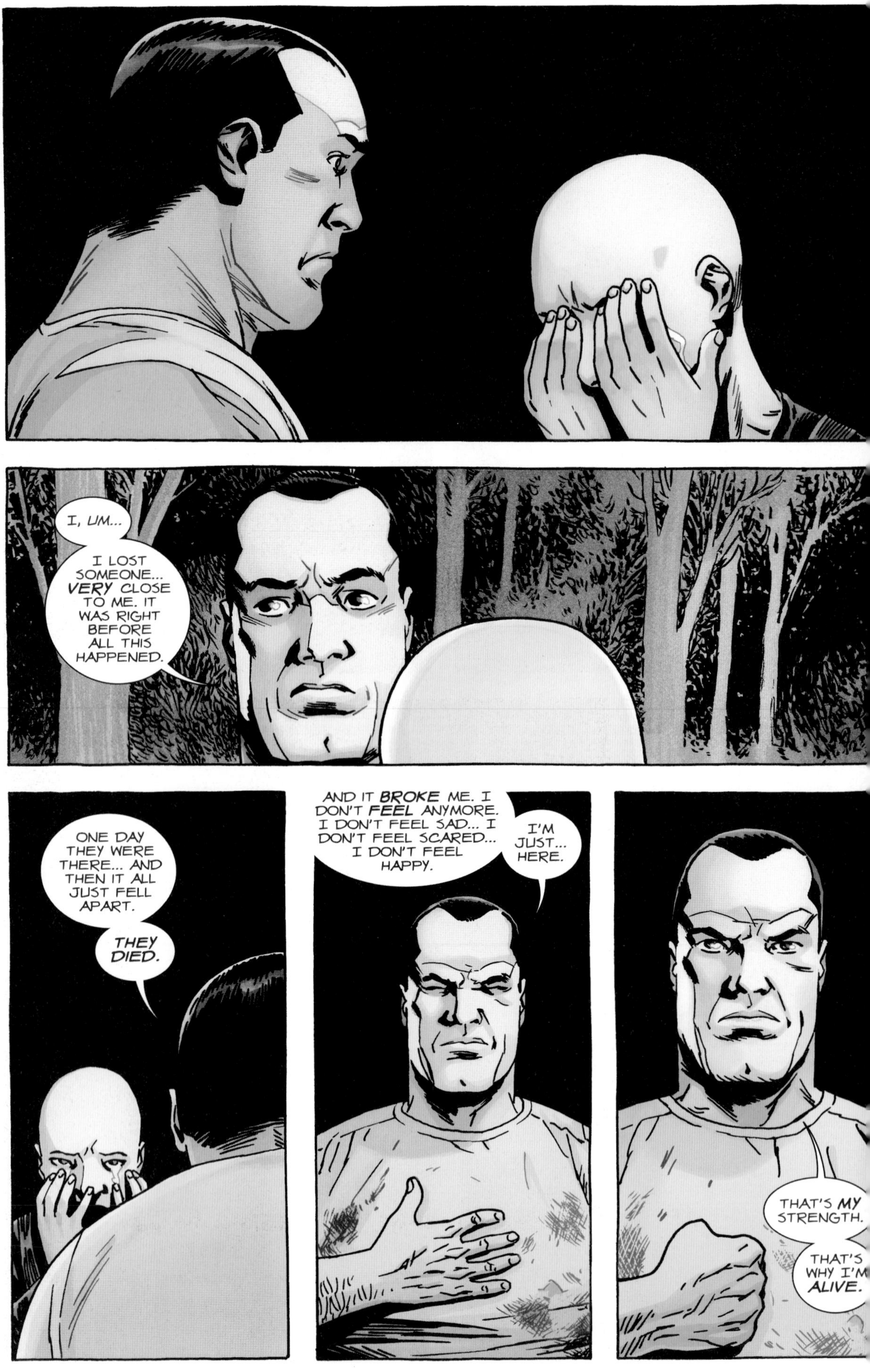

I, UM...
I LOST SOMEONE... VERY CLOSE TO ME. IT WAS RIGHT BEFORE ALL THIS HAPPENED.
ONE DAY THEY WERE THERE... AND THEN IT ALL JUST FELL APART.
THEY DIED.
AND IT BROKE ME. I DON'T FEEL ANYMORE. I DON'T FEEL SAD... I DON'T FEEL SCARED... I DON'T FEEL HAPPY.
I'M JUST... HERE.
THAT'S MY STRENGTH.
THAT'S WHY I'M ALIVE.

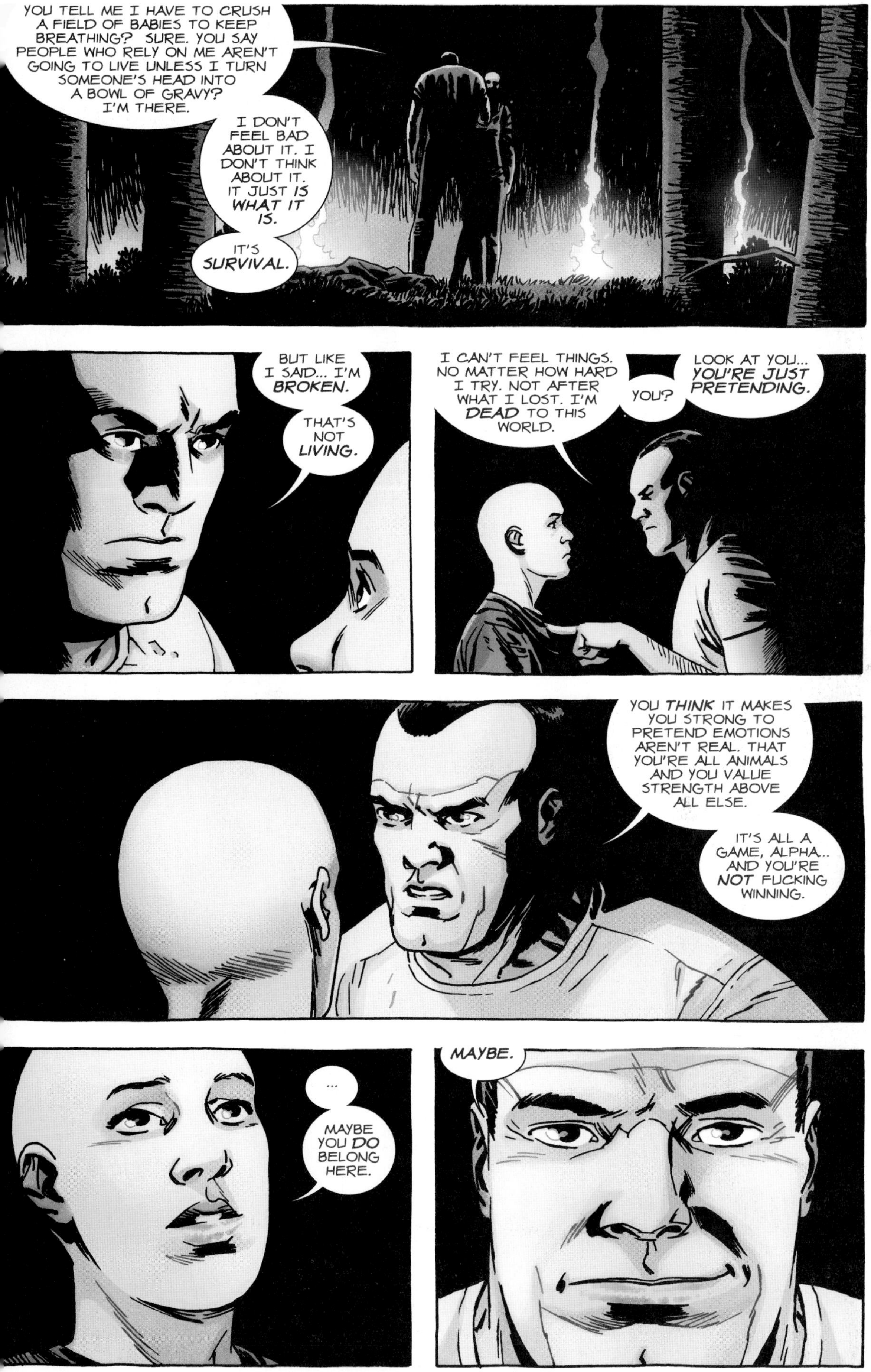
YOU TELL ME I HAVE TO CRUSH A FIELD OF BABIES TO KEEP BREATHING? SURE. YOU SAY PEOPLE WHO RELY ON ME AREN'T GOING TO LIVE UNLESS I TURN SOMEONE'S HEAD INTO A BOWL OF GRAVY? I'M THERE.
I DON'T FEEL BAD ABOUT IT. I DON'T THINK ABOUT IT. IT JUST IS WHAT IT IS.
IT'S SURVIVAL.
BUT LIKE I SAID... I'M BROKEN.
THAT'S NOT LIVING.
I CAN'T FEEL THINGS. NO MATTER HOW HARD I TRY. NOT AFTER WHAT I LOST. I'M DEAD TO THIS WORLD.
YOU?
LOOK AT YOU... YOU'RE JUST PRETENDING.
YOU THINK IT MAKES YOU STRONG TO PRETEND EMOTIONS AREN'T REAL. THAT YOU'RE ALL ANIMALS AND YOU VALUE STRENGTH ABOVE ALL ELSE.
IT'S ALL A GAME, ALPHA.. AND YOU'RE NOT FUCKING WINNING.
...
MAYBE YOU DO BELONG HERE.
MAYBE.

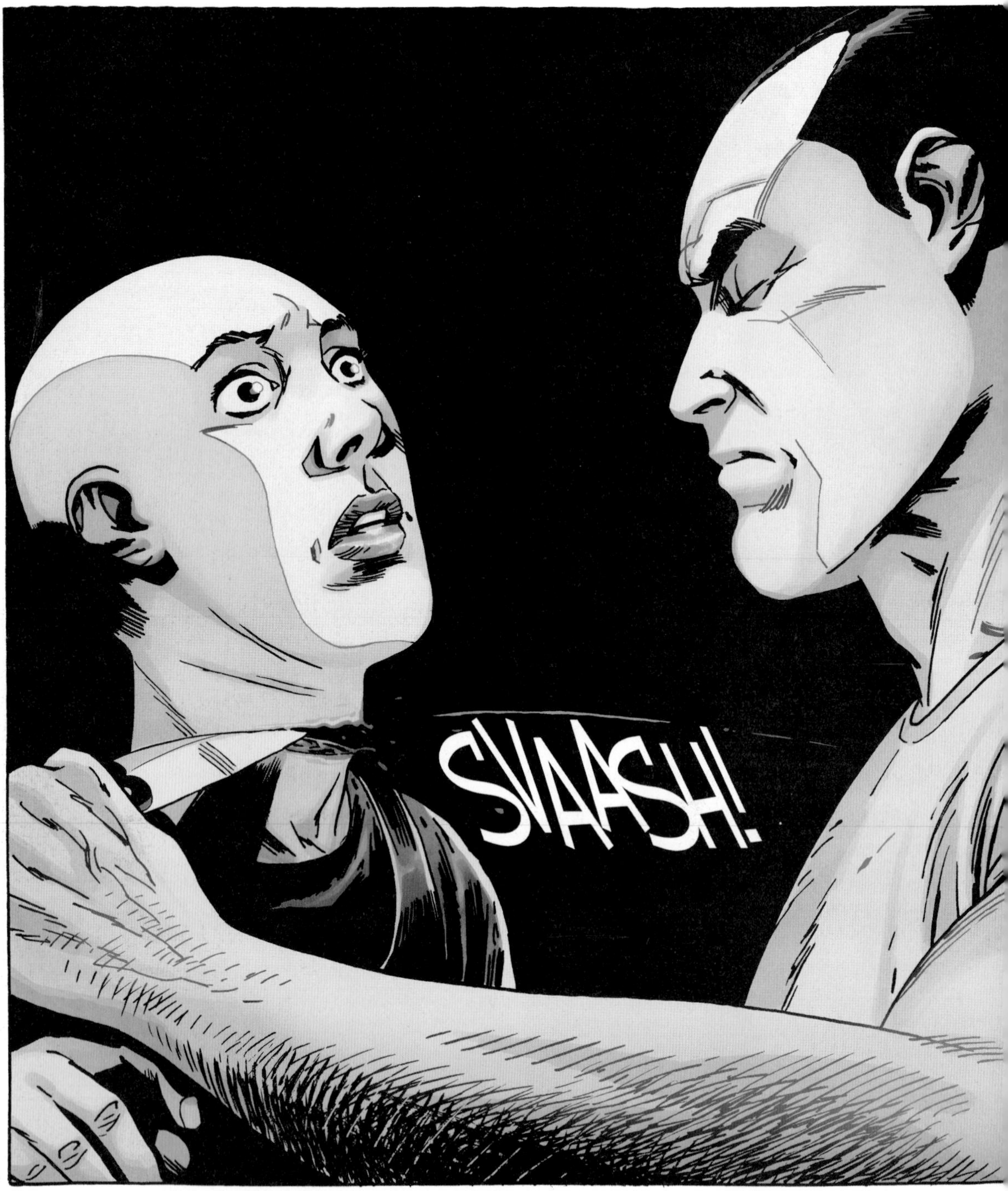
SWAASH!
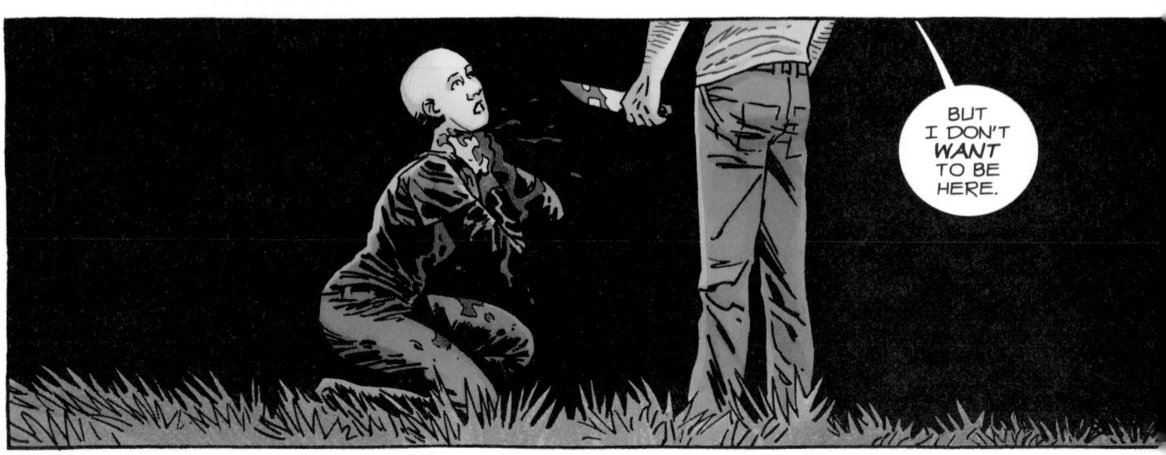
BUT I DON'T *WANT* TO BE HERE.

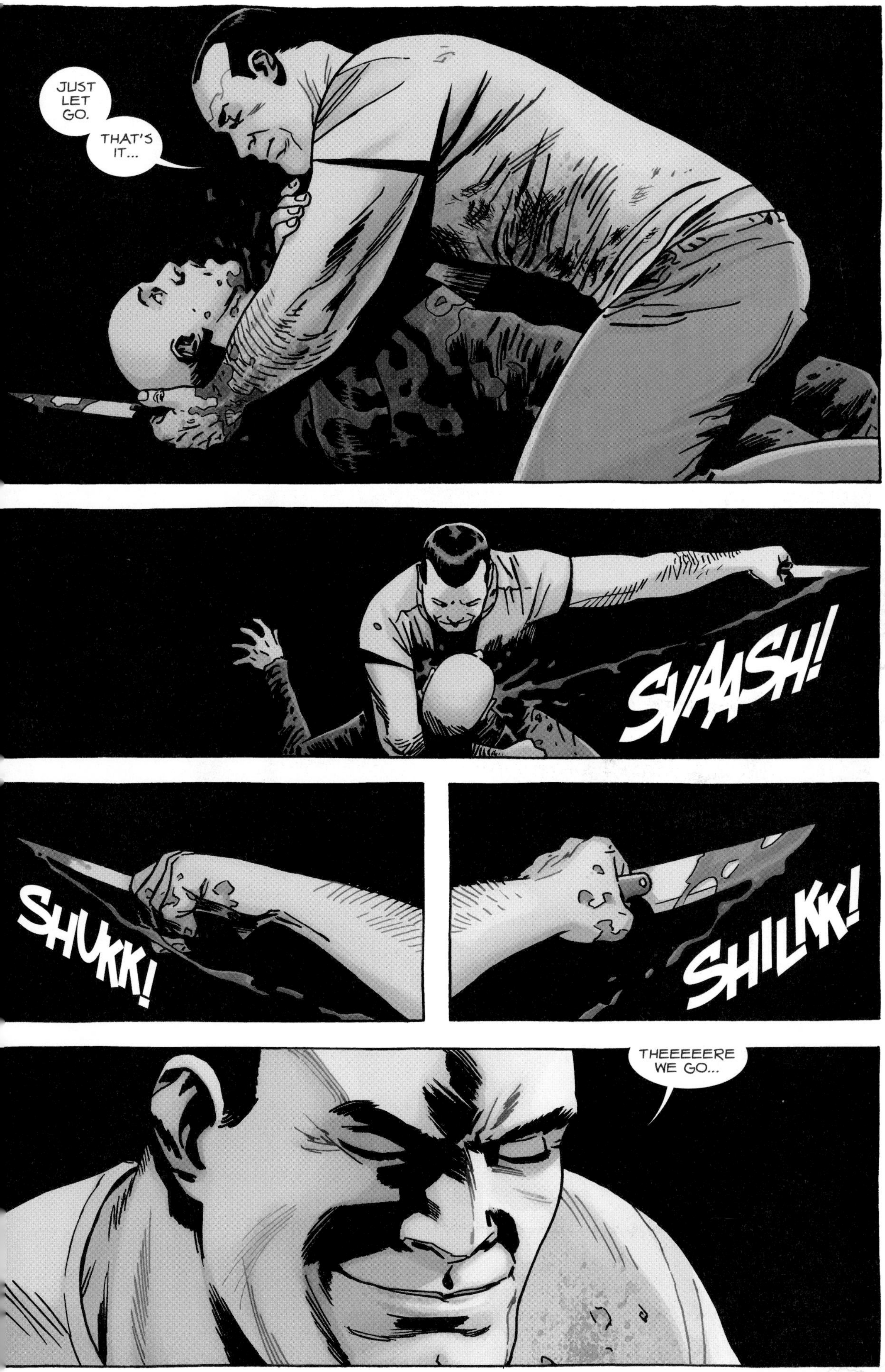
JUST LET GO.
THAT'S IT...
SVAASH!
SHUKK!
SHILKK!
THEEEEERE WE GO...

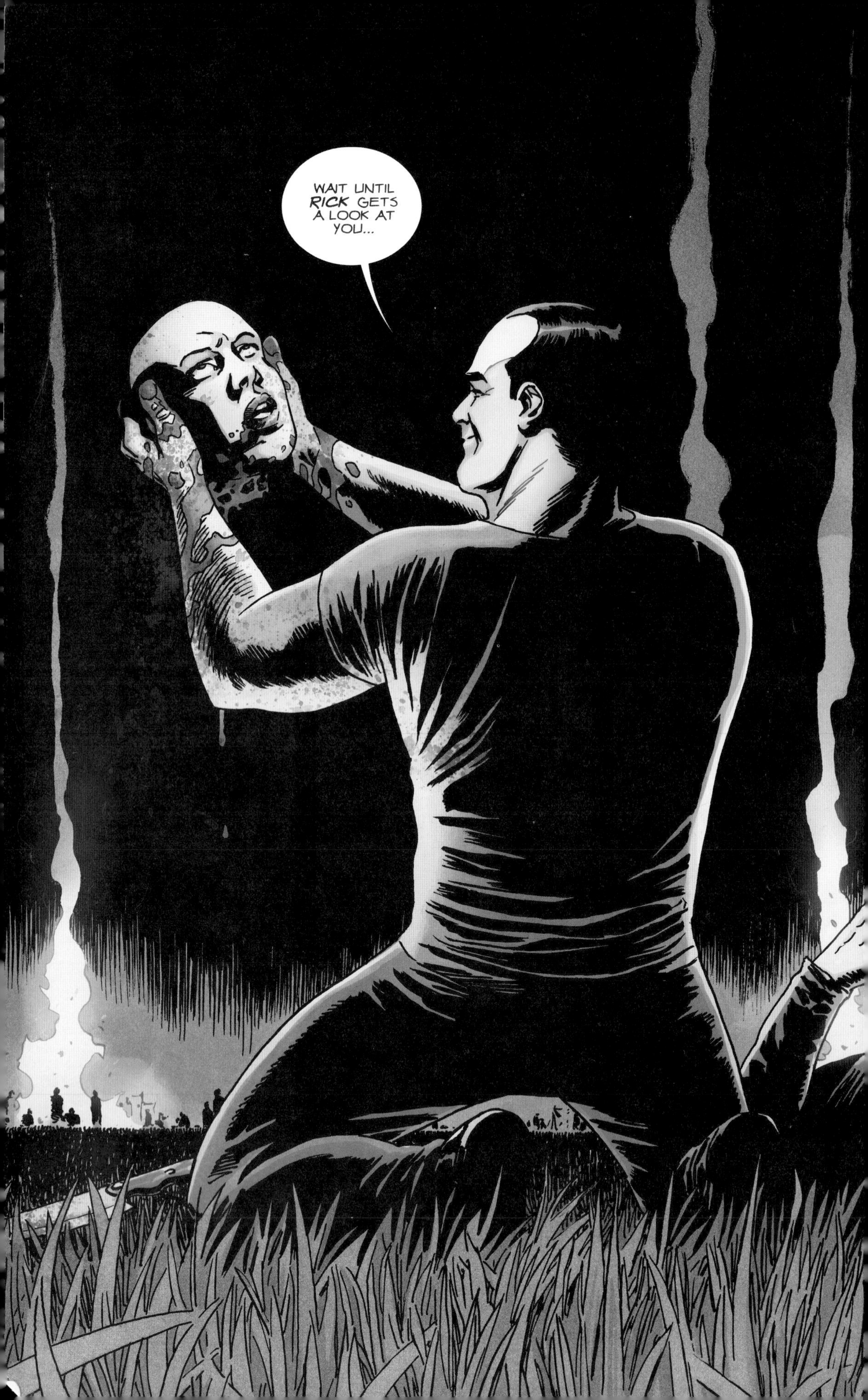
WAIT UNTIL RICK GETS A LOOK AT YOU...

TO BE CONTINUED...

for more tales from ROBERT KIRKMAN and SKYBOUND

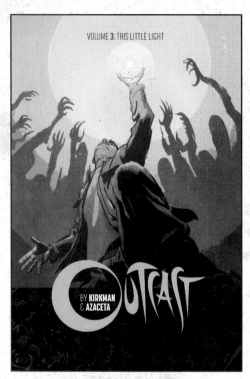

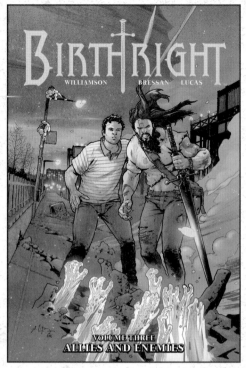

VOL. 1: A DARKNESS SURROUNDS HIM TP
ISBN: 978-1-63215-053-0
$9.99

VOL. 2: A VAST AND UNENDING RUIN TP
ISBN: 978-1-63215-448-4
$14.99

VOL. 3: THIS LITTLE LIGHT TP
ISBN: 978-1-63215-693-8
$14.99

VOL. 1: HOMECOMING TP
ISBN: 978-1-63215-231-2
$9.99

VOL. 2: CALL TO ADVENTURE TP
ISBN: 978-1-63215-446-0
$12.99

VOL. 3: ALLIES AND ENEMIES TP
ISBN: 978-1-63215-683-9
$12.99

VOL. 1: FIRST GENERATION TP
ISBN: 978-1-60706-683-5
$12.99

VOL. 2: SECOND GENERATION TP
ISBN: 978-1-60706-830-3
$12.99

VOL. 3: THIRD GENERATION TP
ISBN: 978-1-60706-939-3
$12.99

VOL. 4: FOURTH GENERATION TP
ISBN: 978-1-63215-036-3
$12.99

VOL. 1: HAUNTED HEIST TP
ISBN: 978-1-60706-836-5
$9.99

VOL. 2: BOOKS OF THE DEAD TP
ISBN: 978-1-63215-046-2
$12.99

VOL. 3: DEATH WISH TP
ISBN: 978-1-63215-051-6
$12.99

VOL. 4: GHOST TOWN TP
ISBN: 978-1-63215-317-3
$12.99

VOL. 1: FLORA & FAUNA TP
ISBN: 978-1-60706-982-9
$9.99

VOL. 2: AMPHIBIA & INSECTA TP
ISBN: 978-1-63215-052-3
$14.99

VOL. 3: CHIROPTERA & CARNIFORMAVES TP
ISBN: 978-1-63215-397-5
$14.99

VOL. 1: "I QUIT."
ISBN: 978-1-60706-592-0
$14.99

VOL. 2: "HELP ME."
ISBN: 978-1-60706-676-7
$14.99

VOL. 3: "VENICE."
ISBN: 978-1-60706-844-0
$14.99

VOL. 4: "THE HIT LIST."
ISBN: 978-1-63215-037-0
$14.99

VOL. 5: "TAKE ME."
ISBN: 978-1-63215-401-9
$14.99

BIRTHRIGHT™, CLONE™, GHOSTED™, and MANIFEST DESTINY™ © 2016 Skybound, LLC. OUTCAST BY KIRKMAN AND AZACETA™ and THIEF OF THIEVES™ © 2016 Robert Kirkman, LLC.
Image Comics® and its logos are registered trademarks of Image Comics, Inc. Skybound and its logos are © and ™ of Skybound, LLC. All rights reserved.